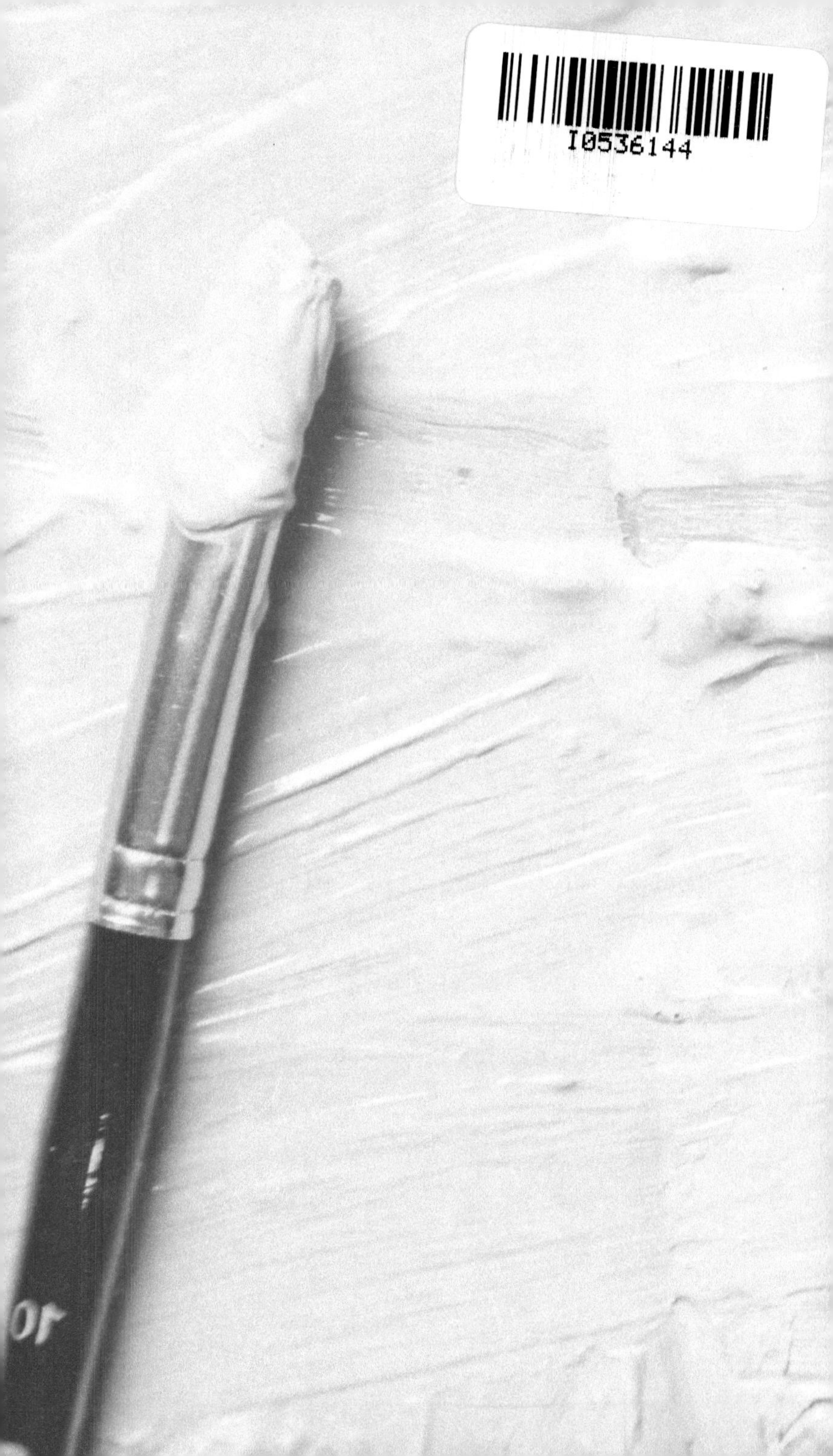

Seven

SUNNY

"THIRTY MINUTES?!" I huff.

I instantly panic, which is almost as ridiculous as expecting me to be punctual when I have a thirty-minute warning before walking into an interview with a potentially very intimidating man.

Jillian is distracted. She's hardly listening to me on the phone. "Just throw on some lip gloss and head out the door. You're probably more likely to get the job if you show up in sweats and messy hair versus your typical cutesy self."

I quickly splash some water on my face and run my fingers through my hair. "I'm not cutesy!"

"You're a ball of sunshine, babe. You are cutesy. Get going. I just sent the address. Oh, and he said not to be late."

Jillian hangs up the phone, and I give myself one more look in the mirror before hoping for the best.

My long brown hair is thrown up with a claw clip. I know some of the strands will fall out by the time I make it to the coffee shop. I have on my cream-colored sweater that falls off my shoulder a little from being stretched out, but there's not much I can do about that, considering all my clothes are piled up in the corner of the Airbnb, needing to be washed. I wish I had jeans that weren't torn in the knees, but at least they're sort of stylish and not too tight.

The cool Chicago air coats my face as I rush down the street with my crossbody in tow. I follow the directions on my phone, ignoring the bustling of the city, and stand in front of a little hole-in-the-wall coffee shop that has the most decadent smell floating out from the open door.

My mouth waters.

I'm immediately drawn to the counter beside the glass bakery section with the prettiest ceramic cake stands displaying various breakfast pastries.

"Hi! Can I help you?"

I stand straight and swing my gaze to the young woman behind the counter. "Hi! Um..." I glance at the prices and hesitate. *Chicago is pricey.* "Can I just have a coffee with a little bit of cream and sugar?"

I'll feel like a loiter if I don't order anything and just sit down at a table.

"Sure."

It only takes her seconds to get my coffee and ring me up.

I spy a tip jar on the edge of the counter, and being raised the way that I was, I place my last dollar inside.

"Thank you so much!" she exclaims as if she isn't used to tips.

I leave her with a genuine smile and turn to find a spot that faces the door so I can see when Rhodes walks in.

Or is it Mr. Volkova?

Shit, what do I call him?

The back booth is open, and I make my way over with my steaming coffee while still arguing in my head over what to call him.

I have four minutes to spare.

Maybe I'll call him Mr. Punctual since he didn't want me to be late after giving me a half-hour notice.

Every time someone steps into the coffee shop, my heart does a little flip. I'm nervous, and I know it's because I have a lot riding on this job. Going back to Washington is my very last option, though I'd love to be back with my nana, even if she is in the nursing home.

It's just that I *can't.*

For reasons unbeknownst to her.

After fixing my clip and taking a deep breath, I sip on my coffee and wait.

The street is lined with cars and passersby walking their dogs. My stomach fills with nerves the longer I wait.

I turn toward the door, and as if he was waiting for the clock to strike 10:30 exactly, Rhodes Volkova walks into the coffee shop, stealing all the air in the small establishment. His presence demands *everyone's* attention, even the sweet little toddler sitting on his mother's lap.

A tight swallow moves down my neck as I watch him from afar. His broad shoulders take up the entirety of the doorway, and his black sunglasses do nothing to hide the stern look on his face.

My gut is never wrong.

Rhodes Volkova is every bit intimidating as he is attractive.

I continue to stare while he takes two long strides and makes it to the counter. A coffee is placed in his hand, and he puts a twenty in the tip jar before spinning and scrutinizing everyone in the restaurant.

I should stand up and get his attention, yet I can't seem to move.

A little boy runs inside the door and stops abruptly in front of Rhodes. He looks down, and the little boy's curls flop backward as he tilts his head. Rhodes bends and pushes his sunglasses up to his thick, effortlessly messy brown hair and gets on the boy's level. I try to make out whatever Rhodes is saying to him by reading his lips, but it's too hard to decipher. The boy's father runs in after him, and just like that, Rhodes is back to standing up and swinging his gaze around the coffee shop.

I glance behind me to see if there is something there that is making his jaw tighten with anger.

But no, it's just me.

In this tiny booth.

All alone.

Rhodes pulls his sunglasses down, and it does nothing to hide the annoyance. In reality, it takes no more than five seconds for him to make his way over to me, but it feels like an entire lifetime has passed.

I tilt my chin and stare at him from the leather booth.

"Hi," I squeak.

His eyebrows rise above his Oakleys.

Hi? Oh my god. I silently groan.

I quickly slide out from the booth and stand. I hold my hand out and act like I'm a twenty-five-year-old woman instead of a preteen who's talking to a boy for the first time.

"I'm Sunny," I say with a smile. "It's nice to meet you, Rh...Mr. Volk—"

Before I can finish my sentence, he shakes his head and turns and heads straight for the exit.

Eight

RHODES

NOPE.

The second I lay eyes on her, my shoulders tense. What I expected was an unattractive woman to nanny my child. What I got was a punch-to-the-gut beautiful woman with glowing skin, a sweet-as-sin voice, and a rocking body that curves in all the right spots.

She looks like all the rest of the nannies that I've hired—the ones who take the job because they have dollar signs in their eyes and see a spot in my bed that could be filled. Past nannies used my daughter to get closer to me, and I don't see how this will be any different.

"Wait." Her warm hand lands on my elbow, and I almost lose my footing. "You're Mr. Volkova, right?

I scoff with my back still turned toward her. *As if she doesn't know.* Everyone in this coffee shop knows.

Peering over my shoulder, I grimace again. She flutters her thick eyelashes, and the act makes her seem innocent. A small line digs in between her eyebrows as she waits for my answer.

"You're not what I'm looking for," I say as deadpan as ever.

She flinches at my words, and for a split-second, I feel bad.

Not bad enough to hire her, though.

I leave her standing there in the middle of the coffee shop. My jaw cracks with the grinding of my teeth.

I'm such a fool.

I thought the reason her photo wasn't on the website was because she wasn't attractive enough. It's the complete opposite. She has this innocent vibe to her too. When I told her she wasn't what I was looking for, shock flashed across her features, like I'd hurt her feelings.

I know I can behave myself if I were to hire her. I'm just not sure *she* can. My experience is that the innocent-looking ones are always the ones you have to look out for.

"You need a nanny, don't you?"

I pause in the middle of the sidewalk.

Color me fucking surprised that she followed me.

Loose pebbles crunch beneath my shoe as I twist and eye her from outside the establishment. Out of habit, I slowly run my eyes down her frame.

I give her brownie points for not dressing up for the interview.

The last two women I had interviewed and hired—out of pure desperation—wore high heels and short dresses that left nothing to the imagination.

I almost told them that it wasn't an interview to be my wife, but an interview for a nannying position.

"How old are you?" I ask.

The lines on her forehead appear again, and she darts her eyes away.

"Twenty-five."

I scoff. "You're too young."

Her arms cross with defiance, and I have the sudden urge to smirk.

"I turn twenty-six in a few weeks," she argues.

I detect a hint of annoyance in her tone, and it's a pleasant surprise. Every other nanny I ever interviewed tried too hard to please me. Half the time, I think they mistook my irritation and clipped responses as foreplay instead of what it really was: *annoyance*.

I cross my arms to mimic her stance. "Twenty-six?"

All I get is a curt nod.

"I'm thirty-two," I add.

Sunny's lips curve. "Well, then...I guess I should call you grandpa."

I blink a few times and try to clear my head, because she surprised me again.

"What does your age have to do with mine?" she adds.

It doesn't. Her age has nothing to do with nannying my daughter. In fact, Gia was around twenty-six when she had Ellie.

"I worry about your intentions," I say.

There it is again—the worry digging into her features.

"My intentions?" She clears her throat. "If you were to hire me, my only intention would be to care for your daughter."

Silence surrounds us. The noisy city fades, and all I can hear is my heartbeat pounding in my ears. Heat creeps up my neck and spreads across my skin with the amount of stress I've been carrying around.

I give her one more long look. She looks sweet, and I do think she has a good head on her shoulders. Her determination runs deep. I can feel it like my own.

But I've been fucked over one too many times.

My trust in pretty women is nonexistent at this point.

"I'm sorry." My apology is more of a grunt. "But again, you're not what I'm looking for."

Sunny's shoulders fall, but the disappointment only lasts a second. There's a little crevice in between her eyebrows that disappears when she finds whatever she started to dig for in her bag.

A small piece of paper is trapped between her thumb and finger. I take it hesitantly before stepping away.

"I'll be in town for a few more days if you change your mind."

I shove the crumpled piece of paper in my back pocket and grumble under my breath, "I won't."

———

Ice flies up with the cutting of my skate. I have the urge to snap my stick in half, but that'll make me look like an overgrown toddler, so instead, I flex my jaw and climb over the side toward the bench.

"Why are you pulling me in?" I shout to Coach Jacobs.

I sit down with anger rushing through my limbs.

"Emergency."

My heart stops. I stand right back up. My stick slips out of my hand, and Malaki swoops it up without even looking in my direction. I nod at Coach Jacobs, thankful that he and I have the type of coach/player relationship that allows me to put my daughter first.

It was my only stipulation when I switched teams. My agent hunted for a team that would accommodate my lifestyle of being a single father, and the Chicago Blue Devils were the only ones willing to bend while still offering me a hefty salary.

We sucked at first. I'm not going to lie.

But this year is different. That's partly why I'm so dead set on finding a nanny who I can trust so I'm able to focus on the team and the rest of our schedule.

One of the managers hands me a phone. "Hello?"

The crowd's chants die out slightly as I round the corner toward the locker room. Nerves rage in my lower stomach with anticipation peeking over my shoulder.

Ellie's panicked voice hits me right where it hurts. "Daddy?"

"Printsessa, what are you doing? I'm in the middle of a game."

She sounds scared, and I'm not sure if it's because she's afraid I'm angry with her or because of something the new nanny did.

"Can I go to Scottie's?"

I pinch the bridge of my nose. "Scottie is here at the game. We're several hours away. You should be in bed. Where is the nanny? Hand her the phone."

"Um..."

"Ellie." I sigh with agitation. I'm not frustrated with her. I'm frustrated with the situation. "Where is the nanny?"

"She locked me in my room."

I think I pop a blood vessel.

My voice doesn't allude that I could strangle the new nanny—who I *thought* was a good pick—but on the inside, my heart is beating a million miles a second. "She..." I clear my throat and glance toward the game. "She locked you in your bedroom?"

"Mm-hmm." Ellie sniffs. "I remembered how to call you from my tablet. I don't have Scottie's number, so I called you instead. I'm sorry, Daddy."

Fucking Christ.

"Don't worry, Printsessa." I sound calm. "Just hang tight."

After telling her that I love her, I shoot a quick text to

Emory's wife and have her call Ellie's tablet so she can keep her calm while I try to fix things.

The game is seconds from being over.

Not only have I let my team down, but I've let Ellie down too.

Why is this so fucking hard?

My phone cracks in my tight grip as I pull up the number that I saved on a whim.

Alright, Sunny. You're up.

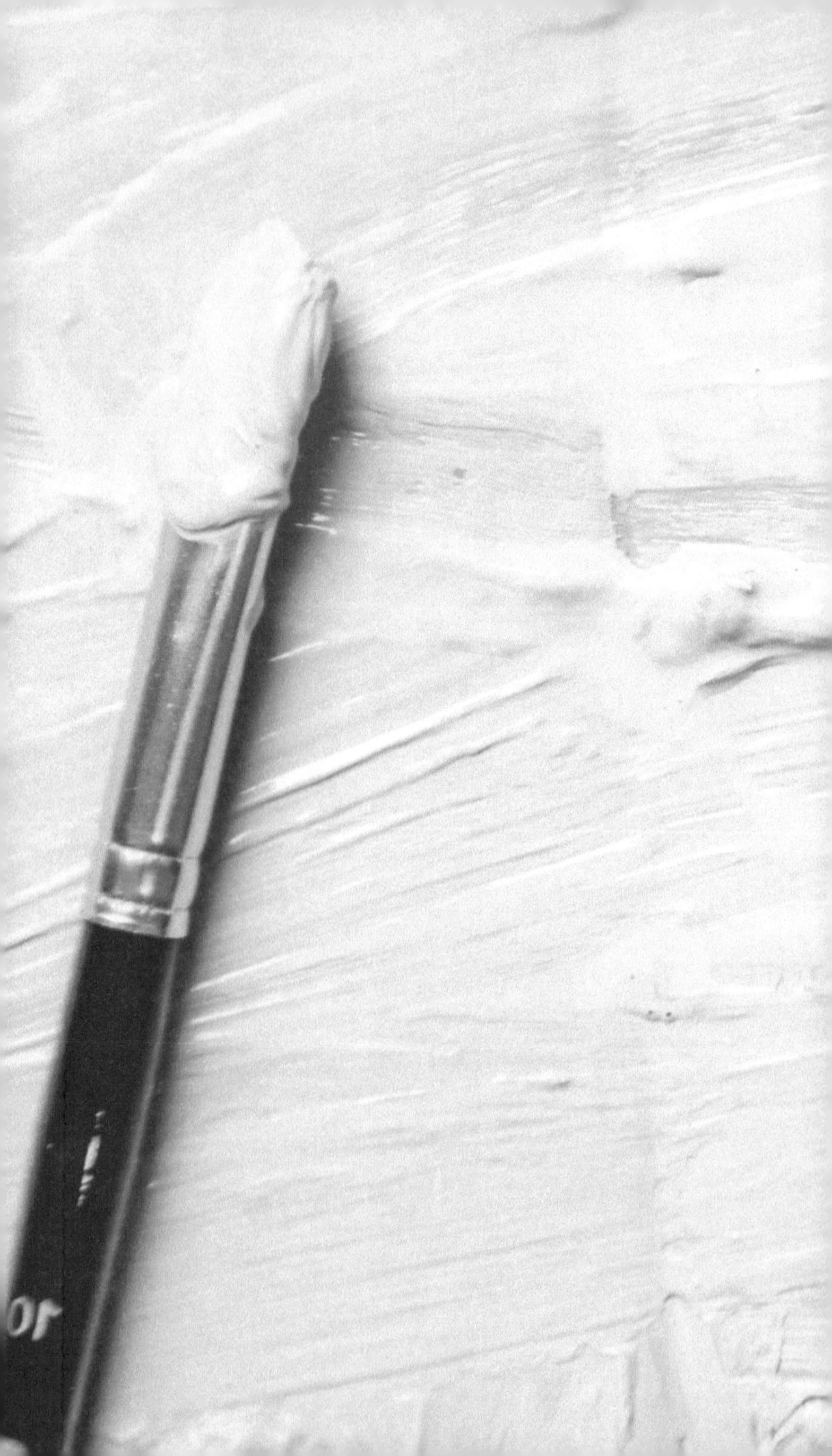

Nine

SUNNY

I SALUTE THE TALL, skyscraper buildings after I step out of the Uber. The driver looks at me funny, so I salute him too. It could be the fact that I'm decked out in The Art Institute gear from my quick trip into their campus store—a little parting gift—or maybe not.

The cool night air blasts my cheeks as I drag my suitcase behind me and head toward the airport doors. Chicago was a hopeful dream that unfortunately didn't come true. It seems I was right in my reservations about Celeste and her tarot card reading.

I pull open my phone while standing in line to check my bag to text Ruby with the disappointing news. Except, a strange number is calling.

I hesitate, afraid that it could be the past catching up to me, but it could also be fate calling, so I answer it on a whim.

"Hello?" I move to the side and let a family of four go ahead in the line.

"Sunny."

My palm covers my other ear so I can hear better. "Yes?"

"It's Rhodes."

My heart halts. I'm stunned. *Fate?!*

"Oh–"

"Are you still in town?"

Technically. "Yes."

His loud sigh filters through the phone. "Good. You're up."

There's chatter in the background, and it's hard to hear him, but I'm certain he just threw me a lifeline. Before I can inquire, I hear my text tone go off.

"I sent you the address to my house. I need you there as soon as possible. If you can manage to handle the situation by the time I get there and keep me out of jail, then the job is yours."

I'm already heading for the airport door with my bag in tow. "See you soon," I quip.

He hangs up the phone, and I stare at the blank screen for a few seconds and try to crawl through the confusion. Rhodes is every bit of gruff and intimidating, but the way his voice trembled with panic has me hurriedly calling another Uber to head to the address he gave me.

If I can manage to handle the situation and keep him out of jail, then the job is mine?

Say less, Mr. Volkova.

———

I don't salute this Uber driver.

Instead, I climb out of the backseat and stare at the tall, luxurious home.

My neck gets a cramp the longer I gaze at the intricate

detail of the limestone, and don't even get me started on the ironclad door.

"Here." The Uber driver drops my suitcase beside my feet with a thud and scares me out of my stupor.

"Oh, right. Thanks." I hand him a tip, and he takes off while I drag my suitcase up the concrete stairs.

I rap my knuckles quickly on the door. I'm not sure what to expect on the other side. Rhodes didn't give me much to go on, and although I wanted to text him on the way over, I decided not to because part of me wonders if this is a test. I refuse to fail it, so whatever is on the other side of this iron, so be it.

There's no answer, which puzzles me.

I walk back down the steps and leave my suitcase on the porch. I peer up the side of the limestone again. Several windows line the front, and I'm certain it's considered a historical home. It is beautiful even without seeing it in the daylight. My eyes snag the window on the left, two stories up. There's a tiny shadow behind the curtain with the dim light of a lamp from behind.

Is she alone?

My heart skips a beat, and I rush up the stairs again.

I knock again and again. No answer.

Bending at the knees, I lift up the rug to see if there's a spare key, but then I hear the creaking of iron.

"May I help you?"

I expected a little girl to appear.

Not a woman who doesn't look much older than me, and especially not one who has a look of displeasure curved in her features.

Springing into action, I stand quickly and pretend I know what I'm doing.

"Yeah, hi. I'm here to take over care for Mr. Volkova's daughter."

Shit, I don't even know her name!

Shock moves across her face.

"Oh? I wasn't told someone was coming to relieve me of my duties."

I smile sweetly because my nana always said that you get much further in life when you're kind, even if you want to be a bitch.

"Yes, Mr. Volkova called me just a little while ago and asked me to head over."

The woman eyes me cautiously. I eye her with complete skepticism. She has bleach-blonde hair that's in desperate need of some conditioner and eyelashes that look like caterpillars.

My gut tells me there's something weird going on, and with Rhodes's warning of keeping him out of jail, I run with it.

I reach forward and gently pat her hand, gripping the door. "I suggest you leave before Mr. Volkova arrives."

"And why is that?" she snaps, proving my gut right.

"Because if he gets here before you leave, he'll end up in jail, and well..." I make a worried face. "I'm not sure where that leaves you."

I slide my foot forward in case she tries to slam the door in my face, but she doesn't. She appears a moment later with her purse in her hand and rushes past me, proving her guilty of something.

I don't linger long.

I grab my suitcase and enter through the door. It's dark inside except for a little lamp off to the side in the living room. The entryway opens up to a wide set of dark stairs that wrap around to several floors. Locking the door behind me, I slip off my shoes and start to head up the stairs.

"Hello?"

Listening carefully, I hear nothing. From the looks of the

shadowy figure through the wispy curtain I'd seen while on the sidewalk, I think she's on the second floor.

I turn to the right. "Hello? Is anyone there?"

"Scottie?!"

I breathe out a held breath. "I'm Sunny," I say softly.

A light is peeking from below the crack near the floor, and I smile to myself at the pink and purple hearts taped all over the front of her door.

In an attempt not to scare her, I let her know who I am. "Your dad called and asked me to come over. Can I come in?"

My hand is on the doorknob, but I know how kids like to have some control, so I wait until she answers me.

"You can try."

I can try? Is that a threat?

I turn the doorknob, but it doesn't move. My fingers wrap tighter around the black knob, and I wiggle it again.

"Is it stuck?" I ask, confused.

"Locked." Her little voice is closer, and she sounds scared. "Where is Ginny?"

"Ginny?" *From Harry Potter?*

If Rhodes is watching me from somewhere and thinks this is a funny test of my nanny skills, I may just head back to Washington regardless, because *really?*

"The new nanny my daddy hired. She locked me in here."

My jaw drops.

I instantly regret letting her walk out the door without tripping her first.

"She locked you in here?" I repeat.

My fingers fly to my mouth. I turn around and try to find a key somewhere, but there's nothing around except a Chicago Blue Devils night-light plugged into the outlet along the hallway wall.

"Okay, don't worry," I say through the crack of the door.

"Grumpy Ginny is gone." I try to lighten the mood to *maybe* make her feel a little less scared. "I'll get you out, Rapunzel."

"Rapunzel?" she gasps. "That's not my name."

"Haven't you ever heard the story of Rapunzel? The old witch locks her away."

"My name is Ellie," she says.

Instead of looking for the key or for tools in this mansion-like home and leaving Ellie alone, I open up my crossbody and pull out my debit card. While sliding it in between the door-jamb and lock, I continue to talk to her.

"Hi, Ellie. I'm Sunny. It's nice to meet you."

"Are you my daddy's friend?" She pauses. "Because he doesn't really have friends."

I laugh out loud and continue working with my debit card.

"And I'm not supposed to talk to strangers."

The lock finally gives, and I use my elbow to turn the doorknob while pushing the door in. "Whew," I blow out a breath and nearly tumble on top of Rhodes's daughter.

Her eyes are wide with fear, but all it takes is one smile from me, and her shoulders relax.

"Are you okay?" I get down on her level.

Her lip wobbles, and my heart aches.

"I'm okay," she answers softly.

Oh. She's a tough one. Her chin dips as she tries to hide her emotions, and I give her the grace she needs until she pulls herself together and meets my eye again.

I hold my hand out. "Hi, Rapunzel. I'm Sunny."

Her eyebrows fold in on themselves, and a little giggle falls from her mouth. "I'm not Rapunzel! I'm Ellie."

I smile at her, and she does the same.

"What do you say we go down to the kitchen for a little midnight snack, and you can tell me all about that evil witch who locked you in here."

Her pretty eyes linger on me for a few seconds, like she's trying to figure out if she wants to trust me.

Eventually, she gives in to the thought and slips past me. I let her take the lead because, after being locked inside her bedroom, I'm certain she's a little distrusting.

That's something she and I have in common.

Ten

RHODES

THE FLIGHT DRAGGED.

It was an hour-and-a-half, but somehow it seemed like ten hours.

I didn't even say goodbye to my teammates. I practically ran to my truck and took off without even letting the engine warm. I blew past several yellow lights that had turned red at the last second and put the pedal to the metal. My door barely shut as I parked on the side of the street and rushed up the concrete stairs.

Ginny didn't answer my phone calls, which was one of my strictest stipulations before I left. I knew that Ellie wasn't particularly thrilled to have her as a nanny, but she isn't happy with any of the nannies. Half the time, she speaks in broken Russian, just to confuse them and to irritate me.

"Ellie?" My voice echoes throughout the entryway. I glance down and see a light-pink suitcase near the door and a pair of tennis shoes kicked off to the side.

I bypass them and head upstairs, taking two steps at a

time. This house is too big for Ellie and me. But I needed a safe neighborhood with a yard. Those were my requests, and this historical, freshly remodeled home had the biggest yard. It still isn't anything near what I'm used to nor what I grew up with.

But we're in Chicago, not upstate New York.

"Printsessa?" I keep my voice low.

A faint glow shines into the hallway from her open door, and I exhale. I'm on edge because either Ginny came to her senses, or Sunny did, in fact, swoop in and save me while in an impossible situation. Though Sunny would be the lesser of two evils, I'm not necessarily prepared for either scenario.

My body is tight from the game, and the added stress from Ellie's phone call hasn't made things any easier.

The closer I get to Ellie's bedroom door, the more I realize that it's Sunny who's here instead of Ginny. Her soft, melodic voice flows into the hallway, and it takes me a few seconds to realize that she's reading Ellie a bedtime story.

It's late.

Ellie should be sleeping.

But a bedtime story from someone like Sunny is less scarring than being locked away in her bedroom by someone like Ginny, so I let it go.

Ginny proves that not all background checks are foolproof. I'll have to let my old-time friend, SGT Mel, in on that since he has assured me that they are.

"In order to save Rapunzel, Flynn Rider sacrificed himself with the help of his trusty companion, Pascal..."

Sunny, dressed head to toe in what looks to be merch from the art college up the street, is sitting cross-legged on Ellie's floor below her bed. Her dark hair is piled on top of her head so high I can hardly see my daughter, but after craning my neck, I see Ellie's rosy cheeks and closed eyes, resting on her pink pillow.

Sunny, unaware that I'm standing in the doorway,

continues to read. She seems lost in the story, almost as if she doesn't even realize Ellie is asleep, but every few seconds, her head tilts, and she looks at her.

Fuck, fine.

I should have hired Sunny instead of letting past experiences ruin all the rest.

My fucking bad.

I clear my throat once Sunny gets to the happily ever after, and it startles her. The book full of fairy tales goes flying into the air, and her shoulders end up by her ears. By some miracle, she doesn't yelp and wake Ellie. Instead, she covers her mouth with her hand.

I watch her ribcage deflate when she recognizes me. I flick my chin to the hallway and turn. She leaves the door ajar after she slips out, and if I didn't look back and see her tiptoeing behind me, I wouldn't have even known she was there. She's quiet like a cat.

For the record, I hate cats.

Silence fills the gaping space between us when we're back downstairs in the entryway. Sunny stares at me with bashful eyes. I should probably thank her for coming to my rescue.

Instead, I insult her.

"You look like a walking billboard for the Art Institute."

I glance at her maroon sweatshirt with the logo smack-dab in the middle and then move to her black yoga pants that have the same logo printed on her thigh. Since she took her shoes off when she came in, I can see that she's sporting their socks too.

"Oh, this?" She dips her chin and stares at her clothes. There's a little bit of pink on her cheeks when she puts her attention back to me. "Next time you need me for a rescue mission, I'll wear my cape."

I want to laugh, but it surprises me so much that it comes out sounding like a grunt.

Sunny's eyebrows shoot upward, and I clear my throat.

"Was Ginny still here when you arrived?"

I tried to access the video footage from my cameras, but with the poor service on the flight, it wouldn't come through.

My heart claps behind my ribs. I grow angry at the thought of someone locking Ellie in her room.

Sunny crosses her arms angrily and nods. "You should have told me what she did. I would have tripped her on her way out."

This time, I can't help it.

I laugh.

Sunny's lips turn up at the sides. Her angry stance loosens, and she looks pleased with herself.

Again, I should thank her, but there's another thought on the forefront of my mind.

I glance away, unable to look her in the eye, because although it's standard for me to ask the question, I don't like appearing vulnerable in front of strangers.

I don't like appearing vulnerable in front of anyone, actually.

"Was Ellie okay when you got here?"

Her soft exhale catches my ear. I glance at her from the side. "Mostly. Nothing that a little snack and a bedtime story couldn't fix after I broke in."

My blood pressure lowers significantly. *She's fine*—well, as fine as Ellie ever is.

I repeat her words in my head. *Wait*. "After you broke in?"

Sunny's lower lip disappears beneath her teeth. She rocks back on the heels of her gray-and-maroon striped Art Institute socks.

"Did you break the door?" I wouldn't care if she did. It'd be nice to have someone else care for Ellie enough to break down doors, honestly.

All Ellie has is me and the team, plus the few wives, like

Scottie, that tend to pitch in when they know I need it the most. My mom and Ellie have weekly calls, but she's too far to be here in a pinch. It never feels like enough. There's a gap in Ellie's heart that I'm not sure I'll ever be able to fill. No matter how many piggyback rides Kane gives her, or skates on the ice with Malaki, or big, blue Chicago Blue Devils hair bows that Scottie ties in her hair, she still has a withdrawn feel to her.

Sunny is quick to answer. "I didn't break the door. I used a credit card."

Ah, so we have a little rulebreaker on our hands.

My arms fold. "And where did you learn to do that?"

There's a tight hitch in my breath when she smiles softly. "My gramps."

"Your grandpa taught you how to break and enter with a credit card?"

Her light laugh fills all the empty spots of the foyer. "He did. But it was only because he used to take me with him to work, and some of his older tenants would lock themselves out of their apartments."

I stand back and watch her without saying anything. I try to spot a lie or some ulterior motive to her response, but instead, all I get are a few flutters of her long eyelashes and warm cheeks. She seems so...genuine?

"So..." Sunny glances at her pink suitcase. "Since the police aren't here to arrest you for...whatever went through your mind when you learned that Ginny had locked Ellie in her room, does that mean I get the job?" Her face twists. "Though, I would have totally bailed you out. *She* deserves to be in jail, in my opinion."

I watch her closely as she recrosses her arms and mutters under her breath about tripping the *blonde bimbo.*

In an attempt to save face, I rub a hand over my scruff and hide my grin. "If you can agree to my terms, I'm willing to give you a spin."

A spin.

That came out wrong, and unfortunately, Sunny caught it. Her eyebrows dip, and she squints as if she, too, is wondering if I really just said that.

I did.

I clear my throat and pull out my phone to check my calendar. "Can you meet here tomorrow at ten? We will go over the contract and salary. If you can agree to my terms after tomorrow, then the job is yours."

If she doesn't agree, I'm going to have big fucking problems.

My mom has offered a few times to come stay for a while, but with her back in Russia, that's nearly impossible. I'm not willing to make things more complicated by forcing her to find someone else to take care of her eighty-two-year-old aunt who requires full-time care just so she can come take care of me.

"I'll be here at ten on the dot. I know how you like punctuality."

She doesn't even work for me yet, and she's already aggravating me with the little teasing evident in her tone.

So what if I like punctuality?

Sunny bends and grabs the handle of her suitcase. I raise an eyebrow when I eye the Art Institute sticker on the side.

"Do you attend the Art Institute?" I blurt. "If you're attending college while also nannying, that may be an issue. My schedule is unpredictable and—"

A playful scoff leaves her. "You're underestimating me, Mr. Volkova." Her flirty eye roll irks me. "But no, I don't attend the school."

I watch her turn and say nothing as she moves to leave. Her suitcase thuds with each descent of the concrete steps. Before I twist the lock, I pull the door open farther slightly and call down to her sitting on the last step.

"Sunny?"

She glances at me over her shoulder. The moon shines a ghostly glow over her face, and although the light paints her in a cool color, there's still so much warmth to her. "Yes?"

I clear my throat. "Thanks."

There.

I said it.

A little twinkle gleams in her eye, and it annoys me. "See you tomorrow," she quips.

The door latches, but I keep it unlocked and stay within eyesight until she springs to her feet at the sound of a car pulling down the street. Once she hands off her suitcase and climbs inside the Uber, I head right to bed.

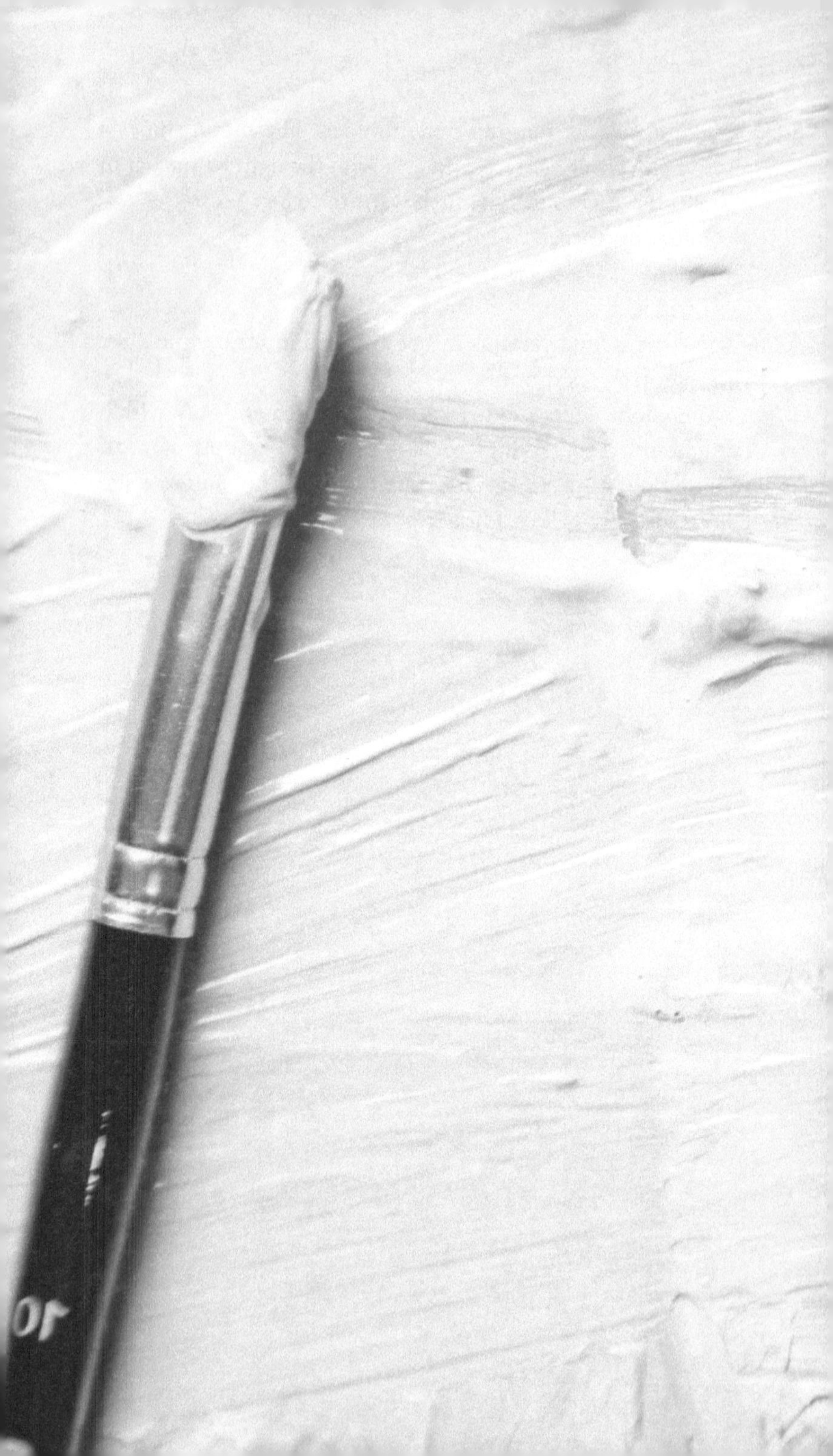

Eleven

SUNNY

HIS HOUSE IS EVEN MORE extravagant in the daylight. The neighborhood is very Chicago-like with tall homes and cars parked along the road, but the bustling of the city is far enough in the distance that it feels secluded.

I check my phone, ignoring the exclamation points from Ruby.

It's 10:01.

I bite the inside of my cheek. It's practically raw. I raise my fist to knock *again*.

Disappointment washes over me when there is no answer.

A car door slams, and I quickly spin around. I'm on edge, and I wish seeing Rhodes round the front of his truck would calm me, but it does the opposite.

God.

Even if I wanted to appear cool and relaxed and pretend I'm unbothered by his one-minute-late arrival, I wouldn't be able to. His very presence demands attention, and I can't look away. With an authoritative chip on his shoulder and edgy jaw, I'm drawn to him like a magnet.

The lock of his truck pulls me back to reality, and I pop up from resting along the ironclad porch railing that I unknowingly leaned against when he started to head my way.

I pull my shoulders back and act professional. "Good morning."

Rhodes glances at me and nods. He is sporting those black sunglasses again, which makes it impossible to gauge his mood. He unlocks the door and heads inside. I follow after him but keep a far enough distance in case he stops abruptly.

Before I get too far, I bend down to untie my shoes.

I stand slowly, and a rush of heat brushes against my skin. My new boss is eyeing me very closely, and he's now without his sunglasses. The longer he watches me slip my shoes off, the harder my heart beats.

Why does he make me flustered?

"You don't have to take your shoes off," he notes. "The place isn't necessarily...clean."

My nana's face flashes through my mind. "Sorry. My nana taught me that it was rude to walk into someone's home with shoes on." I roll my lips and shrug. "It's a habit."

And I beg to differ. His house isn't dirty. It's just a little messy. There's a difference.

Without saying anything else, I follow Rhodes down the hallway lined with various frames of what I assume to be family members on the walls. The last photo catches my attention, and I'm pretty sure it's Ellie's mother. I quickly peel my eyes away and sit in the chair that he's pulled out for me in the middle of his kitchen.

My nana would *die* to have a kitchen like this.

A large island sits in the middle, separating the table and rest of the space, and although the glossy counters are layered with various things like cereal boxes, assorted colors of crayons, and coloring pages, it's expansive, leaving plenty of room to knead dough or make homemade pasta.

Cooking is her passion, whereas creating is mine.

"Here is the contract." Rhodes plops down in the seat across from me and slides a stapled packet of papers in my direction.

I read over it quickly, only glancing up at him every few seconds. It's a dream job. The hours are great, and I can work on my paintings during my time off. The best part is where it's listed that he prefers Ellie stay out of the limelight, meaning no on-camera outings and staying a distance away if he has an after-game interview.

It only takes me a few minutes to read over the rest of his stipulations and initial each one. When I flip to the second-to-last page, I choke on my spit.

A glass of water appears, and I gulp it down while rereading the salary.

"This is..." I peer at Rhodes, who remains standing beside me after placing the water in front of my face. "Too much..."

"What is?" He bounces his attention back and forth between me and the contract.

"The pay," I blurt.

Rhodes flicks an eyebrow. "Well, considering the percentage that The Nanny Roster takes from *your* pay, I think it's reasonable."

I glance at the salary once more. My fingers tingle against the paper. This would easily pay for my nana's nursing home fees—plus some.

Rhodes, who is still hovering over me like a looming shadow, is clearly waiting for me to say something.

"I don't understand why you've had such a hard time keeping a nanny if this is what you're offering them."

Call me paranoid, but regardless of how attractive Rhodes

is, I don't understand how a nanny couldn't abide by his rules and stay employed.

"They didn't want the pay," he says matter-of-factly.

I watch him stride back to his chair and wait until he sits down to question him further.

"You're telling me that they wanted *you* more than they wanted this?" I point at the amount of money to drive my point further.

I'm baffled.

A deep, sarcastic chuckle flows into the open space. Rhodes leans across the table, and my spine stiffens.

What if Ruby had it backward? What if it isn't the nannies who are seducing him and jumping into his bed uninvited but the other way around?

Rhodes's finger slips underneath the piece of paper, and he flips it to the last page. "If that weren't the case..." His voice is low and intimidating. "I wouldn't have to add this into the contract, now would I?"

I quickly scan the black ink and exhale.

In addition to the above contract, the Nanny (Sunny Edwards) agrees to remain professional and will not act in an unlawful manner toward the Parent (Rhodes Volkova). The Nanny (Sunny Edwards) understands and accepts the termination of this contract if the Parent sees fit.

Heat sweeps up my neck. I read it again, and I swear the room gets smaller.

When I finally flick my gaze to Rhodes, he appears cool, calm, and collected. His arms are crossed over his chest, but his face remains smooth and even.

A swallow works down my throat. "Does this go both ways?" I ask timidly.

Something crosses his face that I can't decipher. "I'm sorry, what?"

I glance away because it makes me more uneasy to look at him while explaining. "If you act in an unlawful manner toward me..." Embarrassment stains every free inch of my skin. "Do you accept my termination without a proper advanced notice?"

Heavy silence flows through the room like a wave. I finally gain the nerve to glance at Rhodes. His eyebrows are furrowed, and his lips are parted slightly. Our eyes snag, and I hate that I can't read him.

"I..." He clears his throat. "Yes. It goes both ways."

I inhale shallow breaths until my reservations lessen, and the familiar dark eyes fade from my memory. "Could you add that to the contract?" I ask quietly.

He nods, and I'm thankful he doesn't question it.

I take the pen and quickly initial the rest of the contract before sliding it across the table and into his possession.

His large hand clasps my sealed fate.

"Now that the contract is signed, I'd like to ask you a few questions."

Oh my god, is this an interview?

"Okay." I take a sip of my water because I suddenly feel parched.

"I saw that you took an Uber last night."

I nod.

"I've hired a driver for you and Ellie. That way, she will always have a way to and from places when I am not able to take her. Are you okay with that?"

My nerves instantly lessen. "Yes, of course. I do have my license, but I was afraid my car wouldn't make it here from Washington."

Rhodes studies me. "Washington? That's where you're from?"

"Yes."

He places his elbows on the table and seems more at ease. "Why are you in Chicago?"

I pause.

Lying seems wrong.

There's a weird tug on my morals that begs for me to tell the truth. I don't know if it's my integrity or if it's the way he's looking at me from across the table that has me lingering between a lie and the truth.

The media has labeled Rhodes Volkova as stoic, intimidating, impassive, private, and one of the prickliest hockey players in the league. But there is something about him that appeals to me. Sitting across the table from him, I have my reservations, and it's clear he has his own too. However, I feel like I know him, and I can't even begin to describe that.

"You know what—" Rhodes knuckle raps against the table. He stands a moment later, and I'm suddenly reminded why the media calls him intimidating. "It's none of my business."

I agree. It isn't his business.

But tell me why I felt the littlest push to tell him anyway?

His cologne engulfs me as he walks past. I follow after him like it's some sort of spell.

"Can you start tomorrow?" he asks.

"I'll be here at eight on the dot." I walk past him, desperate to feel the cool windy-city air against my flushed cheeks.

"Marco will take you home." Rhodes flicks his chin toward the sidewalk.

Marco?

I spin and spot an older gentleman standing beside a large SUV, wearing black pants, a black dress shirt, and tie. "Miss Edwards," he greets me with a warm smile.

I turn to say goodbye to Rhodes, but the door is shut, and he's nowhere to be found.

With a roll of my eyes, I put my back to my new boss's disappearing act and descend down the steps toward Marco.

"Hi." I smile. "You are welcome to call me Sunny."

Marco grabs my hand gently and gives it a soft shake. "It's nice to meet you, Sunny."

He opens the back door, and I stare at it awkwardly.

"Can I sit up front with you?" I ask.

The older man looks to Rhodes's home and then to me. He hesitates.

"No worries," I say softly. "We wouldn't want to make Mr. Grumpy angry."

Marco's eyes twinkle with amusement.

Once I'm inside and get over the nice leather seats and cleanliness of the vehicle, I smile to myself.

It'll only be a matter of time before I make friends with Marco.

Rhodes, though?

That's a different story.

Twelve

RHODES

IT TOOK three days for Sunny to spread all that sunshine of hers onto Marco. He's just as smitten with her as he is with Ellie.

Marco and I have known each other for several years. He used to drive the Zamboni for the rink before retiring. It wasn't until I ran into him a week ago when I learned that his wife had passed a year prior, leaving him alone and desperate for something to fill his time. The thought occurred to me that he'd probably jump right onto the opportunity of being employed by me.

He doesn't need the money.

He needs the distraction.

He needs the joy too.

And apparently, *Sunny* is that joy as of right now.

"Whatcha doing, Daddy?"

It's barely noticeable, but I jerk at the sound of my daughter catching me spying on my two newest employees.

"Blet!" I mutter.

Ellie smirks at my curse in Russian—something I rarely do because she's caught on to the meaning.

"Just checking out the weather." Weather. Sunny. Same-same.

I don't lie to Ellie, but there are times where I bend the truth for her own good.

This time, though, it's for *my* own good.

By now, I would've known everything there is to know about my daughter's newest nanny.

Typically, by day two, Ellie's newest nanny would have told me her every last secret and desire. I'd know all her hopes and dreams, regardless of how fucking uninterested I'd seem. It was as if they thought getting to know them would change my mind about not wanting them in a romantic way.

Sunny is completely different, though.

It's been all business with her.

Leaving Sunny and Marco outside to continue their morning catch-up session, I pull the stool out for Ellie and begin brushing her hair.

In broken Russian, she angrily curses.

I cringe and manage to keep myself from laughing. "Ellie," I warn. "Cursing in a different language is still cursing."

She sighs and slumps backward in her chair, giving me access to her long brown hair. It's unruly and tangled.

I'm fucking lost on what to do with it.

Most days, I just hand her a headband, and she pushes back the thick strands.

Today, though, I'm tempted to shave it.

I'm only half-kidding, but frustration skips up my spine as I pull my phone out and click on my trusty parenting hack: YouTube.

How to braid in simple terms.

It can't be that hard. I'm good with my hands.

I click on the first video and begin to follow along. Ellie's head jerks backward for the third time, and the warm chestnut-colored strands are tangled in my large fingers. I'm sweating and frustrated.

"Good morning, Rapunzel. Your chariot awaits." Sunny's cheery voice floats into the kitchen, and tell me why I fucking panic.

Ellie turns at the sound of her new nanny with my hands buried in her hair.

She pauses mid-step, and her smile fades. The confusion lasts three seconds before she slaps her palm over her mouth and hides a giggle, which only pisses me off further.

"Do you need help?" she finally says, creeping toward us.

"No," I snap.

Ellie curses in Russian again, and I shut my eyes. *For fuck's sake.*

I sigh loudly and pull my fingers out of Ellie's hair.

My ears are hot with anger.

I don't take failure lightly, even if it's something as simple as braiding hair.

I bend down and kiss the top of Ellie's head. "I'll see you for dinner, Printsessa." I lower my voice. "And stop cursing in Russian."

She tries not to smile.

Sighing, I turn and let Sunny take over. I keep my back to her, but I can see how quickly she braids my daughter's hair in the reflection of the window overlooking the backyard. She bends and whispers something into her ear. I see Ellie nod, and then I hear her feet slapping against the hardwood on her way over to me.

Her small arms wrap around my leg. "It's okay, Daddy." The disappointment in myself cuts that much deeper with her rosy cheeks and soft eyes looking up in my direction. "You can't be good at everything."

Sunny is right behind her with Ellie's yellow backpack slung over her shoulder.

"Can too," I reply.

———

The puck flies around the ice with so much velocity I'm surprised there isn't fire trailing behind.

"Early again?" Malaki zips onto the ice with his typical high energy.

I chase the puck, warming up my legs for practice. "I'm always early."

It's true. If I'm not with Ellie, I'm at the rink. The only problem lately has been that my nannies weren't reliable, so I've been in and out.

"Yeah." Malaki slips in front of me and steals the puck. "But not this early. You didn't take Ellie to school?"

I shake my head. "New nanny."

Malaki comes to a screeching halt. He rests his arm on top of his stick, and I catch the cheeky grin he's wearing.

Here we fucking go.

"Is she hot?"

"Is who hot?" Kane takes the ice next.

This is why I come extra early—so I can practice and get in the zone before everyone else shows up and starts pissing me off.

Kane begins stretching. "Does Grandpa have a girlfriend? No fucking way."

I haven't had a girlfriend since before Ellie. In fact, I haven't had a girlfriend since my early twenties. I was too focused on my career. Any woman I spent my time with was just someone I slept with occasionally. Gia just happened to be fertile one night, leaving me with something else to focus on.

"Shut the fuck up, Kane," I snap.

Emory, in his goalie gear, chuckles on his way to the net. I shoot him a glare.

"New nanny," Malaki tells Kane and all the other teammates who are listening.

Kane grins before swinging his smug face in my direction. "Well?"

"Well what?" I play with the puck, getting loose in my grip.

Kane skates a circle around me. "How old is she?"

"Twenty-six." Technically, twenty-five, but twenty-six sounds better. It's one of the only things I know about her, actually.

Several of my teammates slow their skating. Their blades come to a screeching halt. Anger flies to the soles of my feet, and I curl my lip. "If any of you even *think* of seeking my new nanny out...I'll make sure you never fuck another woman for the rest of your life."

Silence works its way down the line.

Kane chuckles. I immediately stare him down.

"But it might be worth it..." he says. "Depending on what she looks like. We could go out a winner."

My pupils dilate. My stick drops to the ice, and Kane's deranged smile appears. He loves a good punch to the face, because he's a sick fuck.

My teammates haven't even seen Sunny yet, and they're already starting their shit. I swoop down and grab my stick and head over to Emory, leaving Kane and my anger on the other side of the ice.

I have to mentally prepare myself for the things they're going to say when they *do* see her, because whether or not I want to admit it, Sunny is fucking gorgeous.

It's part of the reason why I didn't want to hire her.

I can ignore her charming smile and the spattering of freckles against her honey-colored skin, but I'm not sure the rest of the population can—especially some of my teammates.

Fuck.

I should have added that to the contract.

Winding back, I shoot a puck toward Emory and wait for him to snap angrily at me, considering he wasn't even paying attention.

To my surprise, he catches it at the last second and drops it to the ice.

"What the fuck was that for?" he asks, pulling his mask down.

I send another puck flying toward him and then another.

When I run out of pucks, he skates toward me in all his gear and angrily whips his mask up. "Feel better?"

"No!" I shout. "Kane pissed me off."

Emory chuckles. "He pisses everyone off."

I stare out into the empty stands, and before I can stop myself, I'm asking Emory for advice.

"Is it wrong of me to require my nanny to sign something that says she won't engage in any sexual relationships with anyone on the team?"

Emory blinks at me.

I blink back and wait for his answer.

There isn't an ounce of amusement on his face when he squints. "I'm sorry. Are you asking me for righteous advice? Do you recall my...fake marriage?"

He has a point. What the fuck am I doing asking for advice? I don't ask for advice.

He elbows me with his thick pad and nods past my shoulder. Coach walks onto the rink, which means we're about to start running plays.

Before we split, Emory pulls his mask down and answers

me. "Maybe get to know her and see if she's the type that would fuck your teammates before you start assuming." He sighs. "Take it from me...never assume."

I turn and skate toward center ice.

It wouldn't be a bad idea to get to know her a little.

After all, she's taking care of my daughter.

Thirteen

SUNNY

ELLIE IS HARD TO CRACK.

She doesn't demand my attention but doesn't discourage it either. I've been her nanny for one week, and although I've gotten her to laugh and smile multiple times, she isn't openly comfortable around me yet.

I suspect there is a lot of pent-up anger inside of her. Or fear? Abandonment? Maybe all of the above.

She watches me closely. If I leave the room, her green eyes follow me, like she thinks I might disappear, but she never asks where I'm going.

"This is a record, you know." A deep voice says.

I spring away from leaning against the kitchen island and spin to meet my new boss, whom I've really hardly spoken to since being hired.

How can someone so large be so quiet?

Like always, he smells decadent. Each time he comes home from his second practice of the day, he's freshly showered with damp hair and a clean, manly scent lingering behind him. It's hard not to notice.

"What's a record?" I ask, gathering my things.

Rhodes leans against the cabinets and crosses his arms over his black hoodie. He stares past me at Ellie, who's putting birdseed into the new feeder that Marco gifted to her.

I've learned more about Marco this last week than I have Ellie or her father. He's much more open than either of them. He reminds me of Gramps, with his soft-spoken tone and kind smile.

"Having a nanny stick around for more than a few days."

I pause. Is he serious?

Silence passes between us.

God, he is serious.

"You're kidding me," I say.

Rhodes glances to the ceiling. "Nope." His gaze shifts back over to me. "By now, they would have tried getting me in bed —or worse."

I'm afraid to know more, but I can't help myself. "Worse?"

Rhodes pushes off the cabinets and rests his hands on top of the island counter. He stares at me intensely. "Yes, worse."

My eyebrow hitches as I wait for him to explain.

He sighs. "Two of them ended up in my bed."

I tilt my chin. "Well...did you invite them?"

His eyes narrow. "No."

"Okay, well...that's—"

Awkward.

He finishes the sentence for me. "Called desperation."

I laugh weakly and continue gathering my things. I put my back to him and glance at Ellie again. She tilts her chin while looking up at Marco, who seems to be teaching her all about birds.

"Do you have a boyfriend?"

My heart slips with his question. I freeze with my hand on the zipper of my bag.

Out of my peripheral vision, I see him stand upright and cross his arms again. The stance seems so defensive. There's an edginess to his tone that I'd usually ignore, but with the question sending the hairs on my arms erect, I can't help but become wary. It's too...*personal*. Too much like *he who must not be named*.

And for once, I'm not referencing *Harry Potter*.

"Wondering why I haven't tried to seduce you like all the other nannies?" I blurt.

Oh my god. Did I really just say that?

Rhodes's throat bobs as he eyes me from across the counter. I wait with a held breath to see what he'll say next. I can see why the other nannies would want to seduce him—his prickly personality is sort of tantalizing. They viewed him as a challenge, just like I was once viewed as one. But there are lines that can't be crossed, and this is one of them.

"No," he answers me confidently. "You're not that type of woman. That's why you still have a job."

I laugh out loud, but it's as sarcastic as it gets. Rhodes tilts his head and observes me.

"Oh? Is that why I haven't expressed some sort of attraction to you? Because I'm not that type of woman?"

His eye twitches. My heart beats fast, and I know I should shut up, but there's something pushing me to lengthen my spine and act with confidence. Otherwise, I may find myself in the same position as I was in before.

"What if I told you it's because I just don't find you attractive, *Mr. Volkova*?"

I pride myself on remaining professional, but there is something frustratingly irking with his tone of voice and question over whether or not I have a boyfriend. It stings, because although he's unaware, I am very much aware as to why I don't have a boyfriend or why I haven't expressed any sort of interest in any male for almost a year.

Not to mention, I'm lying through my teeth.

I'd have to be blind not to be attracted to him. His green eyes rimmed with dark lashes alone are enough to lure anyone into his bed.

I'm not *anyone*, though.

Rhodes grumbles under his breath. I stand completely still while he rounds the side of the counter. He's so close I can feel his warmth. I stop breathing when he leans down beside me.

I'm not afraid of him.

Though, it surprises me.

With any other guy, boss or not, I felt the need to run.

With Rhodes? There's a strong compulsion to turn my head and face him.

"Good." The word is no louder than a breath. "I was only asking because tomorrow is the first game you'll be attending with my daughter." He pauses, and I have no idea where he's going with this. "And once my teammates see you, they're going to advance."

I blink with surprise but keep my features intact otherwise.

"That means they're going to make lewd comments and try to fuck you, Sunny."

My lips part with a soft gasp.

I'm not sure how he made such a racy statement sound ordinary, but he did.

"You're not to fraternize with my teammates, *Ms. Edwards.*"

There's a very child-like response on the tip of my tongue, but I have enough maturity to bypass it. I turn my head slightly and am smacked right in the face with his hot mouth no more than a few inches from mine. I pull my attention to his eyes, and he lifts an eyebrow.

Unfortunately, I see it as a challenge, and I yield too much clout, preventing me from being able to keep my mouth shut.

"What about with the other team?" I ask, testing my limits. *What am I doing?*

His green eyes light up, but before he can do anything, the door swings open, and he steps away.

"Are you ready, Sunny?" Marco asks, shutting the door behind him.

Ellie comes bouncing through the kitchen with her messy braids swinging behind her shoulders. "Hi, Daddy!"

Rhodes sighs before bending down to get on her level. Ellie's bottom lip plops out, and her eyebrows scrunch.

Rhodes has obviously clicked into *dad* mode, which is... sort of adorable. With me, he's stony-faced and somber. From the few clips I've seen of him playing hockey, he's even more intense on the ice. But with his daughter, he's gentle.

"Do you know what I'm going to say?" he asks softly. His eyebrow hitches, and I rest against the counter, watching the interaction play out.

Ellie drops her head slightly and looks off to the right. "No."

Rhodes sighs again. "Don't make it worse by lying to me, Printsessa."

A gush of something warm swoops through me. I know that Rhodes is Russian, but according to the media, he came to the United States at such a young age that he hardly speaks the language anymore. The only tell *was* his last name before he added an A to it in his early twenties for some reason. He doesn't even talk with an accent *unless* he's using the language. Even then, it's minimal. Those snippets, though? They snag my attention.

Ellie blows a big breath out of her mouth. Her forehead

puckers with big emotions before she explodes. "Ugh!" she shouts. "It's not my fault that I don't want to play *family* on the playground with the other girls! It's stupid!"

Ellie runs past Rhodes and disappears somewhere throughout the house.

Part of me wants to go after her, but I know better. She left because she doesn't want to be bothered, not because she wants us to chase her. Ellie isn't like most little girls I know. She's different.

Marco and I catch each other's attention before we both turn and glance at Rhodes. He's abandoned his kneeling position and is standing with his head hung low, with his hands bracing himself against the counter.

I sort of feel bad for him.

His gruff, sarcastic chuckle breaks the silence.

I nibble on my lip and debate whether or not I should insert myself.

Marco nods when I look back to him, and I take it as encouragement.

A shaky sigh leaves me. "Anything we can help with?" I ask, roping Marco into the situation too. We're a team, even if he doesn't know that.

Rhodes twists his neck and stares at me. His knuckles are white from the pressure he's forcing onto the quartz counter. "She climbed the fence on her playground today and walked over to the middle school playground to play soccer with the older kids." He drops his head again and clenches his jaw tightly. "Her teacher keeps saying that Ellie rebukes against any socializing with kids her age. I just don't understand."

Oh.

I step forward. "I do."

Rhodes pops up from the counter and stares at me.

"The other little girls were playing 'family'?" I ask, using quotations around the word family.

He nods. "Yeah, whatever the fuck that is."

I rest my hip against the counter. "It's where they play pretend." I put a finger up for each role that I list. "Someone is the dad, mom, and then the baby. Occasionally, they'll throw a pet in there too."

Rhodes and Marco share a look, and each man looks equally confused.

I shrug. "It's something little girls do. We like the whole make-believe, perfect-family thing. My guess is that Ellie feels uncomfortable playing that because..." There's a twinge in my heart, keeping me from explaining the rest. I'm not sure if Rhodes and Ellie's mother were in love or close in that regard. There aren't any photos of them on the internet, according to Ruby's deep dive, and the only one in the house is one where she's alone. Ellie isn't even in the photo.

The scruffing of Rhodes's hand moving against his five-o-clock shadow pulls my attention. "Fuck," he mumbles.

"Do you want me to go find her?" I ask softly. "I can sort of...relate."

Rhodes doesn't make eye contact with me. He only shakes his head and spins, heading in the same direction that Ellie went.

Marco and I follow him with our eyes before it's just us in the kitchen.

There's a sadness in the room—one that wasn't there before. My own mother died when I was too young to remember her, so I know the emptiness that void brings. It's something she'll eventually fill, maybe not all the way, but little by little, she'll fill it.

The clearing of Marco's throat brings me back to the present. His smile warms the sadness lingering. "Where are we headed this evening, Sunny?"

I sling my bag over my shoulder and pull out my phone for the address to the new Airbnb. It's in a completely different neighborhood, and when I show Marco the address, he grimaces.

Must be in a great neighborhood.

"Don't worry." I pat Marco's arm. "I'll be fine."

He sighs disapprovingly before leading me toward the front door.

Fourteen

RHODES

"GET SOME NEW LEGS OUT THERE!" Coach is nervously pacing the space behind the bench. Kane and I both stand, and the second we get the chance, we change the lineup. We're down by one, but it's only the second period, so I'm not worried.

Yet.

Malaki stays in, playing defense. We let Kane control the flow on the ice, setting the pace. We work together like an old squeaky machine. Hockey is a team sport. I learned that well before I hit the Peewee level. It took Kane a little while to understand, but once we got Emory as our goalie, things started to shift.

The team grew stronger and more serious.

We got our legs back, and they're fucking strong.

"Swiper no swiping." Malaki zips past, and adrenaline flies to my hands. It's a stupid name for the play, but considering Malaki came up with it, he got to name it.

The line is tracking the call, and as soon as Malaki swipes

the puck away, it goes right to my stick. I play with it for a few seconds before sending it to Kane, who sends it back to me.

A Hurricane player comes up on me quickly, and I slip it between his legs, and Kane is in possession.

He's in the perfect spot.

Smack-dab in center ice.

I watch him wind up. He has phenomenal control of the puck. I've never seen anything like it.

At the last moment, I shout to Malaki, "Up!"

He jumps, and the little black puck hits the back of the net, going right between the goalie's legs.

Kane skates off, acting unperturbed. The crowd is going wild as the team skates over to him, patting him on the back. Our helmets hit, and I feel myself grinning.

Kane snorts. "I got you to smile? Let me fix that."

I squint, feeling my smile disappear right away. Kane wraps his arm around my shoulders, and before I can shake him off, he gets close and says, "I saw your new nanny."

My spine stiffens. I know Kane can feel it through my pads. He skates off, laughing. We play a few more seconds before the buzzer sounds, and we head toward the locker room.

I watch Kane like a hawk. His attention swings to the box seats that I gave to Sunny for her and Ellie to sit in. I've done a good job at staying centered and focused during the game. After all, I owe it to my team after spending the first half of the season distracted.

There may be less anxiety that it's a home game too, keeping me from constantly searching for Ellie.

Or is it because you know Sunny isn't like the rest?

I push the thought away because one week of being my daughter's nanny doesn't make me trust her.

Emory comes up behind Kane and nudges him from behind. I see them talking to each other as I slowly skate toward the bench. Before I make it all the way, I watch Emory peer up at the box and then shake his head at Kane.

I groan and pull my mask away from my face. I look in the same direction toward the stands with a knot in my stomach. The last several times Ellie has come to a game, the nanny has abandoned her. A few have left altogether. The redhead, I learned, was getting fucked by one of the other team's coaches in the locker room. Try explaining that to a five-year-old.

My jaw unclenches when I see that Ellie is perfectly fine. Her rosy cheeks are smashed onto the glass as she follows the ice girls who are cleaning the ice shavings for the third period.

Unfortunately, my jaw *reclenches* when I see Sunny standing beside her...wearing my fucking jersey.

Jesus fucking Christ.

I'm spinning with emotions. I stand on the ice and glare into the stands, unable to skate forward.

"Excuse me." One of the ice girls moves around me, and it shakes me out of my trance.

Why the hell is Sunny wearing my jersey? Did she just...go into my room and grab it? What would make her think that I'd be okay with that?

The disappointment is fresh.

My teeth click. I squeeze my jaw tightly.

Not only am I angry that she's wearing my jersey, but I'm angry that I expected something different with her. As each day passed with Sunny as Ellie's new nanny, my optimism grew. I'd watched her closely, and she seemed genuine, like she was there to fulfill her duties and nothing more.

Now look at her.

My fists tighten.

Does she think wearing my jersey makes her mine? Is that her subtle way of getting my attention? I'll admit, the other nannies were a little more obvious. They just showed me their tits the first chance they got.

Sunny, though? No. She went beyond—wearing *my* jersey to *my* game. That's an ulterior motive if I've ever seen one.

It's the ultimate *'she's mine'* play. Whether you're in college or the pros. It's a tale as old as time. Your significant other wears your jersey to the game. It's as simple as that.

Except, Sunny isn't mine, and I didn't approve of this.

I pray the media hasn't gotten wind of it. Not only am I protective over Ellie being in the limelight, but a rumor of me dating her new nanny?

Especially one as beautiful and young as her? They'll think I've corrupted her.

Fucking hell.

With frustration propelling me, I catch the eye of the security guard standing at the end of the hall leading toward the lockers. I tell him that I need him to get the woman in the second box seat—the one with my jersey on. He nods and scurries off.

Now, I wait.

Coach has likely realized I'm not in the locker room, but he'll let it slide since I'm considered a veteran on the team, and we have our trusty agreement when it comes to Ellie.

This *sort of* has to do with her.

My chest grows tighter the longer I wait.

The clock is ticking.

When I hear someone walking toward the end of the hall, my blood thickens.

"Thank you," I hear her say softly. She must be talking to the security guard.

She sounds so...*sweet*. It pisses me off.

My steps are slow and methodical. The closer I get to her, the angrier I become—purely because I can't help but notice how fucking perfect she looks in my jersey. It's been a long time since I've seen someone as beautiful as she is wearing my number.

She is a conundrum, appearing so innocent and sweet but has a tongue on her that catches me off guard at times.

This is catching me off guard too.

There's a hitch in my breath when she stands in front of me. I take a moment to appreciate the subtle softness about her before I ream her.

Warm, brown hair, braided back—probably to match Ellie's. Bright-pink cheeks that I know are spattered with freckles that I noticed yesterday in the kitchen when I got too close to her. Glistening pink lips that are full and often open to a bright white smile that could make any man stop in his tracks.

Damn her.

"Hey! Is everything okay?" she asks, feigning concern and still somehow sounding *happy.*

I'm even angrier now.

Why did I think she was different?

I got my hopes up.

Erasing the rest of the space between us, I scowl. It surprises me when she doesn't back away. I tower over her on any good day, but with my skates on, I'm even taller. She tilts her chin and stares up into my face. For a *split* second, I drop my eyes to her mouth.

Jesus.

It's the jersey.

It's fucking with my head.

"What the *hell* do you think you're doing?" I snap.

A line of confusion works its way onto her smooth forehead. "What?"

I quickly snap my hand forward to grab onto the jersey, but I stop at the last second because...did she just *flinch?*

My tight jaw loosens.

Did she think I was going to hit her?

I know I can be intimidating at times, and with the way

the media describes me, I'm one breath away from shouting at someone, but I don't hit women.

I slowly drop my hand by my side. I only allow myself to linger on her reaction for a second before I snap out of it.

"Wearing my jersey?" I ask. "Is that your way of getting into my head and telling me you're interested?"

Sunny squints. Her forehead furrows even more. She looks down at the Blue Devil on her chest before an amused gasp flees from her mouth.

I don't allow her to come up with some stupid, flirty excuse.

It's too obvious, and I'm irritated.

"Take it off," I demand.

She snaps her honey-colored eyes to mine, and my body buzzes at the thought of her stripping in front of me.

Fuck, what?

"I'm sorry, you want me to take it off?" She's completely perturbed by the thought.

In the worst way, I want to advance on her. I want to grip the hem of the jersey and rip it off her body.

But I don't.

Because who knows what she's wearing underneath it, and also, she fucking...*flinched.*

Sunny takes a step away. "You're angry because I'm wearing your jersey?" She nods to herself, like she understands. "You think I wore it because I *want* you?"

Well, she doesn't have to say it like that.

Like she's disgusted at the thought.

"I understand why you'd think that." Her soft voice is like some sort of melody. "Being egotistical and all."

What—

"I didn't wear your jersey because I want you, *Mr. Volkova.*"

Oh, so now she wants to sass me?

I also wish she'd quit calling me '*Mr. Volkova*' in that insolent tone. It causes dangerous thoughts—ones that I will take to the grave.

In an attempt to gain my control back, I lower my voice. "Then why did you wear it, *Ms. Edwards*?"

Her thick eyelashes flutter.

My dick twitches.

Heat moves through my bloodstream, and I start to sweat even more than before.

"I wore it because Ellie asked me to."

What?

Fucking hell.

Of course she did.

"She wanted me to match her, and since I don't have a Chicago Blue Devils shirt or hoodie, she grabbed this out of your closet." Somehow, Sunny remains calm and self-assured. The explanation flows out of her mouth smoothly, and I know deep down that it's the truth.

Silence passes between us.

The longer I stare at her, the worse I feel. The only thing I can manage is a grunt of understanding. Her mouth twitches at the noise.

"Am I dismissed, sir?" she asks, voice edging on amusement.

Sir.

I shut my eyes and breathe heavily through my nose. There are those dirty, inappropriate thoughts again.

I apparently need to fuck someone.

My eyes remain closed until I hear a shuffling in front of me. Assuming she is heading back toward Ellie, I open my eyes, only to get punched in the gut.

I catch a quick glimpse of her curves and the smooth skin along her torso as she pulls my jersey from her body. My stomach tightens when her lacy bra plays peek-a-boo beneath the thin long-sleeve shirt she has on underneath. She's quick to pull it down, hiding her body from me. She adjusts herself before holding out the bundled-up material in her hand for me to take.

"I'd like to get back to Ellie now—if that's okay with you, *sir.*"

Every muscle locks. There's a challenge present in her eyes, and I fall right for it.

My fingers get lost in the jersey material, but it doesn't take long for me to trap her hand in mine. We're not palm to palm—the fabric rests between us—but I can feel the warmth coming from her hand.

I pull her in close.

She almost bounces against my pads.

A quick gasp escapes her mouth, and I can't help but feel entertained by it.

"Stop calling me *sir.*"

Her throat works along her neck. Her chin dips with a tight nod, and I gently let her go.

Sunny backs away immediately and leaves.

I stand in the dark hallway and replay the entire interaction over and over again until I hear my team leave the locker room. I take the jersey with me and throw it to a fan not too far from the bench.

I'm not sure I trust myself to wear it after it touched Sunny's body.

Fifteen

SUNNY

"HOW IS IT GOING, sweetheart? Are you staying warm?"

I smile at the sound of Nana's voice. It's always been the most comforting sound in the world.

"Nana," I chide. "It's no colder than Washington. I'm used to the chill in the air."

Though, it feels a bit nippier than Washington, considering I'm surrounded by an awfully *cold* man.

"Well…" There's a shuffling on the other end of the phone. "Make sure you wear long johns if you get too cold at night. You know they trap the heat in."

I roll my lips so I don't laugh. *Long johns.* I wonder what she'd think if she knew that the ones she gave me were shoved underneath the creaky, old window at the Airbnb I'm residing in to keep the cold air from gusting in while I sleep.

"Yes, Nana," I say to appease her. "Don't worry. You've raised me well."

"And how is the man?"

She's referring to Rhodes.

"He's...fine. We don't really talk much. I'm only over at the house when he's away, and so far, it's just been a couple of games and long practices."

Nana sighs. "Well, just be careful, sweetheart. I still don't like the idea of you all the way in Chicago without any family near."

Guilt churns in my stomach.

Nana doesn't exactly know the whole reason I moved this far from Washington. After I told her that it's because I'm making enough money to cover the rest of her nursing home costs there—which isn't a lie—she began searching for a cheaper one. I had to guilt her into staying put, thus circling back to even more guilt for me.

My fingers twiddle with clay as I shape it into a small bead. I grab a skewer and push it through the middle, creating a little space for a string to go through after it dries.

Painting is my forte, but that doesn't just apply to canvases. If I'm feeling antsy, I'll make some type of trinket out of clay to occupy my hands and paint it whenever I find the time. I figure I'd make some beads for Ellie so maybe we can bond over making bracelets.

"I'm *fine*, Nana. It makes me feel better that you're in the same nursing home as Gramps, so shush. I'm staying put. The money is too good, and the hours give me plenty of time to paint again."

"Allison, that's wonderful that you're painting again."

I don't bother correcting her when she uses my full name. No one is around to question the slip.

My phone beeps, and I pull it away from my ear. *Mr. Volkova* flashes on the screen, and my stomach dips.

"Hey, Nana, let me call you later. My boss is calling."

"Okay, sweetheart. I love you."

I hang up with my nana and switch the call over to Rhodes.

"Hello?"

"I need you to go to the school to get Ellie."

If there wasn't such an urgency to his voice, I'd probably mention how he didn't even greet me, but after a week of working for him, I've learned that Rhodes isn't the type of man who likes his buttons pressed.

That doesn't stop me from *wanting* to press his buttons, though. I just have enough self-control to ignore the impulse.

"Is she okay?" I quickly climb to my feet.

He grumbles a yes under his breath and follows it with a sarcastic chuckle.

I'll pry later.

"I'm on my way."

"Do you need me to send Marco?" he asks.

Echoing voices cut through the other end, and I know he's at practice.

"No, it's the fifth," I state.

"So?"

"He's at his wife's grave. He goes on the fifth of every month."

Rhodes is silent as I continue to shuffle around to find my coat. The Airbnb is smaller than Rhodes's entryway, and yet, I still can't find anything.

"I'm nearby. I'll just bring Ellie back to my place, and you can pick her up after practice."

"Yeah," he says. "That'll work. I'll be done in forty."

"I'll send you the address."

"Okay."

Silence.

Awkward silence.

"Okay...well, bye!"

"Sunny."

My finger hovers over the *end call* button. "Yes?"

He clears his throat. "Thank you."

My eyebrows shoot to my forehead. "You're welcome, Mr. Volkova."

I smile to myself and hang up the phone, knowing that it makes his eyes narrow each time I call him that.

I guess I'm not mature enough not to press his buttons after all.

———

When I walk into the school, I immediately grow anxious.

I don't relax until I see her sitting on the bench in the hallway. She looks so out of place. Whereas most of the students' uniforms are pressed neatly without a wrinkle to be seen, Ellie's polo is untucked, and her khaki skirt is flipped up on the ends. Her braids are messy with little tendrils falling into her face. Her legs swing back and forth while she looks to be pondering something.

"Hi," I say, taking a seat beside her.

She snaps to attention. Her mouth opens with shock. "Where is Daddy?"

"He sent me instead." I eye her closely. Ellie does a pretty good job at hiding her emotions, but I don't miss the relief that works itself onto her face.

Hmm. "Why do you look so relieved?"

"What does that mean?" she asks innocently.

"It means you're happier to see me than you are him, but there must be a reason for that." I nod to the principal's door. "Did you get in trouble?"

Ellie looks away. Her little hands, stained with marker, grab onto the bench. There's a shift in the air, and my heart falls. "You stay right here," I whisper, tapping her knee.

I climb to my feet and walk to the principal's door and

gently knock. The door opens, and Ellie's principal, whom I see in passing every morning, seems confused.

"Hello." I smile. "I'm Ellie's nanny. Mr. Volkova sent me to pick her up. I should be on the list."

"Oh, right." She blinks a few times, probably shocked that I'm still sticking around since the others were so fleeting. "Well, come in."

I turn and wink at Ellie. Her cheeks turn pink.

Once the door is shut, I feel like *I'm* the one in trouble. The walls are lined with built-in bookshelves with old books in their rightful spots. The office is what I'd expect at a prestigious college, not an elementary school.

Where are the bright colors?

"Is everything okay?" I stand near the door. It seems safer.

"How long have you been Ellie's nanny?" the principal asks.

I guess introductions are a thing of the past.

I shift on my feet. "A little over a week."

Her hands rest on top of the desk, and she nods. "Well, you've made it longer than the rest."

"And I intend to stay much longer. Ellie is a wonderful kid." I soften my voice so she doesn't think I'm being snippy. Though, I want to be.

"She is." There's a dramatic pause. "However, I'm concerned with her behavior."

"I'm assuming that has something to do with me picking her up early?" I ask.

"I've tried telling Mr. Volkova that she's a little withdrawn, but it doesn't seem to be getting better. She's smart and mature for her age. When she's older, that will benefit her, but as a kindergartener, it's concerning. She doesn't have many friends and is very distrusting of adults."

"What happened today?" I ask.

The principal drops her head. "Today, they had a substitute in music class, and Ellie refused to speak or even partici-pate." She looks me directly in the eye. "So, I had the school psychologist evaluate her."

My hackles rise.

"Did her father approve of that?"

She glances away.

I'll take that as a no.

"Well, no. But the reason I called him to pick Ellie up a little early was because I wanted to bring it to his attention that the final outcome was that with Ellie's unstable home life, it is causing her to become apprehensive, mistrusting, skeptical..."

My heart beats a little faster with her implication that Ellie's home life is unstable.

I question her. "Unstable?"

She laughs softly. "I'm not sure you know this, but Ellie has had multiple nannies in the past several months, so yes, unstable."

Anger clouds my judgment.

I suddenly become protective over Ellie.

I know all about not trusting people, and that doesn't mean that Ellie's life is unstable or that Rhodes isn't doing the best he can, like this snotty woman is obviously implying.

"Do you know why he has switched nannies so frequent-ly?" she asks.

I eye her closely.

Does she think this is going to turn into a gossiping session?

"Yes."

She waits for me to explain, but I don't.

I understand her concern, but there is something about her tone that rubs me the wrong way. That may be because I'm distrusting as well, or it may be because she's acting *awfully* judgy.

"Well, then"—she clasps her hands—"I hope bringing this to your attention will make a difference as it has not with her father."

My hand rests on the door handle, and another line of anger works through me. I turn and look over my shoulder, pinning the principal in her spot. "Mr. Volkova is an amazing, caring father. The reason Ellie has had so many nannies isn't because of him. It's because of them. He's trying his best to find the right person for her."

I'm just as surprised at the rising of my voice as she is. A surprising wave of protectiveness comes over me at the thought of her thinking Rhodes isn't a good father.

I've known bad fathers. He isn't one of them.

I open the door and see Ellie standing right in front of the threshold with her ear turned toward the office. I give her a look, and she scurries away, pretending she wasn't eavesdropping.

Before I leave, with Ellie's hand in mine, the principal's parting words linger, "I hope you're the right person. For Ellie's sake."

Sixteen

RHODES

I **SIT** outside of the address Sunny had given me and can't help but be concerned. It's not far from Ellie's school—definitely walking distance—and it's not in a dangerous neighborhood. However, it's where I'd assume a poor college student would reside while they consumed nothing but Ramen noodles and attended frat parties every night of the week.

In fact, there's a frat house three houses down, and I can only imagine what those horny nineteen-year-old boys think when they see her bouncing up those cracked, concrete steps every evening after Marco drops her off.

I pull my hood up and exit my truck. I keep my head down as I stride towards the front door.

Faint music slips out from behind it, and I can make out that it's Taylor Swift—Ellie's favorite. I am man enough to admit that I know every last word to the song that's playing—something Ellie is very proud of and something that half the team makes fun of me for.

My knuckles rap against the thin door, but neither my

daughter nor Sunny answer. I lean over the rusty railing and look through the window. Gauzy curtains hang in front of the glass, but I can make out my daughter's bright smile instantly. Her hair is free from her braids, and wavy pieces of it fling around as she dances to the song.

I lose my footing when I see Sunny grab onto Ellie's hand and spin her around until she's holding her belly with laughter. Sunny's smile matches Ellie's, and something warm comes over me.

I step away and clear my throat.

The guys referred to Sunny as a hot burst of sunshine—emphasis on the word *hot*.

I refused to agree, because she's Ellie's nanny, making her my employee, but I will say that she reminds me of sunshine. Her smile is bright, and so far, everyone that I've known to come in direct contact with her ends up a little more cheerful than before. Ellie, Marco, the fucking security guard from my game... Even Scottie, Emory's wife, mentioned that Sunny had hit it off with the rest of the wives and significant others in the box seats.

I sigh and knock again.

No answer.

I'm not one to invade someone's privacy, but considering I can hear Taylor Swift blasting throughout the small house, I turn the doorknob, only for the door not to budge.

The handle turns, so I know it's unlocked.

But stuck?

It doesn't take much of a nudge from my shoulder for the door to make way. Something topples over near my feet when I step inside.

A chair?

Uncertainty slices through me. I check the doorknob from the inside and twist the lock.

It doesn't work.

I frown.

That's unsettling.

"Hello?" I shout.

I stay near the door and eye Ellie's backpack resting on the floor beside her shoes. Right beside hers are Sunny's.

The place is tiny. I can see directly into the living room where they were just dancing. Now, they're nowhere to be found.

I move a little farther into the house. My finger hovers over a Bluetooth speaker to silence it, and that's when I see them.

They're both on the kitchen floor, sitting cross-legged. Ellie's back is to me, but I can tell she's working furiously on something. Sunny sits beside her and watches her closely with her lips formed into a soft smile.

She's alluring.

I bet she tastes like honey.

My throat bobs.

That was a wild thought.

I crack my neck, shake myself out of the spell Taylor Swift's love song just put me under, and hit pause on the speaker.

Sunny snaps her head to me and jumps in front of Ellie.

I'm taken aback with surprise from her sudden protectiveness over my daughter.

It's only after a few seconds that Sunny's defensive stance loosens, and she places her hand over her rising chest. "Rhodes."

"Daddy!" Ellie zips past Sunny with a wet paintbrush in her hand and moves to hug my leg. At the last second, Sunny plucks the paintbrush out of her hand and holds it up high.

"That's not washable paint," she laughs.

I wouldn't care if Ellie got paint on my clothing, but I don't blame Sunny for assuming I would. After all, I've been nothing but callous since hiring her.

"Hi, Printsessa," I mutter.

"Look what Sunny made!" Ellie tugs me farther into the kitchen.

It's so tight I hardly fit.

Sunny squeezes past me and disappears. I glance at the mess on the floor and try to make sense of it.

"What...is it?" I ask my daughter, confused.

"Beads. Sunny is an artist! Did you know that? She's letting me paint them!"

Oh. I did not know that.

"Beads? For...?" My sentence trails when Ellie's cheeks puff up with air.

She rolls her eyes.

I swear to god, girls are born with that ability.

"To make friendship bracelets! Duh!"

Guess I should have just known that by her tone of voice.

"Alright, well go ahead and finish the last bead before we head home."

Ellie drops my hand and plops back down. There's a thick slab of clay off to the side where Sunny was sitting, various colors of paints, paintbrushes, and some household things that are probably being repurposed as tools for the clay.

I walk back the way I came—so a total of three strides—and end up near the front door.

Sunny is bent over, fiddling with the lock that I've already learned is broken. I can't help but drop my attention to her tight jeans.

I look away as soon as I realize what I'm doing.

"It's broken," I say.

I lean against the wall that separates the living room and entryway. I cross my arms and act nonchalant, though I'm uneasy thinking about her living in a place that doesn't even have a lock.

I was a horny college kid once.

I had a lot more restraint than most, but it would be too easy for one of them to slip right inside and pursue her.

Apparently, I'm just a horny single dad now.

"I know." Sunny taps the cheap chair that I easily shoved off to the side when coming inside. "That's why I had this propped against the door."

"I knocked," I add. "But you didn't answer, so I walked in."

Her lip disappears into her mouth, and she nibbles on it.

I point to the chair. "That means your little security system doesn't work."

A laugh erupts from her. "Obviously."

I step forward. "Would you like me to fix the lock for you?"

Otherwise, you're coming with us.

"Oh." She shakes her head. "No, it's fine. I'm only here for a couple more days."

I wait for more of an explanation.

She waves her clay-covered hand around. "It's an Airbnb."

Wait, what? She doesn't have a place that's hers?

"So for the next two days, you're not going to lock the door?" I stare at her with disappointment.

"I'll...um..." She glances around. "I'll use this!" She pats the couch and smiles.

She's quick on her feet. I'll give her that.

I can't help but chuckle as I imagine her small frame pushing at the couch until it reaches the door, then doing it again when she needs to leave the house.

Sunny's lips twitch, but she does a good job at keeping the bravery going.

I shake my head. "Try again."

"Excuse me?" Her arms cross, and she pops a hip.

It's sort of cute when she tries to stand up to me. I think I like it. It's *refreshing.*

"I can't have you living in a place that doesn't even have a working lock."

I leave her—and the confusion she's obviously working through from my suddenly caring heart—and begin to walk around the place. Something is shoved underneath one of the windows. A blanket? I assume it's to keep the cold out. Or maybe it's another one of her clever security measures.

Right past the kitchen, where Ellie is surprisingly still concentrating on painting, I move to a door. I slowly push against the wood and peek inside. There's a mattress on the floor and an open suitcase. There's another window off to the right with pillows propped up against it, probably to block the wind.

I do one more sweep of the area but backtrack when I see something black on the floor.

Her bra.

A lacy one.

I desperately try to erase the image from my head and end up back near the front door where Sunny is trying to scoot the couch.

"Can you gather your things?"

Sunny turns. "Oh, her things are—"

She pauses when she realizes Ellie is still in the kitchen.

Her soft gaze turns skeptical. "Are you talking to me?"

She points at herself, and I nod.

"You're not staying here."

There it is. A subtle eye roll. "You're just as bad as Marco. I'm *fine*, Mr. Volkova. I promise."

Rubbing my palm against my jaw, I chuckle. "I'm sorry. Let me rephrase..."

Her forehead furrows.

"Get your things, Ms. Edwards, because you are not staying here."

Am I being bossy? Sure.

But I *am* her boss.

She smiles, but I'm almost certain it's sarcastic. She leans against the couch and crosses her arms. "And where would you like me to go?"

"My place." Where else?

Her smile falls.

The air in the room shifts.

"No."

I raise an eyebrow. "Why not?"

"Because..." She drags the word out while she probably tries to come up with a good excuse.

"You'd feel safer here versus my home? I can assure you that it's safe. Otherwise, my daughter wouldn't be living there."

Her eyes dart towards the kitchen.

This is the first time I've ever seen her...ruffled.

"It's not that," she mutters.

"Then what is it?"

Her shoulders drop in defeat, and she swings her gaze back to me. "I don't understand." Her face screws with confusion. "You scold me for wearing your jersey, and you're so against a nanny coming onto you." She glances toward Ellie in the kitchen and lowers her voice. "Yet, now you want me to *live* in your house? What? You finally trust me now?"

If I'm not mistaken, she's changing the subject and turning this around on me.

I let her, though, because clearly, whatever has her all tripped up is something she's keeping close to the chest.

It's not my business, so I don't press.

"If I say yes, will you agree?"

The room is wound tight. Pressure falls to my shoulders while I wait for her answer.

I impulsively decide to be honest with her. I shove my hands into my pockets. "You're the first nanny I've ever had that I feel like I can trust, Ms. Edwards. Ellie likes you." *And I guess I do too.* "Now that we have you, we're not letting you go. So it's either you let me put you up in some penthouse with a real security system, or you move into my house where I can assure you the heater works, you'll have your own bathroom, and I'll put a lock on your bedroom door if that's the issue here. We can even add it into the contract." I inhale a breath because I'm beginning to sound desperate. "It would make things a lot easier for me, if I'm being honest."

Something flashes across her face. Where I normally see smile lines, I see worry ones instead. I leave her to think it over while I go check on Ellie. I tell her to wash her hands since she's nearly done painting, and when I come back toward the front door, I catch Sunny's eye.

"Okay," she says.

Okay? That's a yes.

Her shaky breath fills the small area, and she nods to herself.

"I'll send Marco to grab you before dinner."

That gives her time to gather her things and me time to get the guest room ready. The last time anyone was in that room was when Ellie decided to hide from one of the nannies...for three hours.

"We will see you in a few." I grab Ellie's backpack.

After she says a quick goodbye to Sunny, we make it outside before she glances up at me. "Do you have a game tonight?"

"As if you don't have the schedule memorized."

She puckers her lips and climbs into the backseat of my truck. I buckle her into her booster seat. "Then why is Sunny coming over?"

I step back. "She's going to move in."

Her little jaw opens.

"She'll stay in the guest room, and there will be some

ground rules," I add. "We can talk about it when we get home. Just like we are going to talk about what happened at school today with your music teacher."

Ellie grumbles under her breath, and I know for a fact she learned that from me. That's the hard thing when you're a single parent. All their bad habits come from *you*. I shut her door and glance behind me at the sound of shuffling feet.

A group of jocks, wearing their college letterman jackets, slowly walk past Sunny's. They're all looking in the window like a bunch of fucking creeps.

Yeah, she's definitely not staying here.

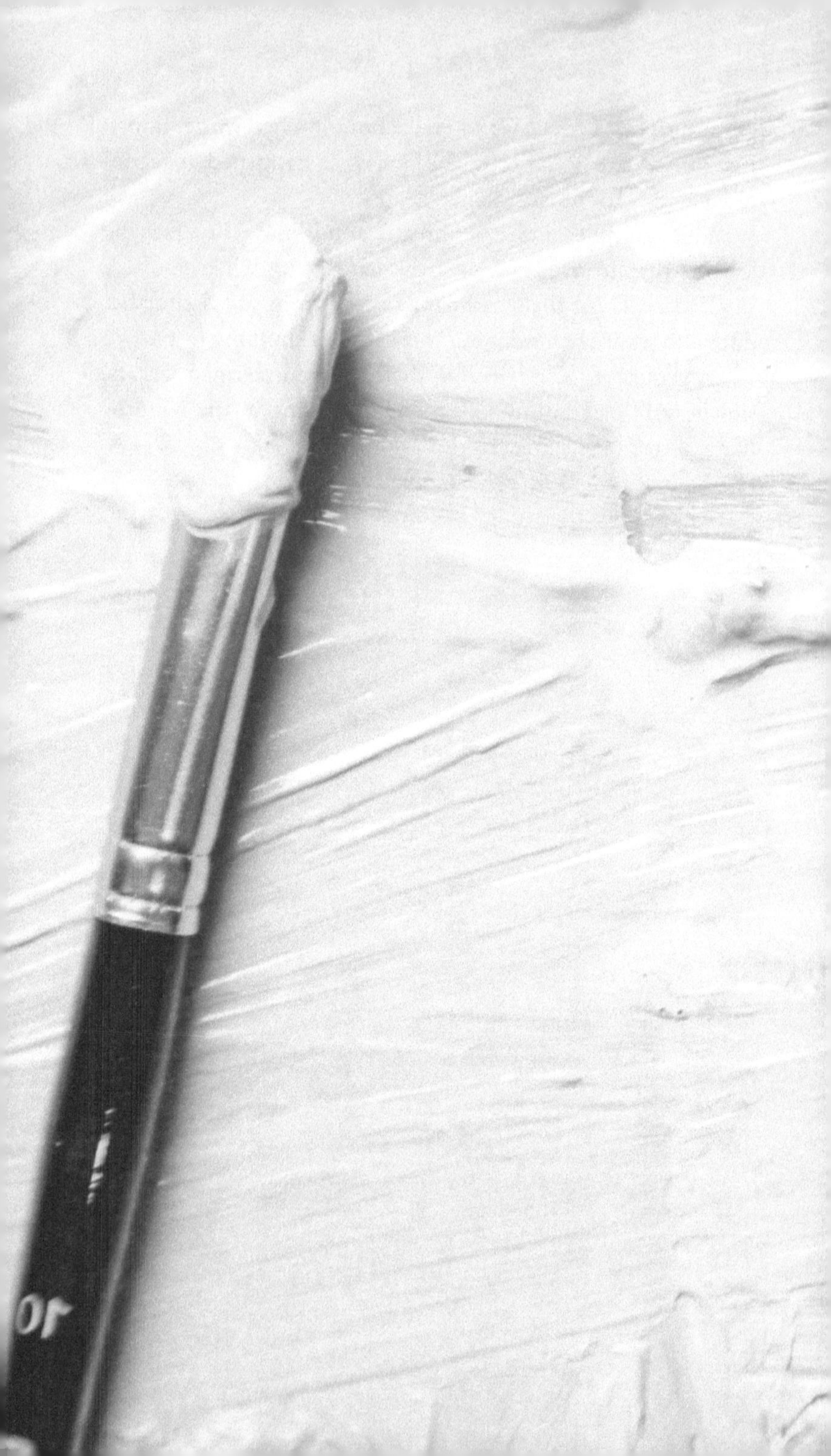

SUNNY

"I DON'T SEE anything wrong with it." Ruby is doing her best to calm me down in my panicked state. I'm surprised there isn't a hole in the floor from my incessant pacing. "Plenty of nannies live with their employers."

"Well, yeah. I know. I used to be one of those." My heart thumps.

"Look at it like this." I stop pacing and stare at the screen. Ruby is slicing fruit for Marybella while she plays in the background. "If you continue to think about the past with every little thing, you're still letting him get into your head."

I make a face, and she points the knife at me.

"Which we *do not* want. Rhodes is different. He's already proven that, right?"

They couldn't be more opposite, so I nod.

Ruby and I share silence, and I know what she's thinking. She's thinking about how I showed up at her doorstep with tears running down my face, a torn shirt, and a busted lip.

"I hate him," she says quietly.

And I hate that he still lingers in my head.

Lights appear through the window, and I'm positive it's Marco pulling up. To save him the trouble of coming to the door, I quickly hang up with Ruby and rush to greet him.

He's somehow already standing there.

"Good evening, dear."

I scoff with amusement. "You're awfully fast for your age, Marco."

He smiles. "I have to keep up with you, don't I?"

I roll my eyes playfully and drag my suitcase behind me. Marco bends to take it, but I pull it away. He shoots me a look, and I smile triumphantly. The street is becoming busier with those frat parties that have been keeping me up at night. Marco glances down the street a couple of times and continues to walk beside me when I go back for my smaller bag.

"Should I add bodyguard to your bio?" I tease.

His lips flatten, hiding his wrinkles. "Just following the boss's orders."

"What orders?"

He hums under his breath, and that's the only answer I get.

I cross my arms after I slide into the passenger seat. "I see where your loyalty lies."

Marco chuckles and takes off down the street.

"I won't hold it against you, considering he *does* pay you," I mumble.

It doesn't take long to get to my new living quarters.

Nerves gnaw on my stomach as I toss around my sudden decision to move into Rhodes's house. It does make things easier—on both of us. If only I could rid myself of the lingering concern.

"Sunny!"

Ellie comes bouncing out the front door in a T-shirt ten sizes too big for her. It's a Chicago Blue Devils shirt that I'm assuming is Rhodes's. Her hair is wet and slaps me in the face when I bend to give her a hug.

I gasp. "Get back inside, Rapunzel! You're going to catch a cold!" I leave my suitcase where it is and swoop her into my arms. I rush us to the front door with her giggle echoing around us.

Rhodes stands there in nothing but jeans and a black tee. When he sees us coming for him, he quickly moves out of our way.

"How does she have so much energy?" I hear him ask Marco.

"Who? Ellie or Ms. Edwards?" Marco replies.

I laugh to myself and place Ellie on the couch. I wrap her up in a blanket like a burrito, something that makes her laugh again, and go back for my suitcase.

Both men are in the entryway with my suitcase and bag.

Rhodes glances at me briefly as I slowly make my way over to him. "Thank you," I say, reaching for my bags.

Without pausing his conversation with Marco, he pulls them out of my reach.

I huff, and he ignores me.

"Alright, Ms. Edwards. I'll be back in the morning to deliver Rapunzel to school."

"Marco," I warn. "It's Sunny."

He salutes me. "Goodnight, Sunny."

"Goodnight, Marco." I salute back.

When Rhodes is distracted, I try to reach for my suitcase again.

He pulls them away. "Will you knock it off?"

I peer at him. "Knock what off?"

Rhodes stares at me. "It's pretty standard for a man to carry your luggage, Ms. Edwards. It's called being a gentleman." He shakes his head. "It's clear you've never been with one."

His eyes drop to my mouth when I stick my bottom lip out with a pout. "I have too," I lie.

The only true gentleman I've known was Gramps.

Rhodes slips past me. I wait until he's halfway up the stairs to say, "I just wasn't aware *you* were a gentleman."

He stops immediately, and a loud snicker erupts from his mouth. He glances over his shoulder at me, and I lose my footing—but only for a brief second. Admitting to myself that he's attractive is fine. I can't expect myself to ignore the elephant in the room.

Rhodes is dreamy. His soft, effortlessly tousled hair flings onto his forehead as he peers down from the steps. It pairs nicely with his olive skin tone and dark-rimmed green eyes. But he has a dangerous vibe to him. He's confident and a bit callous. The scruff on his face doesn't help either.

But just because he's good-looking doesn't mean he's going to pursue me or expect me to fall at his feet like most. He's made it *very* clear that he isn't the least bit interested in me—or anyone, for that matter—and he has no idea how much that calms me.

Rhodes shakes his head and continues up the stairs, releasing me from the spell he didn't even know he casted.

I hear Ellie fake coughing. I glance at her on the couch, and she's still wrapped up in the blanket.

"A little help?" she squeaks.

I laugh and unwrap her before heading upstairs with her on my back.

Rhodes walks out of a room and pauses at the sight of me huffing. "Do you need me to put an elevator in?"

I roll my lips together. "No, Mr. Plays-Pro-Hockey-For-A-Living. I'm just not used to carrying a human on my back."

He quietly chuckles and flicks his head to the bedroom, expecting me to follow him.

Ellie runs off to her room, leaving me alone with her dad.

A tight knot clogs my throat as I stand outside of the threshold.

"I'll get you a real bed," he says. "I didn't bother furnishing the room because—" He turns and stops talking when he sees me standing in the hall. "You can come in, you know."

My gaze skitters away.

Stop it, Sunny.

Rationally, I know I'm being ridiculous. I'm on edge because deciding to live at his house brings up an uneasy memory that still has me reeling with nerves.

I dig the heels of my feet into the floor and eventually step into the room. Rhodes looks at me incredulously but ignores my behavior and continues going on about the room.

"There's a loft-type room above us on the third floor, but it doesn't have its own bathroom, so I assumed you'd want this one."

I nod. He assumed right.

"What do you use the loft for?" I ask curiously. It'd make a nice area to store some canvas and maybe an easel. If there's a window, sunlight could stream in and make way for the natural light needed to see the true richness of paint colors.

"Oh." Rhodes puts his hands in his pockets. "That's where I store all the other nannies. I chain 'em up."

My mouth opens.

Then closes.

Then it opens again.

He snorts before laughing loudly. "Jeez, I'm kidding."

My cheeks burn. I cross my arms angrily and act fast. "Well, obviously! I was just shocked because I wasn't aware that you could make jokes."

He smirks, but it's fleeting.

I'm thankful he turns away, because the heat on my face isn't going away.

The tiniest thought slips into my head that is *highly* inappropriate and shocking. Rhodes chaining women up shouldn't make my belly dip.

"Again, I'll get you a bigger bed. This was all I had on short notice."

I decide to give Rhodes a dose of his own medicine as payback. I shrug nonchalantly. "That's okay. I can just sleep in yours."

He snaps his head over to me so quickly I hear a pop echo throughout the near-empty room. My laughter comes next. "Sorry! I thought we were on joking terms now."

The *smallest* smile—or twitch of his lips is more like it—catches my eye. I turn at the sound of Ellie walking into my new room. She gives it a once-over before her nose scrunches. "Maybe you should paint it..." she says.

"What's wrong with the color?" Rhodes acts offended.

Ellie makes a face. "It's...what's the word?" She taps her little finger on her chin. "Borrrrrring."

I giggle.

Rhodes glances at me and looks as if he's perturbed that I'm half-siding with his five-year-old daughter.

He glances around once more. "I guess you can paint it since it's...*boring*." He directs the last part of his sentence to Ellie, and she smiles.

"Okay, well, let's get you to bed, Printsessa."

Ellie creeps a little farther into the room. "Sunny, will you read me *Rapunzel* before bed?"

She bats her sweet eyes up at me, and I can't help but nod.

"Ellie," Rhodes warns. "Remember our ground rules."

"Ground rules?" I ask.

Rhodes rubs his palm along his face. He tells Ellie to go brush her teeth, and once she's out of his sight, he starts to explain.

"I told her that just because you're living here, doesn't

mean you're always available to her. If I'm home and you're upstairs, then she needs to give you space."

"That's not necessary." I glance over to the door and can see that Ellie is walking as slow as humanly possible.

She's quite the eavesdropper.

I wait until she's fully out of sight before moving a little closer to her father. "I should probably tell you what her teacher said to me today when I picked her up."

He puts his hand up. "You don't have to. Ellie already told me."

I make a noise that resembles a laugh. "She did, now? What exactly did she say?"

Rhodes reiterates everything Ellie told him, and I'll give it to her—she's honest.

"Well, then you can understand why I'd rather be available to her at all times. I'd like to build that trust with her." I pause, and a thought occurs. "Oh god." I slap my forehead. "You probably feel like I'm trying to take over your parenting role. Duh. Just ignore m—"

His hand briefly falls to my arm. He removes it quickly, but the warmth stays. "I don't think that. Honestly, I much prefer the help, Sunny." His gravelly, quiet tone drives his desperation that much deeper. So does the fact that he just used my real name.

He steps away, and I nod. "Well, then. I'm off to read *Rapunzel*."

Before I get too far, he calls out, "By the way, there's a working lock on this door. I left the key on the bathroom sink."

I smile softly and relax even more.

Eighteen

RHODES

"SHE'S MOVING IN?"

I move my skates off to the side and start lacing my shoes. "Well, she sort of already has. I'm picking up new furniture today."

I don't explain *why* I practically forced my new, young, agonizingly attractive nanny to move into my house, because I'd rather not face the jokes that would follow. It's true that I felt sort of protective over her, but she and Ellie have hit it off, and she's the first nanny that I've ever been able to trust for more than a day.

Of course I don't want anything to happen to her.

She's making my life a whole lot easier....until the recent memory of her stripping my jersey slips in, but I'm able to block the thoughts.

She makes my life easier.

Those thoughts do not.

Emory snorts. "Well, that was fast."

I scoff. "Says the guy who married some woman he didn't even know."

He rolls his eyes. "It all worked out. Plus, you love Scottie."

Kane inserts himself to the conversation. "We *all* love Scottie." His shit-eating grin pulls Emory from his seated position. Kane rushes off with his laughter following.

Kane isn't immature. He's simply acting his age.

I'm just the grumpy old veteran of the team who apparently needs to lighten up—at least, according to Malaki and some of the younger players.

Even Sunny had mentioned something along those lines too.

She didn't come right out and say it, but I made a simple joke, and it completely silenced her.

I sigh loudly when Malaki comes up beside me. "What do you want, Young?"

"I was just going to ask if you needed some help getting the new furniture in the house?"

I grab my bag and sling it over my shoulder. I eye him suspiciously. "You want to help haul heavy boxes of furniture up two sets of stairs?"

He shrugs. "I have nothing else to do."

I narrow my gaze. I see right through his helpful gesture.

Malaki is curious. The entire team is. Word has spread after the last game where Kane purposefully pissed me off, per usual, by mentioning my new nanny and how *hot* she was to the entire fucking team.

If we hadn't won, giving my mood an uplift, I probably would have strangled him.

Nonetheless, I do need help carrying the boxes.

"Fine, but if you make some comment about fucking my nanny..."

Malaki pretends to be offended. "I wouldn't do that."

Half the team laughs.

Matthew steps forward and says he'll help too, since his fiancée is out of town. I thank him and head out the locker room where I find Emory out of breath from chasing Kane.

"You and Scottie busy here in a few?" I ask.

"No, why?"

I hate asking for help.

"Can you pop over and help carry some furniture upstairs?"

Emory nods. "Yeah, man. Sure."

I thank him.

At least two out of three who are helping won't beat their dick off to Sunny later on. That's better than nothing, I guess.

———

I pull up in my truck and grumble.

Malaki isn't in his car.

No surprise that he's already inside, probably trying to sweep Sunny right off her feet.

They'd be perfect for each other, actually. She's a bundle of sunshine, and he isn't too far off.

I sigh loudly and open the front door. I'm immediately hit with the sound of loud laughter echoing from the kitchen. I see Sunny's shoes by the door, and Ellie's are right beside hers. It's sort of...nice to see.

I specifically told Sunny that she didn't have to clean my house, but since moving in a few days ago, I've noticed that she isn't listening.

It smells nice in here.

Maybe it's her.

Maybe it's the floors.

Either way, I'm not going to complain.

The farther I walk through the house, the more worried I get. Who else is here?

"Oh, and get this…" someone says. "She literally left a trail of her bras in the hallway to lure him into her bed."

My shoulders tense. *I told him that in confidence.*

Sunny's soft laughter spills onto my irritation and calms it. Barely.

"It's no wonder he was so skeptical of me," she mutters.

"How could anyone be skeptical of that face? I'd marry you right now."

I pause.

My jaw flexes.

That voice belongs to Kane, who I specifically did not invite.

"Nice try," Sunny says. "I don't date."

"What? Why don't you date, love?"

An Australian accent?

For fuck's sake. Why is Cooper here?

I slowly make myself known, though Sunny is unaware. Her back is to me, and I do a very good job at keeping my eyes to myself, even if she is wearing a shirt that I'm sure could fit Ellie. Sunny's tanned skin peeks from below, and I'm certain it would catch the eye of a blind man.

I wait for her answer before walking farther into the kitchen—mainly because I'm also wondering.

Kane sees me and grins like a fucking maniac before putting his eyes back on her. "You off the market, babe?"

Babe?

She shakes her head, and again, I feel a weird sense of protectiveness come over me.

I step forward and save her the trouble. "I made her sign a contract that says she won't fraternize with any of you womanizers."

Malaki stands and throws his hands up. "Is that even legal?"

Sunny spins quickly and seems shocked to see me. Her cheeks turn a bright pink.

I catch her eye and shoot her a reassuring look. *Don't worry. I've got this.*

Leaning against the table—that I can't help but notice is clear of any of its usual clutter—I cross my arms and glance to my teammates. All of them. "What are you all doing here?"

There's an obvious chill to my question.

Malaki smiles to himself and sits back down on a barstool. "I was invited."

Oh, he thinks he's off the hook?

"Yeah, but why are *they* here?" I point to Kane and Cooper—two of the biggest man-sluts on the team.

"Someone spread the word that you needed help moving some furniture."

I wiggle my jaw back and forth and stare at Kane. If it weren't for Sunny being in the room and him being so good with my daughter, I'd probably punch him right in the jaw.

"I had it covered," I say, coming around the countertop to grab a beer out of the fridge.

I'm going to need a drink so I don't accidentally throw Kane and Cooper down the stairs later.

The popping of the tab draws Sunny's attention to my hand. When she pulls her eyes back to mine, I'm half-tempted to ask her if she wants one.

"Ellie is looking at the paint swatches with Scottie and Emory."

I tilt my head with confusion.

"For my room. I hope it's okay that I had Marco take us to the hardware store to grab some paint swatches." Her soft laugh is no more than a wispy breath. "She was pretty insistent we paint it."

I gulp my beer when my phone dings with an alert telling me that someone is approaching the door. "I sure hope you didn't let her pick the colors," I joke.

Sunny rolls her lips together.

Oh, great.

"Let me guess..." Malaki taps his fingers against his chin. "She picked some shade of...pink?"

I grab my phone while still giving Sunny my attention.

"Yes...and..."

I raise my eyebrows.

"Purple?" he asks.

"Mm-hmm...and..."

I chuckle. "The rainbow."

Sunny smiles brightly and points at me. "Ding, ding, ding."

I shake my head. "You do not have to paint your room in rainbow colors."

Although...it's sort of fitting.

"I told her she could pick. I'm not going back on my word now. It's all about trust, remember?" She throws her hands up in defeat, and I keep myself from grinning by glancing at my phone.

I slice my attention to Kane, and he's looking anywhere but my face.

"Did you tell the whole goddamn team to show up?" I hiss.

"Who, me?" Kane acts completely nonchalant. "Must have been Coop."

"Oi, mate. Don't throw me under the bus."

I place my hands on the counter and drop my head.

Sunny clears her throat, and I glance up at her. "This really isn't necessary. I could have just carried the boxes myself."

Malaki, Cooper, and even Kane stare at her like she's insane.

I don't think she's insane, but I do think she's used to doing things on her own, or making due with whatever issue comes her way, just like staying in a house with a broken lock and creaky windows.

I stand upright, and everyone looks at me. "Since you're all so *eager* to help, go get the boxes out of my truck. You can put the furniture together too."

"We're manly men," Malaki announces. "We've got this."

They all shuffle toward the door, glancing at Sunny on their way out. I scowl when Kane winks at her before heading in their direction.

I do the same because the quicker this is done, the better.

"This really is too much."

I stop right away and look back at her. She's nibbling on her thumbnail. "The twin bed was fine," she adds. "Or if anything, I would have helped you carry the boxes."

"What kind of man would I be if I made you lift heavy boxes up two sets of stairs?" I ask.

She crosses her arms defensively.

"I could have done it."

My lips twitch. "Oh, I have no doubt." The more I get to know her, the more I can see that she's *Miss Independent.* "But again, I'm a gentleman, Ms. Edwards—something you clearly are unfamiliar with."

Angry lines appear around her pursed lips.

I turn and smile to myself as I head for my truck. My amusement disappears as soon as I catch my teammates staring at Sunny from the entryway.

"I'll have Coach Jacobs make you guys skate suicides until you vomit," I warn.

They scatter like marbles because they know I'm not kidding.

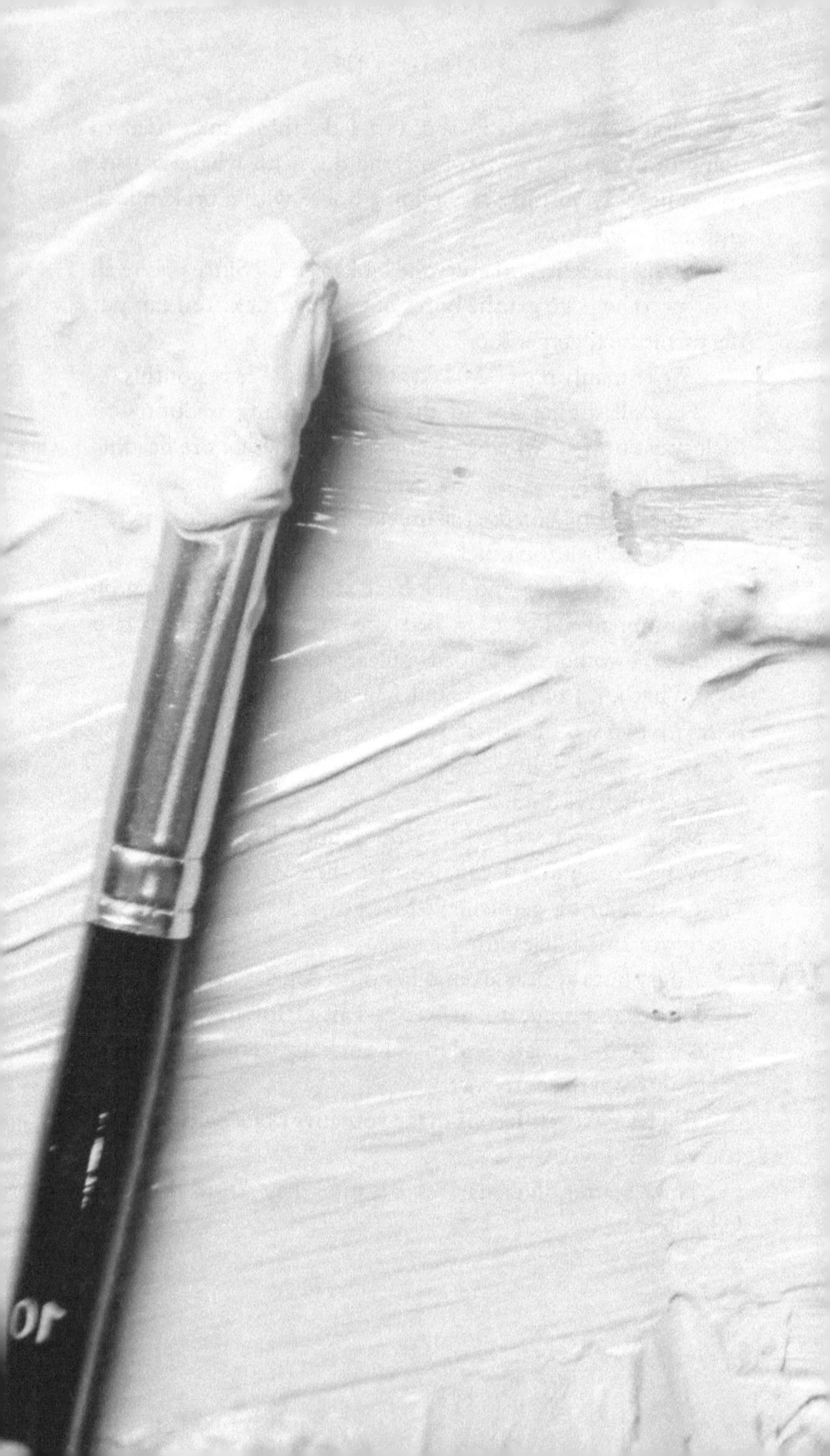

Nineteen

SUNNY

THIS IS A TOTAL DISASTER.

Ellie and I are covered from head to toe in paint. I'm glad Marco recommended I put plastic down on the floor and over the furniture before we opened the paint cans, because otherwise, Rhodes would probably fire me on the spot.

I tap my paint-covered finger on my chin and turn to Ellie. "Maybe we should just do *one* big rainbow?"

There's white paint in her hair, on her nose, and both hands. Thankfully, I lent her one of my old T-shirts—one that I was going to get rid of anyway—as it, too, is covered in paint splatters.

She gasps. "Wait! I have an idea!"

I gasp right back. "Oh, please tell."

"What if you did the sun?"

I glance back at the wall. "The sun?"

"Yeah! One *big* sun!" Ellie scurries over to the sticky wall, now painted white. She traces a huge sun in the air that would practically cover the whole wall.

She turns toward me, waiting to see my reaction.

I smile. "I *love* it. It's like you already knew my favorite color is yellow."

Over the last week, she's opened up a little here and there. She remains fiercely independent—something I can relate to —and is still leery when I go to the bathroom during Rhodes's hockey games, but I'm hopeful for improvements as time goes on.

One morning, before the school day started, Marco and I watched her from the car while she played on the playground. She played alone, but it wasn't for lack of friends. Several little girls came up to her, chatted, and then walked away.

My heart shattered with how *alone* she looked. I didn't say anything to her dad, because he didn't hire me for parenting advice. But I am going to take it upon myself to continue to build a rapport with her—ask for her advice on things, play games, paint together, do activities that someone her age *should* be doing instead of worrying that I'm going to disappear like all the rest.

Maybe then, she'll open up to more people—hopefully, some her age.

"What's your favorite color?" I ask her.

Her little mouth forms a frown. "Blue."

I walk over and find the paint can full of yellow paint. I try to remain busy so she doesn't think this is a test.

"Why do you look sad about that?"

She watches my every move. "Because one of the boys at school said it's a boy color."

I begin to stir the paint. "That's their opinion, and their opinion doesn't really matter."

"It doesn't?" she asks.

I shake my head and turn around to grab her hand. I place it on the paint stirrer and place my hand over hers so we can stir together. "There are going to be plenty of people in your life that don't agree with something that you like. But as long as *you* like it, it doesn't matter what they think."

She nods slowly and accepts my advice. "Okay."

I probe a little further. "Are there any other girls that like blue?"

Without looking up from the yellow paint, she answers, "Jacie. She likes it because it's the color of her soccer team."

"Lookie there," I say, "two girls who like the color blue."

She giggles. "I like it because it's the color of my dad's jersey."

Speaking of.

I glance at my phone.

It's nearly time for dinner.

Rhodes should be home soon.

We've fallen into an easy routine. When he gets home from his second practice, he takes over with Ellie. I usually head upstairs, call in and check on Nana, or if I'm really trying to kill time, I'll sketch or make some sort of figurine out of clay and wait until he's busy with the bedtime routine to slip back into the kitchen to make myself something to eat with the few groceries I picked up.

I can't expect him to make me dinner, and I don't want to overstep and make Ellie and myself both dinner without asking him if he'd like some.

It's too weird.

Too family-like.

Too much like *before*.

"Why don't you go paint the biggest smiley face ever on the wall and then go wash up before your dad gets home?"

"A smiley face?" Her little brows fold inward.

I smile. "I'd love knowing there was an Ellie-painted smiley face on the wall before I painted the sun. It'll make the sun happier."

She giggles and rushes over with a yellow-tipped paintbrush.

I take it upon myself to check out the rest of the room. I dip my own paintbrush in the primer and walk over to the corner while Ellie works on her masterpiece.

I'm not the shortest person in the room, but I still can't reach the spot I need.

Nibbling on my lip, I try to come up with some master plan to get those hard-to-reach spots. Rhodes went a little overboard with furnishing the room, like spending *way* too much money, so standing on the brand-new nightstand is out of the question, especially when he's due home any second.

I jump up and swipe my paintbrush in the direction I need to reach. A huff rushes from my puffed-out cheeks when I miss.

Ugh.

I glance back at Ellie.

She's too busy painting to pay any attention to me.

I jump again, but this time, I drop the paintbrush. It hits me in the head. I try to wipe the paint off my forehead, but I end up smearing it.

I quickly grab my worn and tattered art books—something I'd never leave behind in Washington—and begin stacking them.

Perfect.

My own little ladder.

With careful consideration, I quietly climb on top. It's not that many, three total, but they're thick and raise me at least a foot.

"A-ha!" I exclaim under my breath.

I'm on my tippy-toes, balancing on a stack of books, which is something my nana would scold me for, but if I just stretch a little farther...*there.*

I smile and attempt to lower myself.

Only, the books aren't as stable as I thought.

Oh, shit.

My arms fling backward, and my heart stops.

Except, I never hit the ground.

I'm balancing on a wobbly stack of books, but I'm as steady as can be because two large hands fall to my waist and keep me still.

By the olive-colored skin tone and veins bursting with strength, I know it's not Marco who is behind me.

Instead, it's Rhodes.

My boss.

Twenty

RHODES

IT'S OFFICIAL.

I'm a fucking creep, and now she's going to know it.

Listening to Sunny talk to my daughter without realizing I was listening was wrong. But can you blame a guy with trust issues? I mean, hell, the last nanny locked Ellie in her room.

Of course I'm going to eavesdrop.

Though, it proved that I have nothing to worry about.

In all honesty, it sort of made me jealous.

I've been begging Ellie to open up and tell me things about her classmates, the playground, *anything*, but she just shrugs and walks away, unwilling to act anything but bored when it comes to school.

Two weeks with her new nanny and she's suddenly spilling secrets about some little punk who told her that blue is a boy color?

Sunny is good with her.

She isn't good with being innovative as I rush to catch her, though.

"Rhodes." Her warm breath fans down to my hands on her waist, and I tighten my grip.

She catches my disappointed look and quickly glances away, like she's in trouble.

God, she has a perfect body. I can tell, even in these paint-splattered overalls she's wearing. My thumbs brush against the skin below her cropped white tee, and thank god the rest of my grip is positioned over the denim.

There's a slash of white paint on her face that I want to wipe away in the worst way.

"Good thing you were there, Daddy!" Ellie's voice pulls me to reality.

I peer back at her and bring Sunny with me. I place her on the ground and hastily remove my hands from her body as if they're going to catch on fire at any second.

"I'm quick," I admit, in hopes that Sunny doesn't learn I was hovering outside the door, listening to them.

Sunny rocks back onto her heels with her cheeks sucked in slightly. She doesn't meet my eye.

"What exactly were you doing..." I glance at the books on the floor. "Using your books as a ladder?"

Her cheeks puff with air before letting it all out in one big huff. "Well, I didn't want to stand on the brand-new furniture..."

"Or ask me for help?" I raise my eyebrows. Maybe she's a little *too* independent. "I have an actual ladder, you know. One that you're welcome to climb anytime."

I internally wince. *That came out wrong.*

Touching her flipped a switch in my head, because since when does the word ladder have a double meaning? *She's welcome to climb it anytime? Fucking Christ.*

"It's fine." The soft angle of her chin catches my attention as she looks to the corner of the room. "I got it in the midst of my near tumble." She laughs quietly.

"You got your face too." I shove my hands into the pockets of my jeans so I don't reach out and wipe the paint from her face.

Irritation crawls up my spine. Why am I acting like this?

It's been a while since I've been with someone, but still.

Get a fucking grip.

I'm not sixteen.

She's attractive.

So what?

Not to mention, she's *way* too young for me to even think about.

She isn't that young. She turns twenty-six soon.

I growl silently at the voice in the back of my head.

There are six years between us.

That's too young.

But is it?

Fuck, why am I arguing with myself?

"Oh." Sunny rubs the back of her hand over her face, making the paint smear worse.

I snort, and she shoots me a close-lipped smile, breaking the weird tension that I'm pretty sure I only felt.

"Thanks for catching me," she says, looking embarrassed. "I guess you are quick."

I shrug it off. "I'm just good with my hands."

Jesus fucking Christ.

First, I mention how I have a ladder she can climb anytime, and now I'm telling her I'm good with my hands? To save myself from the absolute shitshow I'm currently the star of, I turn toward Ellie.

"Wow, look at you." I scan her from head to toe. I almost laugh but quickly register the T-shirt that's hanging down to her knees. "Where the hell did you get that shirt?"

"*Daddy.*" Ellie's small fists go to her hips. "You said hell."

I hear Sunny's hushed laughter from behind, but I've since banned myself from looking at her.

"So did you," I argue.

She flattens her lips.

"Now tell me where you got that shirt." I assume it is one of my teammates. They are always telling Ellie to do things that they know will irritate me. Harmless things, but *still*.

The hawk logo is supposed to be on her chest, but the shirt is so big on her it falls to her stomach.

Washington Hawks. Which of the guys played for them? They're in a different division than the Blue Devils, and the last time I played against them, I was a rookie.

"Oh." Sunny steps forward. "That's mine."

She's a Hawks fan?

That makes sense. She used to live in Washington.

I make a mental note to get her some Blue Devils attire because...absolutely not.

"I was planning on pitching it, so I figured it could double as a smock for Ellie. That way, she wouldn't ruin her own clothes." Sunny's usual cheery vibe dulls while she explains this to me.

"Are you sure?" I ask. "I can always buy you a new one..." I clear my throat. "Though it would kill me."

She laughs, and just like that, the spark is back in her eye.

"I'm positive. I wouldn't want you to betray your team like that."

As if she wants to change the subject, she gasps dramatically while looking at the wall behind us.

"Oh. My. *Gosh.*" She quickly brushes past me and moves to stand by Ellie. "Look at your painting!"

Ellie beams. "Do you like it?"

On the wall, in yellow paint, are three little stick figures. I assume I'm the tall one with a... horizontal line for a smile.

Rude. Then there's a shorter one with a huge smile and hair that looks as long as Rapunzel's. And then…

I check back into the conversation. Ellie points to the last stick figure.

"And that's you!" she says to Sunny. "I made you closest to the sun because of your name."

Sunny smiles. "You know what? I *love* it. I'm keeping it."

"You are?" Ellie is surprised but pleased all the same.

Sunny bends down to get on her level. "Of course I am. I'll put a little frame around it. Maybe you'll be an artist like me."

I glance at her "ladder" and read the titles: *Art History, Art from the 1800s, Romanticism in Art.*

Hmm. Does she have an art degree?

"You better go wash up! It's your big movie night."

Ellie told Sunny all about our movie night? What else is she telling her?

Before she leaves me alone with her nanny, she stops at the last second and looks at me with soft and hopeful eyes. "Can Sunny watch the movie with us tonight?"

I pause. "Uh, well…"

Fuck, fuck, fuck.

A movie night with Ellie and her nanny?

I swing my attention to Sunny. *Please say no.*

Her smile is forced. She looks to Ellie and then back to me.

It's like I can read her mind.

She doesn't want to refuse, upsetting Ellie, but she doesn't want to accept and upset me.

Shit.

This is new territory. I've never had a nanny last this long, and I've surely never had one live with us. I lift my hand and squeeze the back of my neck to ease the tension there. "If Sunny wants to join, she can. But remember, Printsessa, she is technically off the clock when I'm home. Now, go wash up."

Ellie quickly looks at Sunny and then turns to disappear down the hall.

The room suddenly feels smaller without her in it, which is impossible.

"I don't have to join if that makes you uncomfortable." Sunny busies herself with closing the paint cans. "I totally understa—"

"It doesn't make me uncomfortable," I lie. "Why would it?"

I said that way too quickly.

Sunny stops what she's doing. Her fingers freeze on the paint can lids. I hear her swallow all the way across the room.

I hate that I'm interested in why she thinks it would make me uncomfortable. Does she know that I can't stop staring at the little bit of skin playing peek-a-boo from her overalls? Does she also feel the undeniable tension between us whenever we're alone?

When she doesn't answer, I take a step closer. She's kneeling on the floor below me, and the thoughts in my head would absolutely make *her* uncomfortable.

Her doe-like eyes peer up at me, and all I can think about is her on her knees, sucking me off.

Wait, what?

"Come or not." My tone is cold, and it has nothing to do with her and everything to do with my incessant thoughts. "It doesn't matter to me."

I turn and walk out of her room.

I quickly pull my phone out of my pocket and text Malaki.

> Me: Ellie is requesting you for movie night if you aren't busy.

Did I just lie and request a babysitter for myself?
Yes. Yes, I fucking did.

Twenty-One

SUNNY

THIS ISN'T awkward at all.

I sink further into the couch, hoping it'll swallow me whole. It's silent in the living room. I can hear every little thing: the shifting of Rhodes on the opposite end, the quick typing on his phone, my heart beating in my ears.

I'm tempted to go see if Ellie needs help doing her chores. Though, that would probably be counterproductive since they're *her* chores. I wonder if Rhodes would think it's weird if I asked for chores too?

An alert goes off on his phone, and I jump. He eyes me quickly with a furrowed brow.

The more he is around me, the more he'll notice how skittish I am.

"Is the pizza here, Daddy?" Ellie slides into the living room on her fuzzy socks. Rhodes catches her by the waist and hauls her up onto his shoulder like she weighs no more than ten pounds.

"Printsessa," he grumbles. "Be careful."

He's two for two tonight. First, he catches me, and then he catches her.

"Why don't you keep Sunny company and figure out what movie you want to watch?"

Ellie nods enthusiastically and tumbles onto the couch cushion beside me. She's mid-whisper to me that she wants to watch *Tangled* for the third time this week when she perks up at a deep voice floating in from the entryway.

The hairs on the back of my neck stand.

"Who is that?" I ask.

Ellie springs from the couch and calls over her shoulder on her way to the entryway. "Malaki!"

"With pizza!" he finishes for her.

I breathe a sigh of relief. *Oh, thank god.* I wasn't sure I was going to survive with just me, Ellie, and Mr. Hot-And-Cold.

I get up from the couch and slip into the kitchen to get plates ready for the three of them.

I listen closely to their conversation.

Ellie: What are youuuu doing here?

Malaki: I thought you requested my attendance?

Ellie: Huh? No, I didn't.

Malaki: Oh, how interesting.

*Rhodes: *makes grunt noise like a caveman**

When they enter the kitchen, I smooth my face and place three plates out onto the counter. Malaki snags my eye, and something flashes across his face. He has boyish features that show every thought going on in his head.

He's surprised to see me, and if the dimples on the sides of his mouth have anything to say, he's also a little amused.

"Ellie invited me," I add, trying to get whatever he's thinking out of his head.

His smile lights up the room. "Funny, she invited me too..."

It seems like he wants to say something else, with the

obvious twinkle in his eye, but Rhodes plops the pizza boxes onto the counter right in front of him, and he decides not to say whatever remark was brewing.

I open the box and grab a slice for Ellie to keep myself busy.

This isn't weird. I'm just making it weird because of a past that has nothing to do with Rhodes or Ellie.

Before I realize it, I'm serving Ellie her pizza and dishing some for Rhodes and Malaki too. My boss stares at me from across the counter with a hitched brow that makes him look even more attractive than usual.

"Oh," I blurt. "Sorry, I'm just used to—"

"Don't be," Malaki interrupts. "You can come to my place and serve me pizza anytime." It's obvious he's joking, with the wiggling of his eyebrows, so I laugh quietly to appease him.

He takes his plate and follows after Ellie, leaving Rhodes and me alone in his expansive kitchen. For a room so large, it's annoyingly difficult to hide from his piercing gaze.

"Here you go." I slide a plate over to him. He catches it with a catlike reflex that I try not to notice.

I turn around and busy myself with yesterday's half-eaten salad, pulling it out of the fridge along with the vegetables I picked up at the store. The cool air of the fridge lessens the heat on my face, and I exhale slowly. I pray he's gone by the time I turn around, but he's still standing on the other side of the island, watching my every move with a slice of pizza in his hand.

My coping mechanism is to pretend he isn't there.

Rhodes who?

My teeth sink into my bottom lip. I pour the salad mix into a bowl and move around the kitchen like it's my own. I grab a cucumber with a firm grip and place it on the cutting board and slowly begin slicing.

"You can eat the pizza, you know."

I pause my slicing and peek at him before going back to what I'm doing. "Oh, no. It's fine. I don't expect you to feed me dinner."

His loud sigh crawls over the glossy counter and hits my ears. "I got you the cauliflower crust."

I stop what I'm doing and glance at him again. This time, he's staring directly at me with a knowing glint in his eye, as if he knows that I'm wondering how he knows I like cauliflower crust.

My mouth waters. "You did?"

His mouth twitches—just barely—but I catch it. "I did."

"How do you know I like cauliflower crust?"

"Because…" He pulls out his phone and does something to it before facing it in my direction. I recognize the front porch footage. It only takes me a second to see that it's a live feed. "I get an alert when the pizza boy comes to the door. He's rattled off your order every time with his shaky, teenage croak of a voice when you answer the door."

I blink a few times. *Oh.* I can't deny the relief that hits me, knowing he has cameras outside his home.

Rhodes leans over the counter and pops open the smaller box of pizza.

Sure enough, it's identical to the pizza I've ordered more times than I'd like to admit since moving in.

"He watches you walk away every time, by the way."

I snap my gaze to his. "What?"

Rhodes pushes the box over to me. "The pizza boy." He takes a bite of his pizza and chews before finishing.

I watch the way his throat moves against his neck. Rhodes Volkova is *all* man. It's almost hard to look at him.

"He practically drools every time you say thank you and turn. He watches you with a little lovesick look in his eye."

A laugh flies from my mouth. Rhodes lifts an eyebrow, and this time, I am *certain* his mouth twitches.

"That's silly. He does not," I argue.

"He does too. Haven't you noticed that it's the same teenage boy that delivers your pizza every time? I'd bet my life that the second he sees the order for a cauliflower crust, extra cheese, no pepperoni pizza, he volunteers to deliver it." He shrugs and takes another bite of his pizza.

My cheeks flame.

He hums in between a chew. "Do you like that the teenager is crushing on you?"

"What?" I squeal. "No!"

A grumble of a laugh comes from deep within his chest.

I panic and start to cut the cucumber faster. I don't like that the teenager is crushing on me. It's just embarrassing to think of some teenager crushing on me and to have Rhodes, of all people, notice such a thing.

"You're not that much older than him," he states. "Only a year or so and he'll be of age."

He is *clearly* amused by this.

I huff before briefly catching his eye. "Says the guy who said I was too young to nanny his daughter."

He rolls his eyes, and I'm blindsided by how attractive the motion is. How can someone roll their eyes and make it look... *hot*?

Flustered by the thought, I slice faster.

He's mid-chuckle when the knife clamors to the counter. My right hand clamps onto my left one before I even feel the burning sensation.

"Shit," he mutters.

Rhodes is over to me before I even register what has happened. His large hand comes down on top of mine, and I almost forget that I've possibly lost a finger underneath our joined hands.

"Let me see," he says.

I shake my head quickly. "I'm fine." *The hell I am.*

His green eyes narrow. "It wasn't a question, Sunshine."

Surprised by the nickname, I let him pull me over to the sink. Cool water rushes from the spout, and he places both of our hands under the stream.

One by one, he unpeels my fingers from the wound. I focus on his furrowed brow and locked jaw instead of the sting crawling up my arm.

"Malaki!" he shouts, placing his hand over my finger.

Malaki enters the kitchen a moment later with Ellie following after him. "You summoned?"

If I wasn't seconds from fainting, I'd laugh.

Malaki's attention moves leisurely between Rhodes and me standing at the sink. He smirks and mutters, *"Interesting."*

Rhodes flicks his chin for Malaki to come closer. I hiss when Rhodes releases the pressure on my finger. "What do you think?" he asks him.

Malaki curses. "That needs stitches for sure."

Jerking my hand away, I shake my head. "No. I'm fine."

I'm not going to the hospital.

My stomach twists. I reach for the paper towels, and the entire roll falls to the floor with my shaky movements.

Ellie is quick to pick them up and hand them to me. "What happened, Sunny? Did you get a boo-boo?"

I force a laugh between my tight teeth. "Yes, but I'm okay. Nothing a Band-Aid can't fix."

Her little brow furrows. She looks just like her father. "You're going to need a big Band-Aid."

Malaki snorts. "And stitches."

I flick my attention to him. "I'm *fine.*"

Rhodes steps forward and looks to Malaki. "You got Ellie?"

"Yep. Uncle Malaki to the rescue."

I shake my head. "I'm not going to get stitches."

Rhodes, who is clearly ignoring me, bends down and swoops Ellie into his arms.

"I'm going to take—" Rhodes pauses and glares over his shoulder at me before finishing his sentence. "I'm going to *drag* Sunny to the hospital so she can get stitches. Be good for Malaki. Eat your pizza, watch *Tangled,* and then it's off to bed for you."

I gasp with frustration, but Rhodes's expression is so steely that I can't even form an argument.

Ellie leans in close to her dad's ear. "Hold her hand, Daddy. She looks scared."

Great. A five-year-old is braver than me.

Malaki steals Ellie from Rhodes's arms and shoots him a devilish smile. "Yeah. Make sure you hold her hand."

Little does Rhodes know, I actually might need his hand.

Twenty-Two

RHODES

I CALLED HER *SUNSHINE*.

The team set me up for failure. They kept fucking taunting me with the nickname, and then it effortlessly slipped from my mouth.

It did shut her up, though, so at least there is a silver lining.

The dish rag stained with blood is bouncing right along with her leg on the passenger side of my truck.

She's filled to the brim with nerves. Tight shoulders, tense spine, firm grip on her injured hand. That plump bottom lip of hers has to be raw from the incessant chewing she's doing. In the worst way, I want to take my thumb and free it from her teeth, but that'd be certifiable, especially for me.

"You good?" I ask. "You're making *me* nervous."

I never get nervous.

Sunny swings her head to me. "I'm great. In fact, we can go back home."

Home.

When did she start calling my home *her* home?

I mean, it technically is her home as of late, but hearing her say it is sobering.

"You need stitches," I say.

She rolls her eyes. *Why is that so tempting?*

The night lights blur against the side of her cheek, accentuating the soft curves of her face as she stares at me. "I really am fine. I can just...go to the doctor tomorrow."

I flick the blinker on. "You'll bleed out by then."

It's not true, and it's dramatic as fuck, but I'm not turning around.

Her sigh fills the entirety of my truck. The fit she's throwing is amusing. I have to actually try not to smile at her scowl.

When I pull into a parking spot outside of the ER, she sits up a little taller and stares at the flashing sign. I observe her from the driver's seat.

Why is she so bent out of shape?

Is she afraid of needles?

It seems unlikely that she's afraid of blood. She didn't act squeamish when I lifted our hands to examine the cut a half-hour prior. It was only when I mentioned going to the hospital that she clammed up.

"Are you afraid of the hospital?" I ask with a tone I only use with Ellie.

Until now, I didn't realize I could use it with anyone else.

She answers too quickly. "Of course not!"

I turn the truck off. "You don't have to lie to me. I won't think anything less of you if you say you're afraid."

"I'm not!" she blurts.

Liar.

"Okay, then." I leave my seat and round the front of my truck. I open her door and stand there, waiting. After a few seconds of her not moving, I sigh. "Come on, Sunshine. Let's go."

Her warm, doe-like gaze clings to mine, and fuck, she's terrified. A layer of moisture muddies the brown color of her eyes, and her lip is swollen from the nibbling. She climbs out of my truck slowly on shaky legs.

Part of me wants to help her, but it feels too...personal. So instead, I walk side by side with her until we're outside of the automatic doors.

They open once, and she makes no move to go inside.

Then they close.

Then they open again.

Fuck it.

My hand slips into hers.

I can't remember the last time I held a woman's hand, but I know for absolute certain that it didn't feel like *this.*

Surprisingly, Sunny lets me guide her inside.

I walk us up to the window and do all the talking without unclasping our hands.

"Do you have insurance?" I ask in a low tone.

That bottom lip plops out from her teeth, and she shakes her head.

"Just bill me," I say to the woman. "I'll take care of the cost."

Sunny attempts to jerk her hand out of mine with a shake of her head, but I refuse to let it go. Otherwise, she may jolt right out the door.

"If you just go ahead and take a seat over there and fill out the paperwork, someone will call you back shortly."

I thank the woman and guide us to a secluded part of the waiting room. A few people side-eye us, but I put my back to them, hopeful they don't come up and ask for an autograph. This isn't the time.

After sitting down, I finally release Sunny's hand so I can fill out her paperwork. She doesn't argue or ask to do it herself. Her leg bounces up and down, shaking both of our seats.

"Will you calm down?" I ask. "You're worse than Ellie."

She snickers and glances away.

I finish most of the paperwork, putting my info down for who is the responsible party for payment, but then I get to the medical history part.

"Are you allergic to anything?" I ask.

She shakes her head but doesn't look at me.

"Have you been out of the country in the last six months?"

She shakes her head again.

"Have you been hospitalized or seen at a hospital in the last year?"

The pen hovers over the *no* checkbox, but no answer comes. I turn toward her and focus on her facial expression. Her thick dark eyelashes flutter. That same lip slips into her mouth again, and she angles her body to the side, like she's shielding herself from me.

Well, this is intriguing.

"So that's why you're nervous," I note.

Sunny turns to me, but before she can say anything, her name is called. She tightens with fear, and I don't like the way it makes me feel.

"I'm going back with you."

It's not a question, and I don't give her a chance to refuse. I grab her gently by the elbow and usher us both toward the nurse.

It takes no more than a few minutes to get her vitals done. The nurse and I make eye contact with one another when the heart monitor beeps loudly from the racing of Sunny's heart.

She pats Sunny's shoulder but quickly releases her hand when Sunny jerks away.

"Do you need me to give you something to calm you down, sweetheart?"

It's admirable the way Sunny angles her chin and shakes

her head, like she's in no need of anyone's help. "I'm fine, thank you."

The nurse, Patty, flattens her lips before leaving the room.

Sunny shifts on the bed, still holding the bloody rag against her hand. She tilts her head and stares at the ceiling.

"Take some deep breaths. It'll help."

Instead of arguing with me, she does what I say.

It seems to be working.

Her chest isn't rising as fast as before, and the spot on her neck that I can't stop staring at is no longer thumping with her flying pulse.

The screeching of a moving curtain draws our attention to the doctor coming into the room.

"So, we have a cut, do we?" he announces, sitting down in a swivel chair.

Surprise flickers across his face when he lands on his patient. It's the same look every man has on his face when they lay eyes on her.

They're stunned by her subtle beauty. It likely steals their breath, just like it did mine.

As if he's caught, he quickly turns to me and tries to mask his thoughts while introducing himself.

I read them as if they're my own, though. My jaw clenches, and I'm not sure if it's because I'm feeling protective over her or if it's something else.

Like *possessiveness.*

There's a deep-rooted part of me that wants to stand up and bang on my chest like a fucking caveman. I want to say, *She's mine, Doc.* But that's absolutely fucking insane. She's my daughter's nanny and nothing else.

Other men can look at her.

Other men can have her too.

"Can I take a look?" the doctor asks, moving closer to her and farther away from me.

Sunny holds out her hand and stays as still as a statue while he pulls back the rag. The wound is split wide open with fresh blood still pooling. "I'd say you need no more than seven stitches." He places the rag back onto her hand. "Have you had stitches before?"

She finally makes eye contact with him. She nods, but that lip stays trapped in between her teeth.

"Okay, good, you understand the process. Can I ask where you've had stitches at?"

Sunny's swallow is loud enough for the patient in the next bay to hear. "My head."

"Your head? Were you young or…"

She shakes her head, and now *my* heart is racing.

"A little over nine months ago," she whispers.

The doctor's eyebrows furrow. He says nothing as he rolls over to the computer and starts typing quickly. I watch him closely. His eyes move back and forth, like he's reading something. Then, his furrowed brow smooths, and a noise leaves his throat.

He peeks over his shoulder at Sunny then to me. "I need to ask her some questions."

I stare at him.

"Alone."

What?

Sunny shifts. "No."

"No?" the doctor questions.

She shakes her head as if she's clearing her thoughts. "I mean, you can ask me questions. But I'd like him to stay. I'm already nervous and—" Sunny stops herself from saying anything else. Her words are rushed.

I don't like seeing her like this. She's full of nerves, and it dulls the sunshiny vibe she always has.

"That's fine, Allison."

She winces.

Is Allison her real name? Why didn't I know that?

It must have generated after they entered her social security number, along with her past medical care.

"Do you currently feel safe?"

I grip the handles of my chair.

"Yes," Sunny answers quickly, and I'm certain she is keeping her gaze away from me on purpose.

"Are you experiencing any more abuse?"

Abuse?

The doctor glances at me, as if *I'm* the one who has abused her.

"No," Sunny answers, quieter than before.

The doctor clears his throat and asks another question. "Are you experiencing any emotional symptoms related to past abuse?"

Is that why she's so jumpy?

I swallow thickly. I am on the edge of my seat, both physically and mentally.

"Not really." She shrugs.

"Not really?" The doctor's question lingers.

I'm seconds from pacing.

Sunny sighs. "Is this really necessary? I just came to get some stitches for my finger."

"And how exactly did you injure your finger?" The doctor glances at me with a look that I can't help but feel offended by.

"For fuck's sake," I snap. "She cut it with a knife as she was cutting up a cucumber for her salad. Now go get the nurse for her stitches so we can get out of here. She's *clearly* uncomfortable at hospitals and even more so with you implying that I've hurt her."

"I'm not implying that," he states calmly.

Sunny sits up taller. "He most certainly did not hurt me, Doctor Cline. In fact, I asked him to stay here with me because he's right...I'm uncomfortable at hospitals. The last time I was seen at a hospital..." Her words trail, and I silently beg her to finish. "Well, you know." She nods to the computer. "I appreciate you asking the right questions and inquiring, but that is in the past, and I'd really like to be on my way."

Doctor Cline clasps his hands. "Okay. Well, I'll have the nurse in within a few minutes to get you stitched. However, if you need...help...you know where to find me."

He can fuck right off.

If she needs help, she can ask me.

Sunny nods once, and then he's gone.

Tense silence fills the tiny space, and she won't meet my eye.

That's perfectly fine with me, though.

I'm not going to question what just happened.

Not yet, anyway.

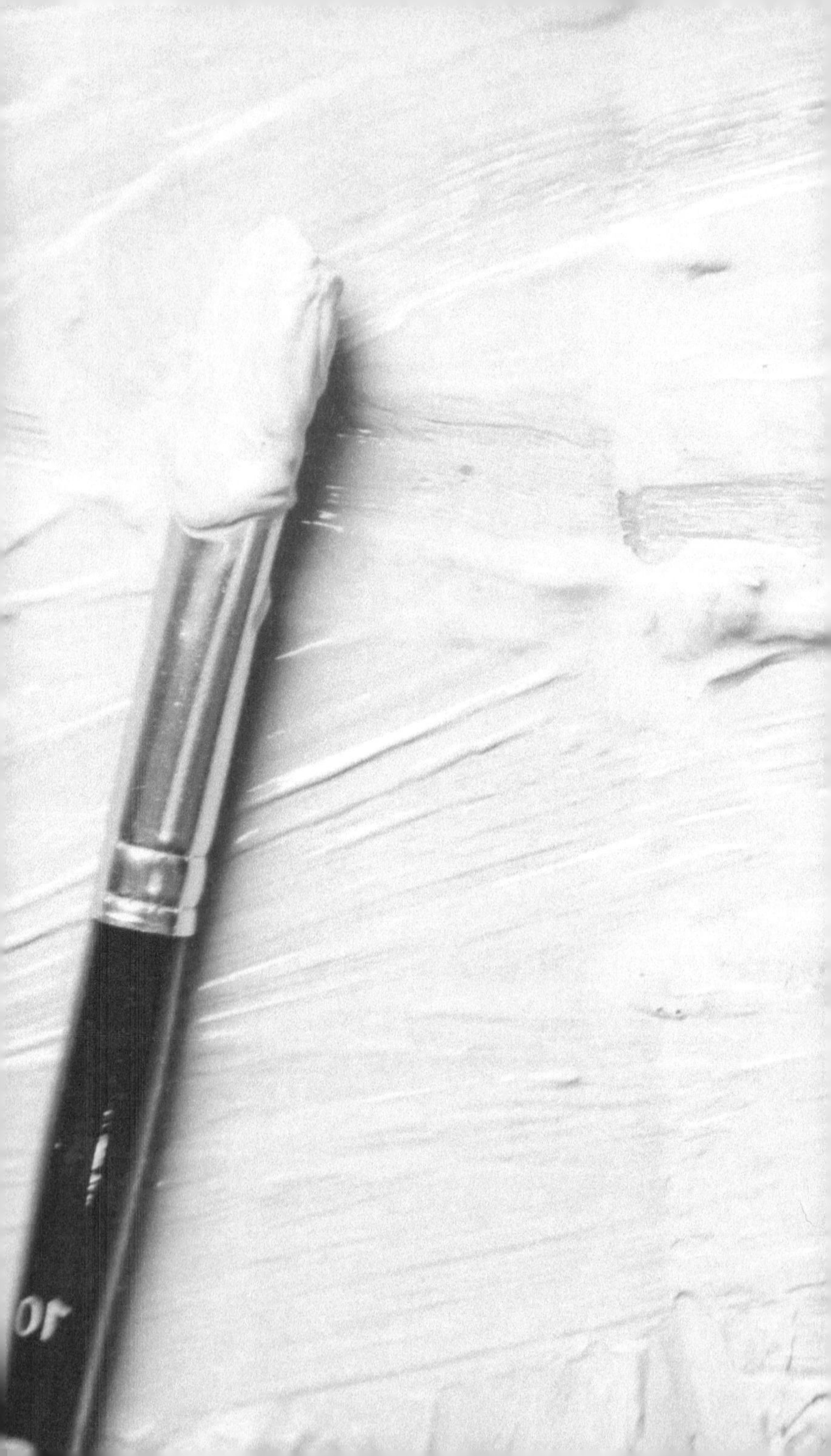

Twenty-Three

SUNNY

I PRETEND to sleep on the way home to avoid talking, which is probably something Ellie would do. Therefore, I'm acting like a five-year-old, but who could blame me?

Not only did Rhodes—*my boss*—witness me in one of the most vulnerable states I've ever been in, but he is now very much aware of something I wanted to keep private.

My body heats.

What if he wants to fire me because he thinks I'm too weak to watch his daughter now? What if Ellie has to go to the hospital, and he thinks I can't handle taking her because of my near panic attack?

I'll have to get a different job to survive living out here. I could waitress. Or sell feet pics. *Anything.*

"We're home."

My eyes spring open.

I hiss when I use my sore hand to open the door.

Rhodes's sigh doesn't go unnoticed. He mumbles something about me not waiting for him to open my door, but I ignore his muttering and hop onto the sidewalk to race up the porch stairs.

The house is locked, so I have to wait.

Which is unfortunate.

"If you would have waited three seconds, I would have opened the truck door for you." He leans past me to unlock the front door.

His cologne erases the smell of the sterile hospital.

"I didn't need you to open the door for me," I say quietly. "I'm fine."

He angles his head toward me, blocking the entrance. "I know you are. It's called being a gentleman, *Allison*."

My stomach caves. "Please don't call me that."

He squints at me, and I take his confusion for granted to slip past into the quiet house. After kicking my shoes off, I scan the area. Most of the lights are off except for the faint glow of the TV in the living room.

I jump when I hear a loud noise.

Is that a freaking monster?

Rhodes's hand presses on my shoulder. "It's just Malaki," he says quietly, heading to the living room.

I follow after him and see that Malaki is asleep on the couch with a hockey game playing on the screen. He opens his mouth and growls angrily, but he's clearly asleep.

Rhodes bends his head closer to me. "He dreams about hockey. He's probably angry we're losing a game."

I laugh quietly, but as soon as the silence falls between us, I'm back to feeling cagey.

"I'm going to go check on Ellie," he says.

A heavy breath rushes from my lungs as soon as he's gone. I take advantage of it and all but run up the stairs to hide in my room like a child. My hand hurts. The numbing shot has worn off, but I'd rather deal with the throbbing pain than ask Rhodes where the medicine is.

I flop onto my bed and shut my eyes. My bandaged hand is cradled on my stomach, and I focus on my breathing. I replay the entire evening at the hospital. My stomach turns, picturing the doctor's furrowed brow when he pulled up my medical history on the computer.

It's been almost an entire year, and I'm still on edge.

I blow air out of my mouth. "*Ughhh.*"

"In pain?"

I jolt upward, strands of my hair flying past my face. My gaze lands on Rhodes standing in my doorway, leaning against the door as if he doesn't have a care in the world. I'm not dense, though. He probably has hundreds of questions roaming inside his head after being in that hospital room with me.

The rattling of pills pulls my attention to his hand. "I brought you some pain medicine and water."

As callous and grumpy as he seems at times, he surprises me more than I care to admit.

"Oh, thank—" I clear my throat and try again. "Thank you."

Rhodes walks farther into my room and steals all the air with him.

He's so intense that even his long strides draw my attention.

I reach out with a shaky hand and take the two pills he's spilled onto his large palm. He unscrews the top of the water bottle and hands that to me next. I wipe my mouth with my sleeve when I'm finished, and he takes it from me, placing it on the little table beside my bed.

In an attempt to ease the tension, I try to make a joke. "Who knew you could be so attentive?"

He chuckles. "Don't tell anyone."

"Afraid it'll ruin your rep?" A tiny smile curves against my lips.

"The team would never let me live it down," he says. "But I am a dad, after all. I know how to take care of someone."

Is that what he's doing? Taking care of me?

My heart races with the subtle reminder of the last time that very action was implied.

The room spins.

I suddenly feel sick.

"Sunny."

"Huh?" I snap my eyes to the doorway. Rhodes made his way over there at some point, but he's headed toward me again.

"You're shaking." He's concerned. *Great.*

"I'm fine!" The words zip from my mouth so quickly *I* don't even believe them.

"I don't think you are." The scratchy sound of his hand against his jaw grounds me. "What do you need me to do? Do you want me to leave you alone? Do you want to talk about it?"

I silently repeat his question.

My eyelashes flutter with confusion.

I answer him without even thinking. "The only thing I want is for you not to fire me."

"Fire you?" The audacity is clear as day. His heavy brow furrows, and angry lines work themselves into the creases of his forehead. "Were you expecting that I came up here to...fire you?"

I stumble over my words. "Well...I...at the hospital..." I loosen my shoulders and try again. "I just figured that with me freaking out at the hospital, you'd have concerns about the safety of Ellie. Like, what if she needs to go to the hospital, and I—"

The sentence trails when I hear his heavy footsteps heading toward me. My heart pounds inside my ears, and my finger throbs even harder.

"I am concerned," he says.

I stare at my feet dangling off the bed. Of course he is. How could he not be?

When his callused hand grips me by the chin, I suck in air and trap it behind my lips. He tilts my head back, my strands of loose hair falling away. His green eyes are dark and fueled by something I can't decipher.

Rhodes Volkova is like a Pandora's box. I suspect there are a lot of things going through his mind, but I'm too afraid to poke the bear. He's gruff, quiet, brooding, intimidating, and doesn't show many emotions. Yet, with his fingers gripping my chin gently, it's tempting to find out.

"Oh, I'm concerned, Sunshine." His whisper is raspy, and my pulse quickens. "But not about the safety of Ellie in your care."

I peer up at him from the bed. My nerves are spent, exhaustion wanting to take over. The longer Rhodes scans my face, the more I surrender.

"He..." I pause.

What am I doing?

It's like watching a trainwreck from above.

My secret is supposed to be safe and locked away for the rest of my life, yet I hear myself talking, unable to stop.

"I thought I was being dramatic and too harsh. He was going through a divorce, and he was lonely, but when his late-night talks turned into subtle touches and things were implied, I politely declined."

Rhodes's jaw flickers, but it does nothing to deter me.

I'm too far in to stop now.

"He didn't like that."

My heart beats so fast it hurts.

Rhodes stares down at me, waiting for the finale.

There's so much more to it, but my brain fizzles out the more I look into his steely gaze.

His hand eventually falls from my face, and he steps away. My lungs are tight.

I stare at the picture that Ellie painted hours prior and force a breath out. It gives me the push that I need to finish what I started.

"He became..." I force a rough swallow down my throat. "Sort of...consumed."

"Consumed?"

Obsessed is more like it.

I rub the pad of my thumb against the bandage on my finger to ground myself. "He didn't want to take no for an answer."

"But did he?" Rhodes asks with his arms crossed over his chest. He's shoved the sleeves of his jacket up to his elbows, and all I can focus on are the veins bursting with some type of hidden emotion that he likely will keep to himself.

My nostrils flare. There is a very thin line between anger and fear, and that night, I felt both of them. "Eventually," I say.

He was forced to accept my rejection, but I leave that part out.

Rhodes is so quiet he can probably hear my heart pounding all the way from across the room.

In an attempt to calm his racing thoughts—because surely he's concerned that my drama will follow me here—I stand up on shaky legs and garner his attention. He lingers on me, his face smooth and unreadable.

"He isn't a part of my life anymore," I add. "He has no idea where I am. I don't have social media, and I changed my number."

Rhodes blinks once, then twice, and by the third blink, I start to grow weak.

"If there is ever contact..." He clears his throat and reaches up to grab the top of the doorway. His shirt rides up just barely, but it's enough to catch my eye. "You tell me."

I dip my chin, and then he's gone.

I stare at the empty doorway for so long my legs grow numb.

It should make me feel better that Rhodes knows what happened in Washington, but I left out some of the most important details.

At least I still have a job, though.

Twenty-Four

RHODES

I GAVE Sunny the day off.

I texted her early this morning and told her that I'd be taking Ellie with me to the rink and that she was welcome to do whatever with her day.

Giving her the day off was more for me than it was her, though.

I tossed and turned all night. I rehashed everything she told me and memorized the faraway look in her eyes until it was all I could picture whenever I closed mine. In the worst way, I wanted to reach out to SGT Mel and have him run a more in-depth background check on her, maybe pull some police records if they existed...*something.*

But in the end, I didn't.

It felt like an invasion of her privacy.

I have never restrained from digging into the lives of every other person in close proximity to Ellie, but with Sunny, it feels wrong.

I haven't known her for long, but she's the most genuine person I've ever met.

"Ready, Printsessa?" I shake myself out of my thoughts and stare at my daughter.

She looks so small in her hockey gear, but she is as mighty as any boy U6 hockey player. Her determination is palpable. When she falls on the ice, she pops up quickly, curses in Russian—no idea where she got that from—and keeps on skating.

"So..." Kane rushes over to me, flinging ice in his wake. "I heard you had a slumber party last night."

"What are you doing here?" I snap.

Kane's tone challenges mine. "Practicing."

He sends a puck over to Ellie, and she misses it. She curses again.

"In case you didn't know, we play the Flames tomorrow."

"In case I didn't know?" I repeat. "Considering you were at the strip club until two in the morning, I should be the one saying that to you."

Confusion whisks over his face. He has no idea there is an entire team group message titled SOS, where if there is a problem child...Kane...we put it in there, and someone volunteers to fix the problem.

He's the problem nine out of ten times.

"And what are you talking about? What slumber party?" My annoyance is obvious, but I know he won't care.

Kane smiles deviously. "I heard you invited Malaki to hang out with your nanny and that he stayed the night."

For fuck's sake.

"Did he tell you that?" I ask.

"No, she did after I left her bed."

Something hot slashes at my back with his joke.

He tries to escape before I can do anything, but too bad

for him, I'm one of the fastest skaters in the league. With a flick of my wrist, my stick flings forward, and I trip him.

He falls to the ground with a thud and stares at me with anger.

Ellie's short strides catch our attention. She stops beside Kane and traps her puck against the icy floor. "Daddy, two minutes in the box for tripping!"

Kane snickers, and I roll my eyes.

Ellie's eyebrows disappear beneath her fallen hair and helmet. "You heard me!" she shouts.

I hide a grin and turn. I slump down into the sin bin and watch her play hockey with Kane. He makes her giggle, but it hardly takes away my irritation. A few seconds later, Emory climbs onto the ice and gets in the net.

He and Kane must be running some drills.

Or maybe Emory is making Kane work off his hangover, which is good because I was ready to make him work off his comment about Sunny.

It doesn't sit right after learning why she's in Chicago to begin with.

"Come on, Ellie." I stand from the penalty box after a full two minutes. "Let's let Kane practice. He needs it."

"No, I don't," he argues before winding backward and sending a puck directly into Emory's glove.

"Yes, you do," Emory adds from behind his mask.

I nod goodbye to Emory and take off with Ellie.

It takes us no time to get changed and back into the car with a bag full of Blue Devils merch.

"Sunny is going to love these!" Ellie beams with excitement with her hand clutched around the bag.

I grin and turn up the *Tangled* soundtrack. She bobs her head with the music and sings her little heart out. I'd love nothing more than to stick a fork in my ears, but as long as she's happy, I can't really complain.

Since Sunny started as her nanny, I've noticed a change in Ellie. I'm not sure if it's the consistency of having the same nanny for once, or if it's because of Sunny herself.

Her sunshine rubs off on Ellie.

It rubs off on me too. Though, I won't admit it.

I grip the steering wheel tighter with the memory of last night. Sunny's radiant smile was replaced with vulnerability and shame as she sat on her bed with her hands in her lap, explaining her reaction to the hospital.

I think back to the other night when she wore my jersey.

She fucking *flinched.*

My stomach tightens with disgust. I quietly curse in Russian and hope Ellie doesn't hear.

After climbing from the truck with Ellie's hand in mine, I spot Marco on the porch.

Does Sunny need a ride somewhere?

I could have taken her.

My steps seize.

Sure, she's Ellie's nanny and lives with us, but I don't have to take her places.

Ellie zooms up the steps and stops in front of Marco. "Marco!"

"Rapunzel!" He gets on her level. "I brought the birdseed." A bag of seed appears in front of Ellie's face, and she claps.

I unlock the door and let them pass by to fill the bird feeder before grabbing all of Ellie's hockey gear out of the truck and the bag of clothes for Sunny.

The house is quiet—and clean. I shake my head at the thought of her vacuuming and mopping the floors with her bandaged finger.

With a heavy sigh, I head up the stairs. I could leave the bag of merch on the kitchen counter or have Ellie give it to her tomorrow before the game, but I want to clear the air between us.

Last night left me feeling *off*.

Sunny shared something personal, and I don't want there to be any weird tension between us or for her to think I'm going to look at her any differently.

She thought I was going to fire her.

I'm an asshole, but I'm not that *big* of an asshole.

Truthfully, I'm not even really an asshole. I'm just reserved. I grew out of my impulsive behavior a long time ago, and I know how to control the little emotions that I do have. It's called being restrained.

Or stony.

Unapproachable.

Maybe a little aloof.

What the fuck ever.

I stand outside the guest room—*Sunny's* room—and stare at the small crack in the door. Her voice slips out into the hallway, and I watch her move around on light feet.

"Um, what the hell is that?" someone says.

Is someone visiting her?

I didn't approve of that.

My heart beats harder. Maybe I'm not as restrained as I think I am.

Sunny moves past the crack in the door, unaware that I'm standing here.

This time, I see that she's holding her phone.

"Oh this?" She holds up her bandaged hand. "I accidentally cut my finger."

The person on the other end of the phone shrieks, "Allison Edwards!"

"Ruby," Sunny hisses.

"Sorry...I mean"—there's a faint clearing of a throat—"Sunny Edwards!"

Sunny laughs, and I hate that it sounds so sweet. "That's better. Anyway, I was cutting a cucumber and sliced my finger."

I suddenly feel like a fucking creep again as I listen to her conversation, so I step forward and push on the door to make myself known. To my surprise, she doesn't hear me.

At least I attempted, right?

"Are you okay? Did you have to get stitches?"

Sunny sighs. "I did."

"You went to the hospital? Are you okay?"

Okay, so her friend—*Ruby?*—is aware of Sunny's unease when it comes to hospitals.

"I'm fine. Going to the hospital was the last worry on my mind."

There's silence, and Sunny sighs again. She holds the phone in one hand, but in the other, she's holding a little piece of clay, inspecting it closely. "Rhodes took me to the hospital, and I felt obligated to tell him why I was acting like a lunatic."

She wasn't acting like a lunatic.

"You told him?" It's pure surprise on the other end of the phone. "No *fucking* way."

Sunny chokes out a sarcastic laugh. "I had to explain. I nearly had a freaking panic attack at the hospital, and then they started to ask all these questions, and I didn't want to be alone, so I asked him to stay and—"

"Wow."

"Yeah." Sunny's chest expands before it falls with a slow breath easing from her mouth. She eventually places the clay on her bedside table, and it's the perfect time to make my presence known.

Something I should have done three minutes ago.

I raise my hand to knock on the doorjamb.

"Did you tell him *all* of it?"

My eyebrow rises with my fist frozen in midair.

"If you're referring—"

"I am absolutely referring to how you're not only fearful of hospitals but how you're fearful of men in general and haven't had sex in *far* too long. God, when was the last time you had an orgasm?"

I choke on the information like it's being shoved down my throat.

That was not what I was expecting.

Sunny spins and drops the phone.

My coughing and sputtering is so loud that her friend can hear me from beneath the bed.

"Oh god," she says.

I ball my fist and pound on my chest. Sunny falls to the floor and snatches the phone up.

"I'm going to kill you," she hisses at her friend.

She quickly silences her friend's amused apology and tosses her phone onto her bed.

I take one look at Sunny on her knees with her lip pulled into her mouth. I'm going to respectfully ask her to kill me too.

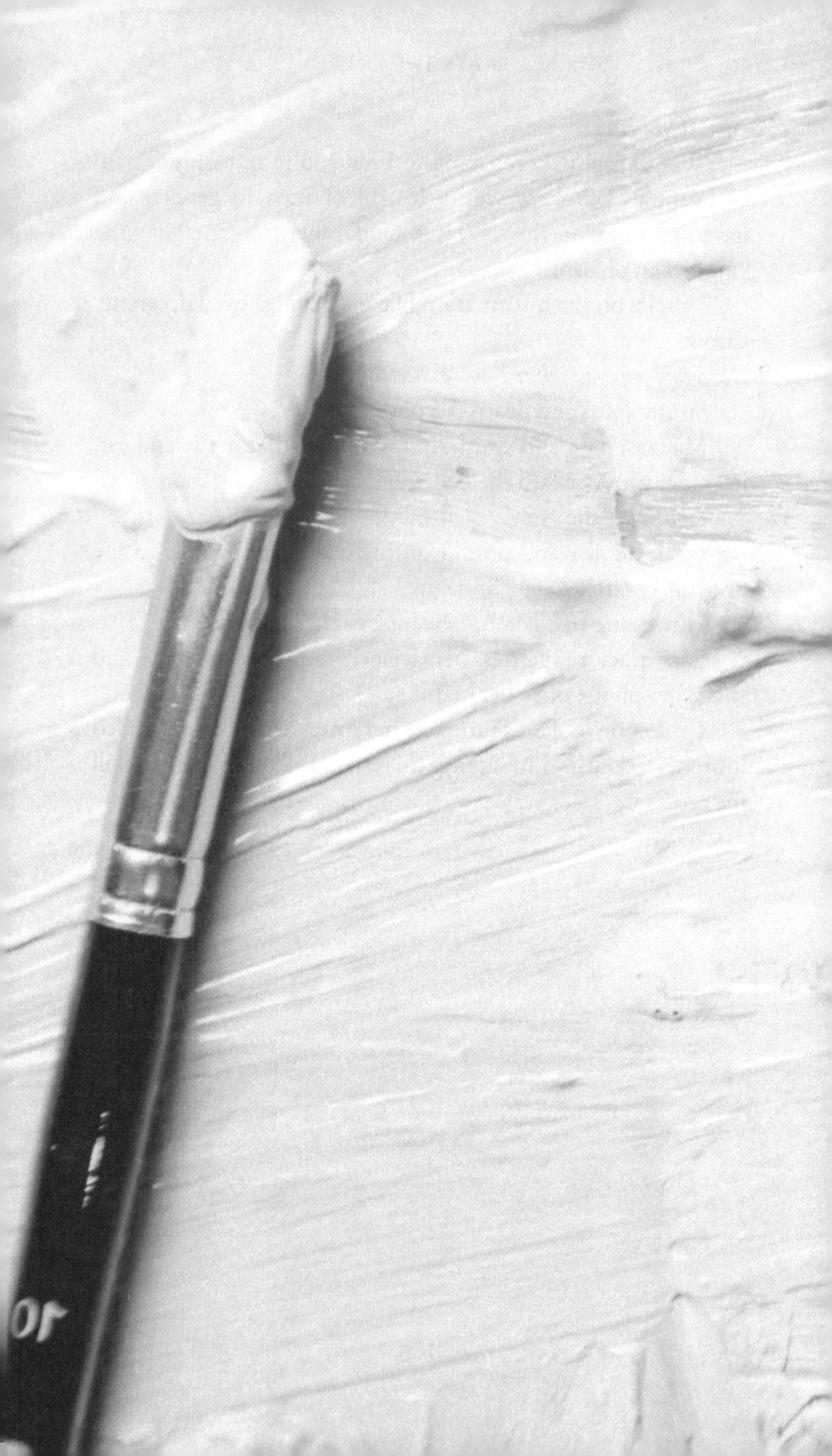

Twenty-Five

SUNNY

I GLANCE AT THE WINDOW.

Should I jump out of it now or later?

Embarrassment crawls over every inch of my skin.

Rhodes, who usually appears impassive, is completely blindsided from what just came out of Ruby's loud mouth, and to be honest, *same.*

"Now I sort of wish you would have fired me last night," I whisper.

Rhodes blinks. The rustling of the bag in his hand catches my attention, but I quickly pull my eyes back to his.

I stand, and silence fills the room.

Both of us are unsure of what to do.

He takes a step farther into my room, and my stomach flips.

"That's why you don't date," he states.

I shut my eyes and hide from his scrutinizing gaze. I'm mortified.

"Makes sense." He's closer now.

I peek an eye open, and nerves jumble me up. "What's your excuse?" I ask.

Did I really just ask him that?

My hand flies to my mouth to hide my nervous laugh. "Sorry, I shouldn't have asked that."

His mouth twitches. "Who said I don't date?"

I slowly lower my hand and cross my arms. My heart pounds so violently I feel it through my shirt. "Every article ever written about you."

Rhodes throws a bag on my bed. I only give it my attention for a few seconds before watching him walk around my room. He runs his finger along my dresser, briefly touching the clay pieces I sculpted to calm my thoughts after last night. His head tilts, his brown messy locks falling to the side. My breath catches when he spins quickly and leans against the piece of furniture, crossing his arms against his chest to mimic me.

"What else do the articles say?" he asks.

Answering is going to make me sound like a stalker, but surely he understands why I looked into him before agreeing to an interview.

"Well..." I bite my lip before letting it go and filling him in. "They typically start off with your stats, how skilled you are on the ice, your speed, things like that." I glance away from his intense stare. "They mention a daughter and how you are very private about your personal life."

He nods slowly.

"Even before Ellie was born... How you never had a plus-one for events, basically indicating that you're the most eligible bachelor in the league right now."

Rhodes chuckles deeply. He drops his head and shakes it slowly. A string of Russian flies from his mouth quietly. I have no idea what he said, but the way he says it makes me want to learn the language as soon as possible.

"That's a little contradicting, isn't it?" he asks, lifting his head. I'm pinned in my spot with the way he's scrutinizing me from across the room.

My forehead furrows with confusion.

"They mention I'm a private person but then go off and say that I'm an eligible bachelor? How does anyone know what I do with my free time? I could be going on dates weekly, and they'd never know."

True.

Without being able to stop myself, I ask just that. "Well, do you?"

Rhodes's mouth twitches. "Are you asking me if I date?"

I nod.

It's not my business, but considering he has found out a lot about me in the last twenty-four hours, it seems warranted.

"I don't." His answer is firm and to the point.

"Well, aren't we two peas in a pod," I joke, trying to lighten the mood.

A faint chuckle leaves him. He glances at the floor again before pushing off the dresser and toward the door.

At the last second, he peers over his shoulder at me. "Yeah, but just because I don't date doesn't mean I'm celibate."

My lips part, and I dart my gaze away.

It wasn't meant to be a dig, and I know he didn't say it to offend me. His tone was matter-of-fact, like he wanted me to know that the articles about him aren't true. But I'm still offended.

Something slashes at my confidence. It's not stupid of me to have reservations about men after what happened, but it's taking me a lot longer than I'd like to move past it.

"Don't feel bad, Sunshine."

My head flies upward, and I snag Rhodes's tall frame still

standing by the door. His intense gaze moves over my face before he shrugs. "When you're ready, you're ready."

A barely-there smile works itself on my face, but it's as fake as can be.

Rhodes grips the top of the door frame, and suddenly, something hot is rushing through me. His biceps ball up with strength, and his black tee rides up just enough that I can see the cut V shape leading to below his Nike sweats. "If you ever want to go on a date with someone, you're welcome to—just on your off nights."

My cheeks burn. "Thanks for your permission." *Ugh.*

His eyes narrow. "Just no one on the team."

I raise an eyebrow. *Oh, is that right?*

"And you can't bring them back here."

I would never.

"For Ellie's sake, you know," he adds.

Obviously.

The room is tense. He stares at me like there's something else he wants to say, but I don't give him the chance.

"You can too. I'm always open to watching Ellie for you if you..."—my words trail, and I clear my throat—"want to... take someone out on a...date."

There's a shift in the air. I drop my gaze to his mouth and briefly wonder what he's like when he's intimate with someone. He's *so* impassive and rarely smiles, but when he does, it's like a punch to the gut. His dark chuckle is hot and—*oh my god.*

My thoughts come to a sudden halt.

I think Rhodes is the first guy I've laid eyes on in nearly a year that has stirred up something other than fear.

"Where's Ellie?" I blurt.

Rhodes pushes off the edge of my door. "With Marco, filling the bird feeder, but you have the day off, remember?"

I watch him pull his phone out while standing in my doorway, and then my phone pings.

"There."

I ignore the three messages from Ruby that are full of fake apologies and laughing emojis and see that Rhodes has synced our calendars.

"Now you'll know when you're available for dates." I flip through the days of the week and note all his upcoming games and practices that are already posted on the fridge downstairs. "And if a date pops up in my schedule, you'll be alerted."

The tiniest seed of envy plants itself inside my lower stomach.

I've had my fair share of dating and one-night stands in my early twenties, but as soon as I began nannying to help my nana with the cost of medical bills for Gramps, I turned... What was the phrase Rhodes used so kindly? *Celibate.*

My anxiety when a man touches me doesn't help any either.

"Great." I give Rhodes a thumbs-up with my good hand. He rolls his lips together to hide a cocky smirk and turns to leave me be.

I wait until he's gone to look in the bag he threw on my bed.

He and Ellie must have gone on a shopping spree while at the rink because there are several Blue Devils shirts, a sweatshirt, a beanie, and a jersey inside.

They're all the correct size too.

I smile as my fingers brush against the knit of the jersey, but to my surprise, it doesn't have the number 87 stamped on the back beneath the last name Volkova.

It's a 3, right below *Barlow.*

Kane Barlow?

He bought me Kane's jersey?

Weird.

I shrug and place it on my dresser before turning and glancing at the half-painted walls in my new bedroom.

Apparently, I have the day off, and I can't think of a better way to spend it than with the familiar wooden handle of a paintbrush in my hand.

Twenty-Six

RHODES

THE WORD ORGASM and Sunny should have no relation in my brain, yet all I hear is her friend's voice talking about how my daughter's nanny hasn't had sex in *far too long*.

I wish I had never heard those words, because they're playing dirty little tricks inside my head.

I kept my distance yesterday. Ellie and I spent the day together, even though I continuously had to remind her not to bother Sunny since it was her day off. I even pulled out the *I'll-teach-you-Russian* card, which is something I only ever do as a last resort to keep her entertained.

"Volkova." I pop up from the sound of Coach's voice.

He nods to his office while I continue lacing my skates.

Malaki whistles under his breath. "Daddy's mad."

Some of my teammates chuckle, but most are too focused on the game to pay much attention to Malaki's jokes.

I walk past him and snort and slip into Coach's office.

"Everything okay?" I stay close to the door. It's nearly game time, and I like to get focused.

"I just wanted to tell you that I've noticed a change in you."

Adjusting my pads, I furrow my brow. "Like?"

Coach Jacobs crosses his arms over his suit. "You are more attentive on the ice. Faster. Determined. You're reminding me of the player you were several years ago."

You mean I remind you of the player I was before I had another responsibility...like a kid.

Anger surfaces, but it's quickly washed away because *fuck.* It's nice to hear.

He has children. They're grown, but he gets it. It's why he's kept me on the team and has dealt with my sudden disappearances from practice and my inattentiveness on the ice.

"What changed?" he asks. "Is it because of Olson?"

I shake my head. "No, but he is a great asset to the team. He's a damn good goalie."

He nods. "It's the nanny, then?"

I make a grave mistake and dart my eyes away, as if he'll be able to read the scandalous thoughts in my head.

"I trust her," I admit. "I can focus on the game because I know Ellie is safe, and I know she's not going to dip out on my daughter because her feelings are hurt that I'm not fucking her."

His abrupt laugh fills the room. "Jesus...well..." He rubs his hand over his face. "Hang onto her, then, and don't fuck it up. Between signing Olson, your sudden focus on the ice, and working out the kinks between the rest of the team, we're looking good."

My fingers tingle.

He's right.

Winning a game sends fire into every one of our bloodstreams. We're competitive and determined, and that's the recipe for a powerhouse team. It's refreshing being able to concentrate on the game for once.

I leave his office and finish lacing up. Noise from the crowd slips into the locker room, and my blood sings.

I check my phone before heading out onto the rink for warm-ups, and my breath catches. There's a text from Sunny. It's a photo of Ellie in her Blue Devils jersey, hair woven in two perfect braids with little blue bows hanging from the ends. She has my number painted on her face in blue paint.

I grin and swipe out of the photo, only to be punched in the gut with another.

It's a selfie of the two of them.

My stomach tightens just as tight as my grip on the phone.

Their faces are smashed together, and they're both lit up like fucking fireworks. Bright eyes, dazzling smiles, and flushed cheeks.

God damn. Sunny truly is a ray of fucking sunshine.

Between her warm eyes, tiny dimples on her cheeks, and killer smile, I start to feel like I'm staring at the sun instead of a photo of my daughter and her nanny.

I quickly exit out of the photo and toss my phone in my locker. I follow my teammates out onto the ice and will myself to focus.

———

The Flames are driving me up a fucking wall.

I like to think of myself as a man with restraint, but if one more red jersey pounds into me and sends me flying into the glass, I may break my fucking stick over their head.

"Fuck you." Barret, one of the Flames's best players, cuts in front of me and tries to steal the puck.

I fling it toward Malaki and ignore the chatter. I slip to the left and then to the right, my feet moving over the ice like I was born to skate.

I follow Malaki, tossing the puck back and forth. We're tied 1-1.

One minute left in the second period.

It'd be a nice touch to score a goal before we head into the locker room and make adjustments for the last period.

Kane rushes to the ice, sending Hayes back to the bench. I grip my stick and pick up the pace. The puck slips out from under Kane's stick.

"*Gavno,*" I grunt.

Alexeyev, a Flames player born and raised in Moscow, growls before trying to throw an elbow into my chest.

I move behind the net, where most players aren't comfortable, and turn and put my back toward him.

We're a good match. Tall, strong, and fucking fast.

The puck jolts to the right, and I have it pressed against the wall.

"*Idi nakhuy.*" The Russian slips from my mouth by accident, but it trips Alexeyev up. He pauses, likely due to surprise, and I smirk. Not everyone knows that I'm part-Russian since I added the A to my last name years ago. I love to use that to my advantage.

I wind my stick back and send it flying across the ice.

In hockey, plays move quickly. Offense switches to defense in the blink of an eye.

But to me, things are slow.

The crowd ceases to exist. The puck slaps Malaki's stick, and it soars through the legs of Barret and hits the back of the net.

I grin and raise my stick in the air.

Malaki does his godforsaken celly, sending the fans into a frenzy.

The buzzer sounds and cancels out the sound of Alexeyev's Russian slander in my direction.

He heads right for me.

My blood runs hot.

I don't engage in fighting on the ice...unless provoked.

One hit to my jaw, and fists are flying.

Though, they're not mine.

To no surprise, Kane is front and center, coming to my rescue.

Or most likely fueling his fill of aggression—as always.

We all have our reasons for getting into hockey. I became dangerously obsessed with it when my father left. It filled a gap in my life. For Kane? I suspect he was an angry child, and he got into hockey for the mere fact that it helped calm him.

It just turns out he's a damn good player.

Angry, but good.

"That's enough, Kane." I grab him by the collar of his jersey.

The Flames back off with the help of the refs, and the teams begin heading back into the locker rooms to reset. Kane brushes me off, no one saying a word about the fight. We both step off the ice, and he glances at me.

His grin is bloody. "Just remember me coming to your rescue later when you want to punch me."

I pause, and he winks.

"Why are you like this?"

My thoughts immediately go to Sunny. He's been talking about her since the moment he laid eyes on her. I know it's only to irritate me, because that's just *him*.

His laugh is manic, and goddamn, he's a crazy son of a bitch.

Before following him, I decided to backtrack. I turn and glance at the suite. I spot Ellie first, as always. She has her back pressed against the glass with her now messy braids swinging over her shoulders. I see cotton candy in her hand. She must have talked Sunny into getting it for her.

I plead with myself to turn around and head to the locker

room, but my eyes betray me. Sunny's warm brown hair pulled into a messy knot grabs my attention like a magnet. I stare at her bouncing bun for a second before something cools my heated skin.

Where the fuck did she get *that* jersey?

My fists clench.

I glance down the long dark hallway, ignoring the curious looks from fans.

First up, Sunny.

Next up, *Kane.*

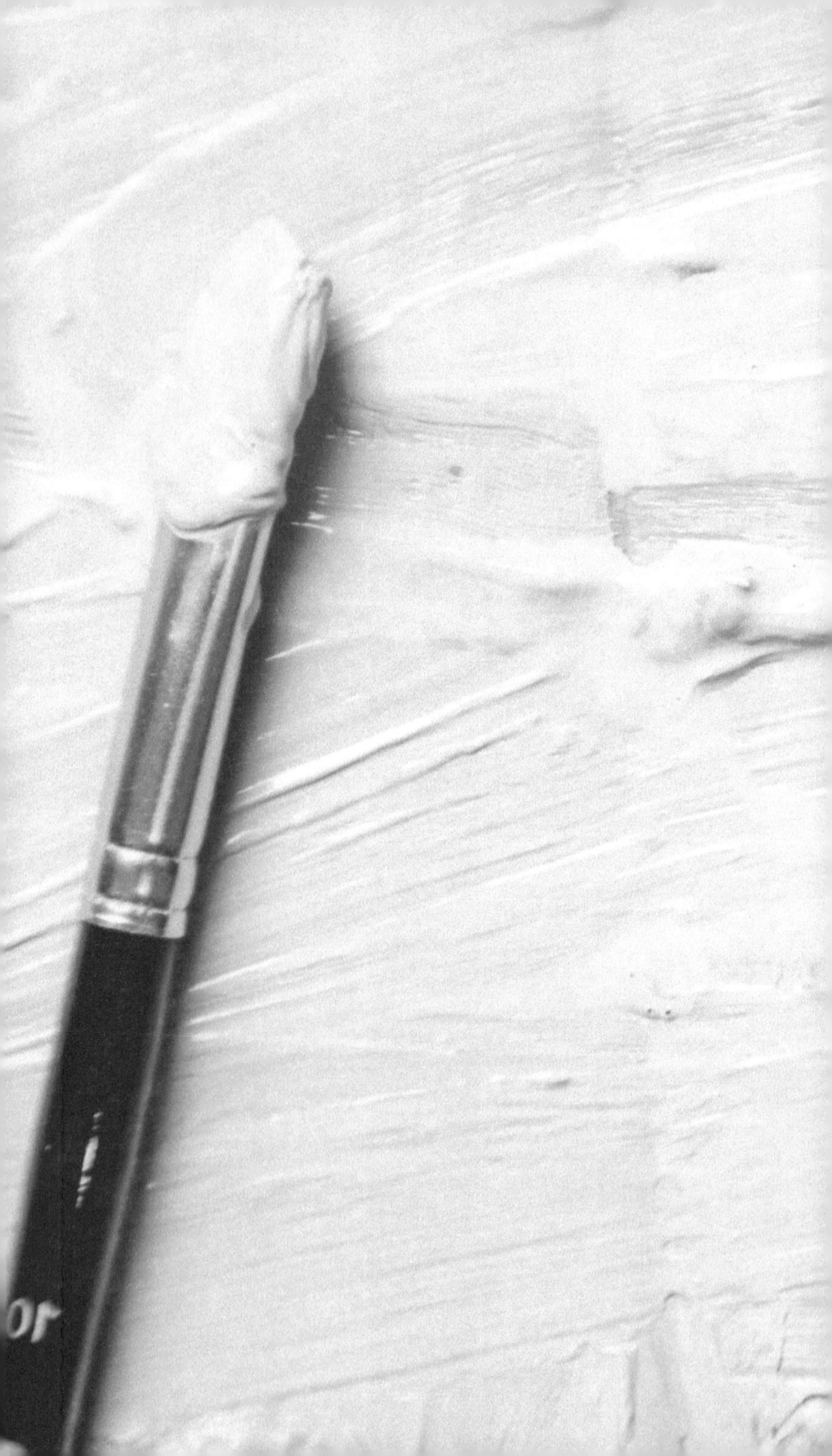

Twenty-Seven

SUNNY

MY PHONE VIBRATES in my pocket. I keep a hold of Scottie's eye while she finishes her story about how she got into photography before pulling it out.

> Rhodes: Meet me in the hallway.

I glance over at Ellie, who is busy making a bracelet with the beads I had her paint a week prior. I bend down and move her braid over her shoulder. "I'll be right back."

She tilts her delicate chin in my direction, stares into my eyes for a few seconds, and then relaxes with a nod.

Scottie shoots me a soft smile before getting on the floor with Ellie and making a bracelet too.

She's kind.

I like her.

It takes less than a minute to reach the familiar hallway.

The last time I met Rhodes down here, he scolded me for wearing his jersey.

He can't do that today, so there's that.

"Let her through," I hear.

The security guard dips his chin toward me and quickly leaves. Rhodes, with his damp, unruly hair, stands in the middle of the hallway, seeming more stern than anything. I meet him halfway and pretend like my heart isn't skipping beats with every step.

"Is everything okay?" I ask.

Rhodes's heavy brow furrows. His gaze skips past my face and lands on my chest. "Did you wear that to irritate me?"

I drop my head and look down. "The jersey?"

This again?

Rhodes steps closer, and it takes everything in me not to back away. "Yeah, Sunny. The *jersey*. Kane's jersey."

Confusion fills me. "Well, considering you were angry when I wore yours..."

He scoffs. "I got over that when you explained yourself, which is why I bought you the same one yesterday, only in *your* size."

A breath that sounds more like a laugh slips from my mouth.

Rhodes jerks backward from my reaction.

I stare up at his tall frame, even taller with his skates on. "Rhodes, this was the jersey in the bag. You must have made a mistake and—"

He pulls his glove off angrily, and I quit talking. He pinches the bridge of his nose and sighs loudly. There's a faint red mark on his jaw, and I think it's from where the other player hit him. To my surprise, he didn't hit him back.

"Chertovski, Kane," he grumbles.

There's that foreign language again.

"What?"

Rhodes drops his hand. "Kane must have switched the

jerseys out to irritate me. I did *not* buy some other man's jersey for you to wear."

I shift on my feet. "Why does it irritate you?"

His green eyes spark with something that makes me do a double take before he darts them away. His faint growl echoes around us in the empty hallway, and I stare at the flickering of his jaw.

"Because—" his voice is throaty. "He wants to fuck you, Sunny. It's his way of trying to get in your pants."

I laugh out loud.

Rhodes immediately glances at my mouth.

"That's never going to happen. Jersey or not."

He squints, like he's trying to read me.

"You heard Ruby yesterday." My cheeks grow warm. "I don't date, Rhodes, and I surely don't let random hockey players *fuck* me."

Plus, why does he even care? Other than the fact that it's his teammate.

Rhodes swallows.

"Not to mention, I'm your employee, Rhodes." I take a step closer to ease his concerns. "I'm Ellie's nanny. I'm not going to let some hot-tempered *boy* be the one to end my year of—"

My words cut off. There's no need to embarrass myself *again*.

We stand in silence. Rhodes stares at me with a look that I can't figure out. I'm hoping my honesty will ease his worries, and we can get on the same page—like putting Kane in his place. I know it's all fun and games. Teammate pranks and all. But I don't appreciate being the center of the joke.

"Well, take it off," he demands.

I cross my arms at his sour tone. My eyebrow arches. "Ellie would put you in time-out for that."

He shakes his head because he realizes his mistake. "*Please* take it off."

I still don't move to follow his command. He rolls his eyes and pulls off his other glove.

Both drop to the floor beside my feet. Next comes his jersey, up and over his head. My eyes follow his every move. He's so sure of himself as he stands mere feet away, towering over me with his jersey outstretched in between us.

"First you're mad that I wear your jersey, and now you want me to wear your *sweaty* one?"

He scoffs. "It's not that sweaty."

I laugh and grab it regardless. "This is ridiculous."

"What's ridiculous is Kane," he snaps.

"Well, what are we going to do about it?" I slip my fingers underneath the enemy's jersey and wait for his clever answer.

Rhodes stands in his thin undershirt and pads with his arms crossed. "There is no *we*. I'll take care of it."

I hum under my breath. "Well, that's no fun."

A laugh, or should I say *scoff*, leaves him. I lift Kane's jersey from my body, thankful I have a tank top underneath, and hand it out for him to take. He stares at it like it's going to catch on fire, but eventually, he reaches for it.

When his warm fingers brush against mine, goosebumps race to my bare arms. I quickly release the knit fabric and free his jersey from in between my knees. I pull it over my head and catch him staring at my chest. His jaw teeters back and forth, like he's still angry about Kane's joke.

After I'm fully dressed, I tie his jersey in a knot so it's not completely swallowing my frame. I hold my arms out and spin.

"Better?" I ask.

A tight nod is all I get.

He moves past me with Kane's jersey draped over his shoulder.

I have no idea what he plans on doing to get back at Kane, but I sort of wish I was there to witness it.

———

The Blue Devils lose by one.

Ellie sighs dramatically on the way home. I sit in the backseat with her and poke her belly. "We already have one Oscar. We don't need two."

Marco smiles at me from the rearview mirror.

Ellie turns in her booster with her blue cotton-candy-stained mouth. "Oscar?"

"That's what I call your dad in my head," I admit, trying to make her laugh. "You know...Oscar the Grouch, from *Sesame Street*?"

Her little brow crinkles. She looks identical to Rhodes when she does that. "*Sesame Street*?"

I gasp. "You don't know what *Sesame Street* is?"

Ellie shakes her head, her braid messy from her jumping up and down during the game.

"Marco!" I shout. "Do you *hear* this?"

He laughs and nods.

"Next movie night, we're watching *Sesame Street*." I sit back in my seat, still dumbfounded.

Ellie looks out the window. "Does my daddy know you call him Oscar?"

I pause. "Not yet." I'm sure the more I'm around him, the more comfortable I'll be, and it'll accidentally slip.

"Sometimes I call Peter a name that he doesn't know."

"Who is Peter?" Marco asks.

I'm wondering the same.

Ellie shrugs. "A boy in my class."

I shift toward her, ignoring my vibrating phone so she has my full attention. I've learned that she doesn't like when someone doesn't meet her eye or talk to her directly—something most kids probably wouldn't notice.

Ellie is different, though.

"What do you call him?" I ask.

"Mudak," she says fluently.

Is that...Russian?

"And that means?"

The tiniest dimple appears on her cheek. "It means asshole."

I slap my hand over my mouth to hide a laugh. "Ellie Volkova," I mutter after pulling myself together. "You aren't supposed to say curse words."

She gawks at me. "That's why I say it in Russian. No one knows what it means."

A grin moves against my lips. "I think I might need to learn Russian."

Marco makes a noise, and I'm pretty sure it means he agrees.

"I'll let you borrow the tapes from my babushka."

I snap my head to her. "Your what?"

She giggles. "My nana. Babushka is nana in Russian, Sunny!" She shakes her head. "You *do* need my tapes."

I'm still laughing when we pull up in front of the house. Marco, the gentleman he is, always walks us to the door when Rhodes isn't there to greet us. After we both give him a quick hug, we head inside and lock the door. I finally glance at my phone and see a calendar notification.

Ellie is placing our shoes in their rightful spot when I swipe up and see an added event from Rhodes.

CALENDAR NOTIFICATION: DATE

He has a date?

I huff.

Is he serious? We just had the conversation yesterday, and he's already taking advantage of it?

Wait, who cares? It's a Saturday evening. I'd already told him I'd get Ellie to bed after the game so he could do his post-interview in peace without having to worry about her being near the cameras. It was nice for me not to worry about being in front of cameras too, actually.

I click my phone off and smile at Ellie. "What do you say we have our own movie night? I'll introduce you to Oscar."

Her eyes grow large. "Right now?"

I nod. "Your dad will be at the rink for a while." *Rink...in between some woman's legs...* "And it's the weekend. No school tomorrow."

Ellie squeals. "I'll get the blankets!"

I mimic my cute little bestie. "And I'll get the popcorn!"

Twenty-Eight

RHODES

SOMETHING IS SERIOUSLY wrong with me.

My hands rest on the woman's hips as she crawls on top of me, yet I can't fucking concentrate on the way she's pressing her lips to my neck and making these sounds like she's seconds from coming.

"Is everything okay?" She pulls back slightly and pouts.

She sits on my lap, and my dick is barely hard. *Well, this is fucking embarrassing.*

It's not her.

It's me.

She's decent enough. Pretty face, nice curves, blonde hair that is pulled to one side, showing off her slender neck.

I'm more of a brunette kind of guy, but considering I haven't fucked someone in close to a year, you'd think I'd be able to move past it.

A thought enters my head like a lightbulb—a *bright* one—and I grind my teeth.

Get the fuck out of my head, Sunny.

Her brown hair is rich and thick. I bet my fingers would get buried in the strands as I pulled on them.

My hands squeeze the woman's hips. "I have to go."

She pouts harder. "What?"

What the hell am I doing thinking about my daughter's nanny while some other woman grinds over me?

That was the entire point of going out—well, sort of. This all started because of Kane.

I took the blonde from him as payback. He had his eye on her, spitting his lame game, and I casually stepped in front of him and pulled her flush against me.

He knew exactly why I did it too. Instead of winding back and attempting to knock me out, like he'd do with any other man in the bar, he smiled like a maniac and walked away.

"Yeah, sorry. I have an early morning."

The woman climbs from my lap on shaky legs. She seems disappointed, and I wish I felt bad.

But I don't.

I leave her apartment without looking back.

It's after midnight.

Sunny and Ellie will both be asleep, which is good because I'm not up to acting like my typical aloof self with Sunny at the moment. I'm exhausted from the game and from keeping my thoughts on the straight and narrow. Seeing her in that darkened hallway with nothing but her skimpy tank top on after I practically convulsed over her wearing someone else's number flipped a switch in my head.

The only explanation is that I need to get laid.

Yet, here I am, entering my house with my dick still nestled inside my pants, *untouched*.

The lights are dim in the living room. I quietly walk through the hall and stop when I see both Sunny and Ellie asleep on the couch. The cushions and blankets swallow them both whole. A smile slips onto my face, and I rub my hand down my scruffy cheek.

There are two bowls of popcorn on the coffee table, half-eaten.

Sesame Street plays on the TV, which is...unusual.

With smooth steps, I walk over to Ellie and gently scoop her into my arms.

She sleeps like a rock, just like me.

It takes no time getting her into her bed and blanketing her with the blue quilt. I place a kiss on her forehead and head back to the living room.

My heart noticeably gains traction as I rest against the arched alcove. Sunny's hair lies over her shoulders in thick waves, and her face is free from any emotion. Perfect golden skin and smooth cheeks that lead down to her bow-shaped lips.

My nostrils flare. I'm obviously attracted to her.

When I met her, my first thought was that she was the type of beautiful that smacks you in the face, but I had my reservations. She's young, which to me means *wild*. I assumed she was untrustworthy and flighty, and I expected her to fuck up at least once, but I was wrong.

That doesn't happen often.

She's mature beyond her years—driven, determined, independent, and a ray of sunshine. When she enters a room and smiles, there's a warmth that follows her. She has a vibe to her that's alluring, making you crave it. She doesn't even have to try either. It's just *her.*

It's admirable that she's still like this after someone broke her trust and damaged a part of her pureness. I've seen the anxiety seep in, yet she has a way of smiling and laughing a moment later.

It's baffling.

I shake my thoughts away and busy myself with cleaning

up the popcorn. I do my best to ignore Sunny sleeping peacefully on the couch, *still* wearing my jersey. A gray knitted blanket is draped over her, only showing small snippets of her body. I wait a few seconds and wonder if I should leave her there, but Ellie is an early riser. She'll wake Sunny up the second she lays eyes on her.

Hovering above her, I place one hand on the back of the couch and lean forward. I give her shoulder a soft nudge, and her face twitches. A small line appears in between her eyebrows, right below a strand of her hair that has fallen into her face.

"Sunsh—" I clear my throat. "Sunny."

She sucks in a sharp breath and pops up so fast I'm forced to step backward. Her bare feet slap onto the hardwood floor as she gasps for air, sending her hair into a blurry brown mess. "Ellie?!"

My hands move before my head even realizes what's happening. My reflexes are quick from years of hockey.

One arm wraps around her waist, and the other cups the side of her cheek. "Breathe, Sunshine. It's just me. Ellie's fine." I skate my attention all over her worried face.

Her eyelashes flutter. I suck in my own sharp breath when her hand winds around my sturdy wrist, gripping onto it for dear life. The rising and falling of her chest is indicative of panic, but I can't help but focus on how her breasts are brushing against me.

A warm, heavy breath flows from her mouth, and my nostrils flare. She smells sweet, like buttery popcorn and something that makes my mouth water.

"Oh, jeez." She closes her eyes and releases my wrist. "I'm so sorry. You startled me. I—"

There's no need for her to explain. I understand why she's on edge sometimes.

I move to let go of her, but she sways, so I quickly reach

for her again. This time, I put my hands around her waist to steady her. I glance down to make sure her feet are stable on the floor, and my mouth runs dry.

Where the hell are her pants?

Fuck.

I gulp, and it's loud enough for her to hear.

"You're still wearing my jersey," I state.

Her silky hair falls and brushes my arm with the dip of her head. "Oh *god,*" she groans. "I fell asleep. I didn't mean for you to...find me like this."

I'm not sure I like the sound of her wobbling voice. I bet if I were to move my fingers to her wrist, her pulse would be flying a mile a minute.

"Sit." With my hands on her waist, I guide her backward and push her to collapse on the couch. When she's settled, I remove my traitorous hands and take a step away. I plead with myself to keep my eyes on her face and not her bare legs. "You're shaking."

"I'm fine," she argues.

There she goes again, acting all determined and independent. "You just scared me. I—"

I make a noise that escapes from deep within my chest when she tries to stand. She pauses, peers up at me with flushed cheeks, and then slowly sits back down.

Khoroshaya devochka.

I freeze at the explicit vision that fills my head.

Did I just call her "good girl" in Russian?

I cough from shock and end up muttering, "Good choice."

What the fuck is wrong with me?

Her lips purse, and I look away.

I sit beside her, putting enough distance between us to where we aren't touching, and clear my thoughts. If this were a few weeks ago, I'd leave her to calm herself down from being startled awake. But now that I know she's skittish for certain reasons, I decide to stay.

Sesame Street plays on the TV in front of us. I look at her and hate that my gaze falls to her bare legs for a brief second. They shouldn't catch my attention, but they do.

I lift my leg and tug on the blanket I sat on. I hold it out to her, and she quickly snatches it, resting it over her bare thighs. *Thank god.*

I reach for anything that will pull my thoughts in a different direction and flick my chin at the flatscreen. "Interesting choice."

A dimple appears on her cheek. "There's a reason behind it."

I give her my attention, and she's smiling coyly. Her hands are in her lap, over the blanket...and why is she so pretty? Her dimple deepens, and there's that warm feeling again.

"Do I dare ask?" My tone is full of boredom, yet I'm anything but bored.

White teeth clamp onto her bottom lip. "Only if you promise not to get offended."

"Offended by *Sesame Street*?" I chuckle. "I think it's a safe bet that I won't be offended."

She laughs nervously. "I may or may not have referred to you as Oscar, and Ellie didn't know what I was talking about."

"Excuse me?" *Okay, fine. I am a little offended.*

Sunny pouts, and unlike my earlier *date*, hers is actually cute. "You promised you wouldn't get offended."

A sarcastic noise leaves me. "I don't make promises, Sunshine."

Her eyebrows come together. "Ever?"

I shake my head and get back on track. "You call me Oscar behind my back?" I ask, keeping my tone level. "Oscar the Grouch?"

"Only in my head," she mutters.

"I'm not even grumpy with you," I argue, looking away. "That's unfair."

"But you *are* grumpy," she says.

It's probably because I need to get fucking laid.

"Sometimes." I stare at Elmo on the screen. "A little less now that I've found a decent nanny to help with Ellie."

It's uncanny how opposite she and I are.

I call her Sunshine, and she calls me Oscar. *Total fucking opposites.*

"Decent?" she exclaims. "That's it? Just a *decent* nanny?"

I turn toward her and grin. "You fishin' for compliments?"

Her lips part, like she's offended. "Uh, no. But I think I'm a little more than decent. I haven't tried to sleep with you like the other nannies, and I never flirt. I don't ditch Ellie *ever*, and I'm practically available to you at all times when you need me."

Available to you at all times when you need me.

Why did that statement wake my dick up?

A thick swallow moves down my throat. "You clean the house too. *Fine*. You're more than decent."

She makes a noise that pulls on my attention like a fucking puppet.

"I know," she quips.

That cheeky grin of hers irritates me. It irritates me because it excites me.

I turn away when she swings her legs up onto the couch under the blanket. I know what lies beneath it.

Nothing.

"Oscar, you say..." I relax back onto the couch, shifting away from her. As if on cue, the green monster appears on the screen inside his metal trash can. "Oh look, it's me."

Sunny laughs quietly.

After a few minutes of watching Oscar, it switches to a different character.

"I do not act like that." My voice is gruff.

Fuck, I do act like that.

Sunny laughs again. "Whatever you say...*Oscar.*"

I glare at her, and she responds with a flirty smile. Those big, brown eyes glimmer beneath the dim lighting of the lamp, and her white teeth gleam like she just used whitening strips.

I scoff. "Why are you so...happy all the time?"

A playful gasp leaves her, but then she turns away from me. The corners of her mouth slowly drop, and she shrugs. "Because."

"Because why?" I prod.

It's late.

We should go to sleep.

Except, I'm still sitting here on the couch with my double in the background, banging his trash can while I question her radiant personality.

I would have never guessed that...one, she was assaulted. Two, she doesn't date nor does she have a boyfriend. And what was it her friend said? She hasn't had sex in *far too long.*

For someone as chipper as her, she has to be letting out some tension somehow.

Is that why she is always fiddling with clay and painting?

"Because I know real sadness..."

My chest constricts.

"It makes me appreciate the smaller things in life. Nothing seems as bad after I've been in...certain situations." She turns toward me. "You know?"

I continue to stare at her. My mind spins in different directions. Is she referring to what she's already alluded to, or is she referring to something else in her life?

Suddenly, I find myself wanting to know everything about her.

What makes her angry?

What has she had to endure in life?

What are her dreams?

Why is she so captivating? Even to a guy like me?

"Plus"—my thoughts scatter with her add-on—"I just like to make people happy."

Gazing at her, sitting with her knees beneath the blanket pulled up to her chin with the colors of *Sesame Street* painting her soft features, I'm not sure she has to even try.

Just looking at her can thaw any man's cold heart.

Except mine, of course.

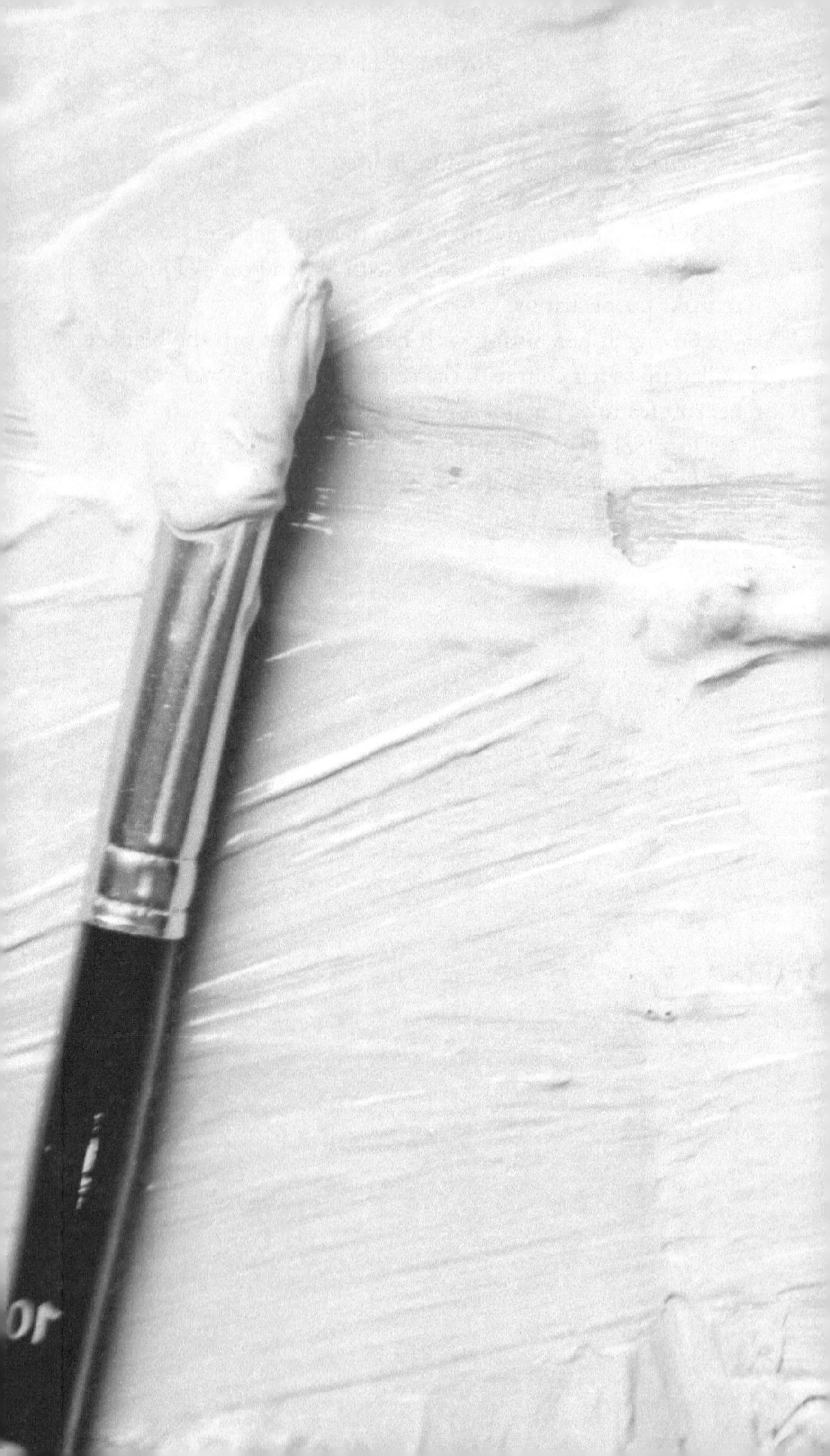

Twenty–Nine

SUNNY

I SIGH WISTFULLY.

I wiggle myself farther onto my bed and pull the blankets up higher. Except, they're stuck? I keep my eyes closed and grumble.

It's too early to be awake.

Or maybe I just stayed up too late.

I tug on the blankets again, but they're unmoving. *Ugh.* I turn to my side and press myself onto the warmth radiating behind me.

A gush of something hot brushes against my neck, and then something heavy lands on my waist.

My eyes flutter open. The dim morning light filters through the window and—*wait*. This isn't my bedroom. I'm in the living room.

I arch my back to peek over my shoulder, and our eyes snag.

Rhodes's eyebrows cave, like he's trying to figure out what's going on and why I'm cuddling against him. His hand never leaves my waist. It tightens for a second before he relaxes. A swallow moves against his neck.

"I either need you to get up or stop moving like that."

The rasp of his sleepy voice does something to my body. Heat brews in between us, and I pray that it's just my head playing tricks on me.

"We fell asleep?" It comes out like a question instead of a statement.

Rhodes nods curtly.

I shift, and he hisses. He presses farther into the back of the couch, but he can't go anywhere.

"I need you to let me up," he says under his breath. "*Please.*"

He sounds pained, like I've hurt him. Concerned, I sit up quickly but not before being forced to brush against him again. Another hiss flies from his mouth, and his hand falls to his lap. I crawl over to the other cushion, a chill wrapping around my legs.

I peer over my shoulder, and Rhodes's lips are parted. He's staring at my backside with a tight jaw.

My eyes widen. *I'm still pantless.*

I flop to sit and pull the blanket to my lap. My cheeks are warm. "I'm sorry." *My god.* "You just keep finding me in the most embarrassing situations," I mutter.

"Embarrassing?" He chokes out a laugh and shakes his perfectly messy hair. "I'm not sure what's embarrassing about *that.*"

He drops his lazy gaze to my mouth and then squeezes his eyes shut. He curses under his breath, "Fuck, I should not have said that."

My body heats again, but this time, it's not from embarrassment.

His long legs swing until his feet hit the floor. He glances at me briefly. "I'm sorry, I'm *obviously*"—he glances to his lap —"not thinking clearly."

Oh.

Oh.

"It's fine. We just fell asleep...to *Sesame Street*."

He snickers, and I grin.

Rhodes sits for a few minutes with his eyes trained to the floor. I stare at the side of his jaw, counting how many times he clenches it.

"Are you okay?" I finally ask.

He snaps his attention to me, and it definitely shouldn't have stolen my breath. "No."

I clear my throat. "I'm sorry?"

A chuckle slips into the quiet living room, and he drops his head. "Stop apologizing."

"Well, I fell asleep and somehow ended up lying on you, and then I move, and I don't have any pants..."

He squeezes his eyes shut. "Please don't remind me. I'm trying to get the nerve to move. You're going to get me stirred up again."

"Sorr—" His neck cracks with how quickly he looks at me. "I mean...is there anything I can do to help?"

His jaw slacks.

I slap my hand over my mouth. "Oh my god."

Unwilling to look at him anymore, I fall back into the couch and hope I blend in with the cushions. "Just pretend I don't exist."

Why does he make me stupid?

A choked noise leaves him.

"I thought you had a date last night!" I blurt. "Did I misread your innuendo there? I thought—"

Why is he all of a sudden acting like a man without restraint?

A breath catches in my chest.

Calm down, Sunny. They're nothing alike.

Rhodes is not crossing a line with me. It's a physical reaction, which is normal. Just like the little tug I felt in between my legs when I accidentally pressed against him.

Attraction is natural.

It doesn't have to be anything other than that.

"I did have a date, and no, you did not misread anything," he stresses. "But..." his words trail.

"But what?"

I stare at the side of his face. He rubs his hand against his jaw.

"You're not the only one who hasn't had sex in a while, Sunny."

I jerk upright. *Wait, what?*

"I left her and came home early."

That should *not* make me happy.

"Why?" I ask.

He shrugs. "Between being a single father—which stemmed from a one-night stand and something I didn't have any time to prepare for—and trying to focus on hockey and my endless nanny problems, I've been a little busy. Not to mention, I've grown skeptical of some women's intentions. I may seem like a cocky hotshot, but it's just as hard for me to trust someone."

I nod. "That's understandable."

Silence comes between us, and as always, I attempt to lighten the mood. "Maybe you should just find someone you can trust. You know, someone other than your hand."

An abrupt laugh leaves him.

I smile at my little joke.

"You're not funny."

I wink at him. "I am too."

He rolls his eyes, but I see the little grin trying to work its way onto his stony features.

A few seconds pass, and he sighs. "I'm sorry if I made you uncomfortable." His glance is fleeting. "With my...current situation."

"Current situation?" I raise my brows and try to hide a laugh.

"You're fired," he grumbles.

I laugh. "Oscar is joking now? Wow."

He scoffs, and I'm certain a comeback is about to fly out of his mouth, but little footsteps catch our attention. Rhodes panics and grabs the pillow, putting it over his lap.

"Printsessa," he says. "Imagine that. You're up with the sun."

"So are you," she argues, rubbing the sleep from her eye. "Hi, Sunny." She turns to her dad. "Can I snuggle?"

A laugh leaves me when I see the unease on Rhodes's face. His arms flex over the pillow. I pop up quickly and come to his rescue–despite the fact that I have no pants on. Ellie and I both stand in nothing but oversized shirts that belong to her father. Me in his jersey, and her in his Chicago Blue Devils tee.

"I have a great idea," I say.

Ellie's eyes light up.

"You know what Sundays are for, right?"

Ellie and Rhodes answer at the same time. "Football."

I place my hands on my hips. "What? No!"

"Says who?" Rhodes mumbles.

Ignoring him, I grab onto Ellie's hand. "Sundays are for breakfasts that are *not* cereal."

She pouts for a second until I bend down and whisper in her ear. "Wanna help me make chocolate chip pancakes?"

Her pretty eyes light up. "Yes!"

"Let's go!" I pull her toward the kitchen.

Rhodes stares after us with an unreadable expression on his face.

I drop Ellie's hand and let her go ahead of me.

"You just go...shower," I say to her dad.

I roll my lips to hide my amusement.

His mouth forms a straight line, and he looks just like Oscar the Grouch.

A *hot* Oscar the Grouch.

"You're welcome," I mouth, shooting him a wink.

He stands and adjusts himself.

The action is too hot for its own good. A thrill skips down my spine and lands at the soles of my bare feet.

Rhodes surprises me when he heads in my direction. I should move, but I don't. My breath seizes when he stops beside me and bends so his mouth is *right* over my ear.

"Go put pants on, Sunshine."

Oh. Right.

I turn at the sound of chocolate chips falling to the floor from the kitchen.

Our mouths are so close, but neither one of us steps away.

"Oops," says a tiny voice.

The slightest growl slips from Rhodes, and then he's gone, and I'm heading into the kitchen to help pick up.

Thirty

RHODES

MY FINGERS GET LOST in Ellie's hair, and I curse quietly. Her head jerks as I tug on the ends.

I'm predicting a meltdown coming.

I glance through the opening of the kitchen and stare at Sunny sitting on a barstool with a laptop in front of her. Her shoulders are tense.

"Hold on," I say to Ellie. I place her on the couch cushion and stride into the kitchen.

Sunny, unaware of me standing behind her, mumbles under her breath at something on the screen. I stop a few feet behind her and glance at whatever has her so worried.

I recognize the social media logo. She's watching a time-lapse of someone painting on a large canvas. *Damn, three million views?* I step closer and catch the handle: @allyepaints.

I gawk at the screen when the painter angles herself toward the camera. Not only is the painting fucking amazing, but the side of her jaw is *awfully* familiar.

It's her.

A faint growl comes from Sunny. Her fingers move quickly. She copies the link, pastes it into an email and furiously types, asking for the video to be removed along with her entire social media account.

This is interesting.

I make a mental note to search her username later when I'm alone and make an attempt at being loud enough for her to hear me as I continue walking in the kitchen so she doesn't suspect I was just lingering over her shoulder.

Rounding the bar, I grab a beer out of the fridge.

I don't drink often, maybe one or two when I'm out with the team. But not being able to do a simple fucking braid calls for something stronger.

I place the bottle down onto the counter and rest my hands against the hard granite. "I need your help."

Sunny raises an eyebrow. "I've met my quota for helping you."

I raise my eyebrow right back.

She shuts her laptop and smirks. "Remember yesterday? When I distracted a certain someone so you could..."

God, please don't bring yesterday up.

Visions of pumping myself in the shower to the thought of her pressed against me come to light. I try to wash the guilt away with my beer, but unfortunately, it doesn't work.

"What do you need, Oscar?" She flutters her lashes and... *fuck.*

The more she and I are around one another, the more I notice the little things about her. Like her long lashes, or how there are a few golden strands of hair woven in between the darker ones.

I am in over my head.

"Braids," I grunt.

What am I? A fucking caveman?

I swallow another gulp of beer and try again. "Can you help me with Ellie's braids?"

Sunny turns on the stool and peers into the living room. She smiles over her shoulder at me before hopping down and rescuing Ellie's poor scalp.

I try to watch from afar, following the movements of Sunny's deft fingers, but it's too hard to see. Instead, I sip on my beer and think about anything *other* than my hot nanny.

Tomorrow is the first away game that I'll have to stay overnight since hiring Sunny.

I'm not worried, but I have a feeling that Ellie is.

Once her hair is pulled out of her face and woven neatly, I place my beer on the counter. "Okay, Printsessa. Say good-night to Sunny."

Ellie, in her oversized T-shirt, turns to look at Sunny. A look of mischief covers her tiny features. "Spokoynoy nochi."

Not this again. This is Ellie's defense mechanism—I swear. Speaking Russian to someone who doesn't under—

"Sladkih snov." Sunny's soft smile catches my eye, and my stomach dips.

"Good job, Sunny!" Ellie wraps her arms around Sunny's neck. "My babushka will be so proud!"

A strange sense of comfort nestles into my chest. Ellie rushes over to me and slides her tiny hand into mine. I let her pull me all the way to her bedroom, and I'm not fully coherent again until she snuggles down under the covers. The blue quilt is pulled up all the way to the bridge of her nose. All I see are two big, worried green eyes peering up at me.

"Are you teaching Sunny Russian?" I tug on the quilt so I can see her face.

She quickly pulls it back up. "She asked to borrow the tapes."

Interesting.

"You know tomorrow evening I won't be home, right?"

She nods so quickly her braid flops over the blanket.

"Are you going to be okay?" I ask.

Sunny and I aren't the only ones with trust issues. It's usually easy for me to move past mine—I just *detach*—but that's the last thing I want to teach to Ellie. The last time I had an away game where I had to stay overnight, Ellie was left alone for several hours.

I have no indications of that happening on Sunny's watch, but Ellie might.

"I fully trust Sunny," I add.

Do I?

"She would never leave you alone or do anything like what's been done in the past."

"I know, Daddy." Ellie slowly pulls the blanket down to her shoulders. "I'll be okay," she says, reassuring me.

I kiss her on the forehead. "Alright, then. Get some sleep."

I'm almost through the door when she perks up. "Daddy?"

I turn, "Yeah?"

"I like her."

How can she not? She's pretty damn likeable. "Sladkih snov." I wink and repeat *sweet dreams* in Russian, just like Sunny, before heading the rest of the way out.

When I reach the foot of the stairs, I overhear Sunny on the phone. This time, I purposefully eavesdrop.

Okay, *fine.* They've all been purposeful, but how else can I learn about my live-in nanny?

"I can't see you." Sunny laughs.

Can't see who?

"What? Oh." The woman on the other end of the phone sighs. "I don't know how to fix it."

"You press the little camera button on the screen," Sunny says.

"Can you see me now?"

Sunny snorts. "No, Nana. I'm looking at the wall. Now the floor." She laughs again. "Now the window."

"Oh jeez. I can't work this old phone. It's too small for me to see the buttons."

"It's okay," Sunny reassures her. "I just wanted to check in. It's evening for me, but I figured this was a good time for you."

"How is the new nanny job, sweetheart?"

Oh, I definitely have to hear this.

I move closer to the kitchen and stop right outside of the opening. Sunny's back is to me as she continues to stare at her laptop.

"It's good."

Just good?

"The house looks nice," her nana says.

I slip backward, afraid her nana will catch a glimpse of me being a total fucking creep.

What the hell am I doing? Why am I sneaking around and eavesdropping on the conversation?

"It is. I actually love Chicago. I even went to one of the art museums the other day."

"Are you painting again?" Her nana coughs, and I'm not going to lie...it doesn't sound good. "Your grandpa was so upset when he found out you had to stop painting as much. If he knew it was so you could work more to help pay for the nursing home, he'd probably demand we put him on the street."

My eyebrows rise.

"And now you're paying for mine."

She's paying for her nana's nursing home?

"It's not that much," Sunny argues. "Insurance covers some of it. You've taken care of me all my life. *Of course* I'm going to take care of you. I make good money nannying, Nana."

I press my head to the wall. She's so...selfless.

"Tell me more," the old woman coughs again. "Is the little girl's dad kind to you?"

My blood pressure spikes. *Hardly.*

"I know you said he's a single father, but what about her mother?"

"I read that her mother passed away at birth or shortly after, just like Mom."

Oh.

"He's a little grumpy, but I think I'm wearing him down a little." Sunny's soft laugh fills the kitchen, and she's right. She is *absolutely* wearing on me.

I'm seconds from strolling into the kitchen. The guilt of spying is catching up to me.

"Do you think he's good-looking?"

I pause.

Maybe I'll wait a few more seconds.

"Nana!" Sunny chastises her.

Before anyone else utters a word about my looks, the faint voice of a woman filters through the computer.

"I have to go, sweetheart. It's time for my breathing treatment."

Strolling farther into the kitchen, Sunny snaps her head over to me but quickly looks away.

I swear her cheeks get pinker.

"Oh, wait. Is that him?"

Sunny is flustered. Her lip gets trapped beneath her teeth, and she mutters, "Uh-huh."

"Hello," I say, leaning down toward the laptop. She isn't visible on the screen, but I know she can see me. "I'm Rhodes."

The older woman laughs, but it's more of a rasp. "Well, I have my answer."

I grin, knowing what she's referring to. I glance at Sunny. Her cheeks are *definitely* pink.

"Okay, bye, Nana. Love you."

"Love you, sweetheart. Bye-bye."

Sunny quickly closes her laptop. Her lips flatten, and she crosses her arms defensively.

As large as my kitchen is, it feels small with us both in here. I round the island and eye her from across the thick stone.

"Well?" I say, crossing my arms to mimic her.

Her big, brown eyes shift away from me. "Well what?"

"Do you?"

I'm not sure what made me ask her. Curiosity? In need of my ego getting stroked? Desperation to know what's going on in her head?

"Do I what?" she asks.

Don't do it.

I lean against the counter behind me and cross my legs at the ankles. "Do you think I'm good-looking?"

I did it.

Sunny's pretty rose-colored lips part. "How—"

I smirk, and she scowls at me.

"You were eavesdropping!"

I push off the counter. "It's not my fault you were on a video call in the kitchen. I was only coming in here for my beer."

"Yeah right." Her eye roll excites me.

I flick my brow. "You don't believe me?"

"Nope." The P pops out of her mouth with sass. "And no, I *don't* find you attractive."

After swallowing the rest of my beer and tossing it into the trash, I round the island and head right for her. Sunny's spine straightens. She pulls her shoulders back and shows off her slender neck.

I lean in close, because I'm *clearly* unhinged this evening, and say, "Well, I don't believe *you*."

She gasps and levels me with an extremely amusing glare.

I chuckle, and her mouth twitches.

"Night, Sunshine," I say, winking.

What the fuck has gotten into me?

Am I flirting?

I do not flirt.

Sunny's cute scowl deepens.

It's the last thing I think about as I fall asleep, which is *clearly* a problem.

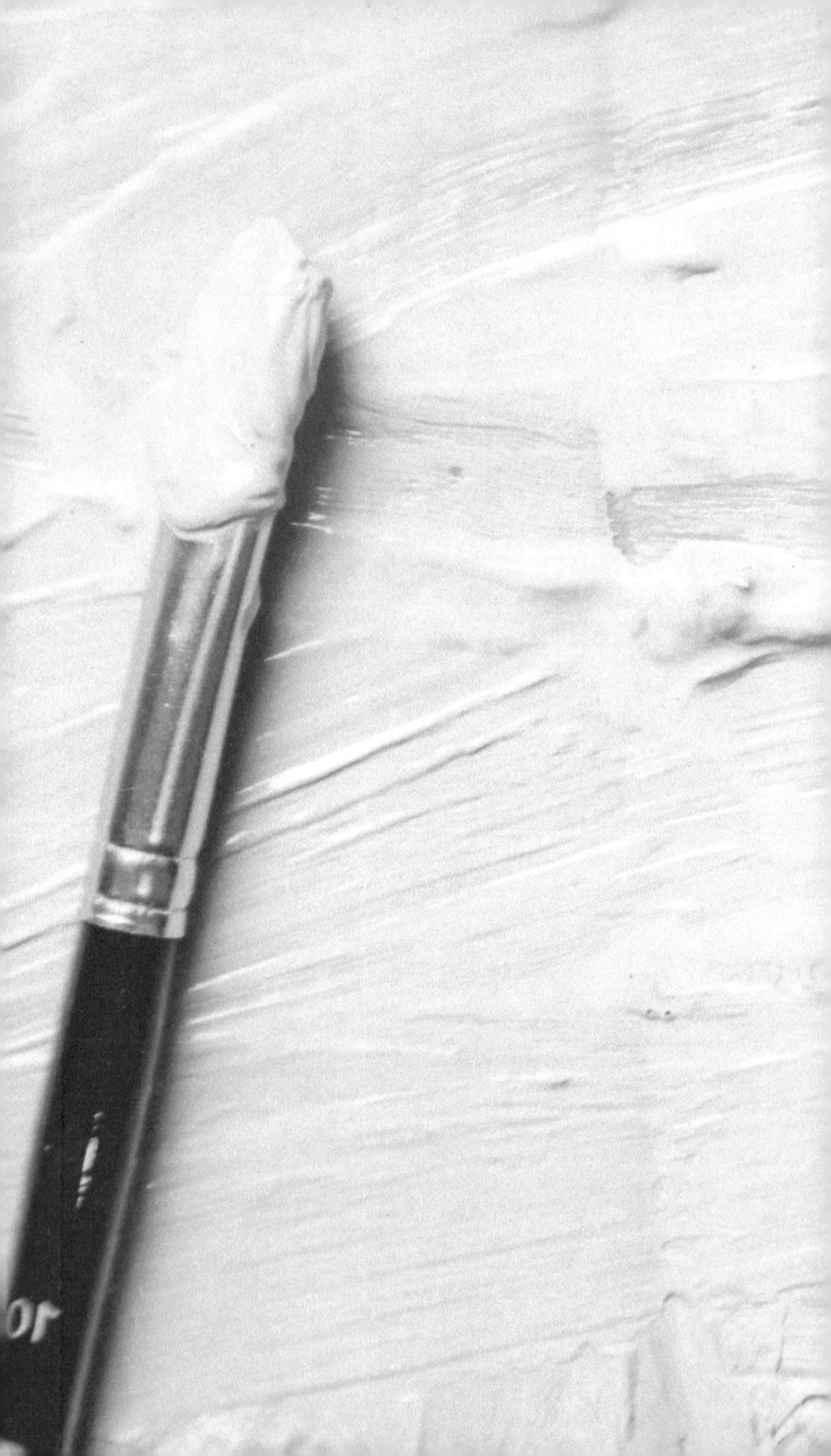

Thirty-One

SUNNY

I PRESS my closed fist to my mouth and mentally cheer for the Blue Devils as they gear up for a shoot-out. Nerves fill my stomach when Rhodes takes the ice. I sit up a little taller on the bed, careful not to wake Ellie.

My heart beats as quickly as he skates.

He winds left and then right.

The cameras follow him like a hawk, and without the rest of the team on the ice, he stands out even more than before.

Come on, Oscar.

My breath hitches when the puck flies off to the top left corner of the net, and as soon as I see his dazzling smile, I silently squeal.

Yes!

The rest of the team spills out onto the ice and circles him. I smile to myself.

For as happy as I am that they won, you'd think I was on the team or something.

I peek at Ellie, who is peacefully sleeping beside me. She is going to be so angry that she missed the end of the game, especially since her dad made the winning shot. After brushing a stray hair out of her face, I place my hand on her back like before. She's cuddled up underneath Rhodes's comforter, which I refused to get under. I already felt like I was crossing a line by coming into his bedroom and sitting on his bed, let alone crawling beneath the covers too.

Ellie begged and pleaded for us to watch the game in his room because he has the biggest TV.

It *is* huge, taking up a large part of the wall in front of his bed. It sort of made it seem like we were there. Only, we are tucked away safely inside the house.

I grab my phone, angle it for a selfie, and do a thumbs-up with Ellie sleeping beside me.

> Me: Good game, Oscar! Just sending a quick photo for reassurance that Ellie is okay!

I continue to watch the post-game eview of the game, where they highlight Rhodes and his winning shot multiple times. Each time they zoom in on his face, something hot whips through me.

He makes it look so easy.

His vibrant green eyes are laser focused while he glides over the ice, so sure of himself. He looks so much larger on the screen too, his pads broadening his shoulders even more. There's a little bit of scruff on his cheeks that's hardly visible, but I know by morning, it'll cover his jaw.

He asked me if I thought he was attractive.

What an absurd question.

He *knows* he's attractive. Why would a man like him need me to feed his ego?

Which is exactly why I lied.

My phone vibrates on my lap, and I look away from the post-game interview to read the text.

Oscar: Thank you.

A man of few words.
Rhodes Volkova.
I laugh quietly, but then my phone vibrates again.

Oscar: Are you in my bed?

My cheeks heat.
Shit, I forgot.
My fingers freeze. There's a slight uptick in my heartbeat, but Rhodes should know me well enough by now to know that I wouldn't climb into his bed for any reason other than Ellie.

Me: Ellie insisted you had the biggest TV.

My teeth dig into my lip as I wait for his response.
It takes far too long.
By the time my phone vibrates with an incoming text, I'm convinced it'll be an angry message from him.

Oscar: She isn't wrong.

Whew.

Me: Don't worry, I'll carry her to bed soon.

He doesn't text back for quite a while.
I look around his room, and it definitely has a manly feel to it.

A dark wall painted a deep gray with a large TV mounted above a sound box of some sort.

It's clean and bare. There is next to no clutter. The only thing on top of his dresser is some hockey memorabilia from past seasons.

I look at his bedside table, which must be the side I'm lying on.

Naturally.

A lamp, the remote, and a book titled *Dads with Daughters: A self-help book for parenting.*

Okay, that's sort of sweet.

He may be gruff and a bit rough around the edges, but he tries his hardest to be a good dad to Ellie.

I reach over hesitantly, knowing I'm totally invading his privacy, and pull on the drawer.

My jaw falls. I freeze like I've been caught robbing a bank.

Condoms.

Lots of them. I start to sweat.

I peer at Ellie's sleeping body, hopeful she doesn't stir and catch me poking around.

The last thing Rhodes needs is Ellie going into school and handing out condoms mistaken for candy or something.

I push the drawer closed and refuse to think of Rhodes and condoms in the same sentence ever again.

My phone vibrates on my lap, and I jump.

I'm not guilty of anything.

Oscar: You can sleep in there with her. I know how clumsy you are. I'd hate for you to hurt yourself carrying her to bed and end up at the hospital again without me there to hold your hand.

Me: Clumsy? I am not clumsy.

Rude.

But also, I am not going back to the hospital.

Rhodes asked them to use dissolvable stitches on my finger simply so I wouldn't have to go back and get them removed.

Which is probably the nicest thing anyone has ever done for me.

> Me: But thank you. If we stay here, I'll make sure to wash the sheets tomorrow before you come home.

I put my attention back on the TV. It's well after the game by now, so some late-night hockey recap show is on with three men wearing ties, talking stats. I perk up every time I hear the name Volkova. When they start talking about other teams in the league, I quickly shut the TV off. The last thing I want to see on the screen is the face of someone I wish to forget.

I lie in Rhodes's bed with one hand on Ellie and the other on my phone. My sleepy eyes flutter with an incoming text.

Oscar: Don't.

My brows furrow.

> Me: Don't what?

Oscar: Don't wash the sheets.

I roll my eyes. He is so adamant that I don't clean or do anything *extra*, but when Ellie is in school, what else am I supposed to do? Aside from painting and making silly little clay trinkets for Ellie, there isn't anything to fill my time. It's not like I can go back to how things were before and become a viral sensation with my painting timelapse videos. There may be a few still floating around on the web, but I'll make sure there aren't any new ones.

Not when anyone could access them.

Not when *he* could access them.

Plus, I don't think Rhodes understands that this is just *me*. I grew up helping my nana whenever I could—or anyone, for that matter. It's just who I am.

Another text comes through.

> Oscar: I wouldn't mind my sheets smelling like sunshine.

My heart skips a beat.

Did he mean to text that?

I glance around as if I'm going to find the answer in his room.

My attention flies to my phone with another text.

> Oscar: I never wanted to unsend a text before, but you're just full of firsts for me.

What other firsts is he referring to?

He's typing again, and now I'm skeptical that he's in his right state of mind.

> Oscar: Can you teach me to braid?

I trap a laugh behind a smile.

> Me: Have you been drinking?

> Oscar: No...yes.

> Oscar: How'd you know?

> Me: You're being nice and asking for my help with something you swear you can do on your own.

Oscar: I'm always nice to you.

Me: Compared to a couple weeks ago, sure.

I'm enjoying this side of him. Tipsy Rhodes is much more relaxed and less intimidating. I change his name in my phone to Rhodes because, at the moment, he isn't being a grouch.

Rhodes: You're the only person I feel okay sharing my weaknesses with.

I snort and quickly glance at Ellie, hoping she doesn't wake up.

Me: Weaknesses? You consider not being able to braid a weakness? 😐

Rhodes: When you're a single father to a little girl, yes.

I see his point.

Me: Try having a weakness like mine. I'm a near 26-year-old woman with all my friends getting married, and I'm practically afraid to even let a man touch me.

I guess he isn't the only one who feels comfortable showing some vulnerability at the moment.

Rhodes: Don't forget you're afraid of hospitals too.

I silently scoff. As if I needed the reminder.

Rhodes: I could help you.

Help me?

> Me: Help me with what? Are you going to try to desensitize me and make me sit in hospital waiting rooms without holding my hand?

I wait eagerly for his next text.

The typing bubbles pop up. Then they disappear. This happens a few times before a text comes in.

> Rhodes: I'm a man.

Just how much has he had to drink?

> Me: I'm aware.

> Rhodes: I can help you face your fear of men.

My heart beats a little faster. I glance at the drawer of condoms. Surely this man, so untrusting of women—nannies in particular—is not suggesting what I think he's suggesting.

> Me: And how would you do that?

It takes too long for him to text back. My hands sweat so much my phone eventually slips to my lap. Too many scenarios run through my head. He's my boss, the grumpy hockey player who scowls when a woman looks at him for too long, and the father of the little girl I nanny for.

Surely, he isn't insinuating that he and I...

I shake my head. Of course he isn't.

Is he?

Why does the thought not make me cower?

I scramble for the phone when it vibrates again.

Rhodes: This is Malaki. Rhodes has asked me to take his phone because he clearly cannot be trusted to text his hot nanny at the moment. Ignore all previous text messages from our drunken grump. Goodnight, Sunshine.

Hot nanny?

Are those Rhodes's words or Malaki's?

Why do I want them to be Rhodes's? Do I want him to think I'm attractive?

No, I most definitely don't.

I'm only thinking about these things because I haven't had sex in what feels like a million years.

That's my problem.

I'm desperate for affection, and I crave things that any twenty-five-year-old woman would...*like the hot, grumpy, single dad thinking she's attractive.*

My stomach drops.

I push my phone away and flop backward onto the bed as punishment.

Of course Rhodes's cologne would waft up from the pillow.

Thirty–Two

RHODES

MY HEAD POUNDS, and every noise sounds like a dying cat screeching.

I slept the entire flight home, cursing the team each time I'd stir. I can't believe I let them talk me into going out after the game, but they made their case, and at the time, it made sense.

Since Emory signed with us, we've all gotten closer. We're better than we've ever been, though still need to work out the kinks, but bonding is a big part of that, even if the thought made me itchy at the beginning of the night.

Two shots in and I no longer felt that way.

Four shots in and I had lost all sense of restraint.

Most of the single guys were on the dance floor with random women.

I was in the booth, texting Sunny in between watching those videos of her painting that she desperately wants taken down from the internet.

What the fuck was I thinking?

Emory snorted each time I'd pull my phone out.

Though, at one point, he was even watching the videos of her furiously working over a canvas with colorful paints. It was pretty damn mesmerizing.

Malaki eventually snatched it out of my hand with a cocky smirk on his face that I wanted to wipe off with my fist.

"Afraid of men?" Malaki asked after reading my screen.

I glanced away, refusing to spill her secrets.

"That's unnerving. Do we need to fuck someone up?"

I grunted. If I knew who it was, yes.

"There. Problem solved."

It took me far too long to read what he'd typed, but he assured me I'd thank him in the morning.

Which I did. *Silently.*

Things could have taken a turn for the worse, and I could have lost the best nanny I've ever had. Ellie would have been devastated, and I would have been granted the *worst dad ever* award.

I pull in front of the house and sit in my truck for a few seconds to mentally prepare myself to face Sunny. I'm man enough to apologize for my inappropriate texts, but I'll only do so if she acts awkward.

Maybe she'll just do what Malaki said and pretend I wasn't drunk-texting her and implying things that are completely inappropriate.

Shit.

My hand moves across my in-need-of-a-shave face.

Since when do I get all bent out of shape over a woman? Usually, I'd be nonchalant, and I wouldn't give a damn what was thought about me or how I made her feel.

I pause outside of the door with my bag slung over my shoulder.

I'm afraid to lose her.

Not in the way that most men would be, I'm sure. But as a

single father who is struggling to make up for Ellie not getting the attention she deserves and for her lack of a mother, I am.

I sigh and go inside. I'm immediately hit with Sunny's signature scent.

Coconut.

My mouth waters.

The floors are shiny, and I'm comforted that her shoes are tucked neatly underneath the entryway table.

At least I didn't scare her off.

I place my keys in the catch-all basket and drop my bag near her shoes.

The sound of feet shuffling on the floor catches my attention. I slowly head toward the noise and find her in the kitchen with her back facing me.

Tight leggings draw my attention to her curves.

A hot swallow works itself down to the pit of my stomach where my conscience lies.

She's bent over, paying close attention to whatever is on the counter, giving me even more room to trace her perfect round peach.

The messy bun on top of her head flops when she straightens and places one hand on her hip. She's wearing headphones and...an apron?

I grip the top of the arch in the wall, digging my fingers into the molding. I suddenly regret rejecting the handful of women who slid beside me last night in hopes of going back to the hotel with me.

"*Poz–*" Sunny mutters.

I narrow my gaze.

Sunny clears her throat and tries again. *"Pozhalusta."*

The word *please* in Russian flows from behind her lips, and all I can imagine is her beneath me, writhing and pleading with me to put her out of her misery—and *for fuck's sake.*

I abruptly drop my hands from the ledge and stalk into the kitchen.

She says a couple more words in Russian. She's obviously gotten a hold of more tapes from Ellie.

She is completely unaware that I'm behind her. Otherwise, she wouldn't be swinging her hips around like she is. As if they're a magnet, I follow them each time. My breathing is suddenly sharp and fast.

When I get close enough, I lift one side of her headphones to make my presence known. Her scream is ear-piercing. She quickly twists, losing her headphones in the process, and knocks whatever piece of clay she's painting off of the counter.

I may be hungover, but I was born with hockey reflexes.

The small sculpture lands in the palm of my hand.

I peer at her from below. "Ty uronila eto."

Sunny's wide gaze drops to my mouth as the foreign language flows with ease into the kitchen. A line of confusion appears in between her eyebrows as she tries to make sense of what I said.

I chuckle while standing upright, now towering over her. "I guess you need more practice with those tapes."

Being this close to her makes me do stupid things. I disregard the one thing I swore I wouldn't do and bring up last night. "I told you that you were clumsy."

Her gasp hits me in the chest. "I am *not* clumsy!" The pink of her cheeks matches the paint smeared on her apron. "You scared me. That was entirely your fault!"

"I told you that the house is secure, though." I place the little clay...*thing*...onto the counter beside her paints. I give her a once-over. She's adorably messy with paint smearing her apron and hands. Her face is clear of heavy makeup, only a pinkish hue to her cheeks and her brown look warmer than usual with some kind of shimmer on her eyelids.

"Yeah, well..." Sunny's gaze darts behind me before she fully turns back around. "You just never know."

"I do know. This house is perfectly safe, Sunny."

I step away, putting some distance between us, because for some insane reason, I have the urge to touch her just to drive my point further.

"Whatever you say, Oscar." Her voice grows lighter, and I'm thankful she isn't harping on last night.

"Oscar?" I scoff.

I head for the fridge, knowing there's something in here that will help me cure my hangover.

Drinking in your thirties isn't what it was in your twenties.

Ah, Pedialyte. Score.

I turn toward her and unscrew the cap. "I let you sleep in my bed, and I'm still being called Oscar?"

Sunny eyes the orange drink I'm gulping and rolls those pretty eyes. "What an amateur," she jokes.

The empty bottle slaps onto the counter. With the back of my hand, I wipe the excess off my mouth. "It's been a while since I've drank more than a single beer. I don't have much tolerance anymore."

A quick smile catches my attention, but her lips roll together before it can fully spread against her face. I know exactly what she's thinking. She's recalling what Malaki said to her in an attempt to save my ass from scaring her off.

That means it's time to nip this in the bud before anything can get twisted.

And by twisted, I mean twisted into the truth, because I was absolutely referring to me fucking her to help her get over her fear of men.

My dick did the talking last night.

He and I are at odds right now.

A soft giggle leaves her, and I snap to attention.

"Something funny?" I ask.

Her denial comes quickly. The bun on her head shakes. "Nope."

I cross the invisible line I've drawn in the kitchen and move closer to her. I can see her glance at me in her peripheral vision. "Are you thinking about my drunk-texting last night?"

"No. Of course not." Her hand pauses with the paintbrush on the...*what the hell is that thing?* "I'm glad you were out having some fun. You deserve it."

"Well, I want to clear something up."

She peeks at me. "If this is about me sleeping in your bed..."

I place my palm on the counter beside the piece of pottery, or clay, whatever it is. "It's not."

The paintbrush, covered in green paint, hovers in between us. "Okay."

I watch her closely. Her big brown eyes peer at me, and for once, I actually feel bad for lying. "I wasn't implying that we sleep together last night when I said I could help you with your...problem."

Sunny's shoulders straighten. Her jaw tightens, and the pink color on her cheeks deepens. "I didn't think that," she declares. "Of course you didn't mean that."

How couldn't I mean that? Look at her.

"Right," I agree with her. "I was referring to giving you time off for dates..." I skip my gaze elsewhere because anyone with a pulse could see right through me. "Or doing a background check on someone if you were to go on a date with them." Sunny nibbles on her lip, like she's trying to decide if I'm telling the truth or not. "You know, just to make you feel safer. Maybe take the edge of fear away."

I'll likely do a background check with or without her request.

Our gazes snag.

There's no way she's believing this.

I have a knot in my stomach, and I don't think it's from the hangover.

Am I nervous? Anxious? Perturbed at the thought of her going on a date?

"That's..." She clears her throat. "Kind of you."

I chuckle. "I don't think anyone has ever referred to me as such."

Her cheek lifts with a turn of her head, and it hits me right in the chest. She goes back to busying herself with her project and says, "You're kind underneath all those gruff layers. It just takes some digging to get there."

I'm only kind to her.

And Ellie, but that doesn't count. She's five, and she's my daughter.

I haven't known Sunny for long, yet it feels like I've known her for a lot longer.

"I'm sorry," I say abruptly. "But what the fuck is that?"

She snaps her attention to me. It only takes a second for a soft smile to spread across her pretty face. "It's Pascal."

I blink, and suddenly my head pounds again. "What?"

She rolls her eyes, and my breath catches. I take a deep breath, hopeful she mistakes it for annoyance rather than what her eye roll actually does to me.

I stare at the clay figure a little longer, noticing two large eyes and the most delicate markings on the entirety of it. Is that a—

Sunny's phone is suddenly in my face, and I can't help it. I laugh.

"The green lizard from Ellie's favorite movie?" I ask.

"Not a lizard," she corrects me. "A chameleon!"

God, why is she so perfect?

"Ellie is going to love that," I say. "What's the occasion? Her birthday isn't for another six months."

Fuck, isn't Sunny's birthday soon?

She beams with warmth. "I told you I like to make people happy. I figured it'd put a smile on her face." It will. "And I miss working with my hands." She thinks for a moment. "I miss painting too."

Good with her hands? I push off from the counter and put some space between us because my mind goes right to the gutter.

"You still need to teach me to braid." I throw the empty bottle of Pedialyte into the trash.

Her back is facing me again, and I can't help but let my gaze skip down to her tight leggings *again*. She bends and grabs the paintbrush, using it to color the lizard's—I mean, chameleon's—tongue.

"Tonight," she says, too focused to glance back at me.

"Tonight?" I repeat.

This time, she pins me with those big brown eyes. "I'm going to teach you to braid, so rest up and rid yourself of that hangover."

I grin. "Yes, ma'am."

She looks pleased with herself. Her coy smile forces me to turn and head upstairs to rid myself of a lot more than a fucking hangover.

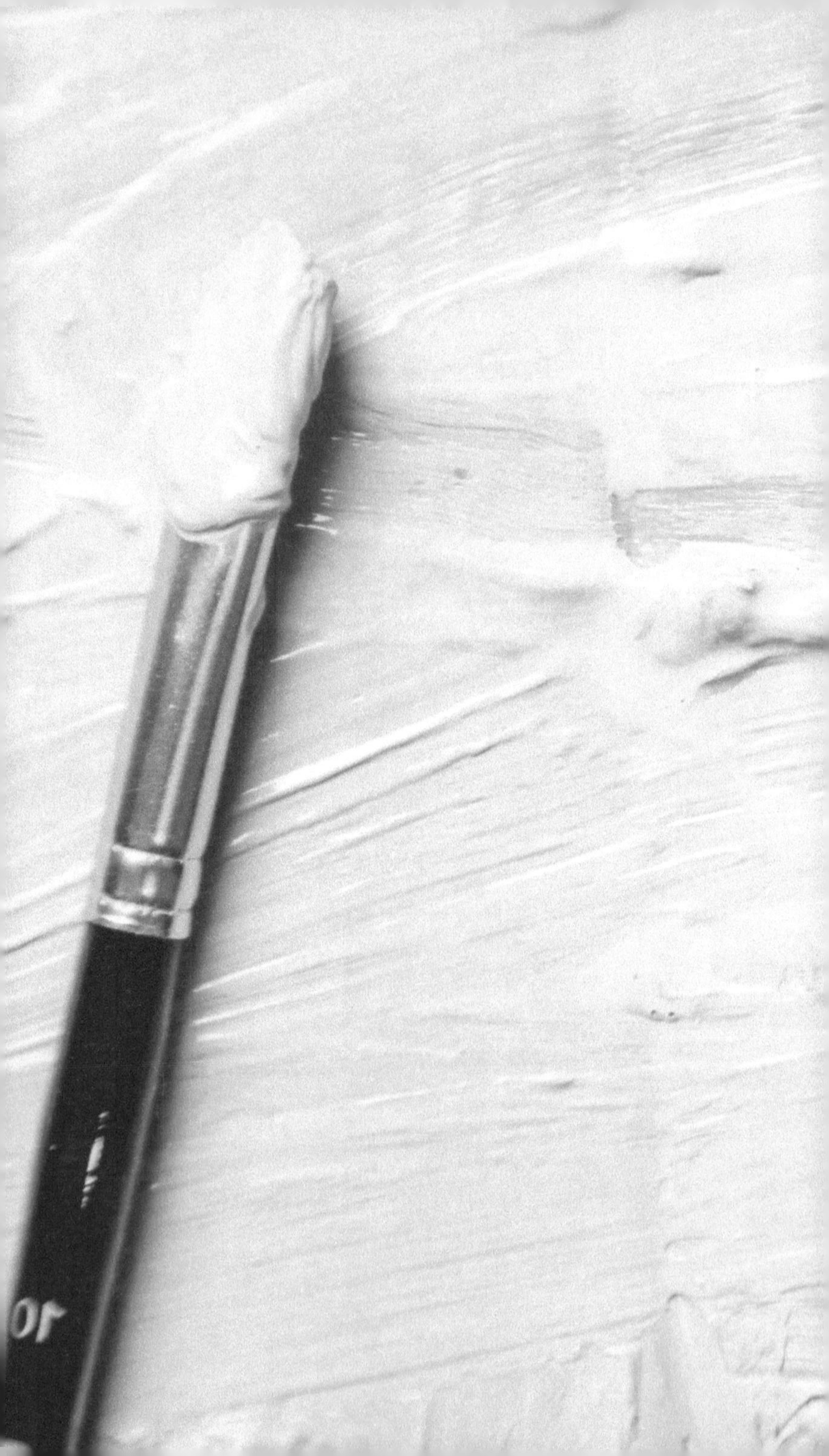

Thirty-Three

SUNNY

I WAIT PATIENTLY on the couch and run my fingers through the strands of my hair. It's still damp from my shower, but I figure working with damp hair will be easier for Rhodes.

Before he carried Ellie on his back to put her to bed, I made him sit beside me on the couch to watch me braid her hair. He sat quietly with his heavy brow folded, concentrating on the steps. Our elbows brushed, and surprisingly, I didn't jolt away.

Heat pooled in the quiet parts of my body, but the nerves that usually cause me to act like a spaz didn't rear their ugly little heads, which is both a comforting and worrying thought.

It's all because of those pesky thoughts I had last night with his drunk-texting. Once he explained himself, it left me feeling like one of his past nannies. I made up this entire scenario in my head that *he* was the one who wanted to rid me of my fear by erasing some other man's touch.

Talk about being absolutely delulu.

A thrill moves through me when I hear his heavy footsteps descending down the stairs.

He appears a moment later, and I quickly dart my attention to the TV, which just so happens to be showing a hockey game.

Gray sweatpants are hung low on his hips, paired with a black T-shirt and a backward hat. *Seriously?* He has every right to change into something more comfortable, but doesn't he know the rule about gray sweatpants?

They're simply not allowed unless you're trying to draw attention to a particular area.

I refuse to look.

"Okay, Ms. Edwards. Your student awaits." Rhodes plops down onto the couch beside me, causing me to fall into him.

He catches me by the arm before I land in his lap and props me upright again.

I attempt to clear my thoughts and reach for my sleepytime tea—something Rhodes already made fun of me for, calling me an old lady.

Which I took as a compliment.

My nana drinks sleepytime tea, and I wouldn't mind turning out like her.

"Okay," I sigh and place my tea back onto the coffee table. "Do you remember the steps?"

He thinks for a moment. "No."

I gasp. "What?"

He gives me a lopsided grin. "I'm kidding, Sunshine. Of course I remember the steps. If I can remember various hockey plays, I think I can remember a few steps for braiding."

I raise an eyebrow. "I've seen you attempt a braid. I wouldn't be so sure."

"I can do it."

His cockiness is highly attractive.

I hide a smile. "We will see."

Sliding onto the floor, I push the coffee table a few inches forward and make some room. I sit cross-legged in front of him. "Go on, hotshot." I peer over my shoulder at him.

His brow furrows for a quick second before he smooths his face and scoots closer. Each of his legs falls beside me, the soft fabric of his sweatpants brushing my arms.

My heart beats a little faster when he gathers my hair and pulls it behind my shoulders. The briefest thought of the last time someone touched my hair slips in, and I tense. My fingernails bite at the flesh of my thigh as I dig them into my skin to ground myself.

"Sunny."

I jerk. "Huh?"

"You're shaking. Are you that afraid I'll fuck up this braid and get tangled in the strands like I do with El?" Rhodes chuckles quietly, and I try to relax.

"No. Sorry, go ahead."

Rhodes leans forward, wafting his aftershave in my direction. He reaches for the brush and settles back on the couch again. My breathing slows with the sweeping motion. There aren't any tangles—something I'm sure he's grateful for.

"Are you going to tell me why you just got nervous?"

"I didn't get nervous." The four words fly from my mouth quickly, telling my lie right away.

I make a face and pout. I try again. "I wasn't nervous."

Rhodes continues to swipe at my hair with the brush, moving slower and slower. *Is he trying to calm me?* Because if so, it's working.

The third period of the hockey game starts, and I stare at the TV, watching the men work back and forth on the ice. I'm not sure if it's the sleepytime tea, the calming sensation of someone brushing my hair, or Rhodes's presence, but I find myself opening up to explain.

"I was afraid," I admit. "But only for a second."

"Afraid?" He separates my hair into three sections.

"The last time someone touched my hair..." I hesitate.

"You don't have to explain," he says.

I've never told anyone this. Not even the nurses when I went to the hospital.

"It might be good for me," I whisper.

Rhodes reaches around and tips my chin backward slightly. I scoot farther against the couch, getting closer to him as he begins to intertwine the strands of my hair.

"I didn't realize he'd pulled my hair until a few days later when some clumps fell out in the shower." Rhodes's fingers pause for a few seconds before he goes back to overlapping the strands. "I guess I blocked some of it out, but after I calmed down, I remembered waking up with his fingers woven throughout my hair."

"You woke up like that?"

I swallow. "That's how it started. I was asleep, and he took advantage of that. I freaked out, obviously, and—"

Rhodes tenses. His breathing turns erratic. I follow the hockey players back and forth on the TV, attempting to think of anything other than that night.

Rhodes mutters under his breath. "He hurt you."

I say nothing.

He did hurt me.

Both physically and emotionally.

"He did," I say. "He refused to believe that I wasn't in love with him, and he slowly became consumed with the idea of there being an *us*."

My hair slips from Rhodes's fingers, and it's parted in three sections again. "Remember," I say, "every other strand."

I hear his teeth rub together with frustration.

"So he was obsessed with you." He crisscrosses strands of my hair and scoots closer, likely trying to get more of a grip on them.

My pulse thrums. "I guess. I found a drawer full of photos of me beside his bed. A secret camera inside my bedroom…" I shrug, trying to play it off. "He hated that his son grew close to me, even though I was his nanny. He became jealous."

"Jesus," he mutters.

Silence fills the living room, except for the sound of the hockey game playing in front of us.

I relax farther onto the couch, unknowingly getting closer to him. My eyes start to droop the longer he works with my hair. The braid is loose, with strands of hair falling into my face, framing it, but progress is progress.

"There," he says, sounding pleased with himself.

I lean forward and touch the back of my head. I faintly run my fingers over the braid, proud that it isn't *as* messy as I've seen him do to Ellie's.

Peering backward, I smile at him. "Not bad, Volkova."

He leans backward onto the couch with his lip lifted on one side and puts his hands behind his head. It screams cocky, and the only thing I can think is that the way he's sitting looks like an open invitation.

Which it absolutely is *not*.

However, his muscular thighs are spread open, and his lap is there for the taking. The smirk on his face makes me do a double take.

Jeez.

He's too hot for his own good.

"You're a good teacher," he says, nodding to the couch cushion beside him.

I gingerly step to the right and sit down. There are seven minutes left in the game, and it's tied.

A minute passes, and suddenly, a blanket appears in front of my face. Rhodes isn't even looking at me as he hands it out for me to take.

"Thank you," I whisper.

He says nothing, but the silence between us is anything but awkward.

I'm relaxed in his presence, which is sort of a big deal, even if he is unaware.

My eyes grow heavy, and I lean my head onto the couch pillow beside me with my fresh braid falling over my shoulder.

The buzzer sounds, and I'm brought back to reality.

Did I doze off?

I glance at Rhodes, and he's watching the TV intently. My gaze falls to my curled legs beneath the blanket. His arm is resting on top of them.

Butterflies fill my stomach, which is ridiculous.

He must not realize he's touching me.

I remain unmoving and place my attention on the TV so he doesn't realize I'm gawking at him.

Two sports reporters are taking turns going back and forth about the game and the upcoming schedule.

My pulse quickens when they say Washington.

The hawk logo appears, and my blood pressure rises.

I zero in on the TV, knowing I should look away, but it's like a car crash. I shouldn't look, knowing the feeling it'll give me if I see his face, yet I can't move.

A knot forms in my throat. I drive my focus to Rhodes's arm resting on my legs.

He makes me feel safe, and I'm not sure if that's delusional or not, but out of desperation, I grab a hold of that feeling to keep me grounded.

Before there's any more talk of Washington, the TV shuts off.

I turn to Rhodes, and he's staring intently at me. Those vivid green eyes move over my face, like he's trying to read me.

Good luck.

It's a mess in here.

"I need you to know that I would never betray your trust like he did."

My heart moves. "I know."

His eyebrow rises. "You do?"

I slowly nod.

With a furrowed brow, he asks, "How?"

"I've learned to trust my gut," I admit. "And my gut tells me that you're safe."

He visibly relaxes. His shoulders loosen, and his chest deflates. "Good," he rasps.

He removes his arm from my legs to sit upright.

I do the same. The blanket falls from my legs, and I move to stand.

We both head toward the stairs, turning off lights as we go.

Before I start up the stairs, Rhodes's hand grips mine gently. I turn, and he's peering down at me. The moonlight from the window shines on the side of his face, encasing the firm look in his eye. "I would love nothing more than for Ellie to grow closer with you."

I blink through the surprise of sincerity in his voice. It's the simplest statement, yet it carries such a punch.

"She needs someone like you," he adds. "She needs more than just *me.*"

How can he think that?

Placing my palm on top of his hand, I shake my head. "You're wrong, Rhodes."

Shadows dig into the confused lines carved into his face.

"She doesn't need more than just you." I smile softly. "Give yourself some more credit, Oscar."

I wink at him and drop my hand.

There's a twitch of his lips that I think about the entire way to my room.

For the first time since moving into his house, I go to sleep with my door cracked instead of closed.

Which is *huge.*

Thirty-Four

RHODES

IF ANOTHER BALLOON smacks me in the head...

Ellie's giggles are out of control, and I'm silently cursing her for talking me into this many balloons.

We're hopeful to get home before Sunny does. I gave her the day off since I don't have a game tonight, but what she doesn't know is that she'll still be busy. Thanks to Scottie and the other wives, Sunny has birthday plans.

In a painfully desperate attempt to tag along, I came up with my own plan. My little white lie from the other night has been on a loop inside my head, and this seemed like the perfect opportunity to make it ring true.

"I wasn't implying that we sleep together last night when I said I could help you with your... problem. I was referring to giving you time off for dates."

What a load of bullshit.

However, going out for her birthday is the perfect opportunity for her to meet some guy, which will hopefully deter me and my inappropriate thoughts, and I can keep an eye on her to make sure no one pushes the limits without her approval.

It's crossing a line, but barely, and aren't lines drawn to be crossed?

According to Malaki, they are, and for once, I'm choosing to believe his thought process.

Another balloon sneaks up to the front of the truck. I smack it away and glance into the rearview mirror.

"This is excessive," I mutter.

All I can see is Ellie's toothy smile and rosy cheeks.

I park the truck outside of the house and round the side to open Ellie's door. A balloon slips out, but I catch the rest before they disappear into the sky. "Daddy! Be careful!"

I huff. "Aren't I the one supposed to be telling you to be careful?"

She hops down with the bouquet of sunflowers in her hand. I *may* have grabbed them from the store before picking her up at school, but if Sunny asks, Ellie was the one to pick them out.

In fact, this entire thing was Ellie's idea, if anyone asks.

Marco pulls up with Sunny, and we hurry through the door. I slam it shut, and Ellie squeals, like she's being caught doing something she shouldn't. A few petals and leaves fall from the bouquet, leaving a trail behind her as she runs into the kitchen.

I laugh and follow.

She's bright-faced and as excited as she is on Christmas morning.

It's fucking adorable.

"You ready, Printsessa?" I ask, getting down on her level.

She nods with a smile. I hand her the bundle of balloons and stand to lean against the cabinets.

I haven't done anything like this for someone's birthday, other than Ellie.

I don't know what that means, but it means something.

Sunny's sweet, familiar laugh faintly flows into the kitchen. She's talking to Marco about something regarding her nana, but the words disappear when she appears in the entryway. Her jaw drops slightly, and I can't help but stare at her parted lips.

So goddamn beautiful.

Her hair is pulled up into a messy bun with rich brown strands framing her glowing face, likely falling throughout the day. She has something chalky on the apple of her cheek, probably clay or something from the art studio downtown that she'd gone to for 'open studio.'

"Happy birthday!" Ellie shouts, pulling my attention away from lusting over Sunny *again*.

Lusting. Observing. Same difference.

Sunny lowers to the ground to get on Ellie's level, and my daughter takes off, bouncing into her arms. The balloons fly high, but I jump into action and grab them before they rush to the ceiling of my kitchen.

Sunny peers at me, still mid-hug with Ellie. Her smile is knowing, like she assumes that this was my idea instead of Ellie's.

I will absolutely deny it, though.

"Sunflowers?" Sunny sits back on the heels of her feet.

Before Ellie can throw me under the bus, I clear my throat. "Ellie's idea."

My daughter turns to look at me as Sunny grabs the bouquet and puts her face to the flowers. I send her a stern look, *Don't you dare.*

If I could trust that Sunny wasn't getting better at her Russian, I could talk in code, but I can no longer trust that.

Ellie shrugs and goes along with taking the credit for the flowers.

"Sunflowers for Sunny! Get it?" Ellie wiggles her eyebrows, and it takes everything in me not to laugh.

Sunny smiles. "These are my favorite flowers. My grandpa used to grow *huge* sunflowers in his garden for me."

Ellie's eyes turn into saucers. "How huge?"

She follows Sunny farther into the kitchen and watches as she rummages around for something. "Taller than you."

"Taller than my dad?"

Sunny glances at me and then shakes her head. "No way. Your dad is huge."

My ego just got huge too.

Marco pipes up from the opening in the kitchen. "You're not going to find a vase, Ms. Edwards."

Sunny spins with her hands on her hips. She pouts for a second and then shrugs. "We will improvise, then."

We all watch in silence as she walks over to the trash, opens up the recycling and pulls out the can of SpaghettiOs that Ellie had for dinner the night before.

Ellie turns to Marco as Sunny is trimming the sunflower stems. "Can I have SpaghettiOs tonight?"

"Only if I can have some too." He smiles.

"Tonight?" Sunny blows a strand of hair out of her face, glancing up at Marco. "Are you staying for dinner?"

He looks at me.

And suddenly, she's looking at me too.

"Well..." I start.

"You're going out to celebrate your birthday!"

I've never been more thankful for Ellie's interruption.

There.

The burden is off my shoulders.

"Whoa, wait." Sunny steps away from the flowers. "With who?"

Never mind.

My hands disappear into the pockets of my jeans. "Me."

Sunny whips her attention over to me so quickly I lose my footing.

"And others," I add. "It wasn't my idea."

It technically wasn't my idea, though I did invite myself, and I convinced Emory to come too.

"The wives of some of my teammates, the ones you sit with in the box, asked me if they could take you out for your birthday."

Sunny's shoulders fall, and a half-crescent smile appears. "That's sweet of them. Totally unnecessary, though. I'd be fine just hanging out here and having SpaghettiOs."

Marco gestures for Ellie to follow him out onto the back porch. They busy themselves with the birdfeeder he gifted her.

I take it as an opportunity to speak without Ellie interjecting.

"You're in your twenties," I state.

Sunny turns her nose in the air. "Twenty-six, thank you very much."

My mouth twitches.

I walk closer to her, crossing the invisible line I drew yet again. I place my palm onto the counter near the cut stems from the sunflowers. "Twenty-six-year-olds don't sit at home on their birthday with a five-year-old."

She rolls her eyes. "Some of them do."

"But not you, unless you're nannying."

Her faint growl makes me want to smile in the worst way.

"Most twenty-six-year-olds get lucky on their birthday, actually."

Her breath hitches.

I see the wheels turning in her head as she tries to spew some comeback. But she comes up empty-handed, and I take full advantage.

"I think you're afraid," I state.

She quickly looks away. "You already know I am."

"This could be a step in the right direction." *Not to mention, it'll remind me that you're not mine.*

I can see why she'd be hesitant. "It's just a club. It's not like you *have* to get lucky, Sunshine. You could just put some feelers out there."

Something passes behind her gaze. I watch her closely while she debates. She shrugs a second later. "Ruby tried to get me to go out shortly after...everything...but I refused."

"Ruby? Your best friend?" I ask.

She fiddles with the flowers and nods.

"Well, if Ruby thinks it's a good idea, and I think it's a good idea..."

She snorts. "Then it's probably a terrible idea."

I chuckle and elbow her lightly. "Come on." *When did I get so...lively?*

Her big brown eyes, full of unease, peer at me.

"I'll be there the whole time. I told you I would help you."

She squints. "What if I don't want your help?"

I smirk. "You do."

Her mouth twitches with a hidden smile, and I take that as a yes.

I stride toward the back door and call over my shoulder, "Be ready by eight."

Fuck me.

Whose idea was this?

Why did I think taking her out for her birthday to watch her mingle, talk, dance, or do *worse* with random guys was going to prevent me from wanting her?

My stomach falls to my balls as soon as she starts down the stairs.

She is sexy as hell.

I try to engage in a conversation with Marco about my next game in an effort to get my shit together.

"Daddy! Look at Sunny."

I'd rather not.

Ellie tugs on my hand, and I'm forced to follow her command.

My glimpse is brief, but I'll likely remember every detail, down to the sheen on her lips, for days to come.

Thigh-high boots, a black long-sleeve dress that hugs every delectable curve, and for once, her hair is down. Thankfully, the dark waves lay over her shoulders, shielding some of her breasts.

She stops in front of us. "Is this okay?"

Is it okay? Is it fucking okay?

I want to tell her no. My hands ache to grab her waist, spin her around, and make her take those sexy boots off, but I can't.

Why can't I do that? Because I'm her fucking boss. That's why.

I shove my hands inside my pockets, and she gives me a once-over. I'm wearing a gray long-sleeve Henley and casual black jeans.

"Ugh," she whisper-seethes. "I'm going to change."

The fuck she is. Despite the fire of protection rushing my veins, she looks *damn* good.

"Absolutely not." I slip my hand around her waist and give her a good spin until she's facing me.

"You look..." *Fuck, what do I say?*

Marco comes to my rescue and finishes my thought. "Like a twenty-six-year-old who is going out to celebrate her birthday with friends." He glances at me with a knowing glint. "Where are you two going? The Vault?"

I nod.

"Ah." He glances back at Sunny. "Very high-end."

I'm certain Marco has never been there, but he isn't wrong.

"Are you sure?" Sunny asks, still unsure of herself.

I answer with a flick of my brow.

She furrows hers, and I notice that she has on more makeup than I've ever seen her wear before.

It isn't a lot, or too much, but it does make her look older.

Which isn't going to help my thoughts at all.

"Night, Printsessa." I dip and place a kiss on Ellie's head.

She hugs both of us, telling Sunny happy birthday once more before taking off for the couch to watch a movie with Marco.

Before I make it out the door, following after Sunny, Marco and I share a look.

His weathered face shows too much.

He shakes his head and chuckles quietly.

The word *behave* is the last thing I hear before shutting the door behind me.

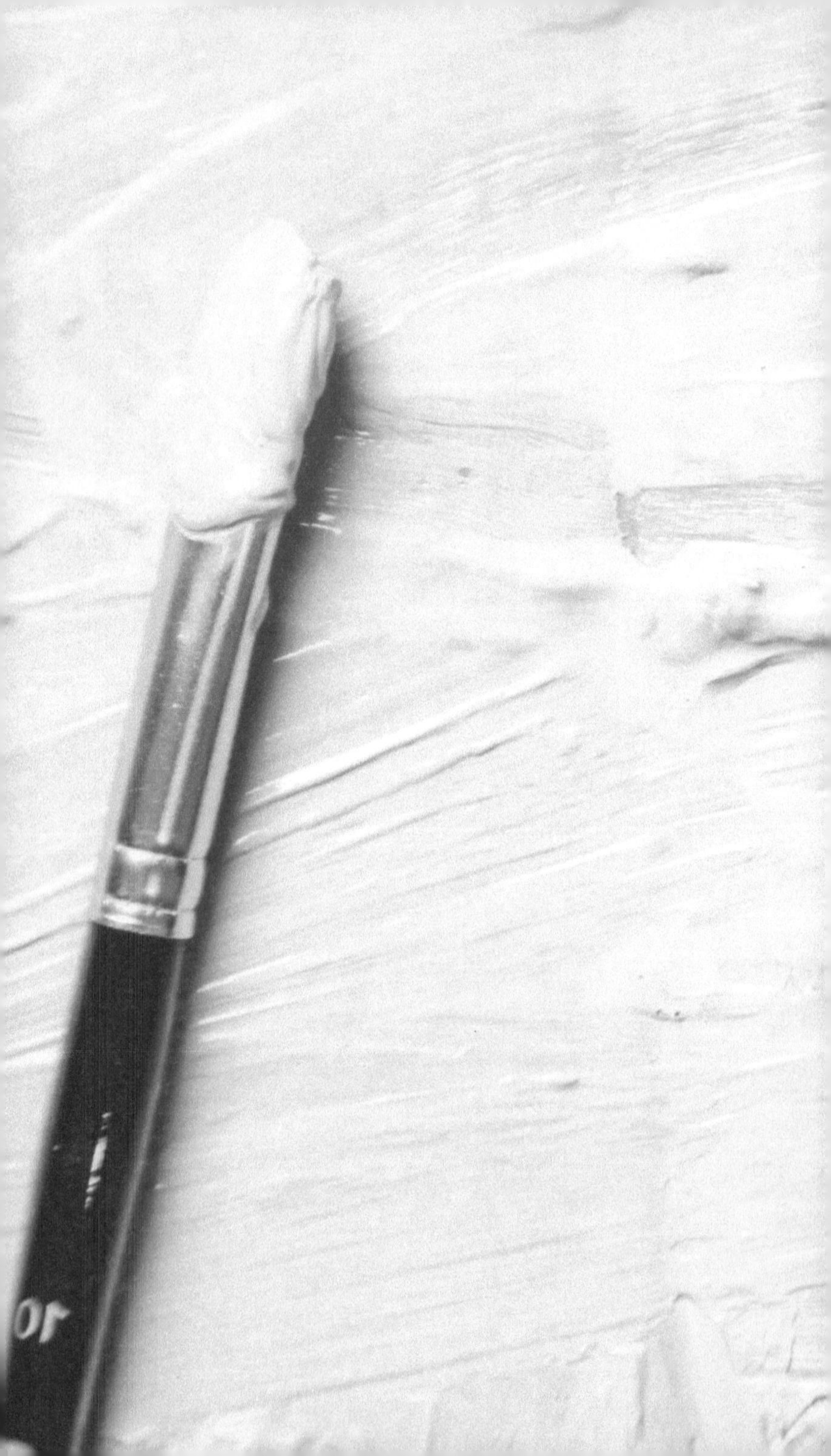

Thirty-Five

SUNNY

RHODES and I are very much out of our element.

We stroll into the club after skipping the line—something I can honestly say I have never done before—and stand awkwardly.

"This way." Rhodes's hand briefly falls to the small of my back. He walks beside me, never letting me trail, until we get to a big booth tucked in the back of the hazy club.

It's dark on the dance floor besides a few strobe lights alluding to all the racy dancing happening. The booth is tucked far enough away that it's not too difficult to hear over the thumping music.

I find Scottie first.

Her eyes light up, and she scrambles out of the booth to envelop me in a hug. "You made it! Happy birthday!"

Rhodes slides next to Emory, who's sitting beside a few guys that I vaguely recognize. I assume they're the husbands or significant others of the other girls I've spent time with watching the Blue Devils.

"We're getting drinks!" Georgia shouts to the guys. She's the loudest one during the games, always buzzing with excitement.

"What do you like?" Scottie loops her arm within mine.

"Um…" I glance backward, a little unsure of myself. Rhodes is in a conversation with his teammates, not even paying attention.

He seems so cool and collected all the time.

It's infuriating.

"I don't know," I finally say. "I guess I'll just do a whiskey sour."

It was my grandpa's favorite.

"One whiskey sour, two cosmos, and I'll have a Shirley Temple."

Scottie's smile comes back into view. "I'm not pregnant," she clarifies. "I just don't drink much."

I nod. "I don't drink much either."

Hattie, one of the wives, puts her arm around me. "But you're making an exception tonight because it's your birthday. Plus, we're officially welcoming you to our pack."

I glance at the three of them. "Thank you for doing this. My birthday isn't a big deal, but I'm happy to celebrate being welcomed into the pack."

Scottie grabs my drink from the bartender. "Your birthday *is* a big deal." She hands it off to me. "Now drink up. We're heading to the dance floor after this."

We cheers our drinks and go back to the booth where Malaki, Kane, and two other younger guys are standing around.

Malaki locks eyes with me and gets the goofiest look on his face. My cheeks turn fifteen shades of red when he starts belting the words to "Happy Birthday."

"*Oh god.*" I dive into the booth to hide from the attention.

Rhodes laughs under his breath, and I elbow him in the ribs.

"It's cute that you think that hurt," he mutters, putting his arm on the back of the booth.

I grumble and take a sip of my drink.

Malaki slides next to me. I'm in a sandwich between the two of them, and it feels like I've known them forever.

Emory, one of the best goalies in the league, according to the reporters the other night, buries his head into Scottie's neck. Even under the dim light, I see the lovey look on her face.

Two drinks down, casual conversation amongst the table, a song change, and the next thing I know, I'm being tugged out of the leather booth on less stable legs than I arrived with.

"Oh no." I shake my head. "I don't dance."

Rhodes scoffs. "Yes you do. I've seen you."

I glare at him. Whose side is he on?

"What? When?"

"With Ellie." There's a challenge in his eyes. Like he's daring me to argue.

He's right. Ellie and I dance all the time.

"Come on, birthday girl," Malaki pleads.

The rest of the girls, even Scottie, dash to the floor.

Rhodes casually moves closer to me and lowers his voice. *"Boc, boc."*

A laugh erupts from my mouth. "Did you just 'boc' at me?"

His lip lifts, and I can't help but notice how my body becomes fully charged at the sight.

The lights play with the sharp curve of his jaw, as if he needed any more help looking hot.

"You're acting like a chicken. So yes, I did just *boc* at you." He straightens his back and rests along the leather.

I sigh.

The booth has mostly cleared out. Malaki is ordering a drink at the bar, and Kane is in a conversation with some blonde paying us no mind.

I raise my chin. "Maybe I should 'boc' back at you, then."

Rhodes peers at me over the rim of his cup. His fingers tighten against the glass. "You saying I'm afraid to dance with someone?"

"I sure am."

The alcohol in my system, even if it isn't much, gives me just enough confidence to throw some jabs back at him.

He's right, though. I'm afraid.

I'm nervous I'll panic and start shaking right there on the dance floor for all to see. I'm too untrusting now. All it'll take is one wrong touch, and I'll spiral.

Rhodes's glass cup clinks on the table. He tips his chin and locks eyes with me. We're at an impasse. My heart skips a beat when he nudges me and climbs out of the booth.

I suck in a sharp breath when he leans into my space. "You should know that I love to prove people wrong, Sunshine."

Every time he calls me that, I grow warm.

He briskly slides past and goes in the direction of the dance floor.

My knees buckle from the way he grabs a random woman around the waist and presses her against his body.

Okay, now I'm *hot.*

I know a challenge when I see one.

Malaki eyes me from the bar. He wiggles his eyebrows at me, and I place my empty drink onto the table.

Georgia spots me heading their way, and the excitement is palpable. Scottie, Hattie, and Georgia quickly surround me, and our laughter fills the air. It reminds me of when Ruby and I used to go out on our nights off. I didn't realize how much I missed letting go until now.

Malaki places another whiskey sour in my hand before heading over to the guys.

They're keeping an eye on us.

Not just the Blue Devils, but others too.

Rhodes, with the woman still pressed against him, keeps his gaze directly pinned to me.

It's comforting and unnerving at the same time.

Not wanting to cross too much of a boundary—because he is still my boss, after all—I don't dance provocatively like every other woman.

Scottie ends up moving over to Emory, and they're slow dancing together, even though the song is thumping with bass.

They're sickeningly cute.

I turn with the feel of someone grabbing my waist.

Disappointment lands abruptly on my shoulders when I realize it isn't Rhodes.

Wait, what?!

"Hi." Two dark-blue eyes stare into mine. A beat of silence passes before he smiles and shakes his head. "Sorry, that sounded lame. I just couldn't not come say something to the sexiest woman in this club."

A sarcastic noise falls from my mouth. "Yeah right," I argue.

I look around, briefly catching the eye of Rhodes. *Stop looking at me like that!*

His eyes flare with...excitement?

Encouragement?

I can't tell.

"Sounds like you need to be reminded what just existing does to a man."

I put my attention back on the blue-eyed guy.

He's close to my age, and he's cute enough.

"Do you want to dance?"

"Dance?" I slowly swallow.

I'm fine.

I can do this.

"Sure."

He wraps his arm around my waist, and I place my hand on his shoulder. The song switches, and it's fast-paced. He tips the neck of his beer to my cup, and then we both take a drink. The more I drink, the easier it gets.

I know my limits, of course, but by the end of the song, my cup is empty, and I'm starting to feel flushed.

"Ready to be reminded?" My dance partner licks his bottom lip, and suddenly, the club is spinning, and I'm facing the other direction.

I snag onto Rhodes.

He locks eyes with me, and I exhale.

He's sitting at the table, alone, with his hand on a full cup of beer.

He squints at me.

I'm fine, I answer silently with a quick shake of my head.

He raises his glass and winks, like he's happy for me. Or proud? Both?

It's definitely the alcohol in my system that's causing me to feel satisfied at the thought of pleasing him.

My attention is pulled away quickly when the hand on my hip flings me backward onto...what is his name?

"Wait, what is your name?" I tip my head against his chest.

His breath is warm and smells of beer. "Simon. You?"

"Millie."

I hear a grunt of laughter from beside me. It's Malaki. We make eye contact, and he smashes his lips, looking elsewhere.

Millie?

Nerves work their way into my stomach. It was a defense mechanism. Simon doesn't need to know my real name just in case he ever decides to look me up after this.

"Here's your reminder of what you do to a man, Millie."

Confusion settles against my face when he pulls me toward him again. I'm flush against his front. My pulse skyrockets with his hands guiding me to move against him. The ridge of his hard length grates against the curve of my butt, and considering I haven't been with a guy in quite a while, it awakens something. Heaving breaths leave him, coating the side of my neck.

"Want to go get a drink?" His voice is ragged.

"Yeah." I'm out of breath. "A drink would be good."

I let him lead me to the end of the bar toward the bathroom.

Rhodes's earlier point drives in further with the heat in my belly and tinge of alcohol in my blood. *Most twenty-six-year-olds get lucky on their birthday.*

"What are you drinking?" Simon asks.

I stare at him.

He stares at me.

Then he drops his gaze to my mouth.

Anticipation crawls down my spine, but if I don't try to push past it, then I'm afraid I never will.

Simon grabs my hand, and I let him pull me toward the bathrooms.

The hue of the club starts to dissipate, and my confidence wavers.

You're fine.

I think about all the drunken makeout sessions in college bar bathrooms that I've had and the times when things went further.

But that was all before...

Simon waits until the passerby, a girl with glassy eyes, disappears into the bathroom before advancing. Suddenly, I'm pressed against the wall with his jean-clad leg in between mine.

He grabs my face, and my pulse flies.

"You're fucking sexy, Millie."

Millie?

Oh yeah, that's me.

His mouth hovers over mine, and I think I'm finally ready to break the streak, but then he grabs my wrists. He pins them both above my head, and I freeze.

I do nothing while he kisses me.

It's like I'm paralyzed.

I tug on his grip, but he's either too drunk to feel it or doesn't care.

My lungs constrict, and I start to shake.

I don't like my hands pinned.

It makes me feel trapped.

"You're coming home with me," he mumbles before sweeping his tongue into my mouth.

"No," I mutter. "Can we sto...stop?"

I need to take a breath.

He grips my chin harder when I try to move. "You are hot as f—"

I bend at the knees when he suddenly disappears.

A tight gasp flees from my mouth.

Why am I like this? God.

With the back of my hand, I press on my swollen lips and slowly stand up straight.

Rhodes towers over Simon with a look on his face that I can only describe as deadly. "She said stop."

Thirty-Six

RHODES

I'M TURNED on and jealous at the same time, which is not a good mix.

As soon as Sunny disappeared from my sight, I stood and followed. Not to be a creep or a pervert. This time, it was purely out of protection.

I told her I'd watch out for her the entire night, and there was no way I was going to go back on my word, even if it was absolutely torturous to watch her dance with some guy.

The torture got worse when I saw them in the dark hallway. Agitation crawled up my spine as I stood and watched some man stick his tongue down my daughter's nanny's throat. I was drowning in envy. So much that I almost grabbed the woman who walked past and started to make out with her, just to ease the jealousy.

But then I heard the faintest *no,* and I became fully enraged.

I want to kill him.

Good for him that I know how to control my impulses. If

I can stand and watch Sunny get tongue-fucked by some guy and do nothing, surely I can stand and verbally threaten the culprit instead of knocking his teeth out.

"Who are you? Her boyfriend?" The idiot glances at Sunny, but she isn't paying us any attention. Her hands are on her knees, and she's bent over at the waist.

She needs me.

"I'm going to give you the benefit of the doubt that you were so blinded by your tongue down her throat that you didn't hear her say stop." I swallow roughly. My voice is more of a growl. "Now go before I change my mind about letting you go scot-free." *With my Sunshine's taste on your tongue.*

The guy scrambles away, muttering something under his breath that has no place in my head. I stride toward Sunny and stand in front of her. Her breaths are choppy, like the sea during a storm, and I don't know what to do. I'm not naturally an empathetic person. I've been told most of my life that I'm emotionally unavailable, cold, and heartless. It's been said that I don't console, coddle, or even attempt to comfort people.

It's not necessarily true.

I just hide my feelings well.

As for consoling, I reserve it for Ellie.

And apparently, Sunny.

"Sunshine," I sigh and crouch down. I peer at her through the thick curtain of hair that envelops the entirety of her face.

"I'm fine," she whispers.

Her breath smells of whiskey, and my mouth waters to get a taste.

"Just focus on your breathing," I remind her. "In and out."

She nods once and slowly straightens to stand. I follow the action and tower over her. The apples of her cheeks are red, and those big brown eyes refuse to look at me.

Gently, I reach forward and place my hands onto her warm face. "Breathe," I demand.

I inhale, wait for her to do the same, and then we both exhale at the same time.

We do this several times before she finally gets the nerve to look me in the eye.

I get lost.

There are so many things trapped behind those innocent eyes that I want to know.

"I'm going to be a born-again virgin for the rest of my life."

I chuckle dryly. "A born-again virgin?"

Sunny's brows fold in on themselves, and she pouts.

It's fucking cute.

"All because that *boy* couldn't seal the deal?" I scoff and drop my hands from her face since she's seemingly breathing better. "Try again, Sunshine. He doesn't count."

"It's not him," she hisses, crossing her arms. "It's me!"

No, it's that jackass who broke your trust in men.

I shake my head. Someone exits the bathroom, and I wait until they're gone before leaning my arm on the wall above Sunny. I grip her chin and make her look at me. Her lips are slightly swollen, and I'm not sure if it's because of the aggressive mauling that her dance partner gave her, or if it's because she constantly nibbles on that bottom lip. "You don't like your hands trapped."

It was an obvious tell.

"If it were me, I would have pressed against the wall myself and let you lead. There wouldn't have been any restraint to your hands because I would have wanted them to explore."

Fuck, what am I saying?

Sunny's shaky inhale catches my ear, and I hate that it makes me excited. Her eyes travel down to my mouth, and my dick twitches. I apparently used up all of my self-control for the night, because I can't stop spilling my dirty little secrets.

"Then what?" she whispers, breaking the last of my restraint.

God damn, I am skating the line.

The hand on her chin loosens since I have her full attention. I drop it and wrap it around her waist, landing on the small of her back. I keep the pressure light, not wanting to set off alarm bells.

"The kiss would start off slow. Tedious." My stomach burns. I should not be saying this.

I can blame it on the need to prove a point to her—that she's not allowing herself to pick the right men to break her past experiences—but it's a lie.

Sunny nods slowly, fully engaged.

"I'd wait for you to sweep your tongue in my mouth before I reciprocated."

As if on cue, that devilish tongue slips out of her mouth and wets her bottom lip.

I swallow thickly. "Then I'd pull you in like this." I spin and press against the wall quickly, bringing her flush against the front of me. Her two legs straddle one of mine, and a sweat breaks out against my neck.

I should take my own advice.

It's not my birthday, but god damn, I need to fuck someone so I stop thinking about fucking her.

Her hot swallow catches my ear.

Is she turned on by this?

My fingers wrap around the slender part of her waist, and I bring our faces closer. *Shit, I need to stop.*

"Then I'd kiss the hell out of you and let your body do the talking." I flex my jaw, my teeth clicking on one another. "That's what you need, Sunshine. A man who knows what a woman wants."

My body is on fire.

She's so sexy it hurts.

She has this needy look in her eye that I'll never be able to forget.

"Sorry to interrupt," Malaki's voice hits the side of my face, and I quickly let Sunny go.

Fuck.

"But there's a cake out here with the name Sunny on it."

Sunny stumbles backward on those thigh-high boots and swings her attention to my teammate.

We're caught.

Or should I say, *I'm* caught.

Without saying anything, she hurries toward Malaki. He puts his arm around her shoulders and leads her out of the darkened hallway and into the club. One glance over his shoulder with his stupid, knowing smirk, and I'm baring my teeth at him.

He laughs silently, and I follow after them with my dick tucked into the top of my boxers.

What the fuck was I thinking?

———

The scent of birthday cake follows Sunny and me to the front door of the house. I'm holding it in one hand, and with the other, I open the door and nod for her to go through.

It's after midnight. The street is quiet, and the house is even quieter.

Marco pops up from the couch as soon as Sunny and I enter the living room. "12:32," he states. "When I was your age, I closed down the clubs."

I snort, and Sunny places her hands on her hips.

I drag my gaze away quickly, because even looking at her does something dangerous to me.

She and Marco are in a heated yet teasing conversation. He follows her to the kitchen where she cuts a piece of birthday cake, chocolate with pink frosting, and places it on a paper plate before putting Saran wrap over it.

"There you go." She smiles sweetly, and it's a nice sight to see.

I'd rather her smile than have that look of lust in her eyes that I can't stop thinking about.

Our gazes snag and stay for a second too long.

My dick twitches.

With my restraint tighter than ever, I walk Marco over to the door and thank him for watching Ellie. I stay near the door well after he drives off and let the cool night air coat my heated face.

Once I get my shit together and mentally prepare to say goodnight to Sunny, I realize she's already gone off to bed.

The downstairs is empty, except for my semi-hard dick and the scent of guilt lingering in the air.

Thirty-Seven

SUNNY

I'M up to three hundred sheep.

Ellie's painting on the wall is starting to move, and it's because every time I toss to my side, I stare at it, just hoping my eyes will droop, and I'll eventually close them without picturing Rhodes's deep, near-suffocating hot gaze that is forever stuck in my head.

I fling onto my back.

What a whirlwind of a night.

It started as an innocent birthday celebration and then turned into some therapy-like experiment that ended with my stomach in knots and my head tangled with fantasies that will never be real.

The way Rhodes grabbed me with possession yet still tender and merciful to the panic I was enduring is stuck in my head. It's playing tricks on my body.

My fingers twitch to move between my legs. I slowly drag my hand over my curves and rest it along the waistband of my sleep shorts.

I can't.

I can't touch myself and picture Ellie's father.

It goes against everything I've stood against since leaving Washington.

But Rhodes is different.

It says a lot about him that he isn't knocking on my door or showing up in my bed in the middle of the night. He didn't even intervene at the club until he could tell I was in distress.

I wonder how long he watched.

My teeth sink into my lip.

Why does it turn me on even more to think about him watching me?

You'd think I would be turned off by that, considering I've been watched in the past. But it's a totally different situation, and it's *Rhodes*. I feel safe with him...and maybe I feel something else too.

"Ugh." I fling the covers off my legs and swing them around until my feet hit the cool floor.

Water. I need a cold glass of water.

Hopefully, it'll wash away thoughts I'm having about my boss.

If it doesn't, I'm just going to pour the water on my head and hope for the best.

On quiet feet, I tiptoe down the stairs and make my way to the kitchen. The house is quiet and calm.

And safe.

Ice clinks against my cup. I pour the water over the cubes and take a few sips. Every time Rhodes slips into my thoughts, I gulp another mouthful down.

I sigh.

This isn't working.

I teeter back and forth on achy legs, refusing to acknowledge where the ache is actually coming from, and grab an ice cube from the glass.

A cool burn bites at my skin as I turn to rest against the counter. I close my eyes and drag the ice cube against my neck.

I exhale shakily. My hair slips behind my shoulders. Concentrating on the cooling sensation from the ice, I shift and move to the other side of my neck until I hear the clearing of a throat.

The deep, rumbly noise surprises me. My eyes spring open, and the ice cube slips. Except, it doesn't land on the floor. Instead, it falls in between my cleavage, leaving a melted trail of water behind, all for Rhodes to see and gawk at with one eyebrow cocked.

"What are you doing?" I ask, panicking.

I quickly push off the counter ledge. There is no sense in trying to hide the whole ice-rubbing situation, so I don't even try.

However, I will try to hide my shame.

"The better question is what are *you* doing?" Rhodes walks farther into the dark kitchen and places his palms face down onto the top of the island. I keep my eyes trained to his face instead of his bulging biceps peeking out from the sleeves of his T-shirt.

I quickly make something up. "I...I was hot."

Technically, I was hot—but not in the way he's likely thinking.

A line of confusion appears in between his eyes. I'm positive he can see right through me.

"You were hot?" he repeats.

I nod. "I couldn't sleep, and I was hot."

Silence fills the kitchen.

I gulp. He stares.

I'm beginning to think he can read my thoughts, which would probably result in losing my job.

I place my cup on the island. "What are you doing?"

Rhodes stands upright, stealing all of my attention. "I was thirsty."

I'm mesmerized by his slow, long blinks. He casually walks around the edge of the island and rests his hip against the counter, mere feet away from me.

I gulp when his hand reaches out for my cup.

His long fingers wrap around the dewy glass, and then his lips wrap around the same edge that mine were on a second ago.

Gulp. Gulp. Gulp.

Rhodes's throat bobbing mesmerizes me.

My chest rises and falls too quickly. I can't hide it.

I need to leave the kitchen.

Right *now.*

"You okay?"

I snap to attention and stare right at his mouth.

"I'm fine!" the lie squeaks out.

Rhodes's head tilts with skepticism. "You sure, Sunshine? You look flushed."

The glass gently clinks against the counter. He keeps his hand on it, but he's staring at me with concern.

"I'm totally a-okay." I fake a smile, and his forehead crinkles.

I take a step backward on shaky legs, and the concern in his eye climbs. "Did you drink too much?"

I laugh nervously. "I wish."

Then maybe I wouldn't be standing in his kitchen with a fire brewing in my stomach.

It's so quiet in the house. It seems like the entire world is asleep, except for Rhodes and me.

My heart races, and my pulse thrums painfully fast.

Rhodes takes another step toward me, but this time, I don't step away.

I tilt my chin the closer he gets, like I'm trying to prove a point.

To myself or him.

I'm not entirely sure yet.

He slowly raises the back of his hand. I stare up at him. My lips part with our close proximity. It's not often that we're *this* close. He is freshly showered with damp hair that smells spicy.

I inhale.

Then I stop breathing altogether when his knuckles gently brush my cheek.

My knees grow weak. I lean backward and try to shake myself out of the spell I'm under.

What the hell is wrong with me?

Rhodes winds his arm around my lower back to hold me upright. His fingers sweep against my hip, and I sway.

"Are you sure you're okay? I don't think you have a fever, but you're warm to the touch." He leans in closer, and those green eyes move back and forth between mine.

I can't take it.

"I'm not okay!" I scramble away and push his hands in the process.

He lets go right away with a flexed jaw. I lean farther against the counter, putting distance between us.

"Is this because of earlier?" His voice is low and gravelly. It does nothing but make me sweat more.

"Yes!" I turn and put my back to him.

A few beats of silence are shared between us. I try to calm my racing heart and push away the thoughts that are zipping through my head. I search for the guilt that should come with the arousal I feel when I look at Rhodes, but it's buried beneath several months of dormancy.

Without looking, I know he moves closer. His warmth brushes against my neck, and I inhale.

"There's nothing wrong with what happened earlier. It was a normal reaction after what happened to you."

If only he knew I was upstairs in bed, thinking about *his* hands on me.

"You aren't going to be a born-again virgin, Sunny." He chuckles, and that's when I realize he has no idea that I'm acting this way because of him. Not because of my freak-out over Simon.

A sarcastic laugh leaves me. I turn and peer over my shoulder. He gazes at me, scrutinizing my behavior.

"You don't get it." I turn all the way around and press against the sharp edge of the counter.

How can someone make confusion look so hot?

His gaze roams my face, like he's searching for an answer.

"I'm not acting this way because of Simon," I say.

"*Simon.*" He says the name with disgust.

"I'm acting this way because of you."

Shit. Why did I admit that?

Each time my heart beats, it's a punch to my chest.

His jaw flickers. He backs away immediately, and I hate the space I inevitably put there.

"Because of me?" He drops his arms in defeat and glances away. He's probably too ashamed to look at me. "Fuck, I'm sorry, Sunny."

"You're sorry?"

Rhodes's shoulders tense. He crosses his arms, and I can't help but notice the veins appearing on his forearms. "I didn't mean to make you uncomfortable. I just..." He clears his throat. "I wanted to help. I shouldn't have touched you—"

An abrupt laugh escapes me. I slap my hand over my mouth.

Rhodes stops mid-sentence and gawks at me. "Are you laughing at me?"

"No!" I throw my hands up and then cover my eyes. "I'm laughing because you have it completely twisted."

He's over to me in a flash. My heart drops when his large hand grips my wrist firmly, but at the same time, there's a gentleness there too. He pulls my hand away and stares at me intensely. "How so?"

"Because..."

Don't. Don't say it.

His earlier warnings are nowhere to be found, and my reservations aren't either. I know he fires nannies for this very thing, and yet, here I am, with an ache so intense I can't *not* say it.

"I liked it when you touched me, Rhodes!"

One second passes without so much as a blink.

Then another.

And another.

I'm out of here.

Thirty-Eight

RHODES

WHY DID she have to go and say that?

I stand alone in the kitchen with my heart beating like a caveman's.

There's an animalistic touch to what's going on inside my body.

Fuck, fuck, fuck.

With agile legs, I turn and search for her.

Like a ghost, she rushes away on quiet feet and heads for the stairs.

I chuckle.

Does she really think I'm going to let her get away after she said something like that?

"Not so fast," I say in a low voice.

My arm comes around the front of her waist, and I press her against me. I lower my mouth to her ear, and she stills in my arms.

"You can't just run off after saying something like that."

Her voice shakes. "You're going to just have to forget I said anything."

Yeah fucking right.

"I don't want to lose my job," she whispers.

Now it's my turn to pause.

Of course she thinks I'm going to fire her over this. Why wouldn't she, given what I've told her about past nannies?

The difference between Sunny and the rest are her intentions. She isn't trying to get me to fuck her. She doesn't crawl into my bed late at night with desperation and hope that I'll marry her and shower her with my wealth.

This is impulsive behavior.

Not sought-out and well-planned.

I mean, I basically had to force her to spill the dirty little thoughts to begin with.

"I'm not firing you because you enjoyed my touch, Sunshine."

My heart is flying faster than it ever has before. It's impressive that she can do this to my body.

Her gulp catches my attention, and I hate that I can't see her face. Not that I can read her. She's always catching me off guard with surprise. But still, I want to see the look on her face when I tell her what I'm thinking.

"I should have never touched you to begin with." It's the truth. I shouldn't have stepped in after that asshole got her all flustered. "But I did."

She surprises me, *again,* by turning around in my grip. We're surrounded by the dark, yet I'm still able to trace the curve of her lips. "It didn't make me recoil or panic..." she whispers. "Instead, it got me all twisted. It woke something up and—"

"Then let me finish."

This is not a good idea.

"What?" Her sweet breath, still smelling like birthday cake, fans against my face.

My mouth waters.

"There are no feelings involved," I admit. "You need someone who you can trust to help you through your fear." I let my words linger for a second. "It can be a one-time thing."

I feel her stare, and it makes me burn.

I'm desperate. My blood runs hot the longer she's pressed against me. The sweet scent of her breath, the way her long hair brushes against my arm. I picture the way she kissed that guy, and my stomach drops.

"If you don't want me to finish"—I creep my hand up the side of her body and push her hair behind her ear—"that's okay. We can act like this never happened—"

"Don't fall in love with me."

My body tenses. "Is that what you're afraid of?"

She nods. "If we do this, it's a one-time thing. Just to see if I can keep it together throughout..."

Throughout me touching you.

My dick twitches, and I'm hungry. So fucking hungry. For *her*.

I grab onto her hand and slowly guide her back to the kitchen. Going to either of our bedrooms seems too intimate, and not to mention, my five-year-old is asleep upstairs.

My hands slip around her waist, and I haul her up onto the counter. The light of the oven shows off her pretty features, and all I can stare at are her lips—the same lips that kissed some other guy earlier.

It was hot watching her kiss.

She's hot.

I was drowning in jealousy, and it's backing this entire spur-of-the-moment idea to *finish*.

Sunny gulps when I set her on the cool counter. I step in

closer at the same time I drag her to the edge. Her legs spread, and I'm right there at the center, silently begging to touch her.

I catch her eye. She's full of desperation. I'm not sure if she's desperate for me to touch her or for her to see if this whole thing works. Either way, it pulls me in closer.

"Promise me this won't affect your ability to nanny Ellie." *Don't turn me away now.*

A breath slips from her parted lips. "Of course I promise. I would never let that happen."

I exhale slowly.

"And I promise not to fall in love with you, Sunshine."

I hate making promises. My father made a lot of promises, and he broke every single one. They have little to no value in my life. But when it comes to Sunny, I'd do a lot more than promise if it meant I got to touch her.

I place my hand on her thigh and gently spread her legs even farther apart.

"The little bit of emotional bandwidth I have goes to Ellie. This won't be anything but physical for me." *Right?*

She sucks in air and lets out a heavenly breath. "I thought you didn't make promises."

I peer up at her while slowly sliding my hand up her inner thigh. *So soft.*

"For you, I'll make an exception."

Her eyes flutter closed as I drag my fingers against her smooth legs. She should probably burn these sleep shorts. They don't leave much to the imagination, and the fact that my dick is this hard, even after I fucked my hand in the shower, says a lot.

I'm highly attracted to my daughter's nanny.

In more ways than one.

"Put your palms flat on the counter." I try to keep my tone even, but my vocal cords strain with need. "If at any time you feel trapped or you want me to stop, you tell me."

Sunny nods. "I will."

Once her hands are face down, I hook my fingers around the waistband of her shorts and panties. I slowly pull the fabric down and glance at her face one last time to make sure she's okay. All I see are two seductive brown eyes watching my every move.

It sends me to a new high.

I drop my gaze in between her legs, and the sight of her is *maddening.*

I can't hide my appreciation. "Perfect."

Her back arches, and the only thing it does is pull my attention to her nipples straining against the cotton T-shirt she's wearing. A yearning rushes through me. I want her completely naked. I want to take my time touching every single inch of her body. Then maybe I can stop fantasizing about her every single time I'm in the shower.

I drop to my knees.

She snaps her attention down to the floor. "What are you—"

"Tikho," I shush her in Russian.

I'm clearly not in my right state of mind if Russian is slipping out.

"Did you just tell me to be quiet?"

I pause my fingers trailing up her thigh. "I did." I pull my gaze away from in between her legs. "Did you just understand Russian?"

The tiniest smile plays against her lips. My chest does something weird, and I immediately place my attention back to the most important thing at the moment: her glistening, pretty little cunt.

"Pick a safe word, Sunshine."

My mouth waters.

Enough talking.

I need to touch her.

Immediately.

She isn't the only one who hasn't been with someone in a while.

"Moscow."

Moscow? She isn't safe in Moscow. Those Russian men would eat her up in a second.

Me included.

"Moscow?" I repeat. "Good."

Her sharp inhale ignites my anticipation. I swipe a finger against her arousal, and every muscle in my body locks.

"So wet," I mutter in awe.

I slowly slide a finger inside of her. She's warm and tight.

It takes my breath away.

It isn't difficult to know what her body needs after touching her for a few seconds. Each time I slowly pull my finger away, she whimpers until I put it back in. She likes it slow, and she likes being teased.

Not trapped, though.

I press my mouth to the inside of her knee and place a kiss there while playing with her pussy.

She makes a noise, and I quickly dart my gaze to her face.

Her nipples strain against her T-shirt, showing off her perfectly sized mounds. Flushed cheeks. Parted lips. Fuck, I crave to kiss her. I want to know what it would feel like to slip my tongue inside her mouth and feel her lips against mine.

Instead of entertaining that idea, I go for the next best thing.

I trace the inside of her thigh with my nose. Her breaths are sharp and fast. I pause, only for a second, to make sure she's still okay. When I'm confident she isn't going to say the word *Moscow*, I blow a hot breath against her wet pussy and start to work her body.

My tongue slides against her folds, and I barely suppress my own groan. She's warm and silky. Tasting her is downright dangerous. If I didn't think it would be a step too far, I'd have her sit on my face. I'd love nothing more than to be fucking suffocated by her.

I'm out of control. Get a grip.

"Oh my god," she moans.

I smile to myself and play with her some more. Her pussy starts to tighten, and I suck her into my mouth. My fingers and tongue work together to bring her to the edge of bliss.

"There it is," I coax, hooking one finger while tugging on her clit with my teeth.

Sunny's rich brown hair brushes against the counter when she throws her head back. My cock strains against my boxers, but it's not hard to ignore as I stare at her hips jerking to meet my knuckle.

"More," she moans quietly.

"*Idealna.*" I mutter in Russian again. My god, she's exactly what it means: *perfect.* Her eyes roll back as her body chases the high.

It's addicting to watch her.

So addicting I can't stand it.

I shut my eyes, suddenly afraid I won't be able to keep my own promise.

Feelings are definitely involved, but they're not the kind she is afraid of. These are the kind that will have me fantasizing about her on her knees in my shower.

"Jesus fucking Christ," I mutter.

Sunny smothers me with her arousal. Her pussy traps my finger, and she moans. I quickly look at her face and watch her come. Her mouth is there for the taking. I have to physically hold myself back so I don't reach out, grip her jaw, and bring her lips to mine.

In an attempt to break free of the trap I'm in, I heave out a breath. I wait until she stops pulsing around my finger to whisper, "Good girl."

Her brown eyes are hazy with lust. Those thick eyelashes flutter against her pretty pink cheeks, and her tongue darts out to wet her lip. I slowly pull my finger out of her and suppress a groan.

Nope. That's all.

A look of satisfaction comes over her, and my job here is done.

I can't touch her again.

I'm as high as she is.

Unable to stop myself, I swipe her panties and shorts off the floor and slowly glide them back up her legs. She lifts her hips to help, and I choke down a swallow.

I want to fuck her so badly I can't think straight.

For a brief moment, I entertain the idea. It'd be so easy to pull her forward, spin her around, push her flat against the counter, and push my dick in her so far she'd never be able to think of another man without remembering me.

Wait, shit. Stop.

I crowd her space while restraining myself at the same time.

She peers at me with a look of awe.

I push her messy hair behind her ear. "Now that's how you do it, Sunshine."

The smallest smile twitches against her lips when I back away.

"Happy birthday, Sunny."

Those white teeth clamp onto her lip, and I see red.

By the grace of God, I take a step backward and force myself to go back to my room.

Alone.

Then I work my dick until I can't anymore, in hopes that I'll be less turned on by her in the morning.

Thirty-Nine

SUNNY

> Ruby: You made out with a guy?! What?!
> And you waited until this morning to tell me
> about it?

I roll my eyes.

> Me: Well, I couldn't immediately grab my
> phone and text you during it. That would be
> rude.

Instead, I came home and basically rode Ellie's father's face instead.

On the same counter that my breakfast currently sits on.

Ellie is beside me, eating her pancakes while humming a song from *Tangled*.

> Ruby: How was it? Did you manage to get
> past first base?

I'm not even sure of the bases anymore. I've been so far removed from this world that I can't remember them.

> Ruby: Did you have an orgasm? What a great birthday gift! 😈

I slowly chew a bite of my pancake.
I did, but not with the guy I made out with.
My body heats. I shove my plate away and stare at my phone before answering truthfully.

> Me: I did.

> Ruby: I knew that asshole didn't ruin you forever. I'm so proud. How was the sex?

I look over at Ellie. She's still eating her pancakes peacefully like the angel that she is.

> Me: We didn't have sex. But his mouth should get an Emmy.

> Ruby: It was that good? #jealous

There's a pressing ache nestling inside my stomach, and I don't know if it's regret or excitement. Maybe a little bit of both?

I'm nervous to see him this morning. Thanks to my encouragement, Ellie decided to eat breakfast with me instead of waking him, so he's still upstairs, hopefully forgetting the last twenty-four hours.

I selfishly need more time to digest what we did.

It was definitely a one-time thing, which I'm sure he agrees with.

But what do I do when I see him this morning? Just act like he didn't send tingles to the soles of my feet and help me past something that makes me vulnerable?

"Good morning."

I shriek, and my phone flies through the air.

Ellie looks at me with wide eyes and then giggles from my outburst.

I wait for the crash of my device to hit the floor, but it never does.

"Morning, Daddy! You slept in for a long time."

Act cool.

I clear my throat and peek over my shoulder. Rhodes is holding my phone in his large hand—the same hand that was in between my legs less than ten hours ago, and he's very obviously reading what's on the screen.

Fuck my life.

I gracelessly fall off my stool and slide over to him on my fuzzy socks. I sink my teeth into my bottom lip and snatch my phone out of his hand. Our fingers brush. A week ago, I wouldn't have noticed. Now, though? My blood sings.

I have to get it together or else he actually might fire me.

"Thanks." I hurriedly click my phone off and rush back to my stool.

Rhodes is frozen with his hand in front of him like he's still holding the device. He cautiously brings his gaze to my red face and stares at me for a second too long.

He absolutely read what I last typed to Ruby.

Now I have to go stick my head in the fridge to cool off my embarrassed-stained cheeks.

After what feels like ten years, Rhodes finally drops his hand and walks casually into the kitchen. I'm almost certain he's carrying himself with a little more confidence than before, so clearly, the compliment went right to his head.

He deserves it.

I shush my subconscious.

So what, he got me off in record time.

It's not like he's the only guy who's ever gotten me off with his mouth.

It's just...been a while.

"Morning, Printsessa." Rhodes kisses the top of Ellie's freshly braided hair while keeping his sights on me.

How he looks first thing in the morning should be illegal. His *gray* sweats hang low, and his half-unzipped jacket reveals a bare chest that is toned beyond belief. He has the hood pulled up over his head but not far enough to where I can't see his freshly tousled hair.

I watch him stride over to the coffee pot. He pours the steaming liquid and slowly spins to lean against the counter.

My heart flips.

"Sunny." He nods at me, and I swear I see a smirk hiding behind his cup.

Oh, is that how this is going to go? He's amused by me and my awkwardness this morning?

Fine.

"Oscar," I say in response. I grab my mug of coffee and also smirk behind the rim.

He grunts, and Ellie giggles.

She and I share a quick smile, and he scoffs.

"I'm not sure that I like you two ganging up on me."

We giggle again. He squints, pretending to be annoyed, but I can see right through the act. There's the faintest smidge of contentment on his features, and it pacifies me.

Things are *fine* between us. We are right back to what we were before we crossed the line.

In fact, we don't even have to mention it.

"How was your birthday night, Sunny?" Ellie's eyes swing to the container on the counter that is full of leftover cake. She clearly wants a piece.

"Yeah, Sunny." Rhodes places his cup on the counter. "How *was* the rest of your birthday?"

I choke on air. Apparently, he didn't get the memo to never mention my birthday ever again.

His eyebrows rise as he smirks.

I shoot him a vexed look, and he snorts.

An exasperated sigh leaves me as I turn toward Ellie. "It was good." I lean in close. "Would you like a piece of cake?"

She quickly nods, little pieces of hair flying out of her braid.

I hop to my feet with a quiet laugh. I move around the kitchen as if Rhodes isn't staring at me like he has something else to say.

"Just good?" he asks.

"Hmm?" I say.

It's hard not to look at him, but I focus on cutting the piece of cake like it's for the Pope instead of a five-year-old.

"Yum!" Ellie squeals excitedly when I slide the plate in front of her. I swipe my finger over the icing and pop it into my mouth while she digs in.

I take a seat and finally give Rhodes my attention. His jaw flickers while he focuses on my finger inside my mouth.

It was an innocent action, and I thought nothing of it, but with the fiery glint in his eye, I could see how it would come off as something other than that. *Whoopsie.*

Rhodes exhales. "I thought your birthday celebration deserved an...Emmy."

My eye twitches.

It did. It really did.

But there is no way I'm letting him win this.

I shrug. "I've had better."

Ellie's fork clanks to her empty plate, but neither Rhodes nor I look at it.

"That cake deserves an Emmy!" She pauses. "Wait. What's an Emmy?"

My lips beg to curve.

Rhodes's twitch.

Then we both laugh.

Thank god for Ellie.

"It's an award for the best of the best," Rhodes explains, placing his cup and her plate in the sink. I can't help but admire his backside as he does the two dishes. If he's home, he makes it a point to beat me to the dishes.

"I've got a game tomorrow night," he states, mid-wash.

"I saw it in the calendar." It's an away game, which means Ellie and I will be on our own.

"Can we go?" Ellie has so much hope riding on the question that it's kind of sad.

He shakes his head. "It's a school night, and it's a few hours away."

"So." Ellie crosses her arm and pouts. That bottom lip of hers slips out, so I quickly swoop in and save the day.

"You have to go to school, silly." I nudge her shoulder with mine. "But maybe I'll have a surprise for you afterward."

She gives me a side-eye. "A surprise?"

I nod. "You'll love it."

"What is it?" she asks.

"Yeah, what is it?" Rhodes repeats from across the kitchen.

I huff. "The whole point of a surprise is that it's a *surprise.*"

They both frown and share a look.

I laugh out loud. "You two better lighten up. Surprises are fun!"

Ellie thinks about it for a second, then eventually, her scrunched face smooths. "Okay...well, we will see."

And just like that, she's bouncing off to do cartwheels in the living room from the sugar boost my leftover cake gave her.

"You're welcome," I muse, sliding off my seat.

"For?" Rhodes crosses his arms and stares at me from across the island.

I glance at the spot he laid me on last night, and I hate that he saw.

"For making her look forward to something so she isn't focusing on you being away."

"What's the surprise?" he asks, coming around the island. "Another clay figurine thing?"

I click my tongue. "No." *She loved Pascal, though.* "But I can't tell you. It'll ruin the surprise."

"But it's not a surprise for me," he argues, leaning one palm on the island—*right* where my bare ass was. "Or is it?"

Something dangerously inappropriate flies through my head, and the second I catch a glimpse of his eye, I'm almost certain he had the same thought.

"I was going to take her to the studio and teach her how to do pottery," I blurt quickly. "I mean, if you're okay with that?"

"Of course I am." He nods. "I trust you with her."

I refuse to look him in the eye.

I'm afraid if he looks at me too closely, he'll be able to read my mind, and what a tragedy that would be.

"Oh." He leans farther across the island. "You're welcome too."

I gradually level my chin and meet his gaze. "For?"

"For the Emmy-deserving birthday gift." He winks, and my stomach dips.

He backs away slowly with a knowing grin and walks out of the kitchen.

I shout over my shoulder at the last second, "Don't let that go to your head!"

"Too late!" he shouts back.

I turn away before he can see the smile on my face.

At least he didn't decide to fire me this morning after remembering how he had a lapse in judgment and broke his own rule of fooling around with his daughter's nanny.

Though, he wasn't the only one who had a lapse in judgment.

Forty

RHODES

THERE'S a dusting of snow covering the road, but that doesn't keep me from heading home. Practice was long and grueling, despite the fact that we have a game tomorrow. Coach doesn't believe in going easy on us the night before. He says it builds stamina, and I don't disagree.

I back off the brake as I travel down the snowy street. I'm driving a little faster than usual, despite the snow, and that has nothing to do with the fact that Ellie and Sunny are at home waiting for me.

Okay, fine.

They're probably not *waiting* for me.

But I'm waiting to be home with them.

My hands tighten on the wheel.

I mean, Ellie is at home waiting for me. Not Ellie *and* Sunny.

I exhale.

I'm fucked.

I should have never gone back to the kitchen last night, and I most definitely shouldn't have touched her *again*. I broke my rule. A rule that's been engraved in my bones since the first nanny crept into my bed.

As soon as I get home, I'm redrawing the line.

The same line that I drew the moment she started working for me.

It was my fault. I'm the one who crossed it—not once but twice.

No more, though.

We have to go back to our normal, platonic relationship. Friendly, casual, but for the love of God, I cannot keep picturing her wet pussy with my fingers inside her. I can't crave her taste either.

"Fucking shit," I mutter.

I turn onto the quiet street without a single tire marking against the layer of snow. A sense of ease backs my movements when I park and climb out onto the sidewalk. Home has never felt more welcoming.

It's been a long time since I've been able to come home after a practice and not immediately tense with what's waiting for me. It's less taxing to have someone I trust around to help me with Ellie, even if I do have to mentally hold myself back from touching her.

I walk inside, and Sunny's classic scent hits me. If I were a blind man, I'd assume we were at a beach resort instead of a home in Chicago with snow covering the streets. Sunshine and coconut fill the air, and I'm pretty sure she has made dinner, because there is a hint of spice too.

"Hello?"

The house is too quiet.

Where are they?

I walk toward the kitchen, spotting a big pot on the stove.

My stomach rumbles with hunger. I've told Sunny countless times that she wasn't required to clean or cook me meals, and for a little while, she listened.

But over the last week, she's made sure to make extra of whatever she's eating so I can have some too.

A squeal of excitement catches my attention. I glance out the back door, and something unfamiliar burrows inside my chest.

My breath catches.

Jesus.

Look at them.

Sunny, with nothing but a thin coat on, has snowflakes trapped in her brown hair with a smile on her face that's so warm I'm surprised it hasn't melted the snow-covered deck. Ellie, who I can't help but notice is fully bundled up in her snow gear, runs around her with snowballs corralled in her gloved hands.

She throws one at Sunny, who acts like she can't dodge them. She's hit in the chest, and her smile grows wider as she looks at my daughter. When she bends down, she swoops up a pile of fluffy snow and flings it toward Ellie.

They laugh, and I somehow find myself outside with both of them, holding my coat for Sunny to take.

"Daddy!" Ellie, with her bright-pink cheeks, rushes toward me.

Sunny and I have the same thought.

She's going to slip.

I reach forward, but Sunny is there before me, sweeping Ellie up into her arms and landing with a loud thud on the hard deck.

"Oof."

A noise leaves her chest, and I stare down at their tangled mess. Ellie is lying on top of her with wide eyes.

"Whoa," she says.

I pull Ellie off Sunny quickly and place her on steady feet.

Instead of holding my hand out for Sunny to take so I can haul her to her feet too, I slip my arm underneath her and place it on the small of her back, slowly pulling her upright.

"You good, Superwoman?" I ask, keeping her steady.

She inhales shakily and bounces her pretty eyes back and forth between mine. She nods gingerly.

I drop my gaze to her mouth mistakenly, giving away all my intrusive thoughts.

Fucking hell.

Her slow swallow is loud enough for the entire neighborhood to hear, and I know it's not meant to be sensual or a tease, but my body doesn't agree.

We're frozen.

I'm bent at the knee with the coat I snagged for her resting over my leg, with my arm around her waist. Her bare hands are buried in the snow, likely red from the bitter cold.

Ellie, unaware of the moment we're sharing, is busy making snowballs.

Are we having a moment?

My mouth runs dry when I see more snowflakes land in her hair.

She's so damn beautiful.

I've never felt a sense of warmth while beneath falling snowflakes, but leave it to her warm, honey-colored eyes to do just that.

"Here." I break our eye contact and drape my jacket over her shoulders.

I catch sight of the tiny smile against her mouth, and for a second, I think it's because she likes that I brought her a coat, but then, something cold smacks me upside the head, and I realize that she and my daughter just silently plotted together with me no more than a foot away.

Ellie's childish giggle pulls me to turn. I slowly inch my head in her direction.

Her eyes grow into saucers, and I raise an eyebrow.

Sunny scurries away from me, while wearing my jacket, and leaps forward to grab onto Ellie's hand.

"Hide!" she shouts.

Ellie laughs the entire time Sunny drags her away.

I smile and rise to my feet. "You two think you can take me in a snowball fight?"

They're awful at staying quiet.

Not only can I see the tops of their heads behind the covered grill, but I hear Ellie's quiet laughter mixing with Sunny's.

Before long, I have six snowballs clustered in my hands. Three in each. I'm certain they have an arsenal too, but they're no match to me.

Slowly, I head to the back door and open it, only to close it a moment later. I put one leg over the ledge of the deck, and with my long legs, I'm able to silently land in the snowy yard. I have to force myself to keep my own laugh under control when I hear the two of them whispering, wondering if I've gone inside.

Ellie is arguing that I left, but Sunny knows better.

This is fun.

When was the last time I had fun like this?

It's like I'm a kid again. My lungs expand with energy, but it's different from when I climb onto the rink for a game. I have a zest for life, and it's been a very long time since I felt this way.

"On the count of three, we'll take a peek, okay?"

I stare at the two of them between two wooden slats. Ellie nods, and Sunny reaches up to adjust her beanie. She pushes the few strands away from her face and bops her on the nose.

Something swells in my chest.

How will Ellie and I ever survive without her?

How did we survive before?

"One," Sunny whispers.

I grin and stand straight.

"Two."

The snowballs shift back and forth in my palms.

"Three," I say.

They both turn toward me. Ellie squeals, and Sunny's eyes fill with something that I can't help but want to chase.

I toss one snowball at Ellie, but the other goes right for Sunny. She gasps when it splatters against her chest, and yes, that was purposefully placed.

Her gaze narrows, like she's ready for a challenge.

I run through the snow and climb the slippery steps, allowing Ellie's snowballs to hit me in various spots.

Like some type of monster, I growl, and she screams playfully. She scurries to the back door, swings it open, and slams it shut. Sunny and I both laugh, but neither of us move to end the fight.

I'm holding four snowballs.

She's holding two.

I raise an eyebrow, and she does the same.

My dick twitches at the thought of her running away only for me to chase her.

I silently beg her.

Run, malyshka.

There I go again, calling her a name in Russian. *Baby.*

She takes one step backward and tosses the snowballs back and forth in her red hands.

"You better run, Sunshine," I warn her.

Her pretty lips split, and I'm blinded by the smile.

A snowball smacks me right in the face.

I'm frozen with shock.

"Oh, you're in for it." I dart forward and throw every last snowball at her backside as she runs toward the door.

She shouts Ellie's name in between her girly laughter.

Ellie stands by the door with her hand covering her wide smile. It's obvious she's laughing at us, and I'm not sure I've ever seen her so child-like.

I dive forward, wrap my arms around Sunny's waist, and fling her around in my arms. Her laughter fills the air, and we fall to the cold powder.

She's on top of me, and suddenly, our laughing comes to a halt. It doesn't take me very long to imagine every inch of her underneath our thick layers. Our body heat mingles, and I've long forgotten that we're lying beneath a snow-fallen sky.

That hot tongue of hers slips out and wets her plump bottom lip. I stare at it, fighting the urge to kiss her senseless. My blood fills with need, and when I flex my hips, her playful eyes turn dark.

Last night opened up the gates of hell.

What the hell am I doing? And why can't I stop?

The door opens, and Ellie stands there.

Sunny and I freeze, but Ellie, as innocent as she is, has no idea that I'm completely twisted with need from her nanny lying on top of me.

"Dad, you're supposed to go easy on us!" Ellie scolds me, and it forces a chuckle out of me.

Sunny tries to climb off me, but my hands tighten against her waist.

Fuck, let go of her. I'm unhinged. I've lost my fucking mind.

She stops wiggling and glances at me out of the corner of her eye.

I wait until Ellie turns away, continuously stripping her snow gear and dropping it to the kitchen floor.

My abs flex as I inch forward.

Sunny and I are flush against one another, and the arousal is enough to send me to an early grave.

With my lips brushing against the cold strands of her hair, I whisper, "I win, Sunshine."

Except, as soon as she climbs off me and swings that smile elsewhere, I feel like I've lost.

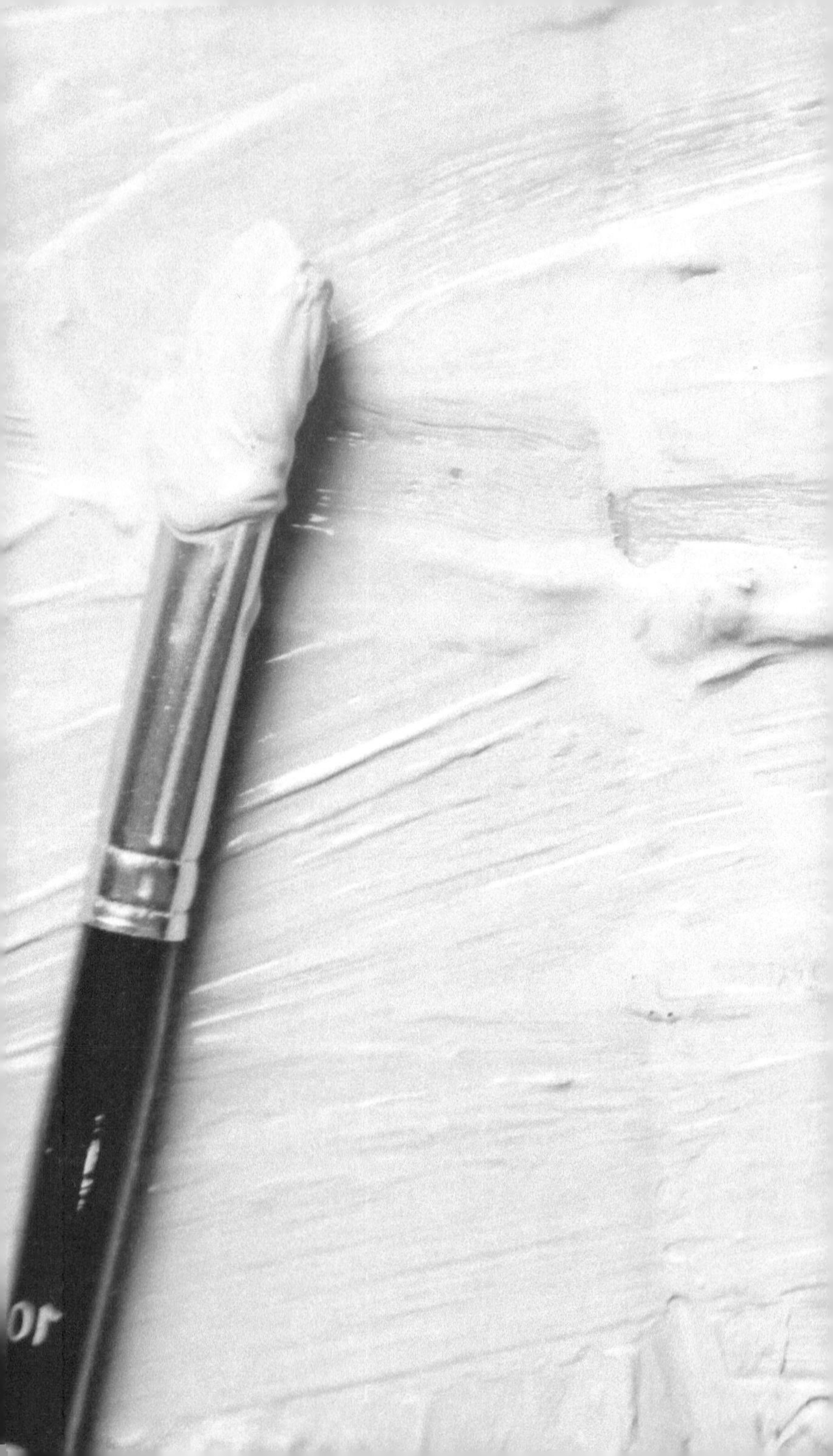

Forty-One

SUNNY

RHODES AND I ARE EVEN.

He takes me out for my birthday, encourages me to act my age, and then later helps me get over the little blip of anxiety I have when it comes to men, and I loosen him up with an impromptu snowball fight with his daughter, which is a memory she'll probably have for the rest of her life.

So there.

We're even.

I shake my damp hair out and cross my arms. My back is to the mirror because if I look at myself, it'll be harder to hide from what I'm really thinking about.

Like Rhodes's husky voice in my ear or the way my toes curled less than twenty-four hours ago with the way he took my body in the palm of his hands and made it sing.

"Stop it," I whisper-shout to myself in my empty room.

It's after ten.

Ellie is asleep.

The house is quiet.

Rhodes is probably sleeping too, because he leaves early tomorrow for an away game.

I wonder if I imagined the look in his eye earlier when he tackled me to the ground during our snowball fight.

The light and airy moment suddenly turned hot and tense. Or did I just think that?

He touches you one time, and look at you!

I spin and glare at myself in the mirror.

The hair framing my face doesn't hide the flush against my cheeks. I look to my chest and spy two pointy buds that give my thoughts away.

And here comes the pacing.

Back and forth, back and forth, back and forth.

Maybe I should try to go out again, on an evening when Rhodes is home with Ellie.

Find another guy like Simon. Only, this time, I won't melt into a panicky mess. If I pushed the limits with Rhodes, I can do it with someone else.

Right?

What if I don't want to?

I flush harder.

An exasperated sigh slips from my mouth, and I flop onto my bed.

What a ridiculous thought.

My phone buzzes, and I expect it to be another text from Ruby since she is one of the only people who have my new number.

I sit up quickly.

It's Rhodes.

Rhodes: You up?

Heart palpitations. I'm literally having heart palpitations over a text.

Me: Yes.

Is this a booty text?
Oh my god. Of course it isn't!

Rhodes: Thank you for earlier.

I calm myself and ignore my shaky fingers.

Me: For what?

For keeping things *normal* between us after your fingers were buried between my legs the night before? No problem.

Rhodes: For reminding me to loosen up every once in a while. I haven't laughed like that in a long time. It made Ellie happy.

I smile.

Me: Who knew it would take a snowball to the face to get you to smile.

He has a really nice smile too. If he smiled more often, I bet he'd have even more admirers.

I pause.

I'm sort of glad he doesn't smile much, now that I think about it.

Rhodes: I'm pretty sure it wasn't the snowball.

My heart stops.
Is he implying that it was me?
I place my phone down on my chest.
There's no way he is, and if he were, shouldn't that scare me?

> Me: Shouldn't you be sleeping? You have a game tomorrow.

There. Perfect. Change of subject.

> Rhodes: I always have trouble sleeping the night before an away game. I don't like to leave Ellie.

Rhodes is such a mystery. How can he seem so apathetic on the outside but be so tender for Ellie? He's shown that side to me a few times too. It's the subtle, barely there, sweet actions that draw you in and give some insight to who he truly is.

The demand for me to move in here rather than stay at the house with the broken lock. Reassuring me that his house is safe and making sure I had the option of locking my bedroom door. Showering me with flowers and taking me out for my birthday. They're such small actions, but they carry such a heavy punch.

> Me: I completely understand, given what you've gone through in the past when leaving her.

I hit send but text again.

> Me: I know you don't believe in promises, but I promise you that she's safe with me.

It doesn't take long for him to respond.

> Rhodes: I believe in promises. I just don't like to make them. And I know she's safe with you. I've never felt more at ease leaving her with someone than I do now.

Pride swells. It looks like I'm breaking through and

gaining some of his trust. The trust that was nonexistent when I first started.

Rhodes: Shouldn't you be sleeping? You're twenty-six now. According to you, that's not far off from my old age of thirty-two.

I snort.

Me: You're the only one who thinks thirty-two is old, Rhodes. But that's fine. I'll keep you young.

I smile to myself.

Me: You up for another snowball fight?

Me: Kidding! But that seemed to spark the youth in you.

Rhodes: Don't tease me like that, Sunshine. I was putting my coat on.

I roll my eyes. He was not.

Me: You were not. If I had to guess, you're in bed with your pjs on.

For a split second, I imagine what he sleeps in, which then leads to me thinking about last night again, when he found me in the kitchen. Gray sweats and a T-shirt that hugged his biceps.

Hot.

Rhodes: I am in bed.

Me: And the pjs?

My pulse races, as if my body knows something my head doesn't.

> Rhodes: If you show me yours, I'll show you mine.

Is he trying to challenge me? As if I won't send him a picture of my snowflake sleep shorts and matching top? He saw a lot more of me last night than this outfit shows.

I snap a picture and send it.

It's nothing racy. My nipples aren't making themselves known like earlier, and although the shorts hit a little above mid-thigh, it doesn't scream "sexy" by any means.

> Rhodes: I didn't think you'd actually send a picture.

A quiet laugh tumbles from my mouth.

> Me: Well, I assumed if I didn't, you'd just come to my room and see for yourself.

> Rhodes: Does that mean you're going to come to my room if I don't send you a picture?

My soul leaves my body. An ache burrows in between my legs so abruptly I look down. I type slowly while I blow a breath out of my mouth.

> Me: I could.

I'm sweating.

Is he egging me on? Waiting to see if I'll come down to his room? I shouldn't. I know deep in my bones that I shouldn't.

I stare at my open door.

How many steps is it to his room? Twenty?

My phone vibrates, and my fingers race to open the text.

He sends me a picture, and all rational thinking goes out the window. My lips part, and a needy breath empties into the room.

He's shirtless.

My blood runs hot.

I'm still affected from last night.

His touch did something to me, and I'm afraid of it. It left something behind that's so strong I'm having insane thoughts of him touching me again.

Sure, I trust him, and that's playing a huge role in this, but I have to get it together!

I count his abs one by one until I get to the waistband of his pants. That's all I see. His strong chest, defined abs, and a pair of sweats that hides the rest of his body.

> Me: What took you so long?

I will *not* comment on his perfectly sculpted body, and I will *not* make mention of how inappropriate this is, because I clearly have no morals at the moment.

> Rhodes: You want the truth?

> Me: Always.

> Rhodes: I sleep…in less clothing. Didn't think it would be right to send my daughter's nanny a dick pic.

I laugh out loud.

> Rhodes: Did you just laugh at me?

I slam my mouth shut. On quiet feet, I jump out of bed

and shut my open door before diving back in bed and reaching for my phone like a teenager texting her crush for the first time.

Nope. There is no crush. I am not crushing on Ellie's father.

> Me: Must be imagining things. I didn't laugh.

> Rhodes: Hmm. I've been imagining a lot lately.

I bite my lip and take the bait.

> Me: Like?

> Rhodes: Like where I'd be if you had entered our lives a year ago instead of a couple of months.

I could have avoided a whole lot of trauma if I were in Chicago a year ago.

> Me: I wish it were a year ago.

Rhodes texts back immediately.

> Rhodes: You like me that much?

I smile.

> Me: I like Ellie that much.

> Rhodes: Fair.

> Me: I wish it were a year ago so I could have avoided what happened to me.

Rhodes: Also fair.

There are more text bubbles, so I wait to see what else he says.

Rhodes: But then last night wouldn't have happened.

I stare at the screen, and my pulse quickens.

Rhodes: I shouldn't have said that.

Oh, but you did, and now I can't unsee it. I play dumb, hoping it'll make him laugh, and we can move past it. Otherwise, I may do something I swore I wouldn't, and that's touch myself at the thought of him.

Me: What happened last night?

Rhodes: You know what happened last night.

My head is spinning.

I wish the memory of last night was hazy so I could forget it.

Because I *need* to forget it.

The way his mouth curved at the sight of me lying on the counter was intoxicatingly hot. His fingers and mouth working together made me come faster than I ever have before, and I was able to stay in the moment with him instead of panicking, which is like a revolution.

Rhodes: Are you thinking about last night, Sunshine?

My fingers tighten on my phone. I secretly love it when he calls me that.

Me: No.

Rhodes: Oh, are we lying now? You know what happens when we lie.

I smile.

Me: You going to put me in time-out like you do to Ellie? 😬

Rhodes: That's not how I'd punish you.

My thoughts turn racy.

They're deranged.

I place the back of my hand to my forehead. *Do I have a fever?*

Without any restraint, I type a message that I know I should delete.

Instead, I hit send.

Me: How would you punish me?

Shit. Shit. Shit.

Now it's my turn to panic. How do I unsend a text?

I'm mid-Google search over how to unsend a text, and my phone starts ringing.

Rhodes is calling.

He's calling me?!

I shouldn't answer. My cheeks are warm. They'll give me away.

Don't answer.

I'm not answering the phone.

Nope.

My finger hovers over the accept button. The room spins. There's a pulse in between my legs.

I hit accept.

I hit accept.

Forty-Two

RHODES

I CANNOT GO to her room.

I'm about to handcuff myself to the bed.

The next best thing is to call her, which is exactly what I do.

"Hello?"

For fuck's sake, even her voice sends me to a new high.

"Hello..." I clear my throat. The rasp is loud and proud.

"Is everything okay?" she asks.

No. Not even a little bit.

I put my phone on speaker and rest it against my chest. My hands clasp at the back of my head, which is good. I'll trap them there so I can't touch myself at the sound of Sunny's voice on the other end of the line.

"Is everything okay..." I repeat her question. "Yes. Everything is fine."

There's some shifting on her end of the phone. "Why did you call me?"

I chuckle darkly. "It was either that or I come up there, and I don't think that's a good idea."

Silence.

What is she thinking?

My jaw wiggles back and forth. I stare at the phone like I can somehow see her through the screen.

I refuse to video chat. If I did that, then she'd see how feral I am, and that'd probably scare her senseless.

"Why isn't that a good idea?" She sounds so innocent, as if she doesn't know she's been skating the line since I first texted her—playing coy, pretending that she doesn't know that I'm picturing her pretty little pussy from the night before. I mean, I couldn't even keep it together in the middle of a snowball fight. What makes her think I could keep it together right now? A sleepy house, her alone in her room wearing those thin snowflake sleep shorts that I want to burn along with the ones she wore last night.

This wasn't my intention when I texted her, but here we are.

I sigh and rub my hand over my face with frustration.

I glance at my sweats.

I'm hard as a rock.

I should hang up, do my business, and go to sleep so I can be rested for tomorrow's game.

But I don't have that much restraint at the moment.

"Because then I'd be tempted to show you how I'd punish you," I admit.

There it goes. The restraint.

Silence lands on the other end of the phone. A dirty thought sparks in the back of my mind. I shut my eyes. I'm playing with fire, and we both know it.

I'm taking every little thing and twisting it to meet my needs, because I swear her question sounded more like a beg than actual curiosity.

"You want me to?" I adjust my dick, and even the light touch sends something fiery into my blood.

I would destroy her if I went to her room.

I haven't fucked someone in a very long time.

I'm not sure I could be the type of guy she needs.

"Sunny?"

Is she there?

I listen closely and almost choke on my tongue when I notice her heavier breathing.

If she's touching herself, I'll die.

The veins on my forearm bulge with need. I adjust myself again.

"I'm here."

She's breathless.

Fuck me.

"What are you doing?" I ask.

"Lying in my bed. What are you doing?"

Dying a slow death.

"Lying in my bed." I pause. "Thinking about whether or not I should hang up the phone."

Tell me to hang up, Sunshine. Please.

This goes against every single thing I'd preached from the beginning. Never get involved with a nanny. What's that old saying? Never bite the hand that feeds you?

She has no idea that she feeds me, but God, she does.

"Don't hang up."

I clench my eyes shut. "You're the one who's supposed to be rational, Sunshine."

"I'm younger than you. Aren't you the one who's supposed to be rational? Set an example?"

She's right.

I am.

But that was *before*.

"You're forgetting one thing, though." I push on my dick,

but this time, instead of adjusting myself, I keep my hand on top and press against it.

"What's that?" Am I imagining that her breaths are becoming heavier?

"I'm a man."

Her airy laugh makes me harder.

"Trust me. I'm aware," she says.

I raise a brow. "Are you now?"

"I've seen your abs. I'm sure."

My lip lifts. The compliment goes right to my head.

"You like 'em?"

"No."

I chuckle dryly. "We're back to lying now?"

She makes a tsk sound, and I picture her tongue clicking inside her sweet mouth. "Are you going to send me to timeout?"

A knot pulls on my stomach. "I told you that's not how I'd punish you."

"Well, you never told me how you would punish me."

She *does* want to know.

"You're tempting me to say things that you can't unhear once I say them."

This is her one out.

If she wants to stop this conversation before it starts, then this is the time to hang up.

I'm not strong enough. Hell, I don't want it to end.

It's hard to remember that she's Ellie's nanny while we're both tucked away behind closed doors inside this big, quiet house. The world is sleeping. There are no witnesses around. It's just us on the phone without anyone else listening.

"Do you want to hear them, Sunshine?" I ask, poking her to make a decision.

"Only if we can act like I didn't after we hang up the phone."

She knows this is wrong, but she must like breaking rules as much as I do.

"Deal."

Her shaky breath causes my mouth to run dry. The rasp in my voice gets worse.

"There are many ways I could punish you." I shut my eyes and imagine her lying in her bed for the taking with a teasing little smile on her face, knowing what's coming for her. "I could tie you up, but we've already learned that's not something you like."

Her loud swallow catches my attention.

"I used to."

Ah, hell.

"We'll have to work on getting you back to liking that."

No, we will the fuck not.

"Tonight wouldn't be the time for that, though." My palm rubs against my dick through my sweats, and I exhale. "Instead, I'd go for edging."

"Edging?"

"Yeah." I hope she can't hear the desperation in my voice. Picturing her alone in her bed, all worked up over what I'm saying, has me pulsing in places I wasn't aware had a pulse. "It would feel like a punishment at first, but it'd intensify your orgasm...when I finally let you have it."

She inhales sharply.

"I'd start by skimming my fingers over your belly and probably dip them under the waistband of those cute shorts you have on." I clench my jaw and press on my throbbing cock again. "I'd do this so many times that you would be dripping between your legs."

I may die from the thought.

"Rhodes." My name falling from her mouth does something to me. I bite my tongue so hard I taste metal.

Fuck.

I grab onto my hard dick and give it a squeeze.

"I'd eventually ease the ache by slipping a finger inside of you, but just enough to make you want more."

She'd be begging me to fuck her by the end.

There's a shift on the other side of the phone.

"Want me to stop?" I ask, attempting to give her one more out. Right now, though, she isn't Ellie's nanny. She's the woman I'm highly attracted to who is just two rooms down.

"Please don't," she begs.

I'm sweating from the inside out.

I inhale sharply and squeeze myself again.

I'm rubbing my dick to my daughter's nanny's voice.

Jesus Christ.

"You'd be writhing so much that I'd have to hold you still so I could strip those tiny shorts from your body. Then I'd do the same with your panties."

I focus on the speed of Sunny's breathing, and I rub myself over my sweats to match the pace.

"What if I told you that I wasn't wearing any panties?"

My heart stops.

"Are you?"

Silence.

"*Sunny.*"

"No."

I exhale, but it comes out more like a growl. "Go lock your door."

We're rooms away, and I somehow feel her everywhere. Those quiet breaths wisp over my skin like an angel.

A dirty, dirty angel.

"Why?"

"Because I'm about to come see what you're doing that has you breathing hard."

There's some shuffling, and I hear the faint click of a lock.

"It's locked."

"*Khoroshaya devochka.*"

Damnit.

"What does that mean?"

"It means good girl. Now tell me what you're doing to yourself that has you out of breath, baby."

Baby? First I call her a good girl in Russian, and now I'm calling her baby?

"I'm doing exactly what you'd be doing. Except, I haven't taken my shorts off yet."

A deep noise leaves me. I shove my hand inside my pants and take a hold of my cock.

"Take them off."

I can hear her shifting around.

I picture her slipping the shorts down her toned legs and kicking them off to the side. I'd spread her wide, just to get a better look.

"Don't touch yourself yet," I warn.

She makes a pouty noise, and I love it.

"We're still in punishing mode, remember?"

She says nothing, and I take her silence for granted.

"After I stripped you bare, I'd take my hands and place them on the insides of your knees." I shut my eyes and picture doing that. My balls tighten, and I milk myself. "I'd push your legs open and stare down at that pretty little pussy."

She whimpers.

"It's perfect. The right size, tastes like heaven, and so goddamn responsive to my touch."

The way her body sang when I touched her last night was more of a miracle than anything.

"*Rhodes.*" My name is a whine, and I eat it up.

"I know, baby," I say. "But this is a punishment."

"I don't want to be punished anymore."

I flare my nostrils. "Don't worry. You'll be rewarded at the end."

She gulps. "What's next?"

What's next? Those nipples. The same ones I saw poking through her shirt last night.

"Next," I attempt to level my voice. "I'd push your shirt up so I could marvel at your breasts."

I hear nothing but her heavy breathing.

"Do it, Sunny. Push your shirt up and feel the cool air brush against your skin."

I listen closely and hear the scratching of fabric against her soft skin.

"Khoroshaya devochka." I call her a good girl again and coax her through the phone. "Now touch them."

She's panting now, and my hand moves faster. I visualize her delicate fingers twisting her nipples and her back arching off the bed. I wonder if she's aching as much as I want her to be.

"Tell me how it feels."

"Um..." She exhales. "It feels..." The faintest moan leaves her, and I almost die. "It feels good...but I want more."

"I guess you're learning your lesson, then." My head tilts backward on my pillow, and I squeeze myself until I can come back down to earth. "No more lying."

"Mm-hmm."

I grip the sheets.

"Let's try this again." A hot swallow works down my throat. "Were you thinking about last night, or are you still going to lie and say you weren't?"

"I was."

I smile at her quick answer.

"What exactly were you thinking?"

"I was thinking about your mouth." I almost don't hear her with how lustful her voice is. It's low and fluttery. It does nothing but make things worse for me.

I grab my phone and press video.

"Answer."

I hear her breathing pick up pace, but surprisingly, she answers.

The moment her face appears in the frame, I lose all train of thought. Pretty pink cheeks, doe-like eyes, plump bottom lip that is likely swollen from her teeth sinking into the soft flesh.

"Let me see you."

She plays coy. "You do see me."

I narrow my eyes. "All of you."

Her throat bobs. She slowly pans the phone down, putting it at an angle that gives me the best visual.

I regret not giving her breasts attention last night when I had her in the palm of my hand. Perfect, rose-colored perky nipples catch my eye before she slants the phone even more, giving way to her flat stomach and open legs.

"Moy." *Mine.*

Her breathy gasp catches my ear.

Did she understand me? If so, I hope it doesn't scare her off.

Her face comes back into view, and as if I predicted it, her white teeth sink into her lip—the same lip that I want to sink my own teeth into. Her eyes are glossy with need, and I *swear* she's begging me to continue this little game.

"Don't move the phone, but switch the frame around."

She hesitates.

"Like this."

Keeping the phone on my chest so I can still see her, I switch the frame so instead of seeing my face, she's now looking at my hand inside my sweats.

Her hot little gasp pairs nicely with the widening of her eyes. Those pretty lips part when I start rubbing myself.

"I watch you. You watch me."

Before she can rethink it, she does what I say. The phone

remains steady, but the frame switches. I'm looking at her bare legs and sweet pussy.

"Are you wet?" I ask, knowing damn well that she is.

My teeth grind together when her hand comes into view. She slips it in between her legs, and I might die.

"Mm-hmm."

I challenge her. "Show me."

I almost black out when I catch sight of her wet finger.

Her hand disappears again, and I groan. All I can see is the circular motion. She's rubbing her clit, and I am going to hell for the thoughts going through my head.

"Proud of you for not lying to me again."

"So where's my reward?"

My hand stops moving. She's constantly surprising me. Her teasing tone makes me give in right away.

"You want your reward?" I waste no time. I push my pants down, and my dick springs forward. I bask in the sound of her breath catching. "Your reward is learning what you do to me." Even though I *hate* it.

"Oh my god..." Her words fade when I grab onto my cock and start rubbing up and down.

"Don't stop on my account. We can both reach new heights tonight, Sunshine."

My balls tighten, and my abs flex. Her hand moves up and down, and her legs spread wider. I grip myself tighter, and the friction is making me sweat.

"There you go," I encourage. "Spread even wider."

The hottest whimper comes through the speaker, and my hand is out of control. I pump up and down, unable to control myself from the pleasure. Seeing her and hearing those sexy noises, knowing damn well I can't have her, is torture.

It's also going to give me the best orgasm of my life.

She's the forbidden fruit that tastes *so damn good.*

"You must be close." My voice shakes. "You're panting."

Her hand moves faster, and when her hips start to meet her halfway, I burn.

"You are the sexiest thing I have ever seen, Sunny. So sexy it hurts."

First time I'm admitting that out loud to her.

Fuck, I'm close.

She's about to get real personal with me after she watches me bust a nut at the sight of her touching herself through the phone.

I want to close my eyes so I don't come first, but I can't. She has me in such a tight grip I'm unable to look away.

"Fuck." I pump two more times and make a noise that I haven't made in a very long time. Hot ropes of cum fly from my dick and land on my stomach as I milk myself, still watching her hand in between her legs.

"Ah," Sunny whimpers not once, but twice. I keep watching as she rides her high, too afraid to miss anything.

For fuck's sake.

There's silence on both ends of the phone, besides our heavy breathing. Her hand slowly moves out from between her legs, and I finally let go of my tight grip.

A rough swallow moves down my throat, and I unclench my jaw.

I want to ask her to come down here for round two, but that isn't part of the deal.

We're going to pretend like this didn't happen and go back to normal.

I'm her boss.

She's Ellie's nanny.

End of story.

I clear my throat, preparing to be casual and nonchalant, but then she switches the phone back to her face, and I lose my train of thought.

I do the same, and the moment she sees me come into

view, she flutters her long eyelashes, looking so damn sweet yet naughty.

I grin at the twinkle in her eye.

"*Sladkih snov*, Sunshine."

Her mouth curves with her new understanding of the Russian language. *Sweet dreams.*

I hang up the phone and glance at the sticky mess on my stomach.

Yeah, I'm fucked.

Forty-Three

SUNNY

THE STEAM of the coffee brushes against my face. I inhale deeply and tell myself that last night was a dream. A hot, *hot* dream. My stomach dips with the thought, but I quickly pull myself back to reality with Ellie's sweet voice behind me.

"I'm all done."

I peek over my shoulder at her empty plate. I smile over the rim of my mug, but it quickly falls when a large presence walks into the kitchen.

My face turns fifteen shades of red.

I start sweating in places that should not be sweating at eight in the morning.

"Good morning, Printsessa."

As if Rhodes needed any help being attractive in the morning, he bends and kisses the top of his daughter's head and sends her the half smile he only reserves for her.

"Go Blue Devils!" Ellie shouts.

I can't help but giggle. She does the same thing on each game day, but today, she pairs it with a cartwheel.

"Wow," Rhodes mutters. "Someone has energy today."

Ellie smiles brightly, proud of herself, and climbs back into her seat.

I sip on my coffee and slip my gaze to Rhodes. My heart leaps out of my body.

He's staring directly at me, and I hate that I have no idea what's going through his mind.

Surely it's not what's going through mine, because the only thing I'm picturing is his hand around his length and remembering what we did last night.

It most definitely wasn't a dream.

Not with the flirty look in his eye.

I'm frozen, pressed against the cabinet.

He starts to stalk toward me.

Am I still dreaming?

"Good morning, Sunny." His tone is neutral, and it's clear he's keeping his word.

We won't bring up what happened last night.

It was...a tiny slip in our restraint.

Now we can resume our normal lives.

"Morning," I squeak.

Stop acting guilty!

He smirks.

How can he be so relaxed? It's as if he doesn't remember watching me finger myself until I had another mind-blowing orgasm last night.

I blush, and he notices. His eyebrow hitches, and his smirk grows deeper. I glance at Ellie, and when she isn't paying attention, I take the heel of my foot and gently stomp it on top of his.

He makes a noise.

"Stop it," I hiss.

I turn and put my back to him.

"You stop it," he says between a chuckle.

"I'm not doing anything," I whisper.

He snickers.

I growl quietly but freeze when he comes up behind me. He's so close I feel his body heat wrap around me like a blanket. His cologne fills my senses, and *great,* I'm spiraling.

What is *this*?

Why am I the one acting like I can't move past this?

His warm breath coats my neck when he leans forward and reaches for my mug. "Your pink cheeks are giving you away, Sunshine."

I'm so surprised by his closeness that I don't protest when he steals my coffee. Our fingers brush, and chills race down my arms. A hot breath caresses my neck. "Your entire body is giving you away."

He backs away, and the airy kitchen comes back into view. I spin and glare at him. I want to argue and tell him he's wrong, but he's standing against the cabinets with *my* mug in his hand, sipping on *my* coffee.

And it's hot.

It's freaking hot, okay?

In an attempt to distract myself, I face Ellie. "Let's braid your hair and get you ready for school."

She perks up. "Can I wear my Blue Devils bow for Daddy?"

I smile, refusing to look at Rhodes. "Of course."

Her face beams, and I lean over the counter into her space. "I'll even wear one too."

"We will be twins!" She claps and runs to get dressed.

Would it be obvious if I ran with her?

I glance behind my shoulder at her father, and he's grinning like a fool.

"I'm going to go get another snowball and throw it at your face," I snip.

He places my mug on the counter and shrugs. "Might have to punish you for that."

My eyes widen, and he smiles. His bright-white teeth catch my attention, and my heart flops. "Oh, wait." He shakes his head with a deep chuckle. "I forgot. You like to be punished."

My jaw slacks.

He winks.

I cross my arms and pout. "You're breaking our deal."

Ellie's footsteps catch our attention. We both pause for a split second before he strides across the kitchen and stops beside me. He leans in close, but I refuse to lose this battle and move away.

"You started it," he whispers.

I've never been so captivated by a man. I'm stuck in place with his closeness. Energy flows through my limbs like he's the very air I breathe.

It's a *huge* issue.

One that I'm going to have to simply just get over.

Is it because he's the first guy I've felt comfortable with in such a long time? Is it because he makes me feel safe while also making me feel wild too?

"See you tomorrow, Sunshine." He sighs, and my hair moves with his heavy breath. "And if you lie in my bed tonight to watch the game, do me a favor."

Oh god.

"Don't wash the sheets. I like them smelling like sunshine."

The pounding of my heart is so loud I hardly hear him arguing with Ellie about her allowing him to braid her hair. He tells her that he's been practicing, and she reluctantly sits below his feet and lets him try.

I make a mental note to give him some more lessons—but most definitely with Ellie there as our chaperone.

———

"Here." I reach forward with the washcloth and wipe Ellie's face in the midst of her bubble bath. "You have paint everywhere."

She shrugs. "I like being messy sometimes."

I lean forward. "Me too."

"Is that why you like art so much?" Water splashes with her quick movements, and it sprinkles my shirt. Ellie makes a face. "Sorry."

"It's okay. I told you I like being messy." I dip the cup underneath the water and pour some on her head, washing away the rest of the shampoo. "And to answer your question, I like being able to express myself in ways that don't require me to speak aloud."

That rang true the moment Gramps grew ill. Instead of talking about it and breaking down like I wanted to, I turned to painting. I'd always been creative, so much that I set out to get my degree in art history, but in order to help Nana and stay strong for her, I used it as my outlet.

That was when I started to record the time-lapse videos of me painting. With the encouragement from Ruby, I posted them online, and I garnered *a lot* of attention. I sold paintings and got requests. It was exhilarating.

Shortly after the incident, I took all the videos down for my own safety and peace of mind.

There were a few lingering, but last I checked, I could no longer find them.

They're long gone, just like my dreams of selling in a museum one day.

"Why don't you like to speak aloud?" she asks.

I glance at the time. It's getting close to puck drop. I pull the plug on the tub and reach for the towel. "Well, do you like to talk about your feelings?"

She looks away. "Only sometimes."

I nod. "That's because it's hard to put into words what we feel sometimes."

I wonder if that's why Rhodes is so quiet.

Ellie digests this for a long time. She remains silent while I get her dressed in one of Rhodes's Blue Devils shirts and even as I pull the brush through her long, damp strands.

"Come on, you." I nod to her dad's bedroom, and she grins. She hops onto the bed and sits cross-legged in front of me, head tilted back, ready for a braid.

For a five-year-old, she's pretty crafty with the TV. She manages to turn it to the correct channel, and there on the screen are the Blue Devils warming up. I'm sure, just like me, she spots number 87 right away.

Butterflies fill my stomach, and my fingers stop weaving the strands of her hair.

"Sunny?"

"Huh?" I shake my head. "I mean, yes?"

"Do you have a mom?"

I pull my attention from the TV and stare at the back of her head. "Why do you ask?"

Her little shoulders rise and then fall a moment later.

I finish her braid in record time and pull her up toward the headboard beside me. She peers over at me with those same green eyes that her father has.

"Everyone has a mom," I say. "But like you, my mom passed away when I was a baby."

Ellie's eyebrows rise, and it's clear she has never met someone that shares the same type of grief. "Really?"

I nod. "But I don't know that I would say I don't have a mom."

The commentators start talking on the TV, predicting that the Blue Devils will lose the game because they're on the road. They go on to talk about Emory, the unstoppable goalie, and they bring up Rhodes too—about how he's become more focused in the last several games, which could work in their favor of coming out on top.

As soon as they're done, Ellie gives me her attention again. "What do you mean?"

My nana's weathered face pops into my head, and a dose of warmth moves to my heart. I pull out my phone and show Ellie a photo. "This is who I consider to be my mom."

"Who is that?"

"This is *my* babushka, though I call her Nana."

Ellie lets out a little laugh.

"She is the one who stepped in to raise me. She and my gramps."

"Oh." Ellie stares at the photo for a long time before she swings her sleepy face toward me again. "Kind of like you and my daddy?"

Um, wait, what?

I start to panic.

What if she tells Rhodes that I said I was her mom?

Oh god.

"Uh, well..."

Her face falls.

"You don't want to be my mom?" She turns away from me, and my heart crashes from the flinch of hurt moving over her features.

I grab onto her hand and give it a squeeze. "It's not that."

Her glassy eyes peek at me. She's confused, and I hope I'm not overstepping by what I'm about to say.

"My point is that the idea of mom can be different for everyone. It's not an easy spot to fill." I swallow. "But I'll do my best to be whatever you want me to be."

That seems to calm her.

"Here."

My forehead furrows. "What?"

She's staring at the photo of my nana. "I just want you to be here. With me. I don't want you to leave."

I glance at the TV and ignore the emotion clogging up my senses.

"I'll always be here." I get closer to her. "If I can deal with your grumpy daddy, I don't think anything will scare me away."

She giggles with me and hands me back my phone. "He's not as grumpy with you around."

I silently argue that she's wrong, but deep down, I know she isn't. I pretend like it doesn't make me happy, because why would it?

I glance at the time. "Hey...do you wanna meet my babushka?"

"Your babushka?" She sits up a little taller. "Your nana? Right now?"

It's not that late in Washington. She'll answer, and she's been dying to meet Ellie.

"Let's call her before the game starts. That way, you can meet my...*mom*." I use quotations around the word mom, and she nods excitedly.

My nana answers after the fifth ring, and surprisingly, her face pops onto the screen, unlike last time we tried to video chat.

"Hi, sweetheart. Aren't you a sight for sore eyes?"

I smile. "I could say the same. You figured out how to answer and have the camera facing the right way? I'm so proud."

My nana flicks a light on, showing off more of her tired face. "Well, you're the one who got me this fancy tablet. It's a lot easier to use. I appreciated the instructions too."

"What? I didn't get you a tablet."

She puts her hand up to her lips and thinks. "Well, your name was on the note."

Ellie slinks down beside me and smashes her lips together, like she's trying not to laugh. She hasn't even met my nana yet, and it seems like she has some secret with her.

"Do you know something about this?" I ask quietly.

Ellie quickly shakes her head and covers her mouth with her hand. Her eyes give her away, though. She's clearly amused by something.

"See!" Suddenly, there's a piece of paper floating in front of the screen. It's hard to read it with my nana unable to hold it straight. After focusing for a few seconds, I recognize his handwriting. My jaw drops. Did Rhodes send my nana a tablet with instructions on how to video chat?

I blink several times, trying to get over the hump of confusion.

I finally manage to say, "Oh."

Ellie is bursting at the seams, and it's hard to be perturbed when she's so giddy over this entire thing. "Yeah, um…"

"Is there a little person beside you?" Nana tries to look past my screen as if she can physically move the camera herself.

Ellie's face pops in view as she snuggles up close. "Hi."

"Oh my goodness. Look at you. She's as pretty as her father!"

Ellie's eyebrows cave. "My daddy isn't pretty."

Tell that to the entire female population, kid.

After several minutes of my nana and Ellie chatting about all sorts of things, I finally pull the phone back.

"Okay, Nana. I have to watch this game with Ellie before she heads to bed."

"I have the game on too!" she says.

I'm shocked. "The Blue Devils?"

She nods. "I have to keep up with them now that you're all the way in Chicago." Her mouth forms a line. "Oh, wait a second. Before you go…"

Worry fills me from the look of concern on her face.

"Is something wrong?" I quickly ask.

The puck drops on the TV, but I keep my attention on the phone. Ellie has crawled toward the foot of the bed. I tell her I'm going to get us some popcorn and that I'll be right back.

"Nana?"

"Yes, honey. Everything is great here. It's just that I had a visitor the other day."

I grab a bowl from the cabinet and put a bag of popcorn into the microwave. "A visitor? Who? One of your friends?"

She laughs. "All my friends are living in this place with me. This was someone looking for you."

I do a very good job at hiding the panic. "For me?"

My blood pressure spikes. Suddenly, I feel like one of those kernels about to pop in the microwave.

"Yes. It was a woman."

Oh, thank god.

I press my hand to my heart. "Oh, okay. Who was it?"

"Goodness, I can't remember."

Not wanting her to feel bad for her short-term memory loss, I shake my head. "Oh, don't worry about it. I'm sure it was an old friend or something."

I have *no* idea who would be stopping in to the nursing home to look for me. Not many people know that my nana is there or that I've moved.

"If I remember, I'll give you a jingle."

I laugh. "Okay, Nana. Sounds good. I love you."

"I love you too, sweetheart. I'll talk to you next week?"

I nod with a smile and hang up.

Ellie is sitting on her knees with her eyes trained to the TV.

"How's it going?"

She eyes the popcorn greedily. "Daddy is doing so good! He already got a point!"

I climb beside Ellie. We lie at the foot of the bed with our feet up in the air and the bowl of popcorn in between us.

"He already got a point?"

Ellie nods and shoves popcorn into her mouth.

That's two for tonight.

One for gifting my nana a tablet behind my back so that our video chats will work, and one for the Blue Devils.

Forty-Four

RHODES

IT'S LIGHTS OUT, though Emory is still on his phone in the other bed. We played a hard game tonight. So hard that I'm positive my younger teammates, the single ones, even Kane, have chosen to stay in instead of going out.

We're all tired. Emory from the blocks he had to make during overtime, and me from being one of three who had to participate in the shootout. The rest of the team is spent from their emotional turmoil of having to rely on three chosen players for the outcome.

Thankfully, it was worth it, and we ended up with the W.

My body aches from the long stints on the ice without a shift change, but I'm too wired to fall asleep.

I stare at my phone.

I shouldn't text her.

I shouldn't text her, because the reason I want to has nothing to do with checking in on Ellie and everything to do with toying with her some more.

It's addicting and dangerous.

My fingers jolt with an incoming text.

I grin to myself when her name pops up.

Speak of the little devil herself.

I quickly open the text and see a picture of Ellie sleeping in my bed with a braid slung over her shoulder and the blankets pulled up to her chin.

Out of the corner of my eye, I eye Emory.

Most veteran players who aren't on an entry-level contract get a room to themselves, but the franchise has had to adjust some funds around, and considering I'm team captain and not concerned with bringing some chick back to my room, I opted to volunteer as tribute—or whatever the fuck Malaki said when I stepped forward.

Making sure Emory isn't somehow reading my texts from across the room, as if I'm doing something wrong by texting Sunny, I type a message back that is, in fact, *wrong*.

> Me: Where's a pic of the other girl in my bed?

Shit. What the fuck am I doing?

I can't help myself.

Sunny brings out a side of me that hasn't seen the light of day in years.

Her text comes in with a photo of her sticking her tongue out. I know it's supposed to be a smart response to me asking for a picture, but I find it highly attractive. I'd like to grab that jaw of hers, pull her in close, and stick *my* tongue in her mouth.

I am so goddamn fucked.

> Sunny: In all seriousness, we need to talk.

And here it comes: *reality.*

She's going to tell me we can't keep doing this. I can't

blame her. In fact, I should man up and be the one to put a stop to it.

I just don't want to.

> Me: About?

I know very well what this is about.

> Sunny: Ellie.

Oh?

> Me: Is everything okay?

Again, there she goes. Surprising me.

She types for a while. The text bubbles pop up, disappear, and then pop up again. This happens for so long that Emory shuts his phone off and rolls over to sleep.

My heart rate spikes when her text finally comes through.

> Sunny: She asked me if I had a mom, and I explained to her that my mom died when I was a baby and that my grandparents were the ones who raised me. I told her that I considered my nana to be my mom.

I remember eavesdropping—I mean, *overhearing*—a phone conversation between her and her nana. Sunny's mother died shortly after her birth, just like Gia.

Ellie doesn't open up to just anyone, so the fact that she's openly asking Sunny these questions means that I'm not the only one who is beginning to trust her.

Sunny: But then she said something that I'm afraid she'll repeat to you and get twisted.

Well, this is getting interesting.

Me: Like?

Sunny: She compared my grandparents... to us.

Us. *Us.*

Why did my pulse pick up its pace at the thought of there being an us?

Sunny: Then she kind of got sad because she saw the shock on my face. She thought I didn't want to be her mom, and I panicked because she looked so hurt. I told her that the mom role is a very hard spot to fill but that I'd be whatever she wanted me to be.

I reread her text so many times the words blur.

Guilt crashes around me, which is unfair because I'm not to blame for this single parenting gig I've found myself in. However, I could also put in *some* effort to find a wife or a motherly figure for Ellie that isn't my hot, too-young nanny who has an entire life ahead of her.

Sunny: After a few minutes, all she said was the word "here".

What?

Me: Here?

Sunny: She said that she just wanted me to be here…with her.

Shit.

That hits hard.

I can't fuck things up with Sunny. If I do something that scares her off, she'll run, and Ellie will be devastated.

Me: That's good. She obviously has a connection with you.

So do I.

Sunny: I have one with her too. I just was afraid she'd tell you that I was the one who said I wanted to be her mom, and then you'd get the wrong idea and end up firing me.

It would take a lot for me to fire her at this point.

Me: The wrong idea?

Sunny: I don't want you to think I'm like all the rest. With us…you know… I just don't want you to think I have certain intentions.

I shouldn't keep toying with her. I really shouldn't.

Me: With us…what?

Sunny: You're going to make me say it, aren't you?

I smirk.

Me: No. But I'll make you type it.

I can almost picture her eye roll.

Sunny: And if I refuse? Play coy? Act like I can't remember?

I adjust my growing dick. I need to end this conversation right now.

Me: Then maybe I'll have to work it out of you.

Shit. I've gotta stop.

Me: Night, Sunshine. See you tomorrow. And don't worry, I won't fire you over your dirty thoughts of me.

———

Taylor Swift plays on the surround sound, and I can't help but laugh. I stand behind Ellie and Sunny unknowingly. I lean back onto the wall and flip my hat on backward.

It's hard not to smile while watching them.

Ellie, still in her school uniform, looking much more put together than when I get her dressed and ready, moves around on the couch like it's her stage. Sunny, with her dark hair piled high on her head, sings along to the song before twisting and grabbing onto Ellie's hand and making her spin on the cushions.

After Ellie completes the turn, I push off from the wall and clap loudly. They both freeze at the sight of me. Ellie runs over and jumps into my arms while Sunny smiles brightly in the same spot from before.

Our eyes snag.

My body burns like there's a wildfire between us.

"Come on, Daddy!" Ellie tugs on my hand.

"No way," I mutter.

Sunny pipes up. "Too afraid to show us your dance moves, Oscar?"

I narrow my gaze in her direction. Her smile is full of mirth, and I smell the bait from here.

I loosen the brakes and let Ellie pull me forward. She jumps onto the couch again, grabs the remote as her microphone, and starts blaring the words to the song.

Sunny stands with a cute grin on her face, cheeks painted with happiness. I raise an eyebrow and snap my hand out and wrap it around her waist. My other hand finds hers right away, and her wide eyes propel me to continue.

This is payback.

She wants to dare me to dance? Then she's going to dance with me.

The song isn't as upbeat as the one before, but the tempo is still fast enough that I can spin Sunny around and pull her back into my chest.

"You can dance?" she asks through a winded breath.

My mouth is right beside her ear. "I have many hidden talents, Sunshine."

She pulls away, turns, and then suddenly, we're only a breath away once more.

Space.

We need space.

Or maybe I just need space.

I squeeze her hand, and she backs away. I spin her once more, and when she comes in close again, her eyebrow arches. "Is one of your hidden talents gifting new tablets to elderly women?"

I look over at Ellie.

Did she tell her?

"I take that as a yes," Sunny says.

I won't admit it. I didn't do it so she'd find out and thank me.

In fact, why did I do it in the first place?

Was it to make her happy? Surely not.

"Can I pay you back?"

Yeah fucking right.

"No."

She rolls her eyes. "*Rhodes*."

"Sunny! Come on!"

We turn toward Ellie. Strands of her hair stick to her sweaty face, and her cheeks are red from all the energy she's burning.

"Get up there, Sunshine." I flick my chin to the couch. "Put on a show for me."

I don't mean for it to come off as dirty, but it does.

Something flashes over her features, and I wink.

Her scoff drives my smile deeper. I bend forward, wrap my hands around her waist, and haul her up onto the couch with Ellie. The look in her eye sparks something I feel in my bones, and it's most definitely because my fingers slipped beneath her *In my Picasso era* shirt and landed on her silky soft skin.

I remain unmoving while Ellie and Sunny dance and sing on the couch, giggling the entire time. Their laughter is louder than the song playing on the speakers, and when it ends, I find myself drowning in amusement.

Ellie beams with a youthful glee, and when I swing my attention to Sunny, she's radiating with joviality.

That's when I realize that it isn't just Ellie's happiness that makes me happy.

It's Sunny's too.

Which is fine.

Right?

It's fine because it means *nothing*.

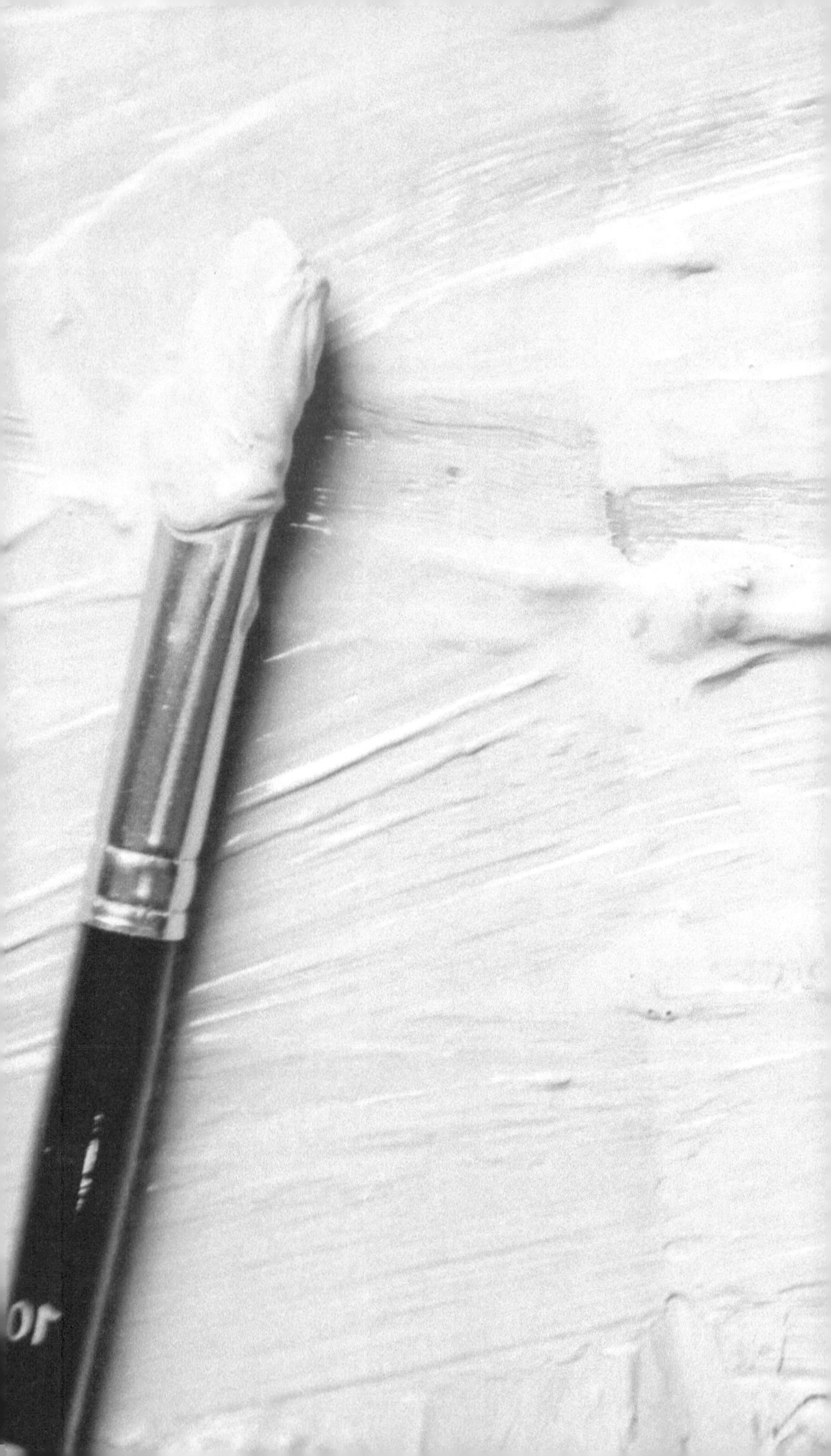

Forty-Five

SUNNY

USING MY FINGERS, I blend the two paints together on the canvas to create a one-of-a-kind color.

It isn't until I'm done that I realize the luscious forest color reminds me of something other than the pine trees I've used as a filler for the background.

Damn Rhodes and his flirty green eyes.

I can't get them out of my head.

Frustration backs every swipe of my paintbrush.

My pulse speeds with each thought circling. There's something about his presence that gets me all twisted on the inside.

I grab my phone and swipe his name away.

Instead, I text Ruby.

> Me: I'm dead serious when I say this…but I think my body is trying to make up for my abstinence.

My finger hovers over Rhodes's name in my messages.

I did the same thing last night.

I debated texting him until I convinced myself that it was okay to message him because it was about Ellie. Plus, it was a lot easier to do so with him in a different state. Tonight, though, he's just a few rooms away. It's much riskier.

My phone vibrates, and I nearly drop it.

I roll my eyes after reading Ruby's message.

Ruby: HAHAHAHAHA 😂😂😂

Me: Unhelpful.

Ruby: Go get some d, bestie. You deserve it.

I snort.

If only she knew I was semi-fooling around with the father of the girl I'm nannying that *she* begged me to move to Chicago for.

Before things turned sour, Ruby might have been more on board with the idea. She has always been the wild one of our duo. But after watching what I went through, I'm not so sure she'd be encouraging this.

I need a true fuck buddy. Someone I can turn to when I need to release some sexual tension, and then we go our separate ways.

It can't be like that with Rhodes, despite his promise of keeping things *physical.*

I have to be around him all the time.

We live in the same house!

It's fine.

I shush my subconscious.

It is not fine.

In an attempt to calm my racing thoughts, I get ready for bed.

Teeth brushed, hair pulled into a high pony, sleep shorts on.

But after tossing and turning for what feels like hours, I shove the blankets away and go back to painting another tree.

Sure enough, it's the same shade of green as before, which is impressive since I made the color on a whim. It's scarily similar to the color of Rhodes's eyes.

My teeth sink into my lower lip.

I wonder what he's doing.

Watching a hockey game downstairs?

Sleeping?

I stare at my cracked door. Butterflies fill my stomach when I think about him in his room, thinking about *me*.

Water.

I need water.

Creeping out of my bedroom on bare feet, I stare over the ledge of the banister.

He isn't down there. There's no faint sound of a hockey game or flickering lights, so I quickly pad on quiet feet and slink down the stairs one by one until I'm gulping cold water in the kitchen.

My nipples perk from the cool wintery air seeping underneath the back door.

Their alertness has nothing to do with my memory of the last time I came downstairs for water.

After placing the cup in the sink, I tell myself to go right back to my room.

Except, there is something pulling my attention to his bedroom door as soon as I take the last stair.

With each step down the hallway, my body grows warmer.

I pause outside his room.

What the hell am I doing?

A voice distantly fills my head as I stare at the closed door.

No one will believe you, Allison. I'll just tell them that you came onto me and then wanted to turn it around so you'd get money out of me. You're a slut, Ally.

His threat is a bitter reminder of who's in charge, day in and day out. Would anyone even believe me if I spilled the truth? Ruby believed me, of course. And my boss. But the league? The world? Rhodes?

Just go back to your room, Sunny.

My shoulders fall, and I force myself to head in the direction I came. I hate that I'm allowing someone who doesn't deserve any part of me to control my actions again, but—

"Sunshine."

My soft gasp fills the quiet hallway. I press a hand to the wall and stare at the very half-naked, dark figure standing mere feet in front of me.

"Rh–Rhodes," I stutter. "What are you doing here?"

He gets closer, and I run hot.

"What am I doing here?" Shadows move over the dips and valleys of his bare chest. "Well, I live here..."

I clear my throat but talk quietly with Ellie sleeping a few rooms down. "I mean..."

"What are you doing lingering right outside my door?"

"Nothing."

I said that too quickly.

His raspy chuckle zips down my spine.

I think fast on my feet. "I was...coming to see if I could borrow some toothpaste."

Great save—never mind the toothpaste taste in my mouth already.

"Oh?"

Why does his voice have to be so...attractive?

"And I wasn't lingering."

I *so* was.

Was he watching me? God, he probably was. For how long? Long enough to see me argue with myself, I'm sure.

"I'm beginning to think you enjoy lying to me." He casually leans his bare shoulder against the wall. The closer he gets, the more I can see: shirtless, too many abs to count without staring, and low-hanging black sweats.

He's quite possibly the hottest man I have ever seen.

My mouth runs dry, but in between my legs is anything but.

"I'm not lying." I glance away.

"Toothpaste, was it? That's what you needed?"

"Mm-hmm." I nod quickly, still keeping my attention far away from his.

Rhodes has been around me too much. He's beginning to see right through me. I don't trust that he won't spot my lies the second our gazes crash.

He pushes off the wall, and I let out a shaky breath.

"Okay, follow me."

He believes me. *Whew.*

I turn and follow behind him. We walk into his dark room, and it takes everything in me not to glance at the bed. The moon shines brightly through the far window, but I keep my back to it and walk over to his bathroom to wait.

The light flicks on, and my heart races. All I can think about is him being naked in here.

He calls over his shoulder as he rummages for the toothpaste I most definitely don't need. "Ellie told me she had fun at the studio yesterday."

I nod while staring at the muscles rippling on his back. *Wow.*

"Oh, yeah? Good. I had fun too."

"She wants me to go next time."

A small smile creeps onto my face. "I'd honestly pay money to watch you spin pottery." I giggle, and he grimaces at me over his shoulder.

"You don't think I could do it?"

I shrug. "It's a lot harder than it looks."

He's definitely going to make it a point to go now. I already see the challenge brewing.

"I'm good with my hands," he says, walking toward me with a tube of toothpaste in his hand. "Something you already know."

His eyes dart to my mouth, and I'm suddenly winded.

"Here's your toothpaste, Sunshine."

I reach forward. "Thank y—"

A squeal rushes from the pit of my stomach. I'm suddenly flush with Rhodes, and he inhales deeply before pulling back, keeping a hold on my wrist. "You *did* lie."

My eyes grow wide.

"Minty." He leans closer. "Fresh." He sniffs the air. "Breath."

Oh no.

"Want to tell me what you're actually doing here, Ms. Edwards?"

My breaths are choppy, and the room spins.

His throaty chuckle brushes against my neck. "Don't be shy. Just tell me what you want."

He pulls back and stares into my eyes while keeping a gentle grip on me, one arm around the small of my back, the other holding my wrist hostage. There's a flirty glint in his eye, but the flickering of his jaw tells me that he's just as hungry as I am.

"I don't want you to think I'm a slut." I wince when the word leaves my mouth. "This isn't something I do, and with your past experience..."

Shock moves across his features. A line digs in between his eyebrows, and the vivid green color of his eyes darkens.

"That's the last thing I'd think of you." He sighs. "I touched you, and it did something to both of us." His pupils dilate as he gives me a once-over. "Might as well get it out of our systems before one of us snaps."

I relax into him, and his eyes flare.

"It doesn't mean anything," I state, letting him back me out of his bathroom.

He shakes his head and pushes me to sit on his bed. "Of course it doesn't."

"And we tell no one." My legs spread slightly with the gentle push of his hands on the insides of my knees.

"Not a fucking soul," he mutters, leaning over me. "I'd never live it down."

Neither would I.

The soft glow of the moon is the only thing separating us.

Rhodes draws his lower lip into his mouth, and he stares at me from above.

I've never felt more desired in my entire life.

"You remember your safe word?" His voice is raspy and tight.

I peer up at him. "Dah."

His mouth curves with my Russian.

My heart flies so fast it may take flight.

"Relax, Sunshine. I've got you."

Forty-Six

RHODES

SUNNY IS such a sweet little thing...until I have her like this. She's panting, and the heat coming from in between her legs is so enticing I couldn't stop even if I wanted to.

Just to be clear: I don't want to.

Touching takes the edge off. I've never been sated from a single brush of skin before.

I get closer to her, leaning onto my bed. My leg slides in between her open legs, and it's taking everything in me not to press my knee into her just so I can feel how wet she is.

"I want to kiss you," I rasp.

My fingers grip her chin, and I stare into her golden eyes. She rolls her lip into her mouth and traps it there with her teeth.

"Okay," she finally says.

The plop of her lip hits my ears, and I go for the kill.

My fingers tighten on her delicate jaw, and our mouths touch. There's a sudden pull in my stomach, and I'm overwhelmed. I press gently at first, easing my tongue into her mouth, but as soon as she flicks hers against mine, I lose myself.

I go in for more, too hungry to stop myself. She arches her perfect body toward me, and I can't get enough. The kiss deepens, and our hot tongues tangle together, giving me a tantalizing glimpse of what's to come.

A sexy noise slips from her, and I'm short of breath.

I pull back, exhale, and curse in Russian.

Her eyes widen, but there's a flirty look buried inside of them.

She's mine.

For the night, of course.

"Take 'em off." I back away and nod to her shorts and panties.

Her movements aren't rushed, and I'm not sure if she's teasing me or if she's hesitant. I slowly move her hands out of the way and take over.

She's naked from the bottom down, and my mouth waters.

I move to her shirt next. My hands glide around her waist, just to get a feel of her smooth skin, and I remove the thin cotton from her body and drop it to the floor.

I have my Sunshine at my mercy, and I swear the sun has touched my soul.

"It's been a very long time since I've had a naked woman in my bed, but I'll do my best to be gentle."

Sunny kneads her lip with her teeth. "What if I don't want you to be gentle?"

I shut my eyes for a brief moment before staring down at her. I give her knee a light squeeze and press it down onto the bed, opening her for my own viewing pleasure. "You're not ready for me at full force, Sunny."

I slowly trail my finger against her thigh until I find her

center. I linger there, embracing the warmth, and finally give in. The moment I dip inside of her, she whimpers.

God damn.

Her pussy is so responsive and willing to let me explore. I glide in and out, watching the pleasure smooth against her features. A sexy noise fills my bedroom, and my eyes glaze over.

"So perfect," I whisper in awe.

Her nipples pucker from my compliment.

She likes praise.

"I could watch you all day, Sunshine."

I'm so hard it hurts, but watching her twist with need is too addicting to stop. I lean down and blow a hot breath on her nipple before pulling it into my mouth. She arches off my bed, pushing her breasts closer to my face. I move to the other side and give that breast the same attention before backing away to watch her some more.

Her eyes are hazy with lust, and those rich, thick waves of hair surround her pretty face like she's some sort of angel.

My nostrils flare with an urgency to fuck her, but if this is a one-time thing, I'm going to take my sweet time.

While keeping my sights on her, I push another finger inside of her tight pussy. A sweet gasp fills the space between us, and her legs widen.

"Such a good girl," I coax, giving her more praise.

"*Rhodes.*" My name on her lips does something to me.

The edges of my vision go black when I see how wet she is.

"You're making quite the mess, baby."

She moans quietly below me, hips moving to meet my fingers.

Fuck, she's the hottest thing I've ever seen.

I know she needs more, though. I can tell by the writhering of her body beneath me.

I slowly pull my hand out from between her legs, and her eyes flutter open.

Being as hungry as I am, I pop my fingers into my mouth and lick them clean.

She watches and parts those lips of hers, almost daze-like.

"Let me clean you up, and then we can get to the best part." I fall to my knees and grip her thighs a little harder than I mean to. My fingers dig into the soft flesh, and I cover the entirety of her pussy with my mouth. I suck hard on her clit, and she moans.

"Quiet, Sunshine. We're not the only ones in the house, remember?"

She stills. "So-sorry." The apology comes out slurred, like she can't form words.

Out of the corner of my eye, I watch her hands grip the blankets.

She's all worked up and truly mine to play with.

This is the only time I'm allowing this to happen, so I'm going to savor every single fucking touch.

I place a kiss on her clit and trail my nose up her thigh. "You're my new favorite thing to eat."

Her hot gasp hits my ears, and I almost come in my pants.

I nip the inside of her leg, and her hips buck.

Oh, she likes that?

Sucking her skin into my mouth, I let go when I know she has a mark and kiss it again.

There.

She's marked.

That'll be a little parting gift to remind her of what we did.

I stand up quickly and shove my pants down, freeing myself. Sunny, still spread open for me to see, props herself onto her elbows and watches me grip my cock. I throw my head back when I squeeze myself.

I don't want to come yet.

I want this to last all night.

I want her in my bed when the sun comes up.

"Look at what you do to me." I open my eyes and see her entirely too close to my dick. She's sitting on the end of the bed, staring up at me like she's mine for the taking.

I wish she wouldn't look at me like that.

It's going to trick me into thinking this isn't a one-time thing.

Sunny's hand reaches out hesitantly. The moment her fingers swipe over the head of my dick, my knees grow weak.

She wipes the precum off the tip and then places her finger into her mouth.

My jaw slacks.

I'm too dumbstruck to ask her what she's doing when she stands on shaky legs and opens the drawer on my bedside table.

A condom appears in her hand.

I cock an eyebrow. "Did you snoop in my room, Sunshine?"

She glances away shyly. I love the blush creeping up her neck.

I pull the condom from her hand and tear it with my teeth before quickly rolling it on. I'm wasting no time at this point, and it's purely because I am out of fucking control.

It's torture not having her in my grasp.

The pull between us is like a rubber band, too taut not to attempt to loosen it.

I grip her hips and gently toss her onto the bed. I position myself over her, and she openly spreads herself wide for me.

"Lie to me and say you didn't snoop," I tease. "That way I can punish you."

A sexy smile appears. "I didn't snoop."

I'm right there, at her entrance. One hand falls to the headboard to steady myself so I don't hurt her, and the other wraps around her waist. My greedy fingers dig into her hip bone, and when the tip is in, she throws her head back and starts to pant. "More."

I hum under my breath. "You want all of me, Sunshine?"

It takes every ounce of restraint I have not to plow into her. I want to fill her so deeply she feels nothing but me. There is a possessiveness brewing in my blood that I'm going to be forced to hide.

"Yes." She's breathless.

I struggle to breathe too.

"In that case, let me go as slow as possible." *Edging.* I'm going to edge her so fucking much that she'll be crying for me to fuck her by the end. "You know, as a punishment."

I also don't want to hurt her. She's so damn tight I feel like she's constricting my dick with every inch that glides inside her.

"It's too..." Sunny's words fade as she moans. She angles her hips. *Fuck, is she going to come?*

Unable to resist, I rub circles against her clit with my free hand. My thumb presses down, and a noise leaves her that I'll respectfully keep in my spank bank for the rest of my life.

"You take me so well, Solnushka." *Ah, there it is.* The Russian term for sunshine.

"Rhodes." My name is more of a whine, and it sends me to the red. I rub her clit faster, and her hips start to circle.

"Finish for me, baby." My teeth clamp onto her earlobe, and I pull on it. Her head rolls to the side, and I tug again.

It doesn't take long for her to break. I'm not even fully inside of her yet, and she's coming. She is *so* receptive, and I refuse to ask if this is how it always is for her, because I want to believe that she's only like this with *me.*

I grab her chin to pull her face back down so I can watch her. Her eyes are closed, but her jaw slacks with pleasure.

I cover her mouth with mine because I can't hold back any longer.

The kiss is hot as hell. Consuming and feverish. I practically choke her with my tongue, but she's so willing to accept it that she meets me halfway. It unlocks something deep within me, and I push farther into her. My hand tightens against the headboard, and once I'm all the way inside, I drop my head to her forehead and break our kiss.

"Don't forget your safe word," I warn. "I'm not going to be able to hold back."

The way her lips turn upward is such a tease. I move in and out, fucking her so hard the headboard hits the wall.

"Fuck." I grit my teeth.

I glance around the room. Where can I fuck her without making too much noise?

She moves under me, wanting me to keep going.

A deep chuckle rumbles from my chest. "So needy," I mutter. "I fucking love it."

Swooping her up without letting us slip away from one another, I wrap her legs around my waist and brace her against the wall. Her hands curl around my neck, and she presses those perfect mounds into my face.

My lips wrap around a nipple, and I suck hard. Sunny presses herself closer, and my dick goes even deeper.

My knees buckle. Thank god the wall is at her back.

I shove her into it, and she loses her breath.

Pulling back, I look down and watch as I enter her over and over again.

"Look at how we fit," I mutter.

I can't stand it.

It's like having a piece of heaven in my hands.

Sunny's hair falls in between us when she looks down. I pull out slowly and ram into her over and over again. The longer she watches, the tighter her pussy becomes.

I do something I'm not sure she'll be on board with, but

given the fact that she's trusting me enough to fuck her like this means something.

While holding her steady with one hand clamped beneath her thigh, I grab her wrists and press them above her head. They're so tiny in my large grip that I'm able to trap them both to the wall.

Her moan is music to my ears.

"You do like being trapped," I whisper in admiration.

I angle my hips, and she tightens around my cock. I move faster and faster until she's coming all over me.

My name is a wispy breath falling from her mouth, and I catch it with mine.

I plunge my tongue in deeply and fuck her so hard I can't see anything *but* her.

"Fuck." My voice is hoarse and strained with pleasure.

I spill my hot cum into the condom for what feels like hours.

I'm still pressed into her when I back us to the bed and collapse. We lie still for so long that the sweat on both of our bodies dries.

"That was…" I swallow roughly. *Hot. Chaotic. Staggering. Life-blowing. Not enough to curb the desire.* The wrong fucking move.

I shouldn't have fucked her, because now, it's all I want to do.

She whimpers when I slowly pull out of her, and I refuse to let myself believe it's because she wants me back inside.

Shit. This is bad.

She falls beside me on the bed and curls onto her side. It takes everything in me not to glance at her bare breasts. "Thank you," she whispers.

"Thank you?" I repeat.

Suddenly, she's her warm, sweet self again. She's back to

being my Sunshine, and after what we just did, I'm not sure which way I prefer her.

I'd take both. Any day of the week.

She nods shyly.

"For giving you multiple orgasms or for breaking your abstinence streak?"

A playful smile appears, and it's official, I've touched the fucking sun. "For both."

There's a funny, unfamiliar feeling burrowing itself into my chest, so I quickly get up and head into the bathroom. After disposing of the condom, I wet a washcloth with warm water and bring it to her.

She looks surprised.

"I'm a gentleman, remember?"

With gentle pressure, I place the damp cloth in between her legs and clean her up.

After I finish, she slowly stands and begins to get dressed. I grab her panties and shorts and slip them back onto her body after she tugs on her shirt. I smile to myself at the mark on her thigh, knowing she'll find it later and remember how she got it.

I hide the amusement and push her messy hair over her shoulders to give way to her face.

She's fully sated. Her features are soft, and her lips are swollen. It's painful to think that I'm making her go back to her room. But this was a one-time thing, and how would we explain her in my bed when Ellie wakes in the morning?

"*Sladkih snov,* Sunshine." I rub the pad of my thumb against her high cheekbone before she turns and heads out my door.

She's all I think about when I close my eyes to sleep, and I have a feeling it won't be the last time.

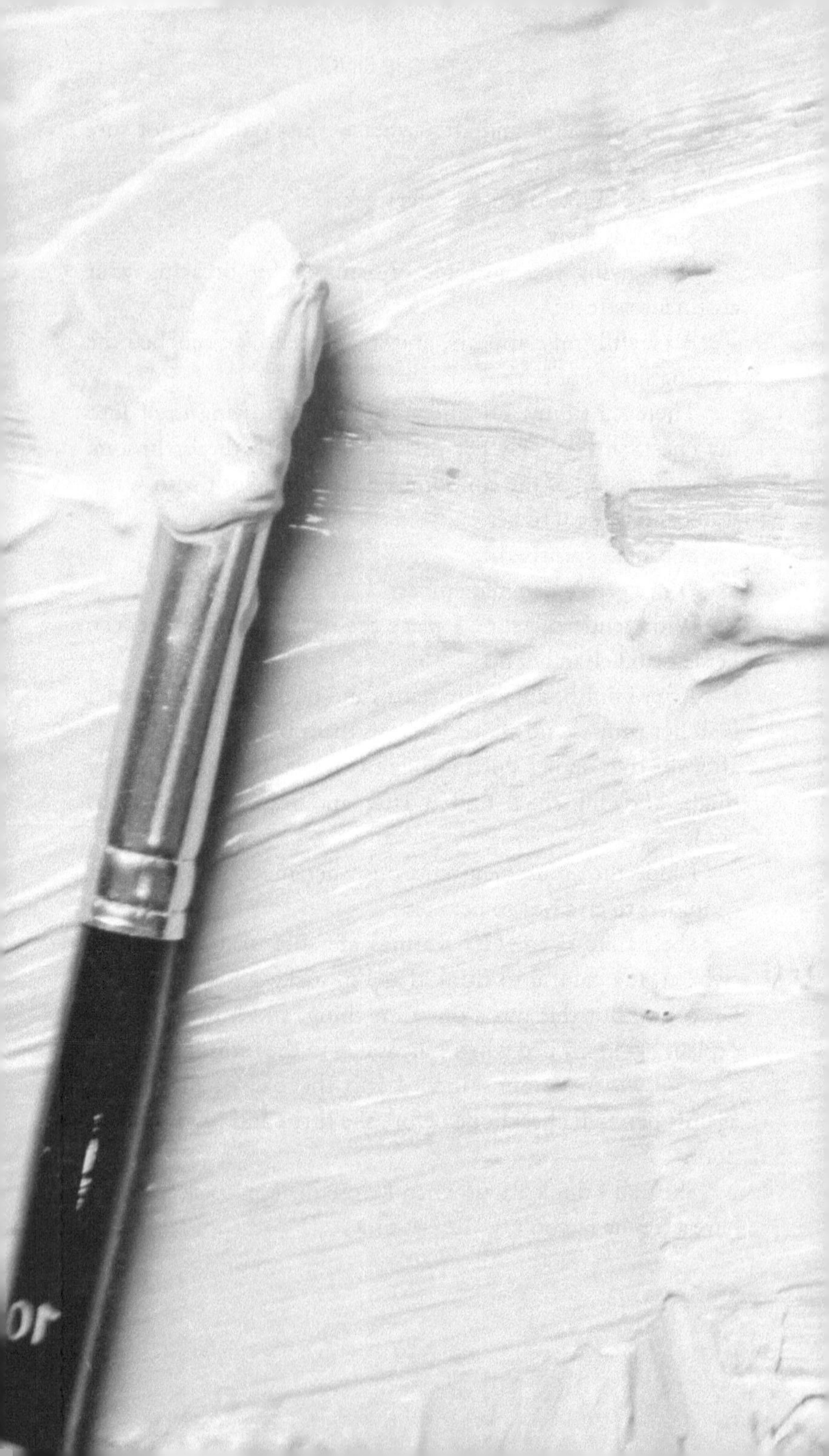

Forty–Seven

SUNNY

IT'S GAME DAY, which means Ellie is up with the sun, holding her Blue Devils bow in her hand, patiently waiting for the game, although it's hours away.

Her little feet kick back and forth while she eats her blueberry pancakes—blueberries for the Blue Devils, of course—and with every little noise she hears, she perks up and gets ready to shout, *"Go Blue Devils!"* the second she sees her dad.

I am also perking up with every little noise I hear. Except, I'm perking up for all the wrong reasons, those of which I will keep under lock and key.

Last night was impulsive and sporadic.

The last few times Rhodes and I have been alone together, we've blurred the lines. It hasn't been on purpose, from either of us, but our chemistry is palpable. Now that I've let him in, I'm having a very hard time keeping him out.

He was the first thing I thought about this morning.

And then again when I hopped out of the shower and saw

what he left on my thigh from our little *escape*. I grew giddy at the thought of his hands on me again.

Except, there won't be an *again*.

The few times we've crossed the line are a few times too many. We're both mature enough to recognize that.

"Go Blue Devils!"

I spin at the sound of Ellie's high-pitched cheer. Hot coffee splashes out of my mug and onto my hand. A hiss slips from in between my teeth, and the mug clanks to the counter.

Rhodes is over to me in seconds. He takes my hand in his and inspects it with that heavy browline of his.

"You okay?"

I nod quickly. "I'm..." I clear my throat and push thoughts of last night out of my head. "I'm fine."

Our eyes meet, and I freeze. His lip tugs at the side, and it's obvious that he's thinking about last night too.

How can we not?

We're *touching*.

Finally, he drops my hand and walks back over to Ellie. I regain my composure quickly and grab my phone as a distraction.

La, la, la. Nothing to see here.

I'm staring at my phone, but I can't comprehend anything on the screen.

My mind is too captivated by Rhodes's voice and his conversation with Ellie about the game.

I glance at the two of them sitting at the island. Rhodes steals some pancakes from her plate.

Before I know what I'm doing, I'm placing a plate of blueberry pancakes in front of him.

He looks at it and then to me. Something unreadable flashes across his face.

"I made enough for you too," I say. "Gotta get you ready for the game." I wink at him, attempting to be casual.

He is stoic.

What is he thinking?

He stares at me for so long I grow uncomfortable.

Eventually, he takes a bite of his pancake, and now I'm the one who can't stop staring.

His eyes close, and he inhales. It's scarily similar to what he looked like last night when he was dick-deep inside of me.

My face grows warm.

I quickly put my back to him.

He chuckles, but I choose to ignore it and pull up our schedule for the day as a distraction.

"So..." I turn and land on Ellie instead of Rhodes, which is difficult because he's standing above her, braiding her hair with concentration.

"Yeah?" he asks, not bothering to look up from his task.

It's cute, watching him focus on something so insignificant to many, yet it means so much to him.

"Today is the anniversary of Marco's wife's..."

Passing.

It's a hard day. One that he'll always dread.

Rhodes glances at me briefly. "I know. I arranged for flowers to be sent to the grave."

He did?

"You look surprised."

I smooth my face. "I'm not surprised."

The look he sends me over his daughter's head goes right in between my legs. His eyebrow hooks, and the flirty twinkle in his eye tells me he knows I'm lying, and that brings up a whole new set of thoughts.

"What kind of flowers did you send, Daddy?"

Ellie does her best to sit still as Rhodes attempts her braid. She winces a few times, and I quietly laugh. Eventually, I walk over and help.

I slip underneath Rhodes's arms and am sandwiched between Ellie's back and his front.

Instead of taking over completely, I place my hands on top of his to guide his fingers. His slow swallow hits the back of my head, but I pretend I don't hear it and help him braid.

"Sunflowers," he says.

A shiver rushes down my spine. He takes a step closer.

Sunflowers?

Because of me?

"Every other strand," I say, moving Ellie's hair in between our hands.

His presence is too much. He leans forward to get a better look. "Got it." His breath hits the side of my face.

I turn my head slightly, and he's *right* there.

My eyes grow wide.

We can't be near each other. Not until last night wears off.

I hastily pull my hands away, drop down like there's a fire, and crawl out from beneath his strong arms.

My hair whizzes past my face when I pop back up.

Rhodes is grinning to himself.

I sort of want to throw my coffee mug at him because he's certainly not helping the situation.

"Anyway," I start with a stern voice. "I asked Scottie to pick Ellie and I up for the game since Marco needs the day." *To grieve.*

Rhodes catches my eye.

"Is that okay?" I ask.

He nods slowly and puts his attention back on Ellie's hair.

The braid isn't bad. I'm proud of him.

"You could just take my truck," he says, grabbing the bow from the counter and tying the end of the braid with it. Once he's done, Ellie hops down and runs to the bathroom to check her braid in the mirror.

"Your truck?" I'm shocked. "You trust me enough to drive the second love of your life?"

The first being Ellie, of course.

I suspect some type of humorous response or a glint of amusement in his green eyes, but instead, I get the serious version of him. He walks away for a second and comes back to the kitchen with his keys in hand. "I trust *you*." He reaches across the island. "I thought I made that clear."

He lifts his palm, revealing the keys. Before I can pull them toward me, he traps my hand there. A spark jolts me.

"Don't wreck it," he warns. "And you'll have to wait for me after the game so we can leave together. I'll have one of the guys pick me up while you take Ellie to school this morning."

The heat from our hands touching rushes to my cheeks.

Rhodes observes me, and when he smirks, I know he knows.

Last night didn't get him out of my system.

Not even in the slightest.

As soon as he lifts his hand, I back away with his keys pressed against my chest.

I can't get away from him fast enough.

He looks disappointed but pleased at the same time.

I can't help but say something.

"Stop looking at me like that," I demand.

"Like what, Sunshine?" He glances at Ellie through the opening in the kitchen.

"Like you're thinking about last night," I say quietly.

Those green eyes darken, and I lose my confidence. "Of course I'm thinking of last night," he admits. His palms lay flat on the counter, and he drops his head. "You're going to have to be the reasonable one."

My phone vibrates against the counter, but I can't be bothered to look at it. "The reasonable one?"

He flicks his gaze to me, and my heart flips. "You're going

to have to tell me no when I come begging." A swallow moves against his neck, his Adam's apple catching my attention. The veins on his arms start to bulge like he's already having a hard time holding himself back.

It should scare me.

But it entices me.

His gaze lazily makes its way down my body, and butter-flies fill my stomach. "Because trust me, Sunshine." He pins me with a dark look. "I will come begging."

My mouth parts, and he notices. He curses in Russian—something I recognize now—and turns to stalk toward Ellie.

This is messy.

I'm the one who has to keep it together?

How the hell am I supposed to do that?

I sigh and glance at my phone with dirty thoughts continuing to dance inside my head.

But as soon as I see an unfamiliar text, they disappear.

The grip on my phone grows heavy. I reread the message on the screen and grow nauseated.

Unknown: Is this Ally Edwards?

Ally.

My phone slips through my fingers and crashes to the floor. I catch the eye of Rhodes and Ellie both staring at me from the living room.

I play it off well and dip down to retrieve it.

Before standing upright again, I exhale and get my bearings together.

Not many people call me Ally, and if it's him, there's no way I'm texting back to let him know he has the correct number.

I quickly block the number.

There.

At least one problem is solved.

I brush away my nerves and busy myself in the kitchen.

I woke up this morning full of giddiness because of Rhodes, but now, I'm full of dread, which is probably just the wake-up call that I needed.

Forty-Eight

RHODES

"VOLKOVA!" A line of guilt slams into me like I've been caught doing something I shouldn't be.

I can thank fucking my hot little nanny for that.

Might as well get it out of our systems...

That came from me. I was the one to say that line of total bullshit. I lured her onto my bed and stripped her bare in an attempt to scratch an itch that I *knew* would only get worse. Now, I'm on edge.

"Yeah, Coach?" I stand, half-dressed for the game. I've been here since we watched films this morning, catching a ride with Malaki since I gave Sunny permission to drive my truck.

"Get in here for a sec."

I catch the eye of Malaki while walking toward Coach's office. He shrugs, and I turn away because, either way, whatever Coach has to say, I'll keep to myself, despite my closer friendship with some of my teammates.

"Close the door."

Now I'm intrigued.

I make sure the door latches and sit in the chair at the foot of his desk.

It takes me a second to realize that this is the first time I haven't immediately tensed with dread at him pulling me aside. My first question is always, *Is everything okay with Ellie?* But lately, I haven't had the notion to even think that.

I know she's okay if she's with Sunny.

"As team captain and someone who has been on this team long enough to see players come and go, I want your opinion."

I remain expressionless and stay silent.

"I'm thinking of bringing in some help."

I lean forward. "Some help? Like some more players for the reserve?"

Coach shakes his head. He leans back and starts to chew on the end of an ink pen. "A skills coach." He pauses and lets me digest this. "We're good this year. Our points are stacking, and we're slotted for the wild card for the first time in a long time."

This makes sense.

I knew the team funds were being rearranged, and this must be why.

I nod in his direction. He's right. We're tighter this year than we've ever been. The media has been saying that it's because we traded Juke and gained an even better goalie, but I've seen tidbits of Kane's lethal ability to fake out the other team with his shots on net. It's probably a bit of both.

The media has also mentioned that I'm more focused than ever.

They're not wrong. Thankfully, they're not aware of the reasoning as to why I'm more focused, but I am. The entire team is focused, though they're still going on about their bullshit of me fucking Sunny to stir things up.

Little do they know...I have fucked her.

"Okay." I nod. "What kind of skills coach are we talking

about? Offense? I'm assuming that's why you're calling me in here."

That will mean more practice. At the beginning of the season, I would have argued that I couldn't add extra time in the rink to my already hectic life with Ellie, but now that I have someone I can rely on and trust, I'll do what it takes to bring the team to the next level.

Since learning that I was a father—a single one, at that—I've felt torn. It was either I gave my all to her, or I gave it to hockey. Over the years, the two have had to share. But now with Sunny in our lives, it doesn't feel like that.

Coach sighs, and it pulls my attention back. "Our defense is strong, especially with Olson as our goaltender. I'd like to gain some more points to put us into the playoffs. We need to hone our skills."

I nod. "I'm on par with this."

"Good." Coach places his elbows on his desk and steeples his fingers. "Now, I have a favor."

It's never good to ask someone for a favor. Doesn't he realize that means he'll owe me?

"Shoot."

"I want you to poke around and ask your former teammates, friends, whatever"—he wafts his hand in the air—"what they think of Washington's former skills coach."

Washington.

And just like that, I'm thinking of Sunny again.

I run through Washington's players—those that I know. "I can ask Blacky."

We played together in college. He's a good guy and would give me the truth.

Coach nods. "Let me know as soon as possible."

"You said *former* coach?"

Why former?

"He was relieved of his job duties, but I know that doesn't mean much when it comes to franchises."

True.

"I'll ask and get back to you." I stand and leave the locker room.

I keep to myself while I get ready for the game. For some reason, there's a fire in my blood tonight. Sunny's face slips into my head, and the fire burns brighter. Is it because she'll be watching me tonight? Is that why I'm so eager to do well?

No.

It has nothing to do with her and all to do with just wanting to play well for the team.

I tighten my skates.

Yeah, keep telling yourself that.

Before heading onto the ice for a warm-up, I check my phone one last time.

My pulse thrums when I read her name on the screen.

> Sunshine: If you see a scratch on your truck, no you didn't.

My jaw clicks. *What?*

I can't read her next message quickly enough.

> Sunshine: KIDDING. Just texting to let you know we're here. Good luck!

I really hate that she makes my lips twitch.

> Me: You think you're funny?

She texts me back right away.

> Sunshine: Ellie thinks I am.

> Me: Well, I don't.

I retie my skate to give myself something to do while I wait.

I wouldn't want anyone to know I'm taking my time climbing onto the ice because I'm waiting for my daughter's nanny to text me back, right?

Sunshine: I think you do.

She's right. I do. I've laughed more with her than I have in a long time.

Me: You know what happens when you lie, right?

If I had to guess, she's blushing right about now.

Sunshine: It was a joke!

The team is starting to head out for warm-ups.

Me: It's almost like you want me to punish you.

Sunshine: I do not!

I stand on my skates. Excitement rushes to my fingers at the thought of seeing her in the stands.

Me: Another lie? Whatever am I going to do with you?

Without waiting for her to text, I fire off another.

Me: I'll let you think about that while watching me score a goal or two.

My phone vibrates as soon as I set it in my locker. I grab it with eager hands.

> Sunshine: If you score, maybe I'll let you
> punish me.

Wrong thing to say, baby.

I told her she was supposed to be the rational one, but I'm so fucking glad she isn't listening to my nonsense.

> Me: Challenge accepted. 

I shut my locker and head for the rink with a lot more confidence than I typically yield.

She wants me to score? Consider it done.

———

Unpopular opinion: I love when we go into overtime.

The crowd is hyped, my team is hungry for the win, and our opponents are testy. It makes for an active and engaging game.

There have been fights, shitty calls, and a whole lot of chirping.

The clock is ticking down, and the rookies are being eaten with nerves.

It's a good thing I'm not a rookie, though.

Kane moves too early on the faceoff—or so the ref says. I swoop in and take his spot, having a damn good percentage of winning them, despite not doing them as often as our centers. I catch the eye of my current enemy, who's looking a little too smug in his teal jersey. I wink, and it throws him off. The puck drops, and I'm the first to connect. It slips out to the left, heading right for Malaki.

We skate like we're on a mission. Malaki, one of the fastest players in the league, zips down the ice, and I follow after him. I block the noise out and focus. Skating toward the corner of the net, I stand with a vengeance and wait patiently for the perfect opportunity.

Malaki fires it off to Kane, and for a second, I think he's going to overturn it, but Hayes is there to swoop it up. It goes back to Malaki again. Adrenaline rushes to my hands. I grip my stick tightly, wind back, and as soon as the puck comes into play, I fire it off to the upper left side of the net.

I don't even have to see it to know it went in. I have the confidence of a player who has been in the league for years, and I know when my shots hit and when they don't.

The guys circle around me and slap me on the back. I grin, unable to keep the smile at bay.

"A fucking hat trick to win overtime?" Malaki grins like a fool. "Now you're just getting cocky."

He throws his stick in the air, and it blends with the falling hats from the crowd. The lights of the stadium flicker back and forth, and my name blares through the speakers from Gary and Rickie, our commentators. I skate forward and head over to Emory.

"I don't know what has gotten into you, but keep it up," he says.

I know very well what has gotten into me. We bring our helmets together like we do after every game, and then I start toward the bench. I stop in the midst of dodging the ice girls and their cleanup of all the hats.

Two blue ribbons catch my eye in a sea of icy dust and hash marks. Slipping my glove off, I swipe them off the ice and hold them in my grip. I glance at the suite, and there she is with my daughter on her back, smiling wildly. Her hair frames her face, messy from undoing the braid to throw her ribbon to the ice.

I try to hide my grin, because I know damn well the camera is on me. It doesn't stop me from holding up three of my fingers though.

Three.

Three goals, Sunshine.

I want to make sure she knows.

She rolls her lips, and I know she's hiding a smile behind them.

I head to the bench where my teammates are waiting for me.

If anyone caught the moment, no one says anything, which is good, because I'm not sure I'll be able to deny lusting after my nanny at the moment.

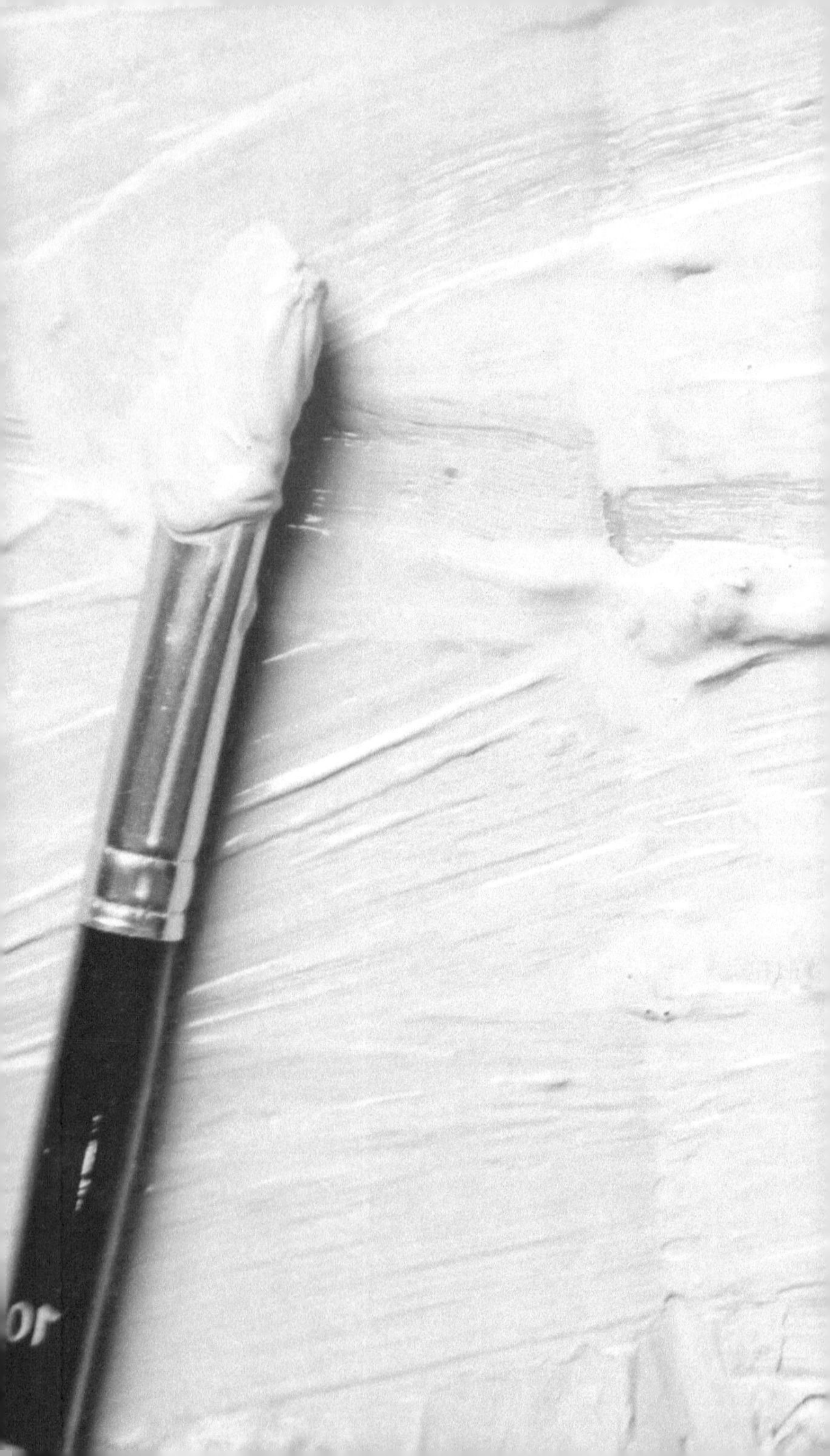

Forty-Nine

SUNNY

ELLIE POUTS in between Scottie and me while we wait for Rhodes to be finished with his post-game interview.

"I'd wait here," Scottie says. "Sometimes during the interviews, they'll swing the camera around, and then Ellie will end up on TV."

I internally freak out. I've been jumpy since the text, and the very last thing I need right now is to end up in the media.

"That's okay." I drop to Ellie's level. "We can entertain ourselves, right?"

"Or…" Scottie bends down and whispers in Ellie's ear loud enough for me to hear. *"Go ask grumpy Emory if he'll take us for ice cream to celebrate the win."*

Ellie beams and runs over to Emory. She taps him on the leg. and he looks down at her with a look of annoyance that we all know isn't real. That's their bit. He acts annoyed with her, and she softens him. It's cute. "Will you take us for ice cream to celebrate the win?"

"Do the lip thing!" Scottie shouts from beside me.

Emory flicks his gaze to his wife, and she smiles.

Sure enough, Ellie plops her bottom lip out, and Emory rolls his eyes. "You think you deserve ice cream?" he asks her.

She thinks for a second.

Despite her father being a millionaire, she isn't spoiled like some of the children I've met over the few years of nannying.

"No," she says. "But I think you deserve it."

Emory smiles, which is sort of rare. Just like it is with her dad.

"How can you say no to that?!" Scottie exclaims.

I laugh.

Emory shakes his head. "I can't." He looks at me. "Ice cream?"

I look at Rhodes's truck keys in my hands. How do I get these to him and let him know that we're going for ice cream without passing by the cameras?

"Do you want to take her since I have Rhodes's keys?" I ask. "I drove his truck, and he wanted us to wait for him after the game. I'm sure he's fine with you taking Ellie for ice cream, and then by the time you are done, we should be back at the house?"

He nods. "Solid plan."

"Are you okay with that?" I ask Ellie, making sure she's comfortable with going with Scottie and Emory without me. I'm certain she is, since she's pretty comfortable with them.

She nods excitedly, and I place a quick kiss on her head.

"Let's go through the back, munchkin." Emory kneels, and Ellie climbs onto his back for a piggyback ride.

I turn to Scottie. "Do you need a booster seat?"

A smile overtakes her face, and she shakes her head. "Emory bought one for Ellie a while back. It stays in his car."

"That's...so cute." And surprising.

These grumpy hockey players have a hidden soft spot, and it goes by the name of Ellie.

Scottie's cheeks ripen with a blush. "It is cute." She leans in and gives me a quick hug. "I'll see you in a few! If you go through those doors, they should let you wait for Rhodes."

I follow her instructions but still plan to steer clear so I don't end up front and center on the sports channel by accident. I could go out to Rhodes's truck and wait, but I'm on edge. The thought of being alone in a dark parking lot makes the hair on the back of my neck stand up.

The security guard lets me through, recognizing me right away. I follow the sounds of reporters and the clicking of cameras. As soon as I hear his voice, my stomach fills with butterflies.

Great.

That's a terrible sign.

"Tell us about your driven focus lately. You've been noted to be quicker, more alert, and more precise with your passing and scoring." The woman reporter pauses with a giggle. "Obviously."

My face scrunches when they come into view. Her hand is on his shoulder, and annoyance cuts right through me. Since when do they touch the players?

Since when do I get jealous?

Rhodes glances to her hand, and she quickly removes it.

He clears his throat. "Yeah, well I've straightened out some of my priorities, and it's helped me tighten my skills and focus on the ice. We've been running some new plays, and I think with each win, our momentum gets stronger."

"You guys definitely have some momentum," she says. "Especially you with that hat trick."

I suck in my cheeks. I teased him earlier and egged him on to score, and sure enough, he did.

Times *three.*

I slip backward, afraid of the camera swinging toward me, and wait until they finish the interview. Not wanting to make an appearance and cause rumors to swirl, I press against the tiled wall near the locker room and twirl Rhodes's keys in my fingers. I practice acting cool and unfazed by this three-goal game.

With the shuffling of feet and low murmurs, my pulse starts to race. Any second now, I'll come face to face with him, and I'll have to act like our entire text exchange never happened.

As soon as he rounds the corner, every one of my senses sharpens.

He spots me right away, and his eyebrow rises. "Are you hiding from me?" he asks.

I scoff. "Why would I hide from you?" As if I didn't tempt him to score goals and *punish* me earlier.

His hand disappears into his sweaty hair as he brushes it off his forehead. "Should I bring up our texts?"

Please don't. "I was just trying to steer clear from the cameras," I admit. "Not you."

Concern burrows in between his eyebrows. "Oh, right." He quickly glances around, and I know he's looking for Ellie.

"Emory and Scottie took her for ice cream to celebrate the win."

His tense jaw loosens.

"That's okay, right? I said she could go with them, and by the time we get home, they should be bringing her back."

He presses on the locker room door with his large hand. "Yeah, that's fine. You didn't want ice cream?"

I scrunch my nose. "Well, I have your keys, and I didn't think you'd be okay with me making you walk home."

Rhodes snorts. "That'd definitely call for a punishment."

That's twice he's brought it up in the last thirty seconds, and I have no one to blame but myself. It's easy to flirt through texting, but now I'm having to face the repercussions, and it's *really* hard to act normal.

"You can wait in here." Rhodes pushes the locker room door open farther and inches his chin for me to follow.

"In there?" I squeak. "I can't go in there."

He laughs under his breath. "The team has cleared out. It's just me."

That sounds like an awfully dangerous invitation.

One that I will willingly take.

"Okay." I slip through the crack in the door and wait until Rhodes directs me where to sit.

Only, he doesn't.

I stand near the door and stare into the vast locker room. Their team colors cover the walls, and to my surprise, it doesn't smell musty or like sweaty hockey gear. Instead, it has a scent of masculinity and cologne.

"You can sit, you know."

I flick my gaze to Rhodes. He stands in front of his locker and sits to take his gear off. I squint when I catch sight of a colorful picture hanging up inside it. I find myself walking toward it with a smile on my face.

A rainbow is arched above what I think is an ice rink with three stick figures. One has insanely long legs and is holding a hockey stick, and the other is a little bit smaller with a big smile on her face. Then, in between them, is an even smaller figure with a big blue bow in her hair.

"She drew that shortly after you started as her nanny."

I glance at him. He has the audacity to sit on the bench with nothing but the lower half of his body covered. His pads and jersey are on the floor near the bench beside his pile of hats from the fans. I can't stop staring at his rippling back muscles as he continues to undress.

I should've waited outside.

When I pull my attention to his face again, he's staring at me. He swallows loudly, and I hear nothing but my heart racing.

"That's…" I clear my throat and look back to the picture. "That's adorable."

He sighs. "She's your biggest fan."

I make a noise of satisfaction.

"Besides me."

I shoot him a look and laugh sarcastically. "You hated me when I first started."

A cheeky grin appears. "I hate everyone at first." He glances at my mouth. "It usually stays that way."

"Don't tell me," I tease. "I'm just too sunshiny to hate."

I expect him to chuckle and say some witty remark, but he suddenly turns grave. His dark brows lower, and he squints those green eyes, surveying my face. "Pretty much, Sunshine."

My smile slips.

The locker room is too quiet. He's bound to hear my racing heart soon if I don't put space between us.

Panicking, I step backward, but the bench is there. A rushed breath flies from my lungs as I prepare to fall, but naturally, Rhodes and his hockey-like reflexes work their magic, and he's there to catch me.

"I swear that was not planned," I quickly admit.

I land in his lap, and all I feel are his strong thighs beneath me. My hand grips his arm resting against my stomach. He stares down at me with a wildly excited look in his eye that does nothing but send my stomach into a frenzy.

I scramble to get away, but his arm tightens.

Instead of it sending a line of fear into my blood, it sends an ache in between my legs.

"What are you doing?" I whisper.

"Making sure you're okay." He keeps a hold of me, and I make no move to escape.

A breath falls from my lips. "I'm fine."

He eyes me with skepticism. "Are you? You've been awfully clumsy lately. A little jumpy too."

I hate that he's noticed I'm jumpy.

Rhodes drags his hand across my lower stomach. I resist the urge to shiver.

"Want to tell me why?"

No.

My lips part when he grabs my hips. Suddenly, I'm flung upright and straddling his lap. I place my palms onto his bare shoulders, and thoughts from last night flood me.

I scan every inch of his face. He's perfectly imperfect and so damn hot. It's hard to ignore his sharp jaw and sexy mouth hiding that teasing tongue.

"You make me scattered," I admit.

His forehead wrinkles. The grip on my hips becomes steadier, like he's trusting that I'm going to stay put. "Scattered?"

I slowly nod and spill the truth. "When we're this close, it's hard for me to think rationally." He scoots me closer, and my entire body flushes with heat. His bare chest presses against the jersey he bought me, and he tenses his jaw. "Last night was supposed to be a one-time thing," I say.

I swear he can touch me with his gaze alone.

"But then you had to go off and tempt me to score some goals to *punish* you," he chides.

My heart stops with the flick of his feverish glare.

"Do you remember how many times I scored?"

Of course I do. I start to shake my head but stop when he opens his mouth.

"Don't do it," he warns, digging his fingers into my sides. "Don't lie to me."

My mouth slowly opens, and my answer falls in between us. "Three."

"You know what that means?" His voice is throaty and hot, like he's trying to hold himself back.

"What?" I'm breathless.

"I score three times..."—he dips his head—"*you* score three times."

My breasts grow heavy. To settle myself, I press my fingernails into his bare shoulders slightly. "That doesn't sound like a punishment."

The look on his face darkens, and I'm pretty sure the thoughts in his head are just as filthy as mine. He sighs. "You're supposed to tell me no, Sunshine, not tempt me further."

I shift over him, and he grits his teeth. His forehead falls to my chest, and my lungs beg for air.

"Your heart is racing." His voice is muffled, strained even.

"That's what you do to me when you touch me," I admit quietly.

I have never been like this with someone before. The way he touches me does something to my body. It's addictive, and I don't know if it's because he's the first person I've let touch me in a very long time, or if it's just Rhodes himself.

He stares at me.

I suck in a breath.

"That's what you do to me when I *think* about you, Sunny."

Neither of us say anything for a few seconds. He shifts his eyes back and forth between mine, and I can't help it. I break.

My heart skips a beat when I press my mouth to his.

It surprises him, but as soon as I slip my tongue inside, his hand cups the side of my cheek, and he pulls my face closer.

I kiss him with an urgency I can't control, and he kisses me back just the same. Our mouths are glued. Not even a breath can pass through. I whimper when he moves me against him, bringing our bodies closer.

God, it feels so good to be possessed by him. He calls the shots without even speaking. My tongue mimics his, my body doing whatever he makes it do. We kiss until we get our fill of each other, and when he pulls apart, we're both out of breath.

I don't feel like myself, and I think that may be a good thing.

"It still means nothing," he presses. "This is just me helping you get over those fears you have of men, okay?"

His nostrils flare, and I nod quickly.

Both of us know this is just an excuse to touch, but I don't think either of us care.

"You said you like being tied up, right?"

Anticipation fuels me to answer. "I used to, but—"

He interrupts me. "I know, Sunshine. He ruined that for you." His tongue slips out of his mouth and wets his lips. "Don't worry, I'll fix what he broke."

My body weakens, like it's willingly handing over the power to Rhodes.

While keeping me on his lap, he leans to the side and swoops something off the floor. My mouth twitches at the blue ribbon in his hand. The same blue ribbon I had in my hair before Ellie and I threw them to the ice after his hat trick.

"Thanks for the ribbon, baby." Any trace of humor that was on his face is long gone and replaced with something much more dangerous. "Now get up and turn around."

Fifty

RHODES

I TURN HER AROUND, too impatient to wait for her to follow my commands. I'm out of control, the adrenaline from the game still flowing through my veins in desperate search of a release.

She only makes it worse.

Or better?

I keep ahold of her wrists with one of my hands and move us over to the locker room door. I flick the lock, and as soon as the sound echoes throughout the empty space, my dick grows harder.

The showers come into view, and Sunny glances back at me.

Her sunshiny vibe is dimmed by something much hotter, and it's enough to make me act out of character. *Clearly.*

There are multiple shower heads placed along the blue and black tiled area. As men, we don't care about privacy, so there's nothing but an open space I'm working with. We're short on time, but with Ellie taken care of, I'm not in that much of a rush.

I drop her hands, but only for a second. Blood rushes to my fingertips with the need to touch her, kiss her, fuck her, *all of it.* Pulling the ribbon taut, I wrap it around her delicate wrists and pull them up above her head. I watch her the entire time, making sure she's still with me and not revisiting an old memory that I wish I could erase from her head. Her white teeth sink into her bottom lip when she catches my eye. *Oh, she's with me alright.* That flirty glint will haunt me for the rest of my life.

It takes me a few seconds to tie the ribbon into a knot around the shower head. With her arms above her head, it exposes her entire body for me to survey.

The only problem?

She isn't naked.

I strip down into nothing but my boxers. A soft whimper falls in between us, and the things I want to do to her are worrisome.

It would take hours for me to touch her the way I want to.

We don't have hours.

Every time we find ourselves in a compromised situation, we're on borrowed time.

One of us is bound to put a stop to this eventually, and it won't be me.

"Tell me to stop if you start to panic, okay?" I step close and cup her cheek. Her fluttering eyelashes tell me that she isn't panicking. She's the furthest thing from being afraid, and it means something to me that she trusts me to do this to her.

Why does that make me so happy?

I flick the button of her jeans through the hole and shimmy them down her smooth legs. "I wouldn't want you to get your clothes wet," I tease.

My heart falls to the pit of my stomach when I step back.

Holy hell.

She's in nothing but panties and my jersey with her long chestnut waves spilling over her rising chest.

"I've gotta admit," I say over my shoulder as I walk to the opposite shower. I turn the nozzle on and stare at her through the stream of water. "I've never been a fan of a woman wearing my number, but seeing you in nothing but my jersey sends me through the fucking roof."

She shifts on her bare feet, and the sexiest little smile curves against her lips. She runs her hot gaze down my body as I step into the warm water.

Seeing her like this makes it hard to remember all the sweet parts about her.

It's the best of both worlds.

She seems so innocent at times, but that look in her eye tells me she knows her body much better than I thought. My Sunshine wants to touch the sun again, and I'm here to give her just that.

After some taunting, of course.

A hiss of breath hits my ears when I strip my boxers.

Our eyes crash, and I grab onto my hard cock.

My muscles are still pumped full of energy from the game, and my veins bulge the harder I grip myself.

"Seeing you tied up like that does something to me." I fling my hair out of my face and step out of the shower so she can see me better.

She swallows while staring at my moving hand.

I shift up and down slowly, watching her become winded.

Her shaky sigh is music to my ears.

"Something wrong, baby?" I tease.

Her gaze flies back to my face, and I grin. Those pretty cheeks of hers are red, and her cute nose scrunches with frustration. "Nope."

My eyes flare. "I think you lie to me on purpose."

I drop my hand and stalk over to her.

Steam begins to fill the open space, and little droplets of moisture cover her skin. I grab her around the waist and angle her closer to me with her hands still trapped above her head. I wanted her to watch me a little longer, get really worked up and beg me to touch her, but it seems like a punishment for me too, so I scrap that plan.

Skimming my hand down the side of her thigh, I grip it hard and wrap her leg around my waist.

The only thing separating us is her panties, and with my dick slick with water, it'd be so fucking easy to move them to the side and slide right into her.

"So soft," I whisper, moving my mouth against her ear.

I'm hungry for her. So hungry I bite down on her earlobe and give it a tug with my teeth.

She arches into me as much as she can with her hands tied above her head.

My palm makes its way to her ass, and I give it a squeeze before slipping in between her legs and pressing onto her sweet, sweet cunt.

"Do you want me to touch you here?" I swipe my fingers against her panties, and she whimpers. "Or here?" I move up and flick her clit.

"Both."

"Or maybe you want my mouth down there?"

I watch the dirty thoughts move through her head, and I see her breathing pick up.

I fall to my knees. "Mouth it is."

I hook my fingers underneath her panties and pull them off swiftly.

She bucks with each flick of my tongue.

"*Rhodes*," she whines.

I bite her thigh and fling her leg up onto my shoulder. I make a mistake and take a peek at her. Her head has fallen backward, and all I see are her wrists tied and her white-knuckling the shower head.

"Yes, solnechnyy svet?" *There it is.* That little pet name in Russian.

I skim my nose up her thigh, knowing damn well I'm teasing the hell out of her. Heat pools in between her legs, and she's so wet I get lost. I lick and suck her clit into my mouth until I can't stand it anymore. I press two fingers into her, and her hips start to move against my hand.

"That's it, baby," I encourage. "Let me hear you."

I watch with rapt attention. Her body moves against my hand, and she moans. I move to kiss her, but she flicks her chin and stares at her hands trapped. "Untie me."

I pause and raise a brow. "Untie you because you're afraid, or untie you because you're so turned on you can't stand it?"

I wait for her safe word.

But it never comes.

Her warm eyes darken, and she moves herself faster over my hand.

I smirk and lean in to kiss her.

It's a sloppy kiss. My tongue explores her mouth, and I wrap my other hand around her neck.

Not enough to send her into a fearful state but just enough to get her attention.

She constricts around my fingers.

Her moan is loud and hot.

"There it is." I break away from her and watch her chase the high. "Look at you letting go for me...and while being tied up. *Such a khoroshaya devochka.*"

She explodes when I call her a good girl. Pleasure paints her face while she comes, and it puts me into a trance.

"I have never seen something more perfect in my fucking life," I say in awe.

I love watching her come.

It sends me to a high that I've never reached before. Ever.

Why is this so good?

I have never in my life wanted to give the reins to a woman, but I could lie on this wet tiled floor and let her fuck me until the team came barging in the next morning for practice.

Unable to wait any longer, I pick up both of her legs and press her onto the tiled wall.

"That was one orgasm." Every one of my muscles strains, even my voice. "Now you owe me two more."

Her eyes flutter open, and I'm at her entrance.

I don't have a condom.

But I don't care.

With the way she opens her legs farther, I don't think she does either.

I shove inside her and stop breathing. My head falls to her shoulder, and she rises up a little more, using the shower head as her anchor.

"*Fuck*," I groan.

She's so warm and tight. It's a perfect fit.

I dig my fingers into her bare ass and move in and out as slowly as I possibly can without losing my control. My balls tighten when I bring my hands up to her waist, diving beneath the jersey. Her rib cage expands in my grip, and I suck on her neck before pulling back and whispering sweet nothings into her ear.

Actually, they're not sweet.

They're downright fucking dirty.

"You feel so..."—I pull back and slowly enter her again— "fucking good."

She makes a noise in agreement. "So..."—her breaths are choppy—"do...you." A whimper leaves her, and I think she's winding up again. "How?" she whines. "I've never... I feel consumed by you."

I grin against her neck. "I don't fuck like normal men, Sunshine."

A sweet moan leaves her, and I reach underneath her bra. I pinch her nipple, and it hardens against my palm.

"If someone is worth a fuck, she's going to get my all."

She's worth so much more.

I'm out of control, possessive, and downright fucking addicted.

Her legs clamp onto me, and I move my hand to her other breast. I play with her nipple, and my name breathlessly falls from her lips.

"You're fucking killing me," I admit. "Each time I get a taste of you, I want more."

I pull out of her, and her eyes flare. I shove into her quick and hard. She gasps, and I catch it with my mouth.

That's right. You're mine.

For the time being.

I kiss her like I mean it.

I kiss her like I own her mouth.

It's possessive, and she can tell.

It makes her come, and it makes me high.

My pace picks up, and I can't stop myself. I ram into her over and over again while her pussy squeezes the life out of me, and before I know it, I'm pulling out of her and coming onto the tiles behind her.

I finish myself off while digging my fingers into her side, and truth be told, I think I black out.

What the fuck was that?

I look at her, dick still in hand, come sliding down the wall slowly as our only audience.

"Well," I rasp. "I think it's safe to say you don't mind being tied up any longer."

An amused breath leaves her, and the color on her cheeks sends me into overdrive.

Sunny all tied up, freshly fucked with a shy smile on her face that I put there?

Yeah, this isn't going to be the last time I touch her.

We can call it whatever the fuck we want, but the truth still stands: Whenever she wants to use me, I'm hers.

Not to mention, I owe her one more orgasm.

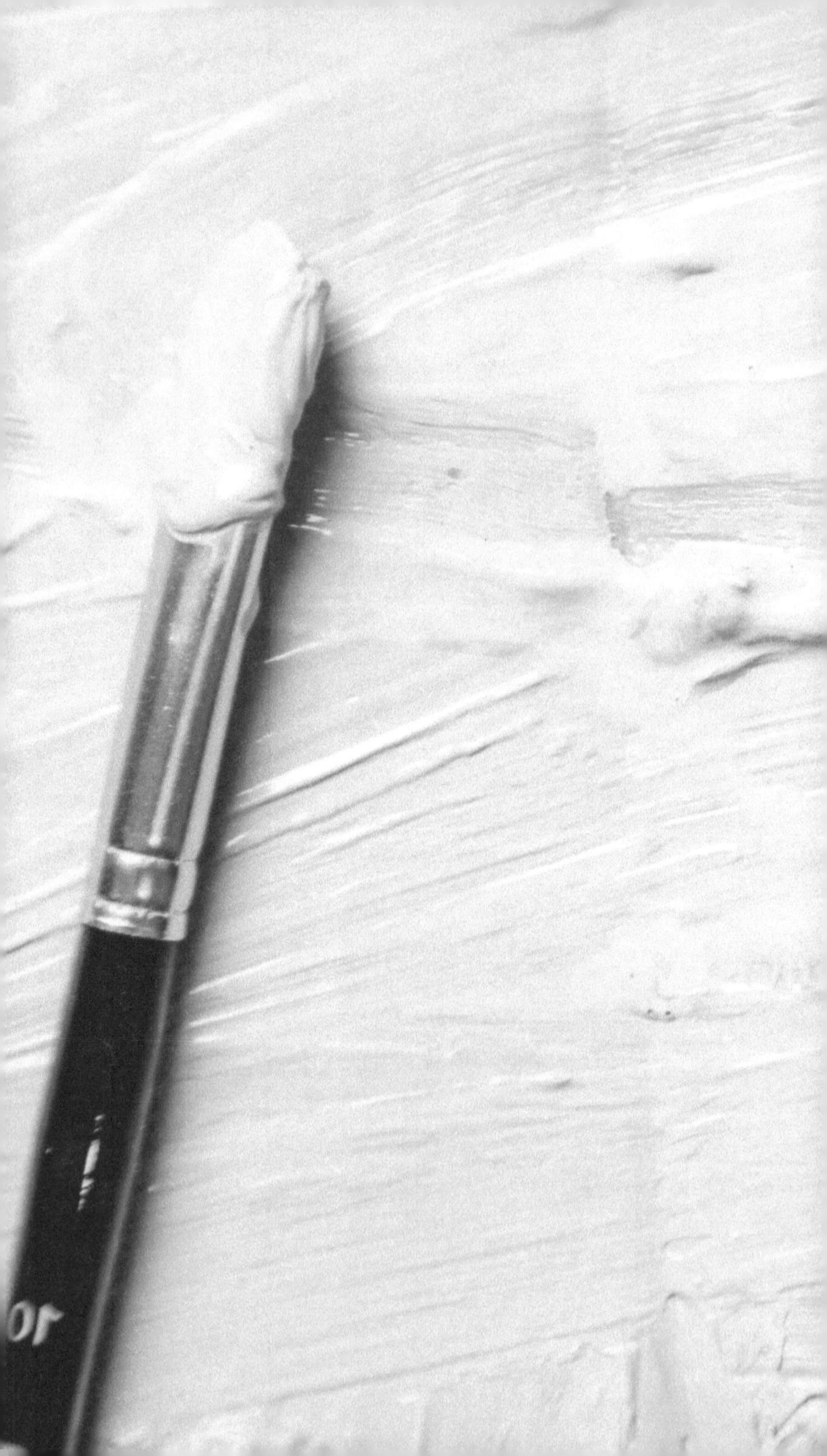

Fifty-One

SUNNY

"WHAT HAPPENED TO YOUR WRISTS?"

Rhodes and I both glance at my wrists with Ellie standing in between us. Her eyes are wide with concern.

I hastily pull on my sleeves. "Uh, I...um..."

Rhodes places his hand on my frantically moving ones. "It's just a rash."

A rash?

A rash from him tying me up in his locker room and completely messing with my head? In that case, yes, it's a rash.

"Should we take Sunny to the doctor?"

"No!" I exclaim. "I'm fine. It'll go away."

Rhodes snickers but hides his amusement with his coffee mug.

I could hardly look him in the eye this morning.

After we drove home, both of us masterminding a good excuse as to why we were showing up late with my jersey damp from Rhodes's wet chest pressing against mine, we went our separate ways. I'm not quite sure if Scottie and Emory bought the explanation, but either way, I fell into a blissful slumber.

This morning, I was hopeful he was already on his way to the away game, but to my surprise, he was downstairs, making blueberry pancakes with Ellie before school.

"Yeah, Printsessa," Rhodes muses. "The rash will go away."

My cheeks are hot. I shove pancakes into my mouth to keep my jaw from unhinging, but as soon as Rhodes's smile deepens, I know something else is coming.

"Who knows when it'll show back up again, though. Rashes have a tendency to reappear."

I almost choke.

I slap my hand on the counter, and naturally, he comes over and pats me on the back.

"You good, Sunshine?" he asks, lowering his voice slightly. "Do you need mouth to mouth?"

He chuckles as he rounds the island again.

Rhodes thinks he's funny, and I really hate to admit that I like this version of him. Aside from me and Ellie, and maybe a few of his teammates, he keeps his teasing, carefree attitude on lockdown.

His airy mood is too enjoyable not to play along.

"Ellie, why don't you go upstairs and get dressed, and then I'll braid your hair before school? I have an early flight so we can get to the rink and get in a practice before the game."

Ellie hops down from her stool and gives him a thumbs-up before dashing away and up the stairs on her own.

I spin and glance at him with shock. "Wait, did that just really happen?"

His eyes widen. "She didn't even say anything about me leaving."

Some parents may be upset by that, but with Ellie's anxiety over being away from Rhodes, this is *huge*.

My hand moves to cover my smile. "I'm so proud of her."

"It's because of you."

I drop my hand and start to shake my head, but he doesn't let me get that far. He places his mug onto the counter and rounds the island. I spin on the stool and face him with skepticism.

What is he doing?

I glance over his shoulder to the stairs as he crowds me. One hand falls to the counter, and I lean backward. The other one does the same, and suddenly, I'm trapped between his large arms and heavy presence.

"Thank you." He swallows.

I blink a few times. "For?"

"For fixing what I couldn't." He shakes his head, appearing vulnerable for the first time *ever*.

I brush it off. "Well, you were the one who hired me despite not wanting to, so technically, you're the one who—"

His hand falls to my chin, and I stop talking.

"Thank *you*."

With the gravity of his voice, it seems like he's thanking me for more than just Ellie.

Which makes me thank him in return.

"Well..." I shrug. "I fixed her, and you fixed me. I guess we're even."

His thumb grazes my lower lip, and my heart races. He glances at my mouth, and if he kisses me, we're in *big* trouble, because what can we blame it on this time?

The moment is too heavy between us.

Too real.

As much as I want him to kiss me, I'm thankful when his phone pings, telling him that someone is at the door.

A slight growl leaves him, and he reluctantly pulls out his phone.

He glances at me once before walking toward the front of the house.

I escape upstairs to help Ellie, only to come back down ten minutes later to Rhodes having an intense conversation with Marco. Except, it's in fluent Russian. *Marco knows Russian?*

I look at Ellie, and after a few more seconds of us eavesdropping, she pouts. "I don't know that many words in Russian."

"Maybe we should listen to some tapes tonight," I say with a laugh.

Rhodes catches my eye and does a double take before ending his conversation with Marco.

Ellie turns her back to her father and taps her finger against her chin. "Or come up with our own secret language."

Rhodes snorts. "The last thing I need is you two having your own language."

Ellie giggles and runs off to pester Marco about knowing Russian. She scolds him for not teaching her certain phrases.

"Everything okay?" I eye Rhodes closely.

He glances at Marco and Ellie, seeing that they're in a heated conversation, and inches his chin toward the living room.

Once we're tucked away, he says, "Make sure you lock the door tonight and set the alarm, alright?"

My brows fold right along with my arms. "I don't need to be reminded to do that," I remind him.

He sighs. "Just tell me you will."

"I will."

A dark cloud of dread heads my way. I'm already on edge because of the text, which Rhodes is unaware of, so why is he acting so protective?

"Did something happen?" I ask.

He stares down into my eyes and answers quietly. "Nothing you need to be concerned about."

I attempt to ask him again, but my thoughts jumble when he slips his hand around my waist and pulls me in close. I forget where I am when his mouth covers mine. Our tongues dance together, and I'm suddenly spinning.

Ellie's loud laughter breaks us apart.

I lick my lip, and he winks.

Then we part and act like nothing happened.

Something absolutely did, though.

I'm just not sure what.

————

I reread the text I got from Rhodes for the third time, and I'm still confused.

Slipping away from Ellie and Marco, who are finishing up a game of Uno before we head to dinner—something Marco insisted on—I read the message again.

Rhodes: Excuse me?

After not being able to decipher what Rhodes is talking about, I text back.

Me: What?

He must have his phone in hand because I hardly hit send before he's firing off another message.

Rhodes: You're going on a dinner date?
Tonight?

I think for a second and then suddenly realize what he's referring to.

I swipe the texts away and pull up the calendar. I put *"dinner date"* in the calendar so he'd know what we were up to with him being states away, but apparently, he isn't aware that Marco is the one taking Ellie and me out for dinner.

He thinks I'm going on a date.

Is he jealous? Or angry?

Does he really think I'd go on a date tonight? With him away and Ellie in my care?

I'm almost offended.

My nose scrunches.

You know what, I *am* offended.

Typing bubbles pop up, then they disappear. I begin to type furiously, angry that he thinks I'd leave her, but then the bubbles pop up again, and my phone vibrates.

Rhodes: Cancel your date.

I thought he knew me better than this.

I hit send on my previously typed message and wait.

Me: You must not know me very well.

Rhodes: Maybe not. But I know your body, and let me tell you, no one else will touch you like I do.

Heat sprinkles against my skin because I know he's right.

My phone starts to ring, and my stomach drops.

I attempt to hold my composure and answer.

"Calling to demand something else?" I tease.

"Who's watching Ellie while you go on this *date*?"

A laugh tries to slip from my mouth. The way he says the word sounds like he's about to strangle me through the phone.

"Rhodes," I drag his name out. "Are you seri—"

"Why are you..." He softens the anger in voice before pausing. "Why are you going on a date?"

Is he hurt by this?

I open my mouth to tell him that I'm not going on a date, especially while he's away and I'm responsible for his daughter, but he cuts me off again.

"Do you want to find a boyfriend? Or do you just want a hookup with someone who isn't the father of the girl you're a nanny for?"

The thought of going on a date with someone makes me antsy—and not in a good way.

He starts up again. "If it's a boyfriend, then fine. Reschedule the date for a night that I'm home."

My thoughts are all over the place. Do I want him to be angry at the thought of me getting a boyfriend?

"Why? Are you going to make sure he's up to your standards?" I meant it as a joke, but I hear the hint of irritation in my tone.

"Yes." I hear some shuffling in the background, and then I hear him call out to someone, *"Give me a minute."*

"And if I say it's the latter?" Curiosity is getting the best of me. I'm tempting him to say something that he can't take back, but it's something I desperately want to hear.

"Like you just want to find some guy to hook up with?"

"Yes."

He scoffs. "Then what I said earlier stands. Cancel your date, Sunny. I'll be home tomorrow, and I'll take care of you."

Butterflies fill me to the brim. My heart flips at the thought.

"I gotta go. The bus is leaving for the arena." His tone is clipped.

"Wait! Rhodes," I rush.

"What?"

"I'm not going on a dinner date with some guy. Marco is taking me and Ellie out for dinner before your game starts. I put it in the calendar because I wanted you to be aware of what we were doing since you're away." *There.*

Silence.

I peek around the corner and see Marco and Ellie still playing Uno.

"Feeling pretty stupid?" I ask him jokingly.

Almost as stupid as I feel for loving that he didn't want some other guy hooking up with me, I bet.

"You could say that," he says.

"I can't believe you thought I'd actually go on a date right now, with you away and Ellie in my care." I can't hide my disappointment. "I thought you knew me better than that."

He makes a noise that resembles a growl. I picture him pinching the bridge of his nose like he does when he is frustrated about something. "You've got me so twisted I can't even think straight."

"One day you'll trust that I'm not like those other nannies you had. Now go win your game. Ellie and I are going to eat dinner and then crawl into your bed to watch you on TV."

"Trust me, Sunshine. You're *nothing* like anyone I've ever met before."

He hangs up, and I stare at the phone for so long Ellie and Marco appear, both of them ready for dinner.

"Right, dinner." I slip my phone into my pocket and follow them out the door, making sure to lock it behind me.

Fifty-Two

RHODES

"BRO, WHAT IS THAT?" Kane uses his stick to point at my skate during the other team's time-out. I glance at the laces and hide a grin. A pretty blue ribbon is intertwined within the laces, something I did right before the game after getting off the phone with Sunny.

"A good luck charm from Ellie," I lie, flinging water down the hatch.

It most definitely isn't a good luck charm from my daughter. I slipped the ribbon in my bag after losing yet another battle with myself at the innocent hands of Sunny, and when I saw it there before the game, I found myself wanting to hold onto it for good luck.

How pathetic.

Am I a teenager or in my thirties?

But that's just it, isn't it? Sunny makes me feel like a teenager again. I'm antsy when we're apart, and now, she's starting to run laps in my head. She's all I can think about, and for the first time in my life, I'm eager to get back home to see my daughter's nanny instead of dreading it.

Sunny in my bed will be the perfect reward for winning on the road—and we will win. We're up 3-1, and as long as we hold the line for the next few minutes, we should be destined for the W.

Malaki zips past, and we get into position. Kane skates up toward the refs and says something mouthy to the other center, and just like that, we're off.

I'm skating with a purpose tonight, and I know it's because I have someone important watching me from home.

Except, she didn't text me back during the last intermission.

Fuck, focus.

I clear my head as best as I can and follow the puck.

It hits my stick with force, and I skate up the line, passing it back and forth between my teammates. There's an opening up ahead, and Kane hikes it toward the goal but misses by a hair.

I slip behind the net and play with the puck, tossing it back and forth before flinging it around the wall with it ending back in Malaki's possession. A defender elbows him and steals possession, giving us a turnover.

Shit.

They're going to pull their goalie to the bench, and it'll be six of them against the five of us.

We've been in this position before, though, and we've practiced the drill too many times to count, constantly tweaking and reinforcing pressure.

I skate quickly toward the commotion but hear my name being called from the bench.

Coach is pulling me in?

We don't need fresh legs yet.

In the end, I listen to him. I trade off. I slump on the bench to grab my water.

"Volkova."

"What?" I snap, glancing down the bench at Coach.

Time is ticking, and the pressure on our guys is heavy.

I need to be out there.

He flicks his head toward someone, and I lean back to see who.

My stomach falls.

And just like that, I forget about the game.

I stand and start to rush past my teammates toward Kevin, the team manager. I've seen this look before. Something is wrong, and it's a blunt hit to my chest. I've grown so comfortable with Sunny taking care of Ellie in my absence that a problem at home didn't even occur to me.

Malaki comes to the bench to rest, and his brow furrows when I brush past him.

"Where're you going?" he asks through heaving breaths.

I leave my stick with him, but I don't answer.

I'm hopeful the cameras are on the ice and not watching me disappear down the hall. The media will start to speculate, and there will be all sorts of rumors.

As soon as Kevin and I are away from the crowd, I turn and wait for an explanation.

"We just got word that there's been a car accident."

My legs nearly give out.

"Where is my daughter and her nanny?" I force out.

I follow my manager into the locker room and start to strip as fast as I can.

I'm several hours away by plane, but they better get me on the next fucking flight.

"I was told that Ellie is perfectly fine." *Thank God.* The dread is still present, though. My hands shake, and the adrenaline is swift.

"And Sunny?"

My manager pauses for a second. The question must've surprised him, but why wouldn't it? I've never shown anything but disdain for my nannies in the past. Sunny is different, though.

"Uh..." He pulls out his phone and scrolls. "She's...banged up, but..." He quickly reads a message. "They're at the hospital now and—"

"They're at the hospital?" My tone is level, but I am anything but.

Fuck, Sunny is probably freaking out.

"Get me on the next flight."

I pull on my hoodie and a pair of shorts, not even bothering to lace my shoes.

"Let's go."

There isn't room for arguing.

My girls need me, and they need me now.

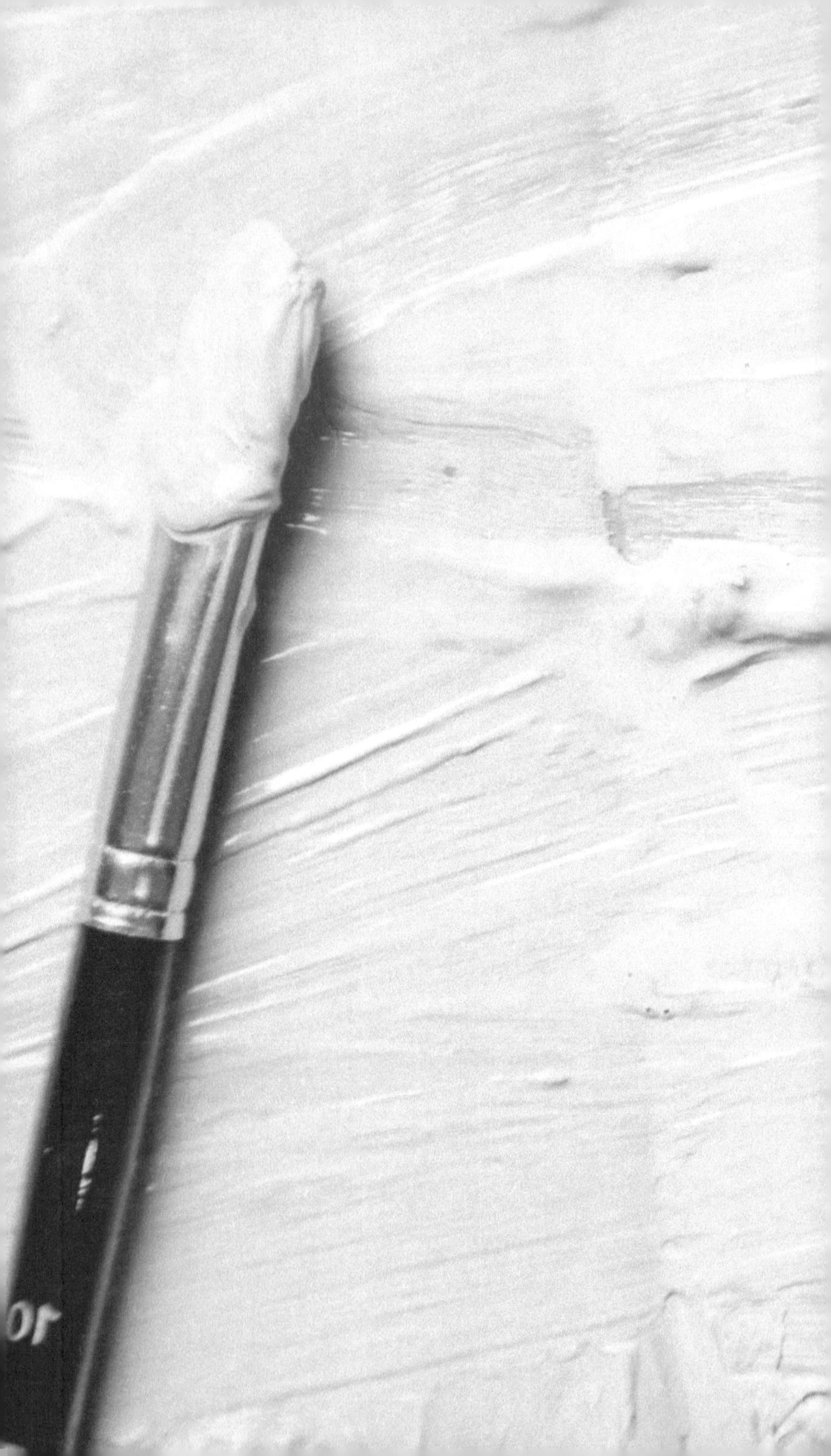

Fifty–Three

SUNNY

ELLIE IS pale from the shock. I reach back behind my seat and touch her leg. She looks okay. Her seatbelt is intact, and other than wide eyes, she looks perfectly normal.

"Ellie, are you okay, sweetie?"

She nods quickly, little pieces of hair falling into her face.

Marco is unconscious, and I know I should be panicking, but instead, I jump into action.

My phone flew somewhere from the sudden hit, so I unbuckle my seatbelt and look around. Unable to find it, I open the car door and slide out of the passenger seat. Glass crunches beneath me from the broken side mirror, so I'm careful to step over it and open Ellie's door. *She's okay.* I give her a quick hug and search the backseat for my phone.

We need to call the police.

And an ambulance.

"Marco." I reach forward and give his shoulder a shake.

"Sunny, you're bleeding."

"Huh?"

Ellie points at my cheek. My cold hand touches the burning sensation beneath my eye, and I wince. My fingers are stained with blood, but I shake my head. "I'm okay. We have to wake Marco up. Do you know where my phone went?"

Ellie's eyes gloss over, and her bottom lip starts to shake.

"Hey, hey." I place my hands on her cheeks. A tear slips out, and I shush her. "We're okay, Ellie. Do you trust me?"

She nods.

"Good. I'm not going to leave you, okay? I'm just going to go around to Marco's side of the car and wake him up and drive us to the hospital, yeah?"

"Okay." She sucks up her tears and nods.

I shut her door and look both ways, hoping for someone to come along to help us.

It's quiet, though. A thin layer of snow covers the road, and besides the tire marks from us and the other car who hit us and sped away, there's nothing.

It's a quiet street, not too far from Rhodes's neighborhood. Someone will come eventually, but can we wait?

Where is my phone?

My head starts to pound.

I open Marco's door with force. The car hit the driver's side, but it was really the backseat that sustained most of the damage.

Thank god Ellie was behind me instead of him.

"Marco!" I say, shaking his shoulder again.

He begins to stir.

I place my cold hand on his chin, trying to get him to see me. He blinks a few times, but his eyes won't focus. "Marco, I need you to get to the passenger side."

"Chto?" he slurs.

Ellie pipes up from the back. "That means *what* in Russian."

I reach over Marco and pull on his seatbelt. "We got in an

accident. I'm going to drive us to the hospital because I can't find my phone. You're hurt."

He says nothing, and I don't have time to waste. I push the dread of going to a hospital away and do what I have to do.

"Come on." I pull on his hand. Glass sprinkles toward me from the broken window when I get him to his feet. I wrap my arm around his waist, and thankfully, he's coherent enough to put his arm around my shoulder.

Our blood ends up mixing together by the end from the little cuts on both of us.

Once he's settled into the passenger seat, I rush to the driver's side and glance back at Ellie.

Her eyes are glossy. "Is he going to be okay?"

I smile, though it's fake. "We're going to make sure he is. Zip your coat. It's going to be a little chilly because of the window, okay?"

She quickly does as I say, and I slowly put the car into drive.

This is unsafe, but what choice do I have? I can't leave Ellie here and search for help, and I don't know how long it'll be until someone comes. The other car is long gone.

I hope Rhodes isn't angry with me for doing this.

Marco groans and grabs onto his side in pain.

"Hang on, Marco. We will be there in ten."

"We need to get you looked at, Allison."

I cringe at the name, hating that the same ER receptionist from the last time I was here recognized me right away. Ellie glances up at me from my lap with her sleepy gaze full of confusion.

"I'm fine," I reiterate. The nurse eyes me with frustration, and I silently mouth, "I'm not leaving her," referring to Ellie.

She sighs but eventually walks away and heads to the doctor at the end of the hall. I can tell she's tattling on me, for the third time since arriving, but I make no move to get up. Ellie and I have been sitting in this chair for who knows how long, waiting for news about Marco.

The ER receptionist, along with all the nurses, immediately stood when we walked through the doors.

It didn't take long for them to take Marco back due to his confusion. When they came for me, already having my file in hand, I politely refused. I told them I wasn't leaving Ellie with someone random, and I'm sticking to that.

My nerves are already spent, and the thought of being separated from her makes my heart rate go through the roof.

So, we wait.

The longer we wait for news about Marco, the harder my head pounds.

Rhodes is going to flip out when he finds out what happened.

"I'm tired," Ellie whispers.

I glance at her long blinks. "Me too. We will go home soon, okay?"

She nods and snuggles in closer.

I'm not sure how we're going to get home. Without my phone, I've had no way to call anyone for help. The only numbers I have memorized are my nana's and Ruby's—and they're not going to be of any help.

Ellie eventually falls asleep against my chest, and I clamp my arms around her. I place my head on top of hers and try to keep my eyes open for as long as I can, because I think I might have a concussion like Marco.

But with Ellie draped over me, safe in my arms, I eventually doze off. The doctor will come get me when Marco is through with his tests, and then we can figure out what to do next.

Fifty–Four

RHODES

I'VE CALLED her at least a dozen times, and each time, it goes to voicemail.

The hospital got a hold of my manager as soon as Sunny came in because I put myself as her emergency contact the last time we were there.

There hasn't been much information since, though, and with each minute that passes, the dread gets heavier.

Knots form in my stomach when the airplane lands. I call Sunny's phone again, only to be disappointed when she doesn't answer. I have multiple messages from my teammates, all saying something semi-comforting, with the exception of Emory and Malaki who are demanding information.

Despite the snow, I make it to the hospital in record time.

I slam my truck into park and rush toward the doors, only to stop when I recognize Marco's car. It isn't until I round the side of it that my heart falls. It's banged up on the driver's side. The window is shattered, and the backseat door is caved in. *How did the car get here?*

I pull my hood up to hide from the cold and head inside. Embracing the warmth, I go right past the security guard and over to the ER window.

I'm not sure if I'm recognized, and that's why people are parting to give me a path, or if it's because they see the panic and determination on my face, but regardless, everyone moves out of my way.

"Sunny Edwards." I tap my fingers on the counter. "Where is she?"

The woman clearly doesn't care for my demand. She rolls her eyes and flips through a paper. "Sunny?"

Wait.

"Allison. Allison Edwards."

"Oh. Her."

I don't have time for this. "Yes, *her.*" If someone doesn't point me in the direction of Sunny in the next second, I'm going to lose my mind. "Where is she?"

The woman sighs. "She's over there. Can you please convince her to let us take a look at her? She's stubborn—"

I turn, and everything around me disappears.

My heart moves behind my ribcage with something I can't explain.

It takes me seconds to make my way over to them, but an entire lifetime passes.

There, sitting in the corner of a crowded ER, is my daughter curled up on the lap of one of the purest, most kind-hearted women I have ever met, safe and sound.

I stand in front of them and stare for so long people start to murmur.

Ellie is pressed against Sunny's shoulder, and Sunny's cheek is smooshed on top of her head. Both of them are sleeping with a coat that I don't recognize draped over their bodies like a blanket.

"I covered them up," an older woman whispers from a few chairs down.

I glance at her, my mind swimming with thoughts of the future that have *no* business being there.

"She's a tough cookie." She inclines her head to Sunny and Ellie.

I furrow my brow. Which one?

"Is she your wife?"

I open my mouth but say nothing because the answer that wanted to come out was *yes,* and that's enough to make my knees weak.

Wife? No.

"She refused to leave your little one. She's in pain, though. I've watched her wince in her sleep a couple of times."

Your little one.

My throat tightens with emotion.

"See," she says.

I put my attention back on Sunny, and a line of pain appears in between her eyebrows while her eyes remain closed. Her cheek, caked with dry blood, scrunches. There's a thin slice beneath her eye that needs bandaged at the very least. For fuck's sake, there's a piece of glass in her hair too.

My heart beats hard, and I bend at the knees. I place my hand on the side of her thigh and gently tap her awake. When her eyelashes begin to flutter, I stare up at her and pray that she's actually okay.

I'm not, though.

I'm far from it.

The thought of losing her makes everything seem so fucking bleak.

"Sunshine," I whisper, rubbing my thumb against her jean-clad leg.

It takes her a second to come to. She flinches when she

picks her head up. I ache in a way I never have before to take her pain away.

"Hey," I whisper quietly, careful not to wake Ellie. "Look at me, Sunshine."

"Rhodes?" She blinks through the haze, and as soon as she latches onto me, her eyes widen, and she gasps.

My palm falls to her leg, and I shush her. "You're okay."

The beating of my heart is so thunderous it hurts. My blood pressure climbs, and the need to grab onto her face and press my lips to hers is almost too much.

I'm relieved to see them both sitting here, but there's so much emotion laced to this moment that I can't think straight. There's pressure in my chest that can't be ignored.

"You're here?" She swallows and winces again.

She needs to get checked out.

"I'm here." I check out her face again, eyeing the cut.

"Ellie is okay," she adds, glancing at my sleeping daughter.

I gently reach forward and brush her hair out of her face. I rub the pad of my thumb beneath the cut. "But you're not," I remind her. "How did you get here with the car like that?"

"I drove us."

What?

Sunny's bottom lip starts to shake, and I could die from the sight. *She's crying?* Why does this hurt me so much? It's like salt being rubbed in a wound.

"I am so sorry, Rhodes."

My jaw flexes. She's apologizing to me?

"I didn't know what to do."

She's getting worked up. This is a version of her that I have never seen before, and I have to admit, I don't fucking like it.

"I lost my phone in the accident, and Marco was hurt. I made sure Ellie was okay, but since there was no way to call an ambulance and the other car had left, I didn't have a choice. I had to drive us here. I was afraid to waste time and wait for help." She gasps for air, and I'm frozen with shock.

Did she just say that the other car left?

Once I find out who hit them, they're dead.

"Sunny."

Ellie starts to stir.

A tear slips over Sunny's cheek.

"I'm so sorry—"

"Stop it," I blurt.

Her lips clamp shut, and I weave my fingers through her hair, letting the small shard of glass fall to the floor. I grip the side of her face with enough force to get her to focus on me.

"I'm not angry with you," I say. "How could I be angry with you for worrying about everyone *but* yourself?"

Sunny bounces her watery eyes all over my face, but I'm pulled away when I hear Ellie.

"Daddy?"

"Printsessa." I lean forward and press a kiss to her forehead and pull her into my arms. I make no move to stand, though. I refuse to give Sunny any more reason to think I don't care about her too.

Ellie's arms wrap around my neck, and I stare at Sunny.

"Here's what's going to happen." I look deep into her eyes and silently ask her to let me take care of her like she's been doing for us for the last few months. "I'm going to call Scottie, and she's going to take Ellie home, and then you're going to go get checked out."

She opens her mouth, but I keep going.

"I'm going to get information about Marco, and then when you're cleared, we're going to go home. *Together.* Okay?"

Sunny slowly closes her lips, and those glassy eyes turn doe-like. She nods, and I pull out my phone to call Scottie with Ellie safely in my lap and one hand on her.

It may have taken something drastic to wake that thing up in my chest, but Sunny is about to realize that Ellie isn't the only one I care about as of late.

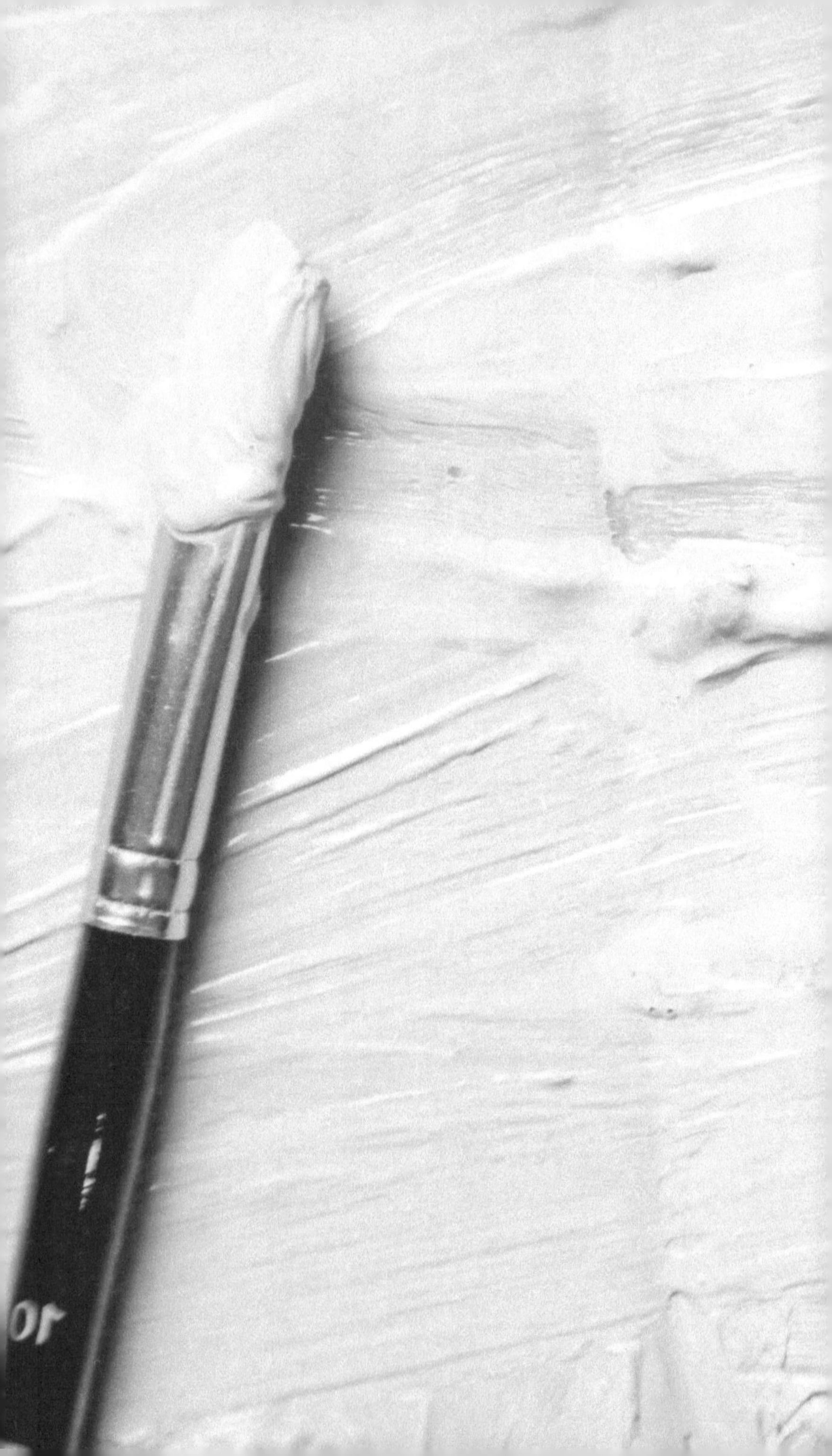

Fifty-Five

SUNNY

I PUT my hand on the passenger side handle, but Rhodes clears his throat from the driver's seat.

"Rhodes, I can open my own door." I laugh softly because if I laugh too hard, it'll hurt. The soreness set in as soon as Rhodes showed up and acted all hero-like. It was like my body refused to feel anything until he was there and Ellie was fully taken care of.

"I know you can," he says. "Doesn't mean you have to."

Warmth spreads to my cheeks. I stay unmoving in the passenger seat while he climbs from the truck and rounds the front of it. When he gets to my side, he opens the door and leans inside so closely that his arm brushes the front of me.

He unbuckles my seatbelt, and I playfully roll my eyes. "Don't even think about carrying me."

He grumbles something under his breath but settles for my hand, helping me down to the sidewalk.

"It's slippery," he warns. "So hold onto me."

"I really am fine, Rhodes," I remind him. "It's just a mild concussion and a few scrapes."

Marco had the worst of it and is required to stay in the hospital overnight for observation. Two broken ribs, a concussion, and some stitches. He's reassured us that he's okay, but Rhodes is still planning on checking on him tomorrow.

"I don't care." Rhodes shuts the front door behind me, and to my surprise, he bends down and starts to unlace my shoes. "Just be quiet and let me take care of you."

The dip in my belly shuts me right up.

His hand on my calf is warm, and when my shoes are off and to the side, we're greeted by Scottie.

"Oh my goodness, Sunny." Her hand goes to her mouth. "Are you okay? What do you need?"

"I'm fine," I reiterate with a smile. "I promise."

She looks at Rhodes.

He scoffs. "She's just like you."

Scottie, with her blonde hair piled on top of her head, places her hands on her hips. "He doesn't mean that as a compliment. He means that you're acting as independent as I do when it comes to someone taking care of me."

I frown.

He isn't wrong.

"I still take it as a compliment," I say.

Rhodes rubs his hand over his scratchy face. He looks exhausted. His hair is tousled, like he's run his fingers through it a million times, and he's wearing nothing but a thin Blue Devils hoodie and a pair of shorts.

"Do you want to stay?" Rhodes asks Scottie. "It's late, and the team won't be back until morning. You can take Sunny's bed."

"Wait, what?" I ask.

"You have a concussion," Rhodes reminds me. "I have to keep an eye on you."

Scottie looks at me, and we catch each other's eye.

Call it girl intuition, or whatever you want, but it's clear that she knows something neither Rhodes nor I have admitted to anyone.

"Yeah, I probably should." Scottie tries to hide her smile. "If it's okay?"

My thoughts of Rhodes and his attentiveness scatter. "Of course." I slowly walk toward the stairs. "You can use any of my stuff if you want to shower—"

"Where do you think you're going?" Rhodes's hands fall to my hips, and I pause.

I glance over my shoulder and meet his intense gaze.

"To get Scottie settled?"

He flicks a brow. "Taking care of others still, I see." He looks over at Scottie. "You know the way, yeah?"

She laughs and slides past us. "Yeah, I'll see you two in the morning. Come get me if you need something."

I say goodnight to her, and when she's out of sight, Rhodes gently scoops me up into his arms and begins to carry me up the stairs. I snort quietly. "Rhodes, you are being ridiculous. I can walk!"

He shushes me and follows it with, "Tikho."

My lips clamp together, and I do as he demands and stay quiet.

Stopping in front of Ellie's room, we both peer through the crack of the door and see that she's peacefully sleeping in her bed with her nightlight on.

"She doesn't have a scratch on her," Rhodes sighs in awe.

"That's because she has a guardian angel." *Her mother.*

"I think you do too," he says.

My own mother comes to mind—and Gramps. I smile at the thought of them both.

Bypassing his bed, he takes me right to the bathroom and slowly sits me on the vanity counter. He keeps the light off and brushes my hair away from my face, careful not to touch the butterfly strips on my cheek from my cut.

"Does your head hurt? I figure keeping the lights off is best."

"A little," I admit. "But I'm—"

"If you say you're fine..."

Even through the darkness, I see the severity in his gaze. I sigh and glance away while nibbling on my lip.

I'm not used to someone taking care of me. Sure, my grandparents gave me a wonderful childhood full of love and nurturing, but I haven't been a child in a very long time. As soon as Gramps started to go downhill, I had to step up to the plate and take care of them.

"Do you want to shower?" Rhodes asks. "The warm water might help loosen your muscles."

"You're tired," I say.

He chuckles. "So?"

I shrug. *Oh, my muscles are tight.* "I feel bad. You played a full game of hockey and then flew home to this mess. You should get some sleep."

Rhodes grinds his jaw and walks over to the shower and turns it on. When he comes back, he lowers his voice. "You're gonna make me say it, aren't you?"

I peek at him through the darkness. "Say what?"

"Do you understand the fear that flew through me when I heard there had been an accident?"

"Of course," I say. "That's why I made sure Ellie was okay before anything else."

Rhodes chuckles darkly. He drops his head, placing both of his hands beside my thighs on the vanity top. "You don't get it. I wasn't just worried about Ellie."

My stomach flips. I'm too tired to fight the irrational thought that he was worried about me too. He should be worried. I take care of Ellie. That makes sense.

Rhodes slowly raises his head. The look he gives me brushes against my soul. His neck bobs with a swallow, and I wait with bated breath to hear his next words.

"I was scared out of my fucking mind that something happened to you." He exhales slowly and grips the hem of my shirt. "And it isn't only because you take care of my daughter."

"Rhodes," I whisper. "I think you're still in panic mode, and that's why you feel that way."

I will admit, things seem more serious than before, when we were giving in to attraction. But that's probably just the lingering panic speaking, right?

Even if it isn't, I'm not sure I have it in me to push him away and force us to think rationally. I don't *want* to.

"I'm going to take care of you, and you're going to let me, okay?" The way he looks at me sends chills to my arms, despite the bathroom filling with steam.

I bite my lip and nod.

Rhodes strips the shirt from my body, careful when pulling it over my head. His hands move deftly to my jeans, and he slowly pops the button through the hole and slides me off the vanity to stand. My jeans fall in a pile beside my shirt, and next, he reaches around and unclasps my bra, slowly dragging the straps down my arms and tossing it to the floor.

He's on his best behavior as he hooks his fingers into the sides of my panties, slowly tugging them over my hips and helping me step out of them.

I swallow and let him help me into his shower. My eyes have adjusted, so when I see him begin to strip too, I force myself to turn around so I don't accidentally glance below his waist.

My body is jumbled, and my thoughts are messy.

When I feel his presence behind me, my breath hitches.

I don't recognize the feeling buried in my chest when his

arm slips around my waist to spin me toward him. Steam surrounds us, and butterflies make a home in my stomach.

"I have no idea what I'm doing," he whispers.

Our bodies are flush, and I find myself reaching up on my tiptoes.

"Me either," I admit.

Rhodes skims his nose down mine at the same time his fingers knead my back muscles. I shiver, and he pulls back slightly to look into my eyes.

"*Damn,*" he mutters.

Then his mouth is on mine, and I suddenly feel like I'm *his*.

Fifty-Six

RHODES

THIS WASN'T SUPPOSED to happen, but it is, and I'm too drunk with her mouth on mine to stop it.

She's in my arms, slick from the moisture of the shower, and she tastes too sweet for me to resist. The night has lasted a year. I've been in two different time zones, felt an entire lifetime pass, but this makes it worth all the worry I felt on that plane ride home.

I graze every part of her body with the palms of my hands, memorizing her curves, before reaching up to grab the shower head. With the pad of my finger, I tilt her chin so I can run the water through her hair. I said I'd take care of her, and that's what I intend to do.

After lathering the shampoo, I slowly massage it into her hair, careful not to tug on the strands and give her an even bigger headache.

"That feels nice."

Even her voice is a temptation. She drags her breaths out, and I crave to feel them against my neck.

"Good," I murmur, massaging my fingers through the suds. "Tip your head again, baby."

She does what I say without protest.

Finally.

Water runs over her scalp until her silky dark strands are clear of shampoo, and I grab the body wash.

This is going to take some serious willpower.

I turn her around, and she peers up at me with a hazy look on her face. She blinks through the beads of water on her face, and as soon as my sudsy hands touch her, I know we're fucked.

She gasps and backs herself to the tiled wall for support.

She doesn't need the wall, though.

She's got me.

My hands glide over her shoulders, and I slowly rub both of her arms before moving to her chest.

I wish I were a better man and could keep my eyes to myself, but I can't.

Her breasts beg for my attention.

I dig my heels into the floor of the shower to ground myself, but it doesn't work well enough to keep my dick from hardening. She's irresistible, and the hot little gasp that slips from her lips eggs me on.

Getting her off is taking care of her, right?

I argue with myself while sliding my hand in between her cleavage. When her nipples pucker, I smile to myself. Getting her off is most definitely taking care of her.

"You want to be touched, Sunshine?"

I rest my hand against her stomach until she gives me the go-ahead. I'll do anything she wants, even if that means not touching her there.

"Please," she begs.

Anything for you.

"Hold onto me," I say, moving my hand between her legs.

Her fingers fall to my shoulders, and the bite of her nails against my skin is the biggest turn-on. Her head slowly falls backward when I start to play with her.

"Beautiful," I mutter.

Her hips start to rock forward, and the way her pussy grips my fingers is a fucking drug.

"Are you always this responsive to being touched?" I'm mesmerized.

Her answer is more of a moan. "No."

Mine.

Apparently, my dick has a brain of his own, because the only thing I can think of is how I'm never letting another man touch her like this.

I've known men to be possessive, and I've never really understood it.

Until now.

"I need you," I admit, not giving a fuck that it makes me sound desperate.

I am desperate.

Maybe it's just left over from the thought of losing her earlier, or maybe it's something else.

She peers up at me through her wet lashes. "Then have me."

I am unhinged.

Willing myself to take it easy, I drag my hand out from in between her legs and grab her thighs. I haul her up gently, and she clasps her fingers around my neck. I press her against the tiled wall. I'm at her entrance, and it's her that wastes no time. She pushes herself onto me, and I lose my breath.

"Fuck, Sunny. You're killing me."

A moan leaves her mouth, and I catch it. I groan when my tongue slips inside. Even my kiss is possessive, like my body is trying to tell her that she's mine. Her back arches, and it makes me take her deeper.

Fuck, she feels like heaven.

Suddenly, she starts moving against me with speed, and I'm forced to pull back. "Slow down," I warn. "I'll take care of you, but we have to go slow. You're sore from the wreck."

She pouts, but it disappears when I slowly enter her again.

We move in sync. Slow and steady. With each thrust, a soft moan floats from her, and it twists me up inside.

I bring my eyes to her face and notice that the moon has crept its way through the bathroom window. I can see her perfectly now. She's staring at our joined bodies, and I selfishly want her to see what she does to me.

Holding her with one arm, I lift my hand and tip her chin up so she catches my eye.

"Eyes on me, Sunshine."

Our gazes crash, and I feel her everywhere. She's digging her sweet self into my bones, and I know another woman will never match her.

This doesn't happen more than once in a lifetime. I'm not dense to think this is just a simple fuck between two people needing a release.

It's more.

"Fuck," I grunt, pushing into her deeper.

Her mouth opens with pleasure, and it's me who closes her off. I can't watch her like this because I'm afraid I'll fucking fall in love with her.

I groan, pulling out of her and pressing in deep.

"Rhodes." My name sounds like a prayer from her mouth. Her teeth sink into my shoulder, and she comes around my dick, making my knees grow weak.

Not being able to hold on for another second with her squeezing me like a vise grip, I pull out of her and come.

I can't even stand.

Keeping a hold of her, I bring us both to the floor. She's still tangled around me, and I don't want to let her go.

"What are you doing to me, Sunshine?"

I'm in disbelief. Utter fucking disbelief.

I'm in my thirties, have been with multiple women, even having a child with one, and I have never felt so connected to someone in my entire life.

"The same thing you're doing to me."

Her quiet admittance stays with me through the rest of the night. I braid her damp hair and watch her fall asleep in my bed, knowing that if it were up to me, I'd have her in here with me every night from here on out.

or
10

Fifty–Seven

SUNNY

I ROLL over in bed and groan quietly. My back is tight, and I feel hungover, though I didn't drink a drop of alcohol.

Thoughts of the wreck filter through, and my heart starts to race. I think of Rhodes, and my heart starts to race even faster.

I peek an eye open, and his room is basked in pretty sunlight. The bedroom door is open, and I stare at it, wondering where he and Ellie are.

Does she know I'm in his bed?

As a five-year-old, she probably will buy the excuse that he was watching me because of the mild concussion, so I don't worry too much.

What I should worry about is the feeling he gives me with a single look. Or the butterflies in my stomach thinking about what we did in the shower.

"So there's no lead at all?"

My attention is pulled at the sound of his voice floating in from the hallway.

I shush the butterflies and listen harder.

"Marco said that he saw the car head right for them, and according to the report, the tire marks show a direct line to their car, as if the car didn't spin out of control and slam into them by accident."

What does that mean?

"I know. It doesn't make me feel..." Rhodes's voice fades.

I lie in bed for a little longer and nibble on my lip. I go over the events after dinner, but nothing unusual stands out. It was a fluke accident. I'm just thankful we're all okay, for the most part. I decide not to tell my nana, or else she'll worry. But Ruby will be angry if I don't tell her.

Sitting up in bed with a wince, I see my phone laying on the bedside table with a few cracks on the screen. Rhodes mentioned that he'd found it underneath the driver's side seat when he went out to Marco's car to make a report with the police while I was being discharged from the hospital.

I video chat Ruby and do a double take at my face on the screen.

The thin cut on my face is red and inflamed, and I look beyond tired. The braid that Rhodes did for me is messy with tendrils popping out around my cheeks, and his shirt is three sizes too big.

"Hey, you—" Ruby's face falls the second she sees me. "What the hell happened? Do not tell me that he found out where—"

Her first thought goes to the last time I had a cut on my face, and I don't blame her.

"No, no!" I stop her. "It was a car accident."

She blows out a heavy breath. "Can you start with that next time? Jeez. I was going to tell you to get my bail money ready."

I snort and wince right after.

"What happened?" she asks. "Are you hurt somewhere else too?"

I sit up a little taller, and her eyes drop to my shirt. Her brows furrow, but she remains quiet.

"It was a random accident. Well..." I pause. Was it? "It was a hit-and-run. But Ellie is fine. I have this cut, a mild concussion, and I'm sore. Everyone is okay."

"A hit-and-run?" she scoffs. "I lied. Get my bail money ready."

My mouth curves into a smile.

Her eyebrow hitches. "What are you wearing?"

I look at Rhodes's Blue Devils shirt.

"And whose room are you in?" she asks.

I'm suddenly hot.

"Uh, well..."

"Allison!" she snaps.

I flick my eyes to her with the use of my first name.

"Oops, sorry, I'm just recovering from utter *fucking* shock. Have you been holding out on me?"

"Shh," I hiss. "No. Well, yeah, kind of, but it's...I don't know."

How do I explain this?

I can't even explain it to myself, and if I'm being truthful, there's a tiny seed of shame buried in my stomach at the thought of telling anyone that I've slept with Rhodes. He's my boss and the father of the little girl I nanny for. But then I think about how safe I feel with him and how I truly care about him and Ellie both.

It outweighs the shame and guilt.

God, I'm a jumbled mess.

"Are you two a thing?"

"What? No!" *Are we?*

Ruby looks at me funny.

"Stop it," I whisper. "I know what you're thinking."

She smooths her face.

"You're thinking what everyone else will think if they find out."

My allegations won't stand a chance if it gets out that I'm messing around with Rhodes, because who's to say that I didn't do what was accused of me? If I "seduced" another father of a child I was nannying, I must have done the same to Rhodes, right? They'll say, *it's no wonder things turned out the way that they did.* I'll be the one faulted.

"That is *not* what I'm thinking," Ruby says.

I glance at the screen and can't even bother to look at my face. I stare at her instead.

"I'm thinking that I hate that you even had that thought to begin with."

Me too.

I snap my attention toward the bedroom door. The small opening gets larger, and I expect to see Rhodes, but instead, it's a little face with sleepy eyes.

"Good morning." I smile.

Ellie rubs the grogginess away and walks over to me.

"I gotta go," I say to Ruby, pulling the blanket up so Ellie can get into bed with me. "Love you."

"This conversation isn't over, but I love you too."

I blow her a kiss before hanging up.

Ellie crawls toward me, and I cover us both up with the blankets.

"What are you doing in my daddy's bed?" she asks.

Great question.

"I had to make sure she was okay after the wreck."

My senses heighten when I see Rhodes leaning against the doorway with a mug of coffee in his hand. Damn him for being so attractive in the morning. My body is highly aware of his every move, even down to the faint bob of his throat when he swallows.

Ellie slants her chin to look up at me. "Are you okay?"

I nod through the slight throb in my head.

"Are you?" I poke her belly, and she giggles.

"Yes." She stands up quickly and gets out of bed to do a cartwheel. "See!"

Rhodes and I both laugh.

"Hey." Rhodes gets down on her level. "Some of the team is downstairs with *donuts.*"

Ellie's eyes light up. "Is there one with sprinkles?"

He stands and shrugs. "Yeah, but I saw Malaki eyeing it."

She takes off, shouting Malaki's name as she goes.

I laugh again, but this time, I don't hide my wince. My head pounds, and the longer I sit in bed, the worse it gets.

Flinging the covers off my legs, I move to stand.

Rhodes is there within a flash. He sets his mug on the side table. "Does your head hurt?"

I peer at him from his bed. His brow is furrowed as he stares down at me.

"It does." I shoot him a half smile. "But I'll be fine, you ol' softy."

He grips my chin lightly. His lip twitches with a grin so small it's easy to miss. "Softy?"

Warmth flows to my chest, and I'm marveled by it.

Rhodes lifts a shoulder. "I guess I am a softy when it comes to you."

"And Ellie," I add.

He nods slowly.

"Rhodes Volkova," I tease, "the most intimidating winger on the Blue Devils is a softy. Who would've thought?"

To my surprise, he doesn't deny it or, at the very least, scoff. His hand falls to mine, and he gingerly pulls me to my feet.

"What can I say?" He wets his lips, and I'm captivated. "I'm a softy for my girls."

His girls?

My stomach dips.

"Let's get you some medicine, and if you're up for it, the guys brought donuts."

"The guys?" I let him lead me to the bathroom.

Rhodes glances over his shoulder at me. "The team. I guess they're softies for you too."

I make a face. "They're here for you. Not me."

He chuckles. "I can assure you that they're here for you, Sunshine. Not me."

My cheeks grow warm.

"Welcome to the fam, baby. I guess you're one of us now."

Fifty–Eight

RHODES

COACH JACOBS STANDS at the foot of the locker room, and silence fills the tight space. With the entire team in here, it gets congested, and adding in each of our egos, it's even worse.

"Listen up."

Kane mumbles about it being silent, so clearly we're all listening.

I send him a glare, and he lazily swings his attention back to Coach.

"We're going to be making some changes with the playoffs in our future. We're slotted for the wild card right now, but if we can get our points up for the next few games, we'll be able to secure a spot for the first time in ten years."

The locker room erupts in chants, and some throw up the new fan salute: their first finger and pinky up like devil horns. Some chick did it at one of the games, and it went viral. Now everyone is doing it.

"Alright, alright, alright." Coach sounds eerily similar to Matthew McConaughey.

"The franchise has hired a skills coach to help tighten the line and work out the rest of our kinks."

A murmur works through the locker room, and Coach continues.

"And we've added a few more players to our roster. It could change before the trade deadline, but I need you all to be aware of your new teammates and coach."

This is nothing new. There are trades all throughout the season with injuries, unfit players, and more, yet Coach Jacobs always gives us a heads-up.

Some of us, like myself, have even more of an advantage of knowing privy information. Like promised, I reached out to those that I knew playing in Washington, and their facts all remained the same:

Nicholas Tarvo knows his shit.

Nicholas Tarvo is skilled.

Nicholas Tarvo took our offense to the next level.

The only negative thing I was told was that he had some personal issues he needed to work through, which is what has propelled his decision to move closer to the Mid-west, and that he had a temper. But who in hockey doesn't?

The locker room door opens, and two guys shuffle through, decked out in full Blue Devils attire. Emory catches my eye from across the room.

"This is Lars Perrson—"

And Crew Hart, I finish in my head.

Hart is a hot commodity. It's no wonder Emory and I had to share a room the other day. Crew Hart is where our funds went. He's not the youngest player in the NHL, but he's one of the best of his age.

Emory walks right over to Crew after Coach introduces

our new teammates. If I have my facts straight, they went to Bexley U together.

Coach Jacobs claps his hands. "Now that we're through with introductions, get dressed. Your families are here to watch you practice, and it's the only time it's allowed, so go."

The team breaks, and he pulls the two new guys over to talk. The rest of us shuffle out of the locker room and head for the ice to work on last minute drills for our game tonight with our families getting an early glimpse.

Practices are usually closed, even to family, except for today.

Family Day, where our loved ones are allowed to watch us, is always the practice before a rival game. Either Coach knows we need the extra support on days like today, or he wants to remind us that we can't get too ahead of ourselves with the fighting.

The second my skates touch the ice, I glance to the stands.

I relax when I see two blue ribbons and smiling faces behind the glass. Ellie throws up her horns, and I slip my glove off to do it back to her. Sunny scrunches her nose when Ellie grabs her hand and forms the horns, making her hold it up.

My cheek lifts. When Sunny stops laughing, she swings her gaze over to me.

I haven't even begun skating, and I can't seem to catch my breath.

I left her alone last night, making sure she got much-needed rest in her own bed. I knew if I had her stay in my room again, Ellie would ask questions. Not to mention, I can't keep my eyes to myself, let alone my hands.

The thoughts are just as bad.

The dirty ones and the ones that are picturing her as something more than a nanny.

Ice flings up beside me, and I pull my gaze from Sunny.

It's the new guy, Perrson.

"Hey, man." He taps me on the shoulder with his stick, and I instantly want to snap it.

Who does he think he is?

I slant my head, deciding whether or not to give him a little leeway since he's new.

"I'm Lars." He speaks with a Swedish accent.

"Volkova." I skate forward, and he follows me.

Does he want a friend? If so, he's coming to the wrong guy.

I won't haze him or anything, but I'm also not going to befriend him three seconds after he joins our team.

"I know who you are," he says.

Crew Hart climbs onto the ice next and skates around a few laps, nodding at his new teammates with a tight smile like any normal man would do.

"So, Family Day?"

I grunt and play around with a puck, trying to loosen up.

Go away.

Not that he knew he interrupted my thoughts of Sunny, but he did, and now I'm irritated.

"Who do you have watching you today?"

I send a puck toward Emory.

He smirks at Lars following me around like a lost puppy.

"My daughter," I answer curtly.

"Oh, nice. You married, then?"

A puck comes in my direction, but he steps forward to take it.

I come to a sudden halt and shoot him a *who-the-fuck-do-you-think-you-are* look. "If you know my name, then you probably know I'm not married."

He nonchalantly shrugs.

Is this another Kane-like situation? A young punk who is

talented enough to be pulled up from the minors but needs some help maturing? Surely Coach didn't think this would put us in the playoffs?

"Your life is pretty private, actually. I did some research on the best players, and you're the only one that is a mystery."

I squint. "Yeah, there is a reason for that. I want it to stay private."

Glancing around, I look to see if any of my teammates are watching this interaction.

Kane is leaning against the wall in front of our bench, staring right at me with a shit-eating smile on his face.

I shift over to Malaki, who is standing entirely too close to the penalty box. When he sees me looking, he opens the door and wafts his hand in front of it. *What is this?*

If Lars doesn't skate the fuck away from me, I might just end up in there.

Thankfully, he takes off skating down the line, leaving me alone.

I head toward Kane.

"Wipe that look off your face, or I'll give him your address, and you'll have yourself a new friend."

Kane snorts. "You don't know my address."

I chuckle.

He eyes me closely.

Of course I have his address. The entire team does, because he continuously gets too wasted to drive home.

I steal the puck from him and slide it over to Malaki, who is shaking his head at Kane behind me.

I peer over my shoulder.

Kane looks guilty.

"What did you do?"

Malaki slides me the puck, and I send it to Kane with a little more force.

"Welcoming our new teammate with an innocent prank." He shrugs. "The usual."

If I didn't have some sunshine running through my veins from a certain someone, I'd probably be irrationally annoyed with Kane and his constant bullshit. But it doesn't hit me as strongly as usual.

"Well, don't include me in this. Unlike you, I'll be focusing on tonight's game."

I bend at the knees to stretch.

"Too late," Malaki mumbles.

As soon as his words hit my ears, I look for Sunny and Ellie.

My stick falls to the ice.

I flick my glare to Kane.

"What?" He acts innocent but makes no attempt to hide his smirk.

"Did you tell the new guy to go over there? Or did he do that all on his own?"

Am I going to have to make a scene?

Kane's cheeks cave in as he tries to hold in his laughter.

Irritation fuels me to stand at my full height. I drag my glare back and forth between Kane and Lars, trying to decide which one to go toward.

"There's one thing you don't do when it comes to me." My voice is entirely too calm for the jealous rage zipping through me.

"I know." Kane rolls his eyes. "Stop fucking with you. But relax. It's just a joke. Everyone knows that Sunny is off-limits, and she has no problem telling us that she doesn't date hockey players, remember?"

I shake my head with the flex of my jaw. I skate over to him and lower my voice. "No. The one thing you don't do is fuck with what's mine."

Kane eyes me with confusion but quickly smooths his features when the realization hits him.

I narrow my gaze. "You get what I'm saying?"

He smiles like a fool next. "I got you. I'll take care of it."

"Good," I snap.

He begins skating toward Lars. "And my bad. I honestly never would've guessed that you'd be fucking your little nanny at your disposal."

I quickly swipe my stick off the ice and put it out to trip him.

He goes flying.

"Damnit, Volkova! I said I was sorry. Take a fucking joke."

A sick smile paints my face as I bend to help him up. If the families weren't watching, I'd probably place my stick against his neck, but since I have to play nice, I decide to act even more insane and help him to his feet.

It probably sends more fear into him than if I were to use my fist on his face.

"I know you said sorry." I grab his stick off the ice and hand it to him with force. I press it into his chest. "But I need you to understand that I'm not just fucking her like she's a goddamn toy. Show some fucking respect."

Kane flicks a brow.

"Don't say that shit again."

"Wow." He glances at her over his shoulder. "You really care about her."

I do, but I'm not going to admit that to him before I do her.

"I'll take care of Lars," he says.

I turn away and grip my own stick a little tighter than before. I catch Sunny's eye, and she's watching me closely.

It calms me enough to send her a wink. Her cheeks ripen with color, which is something I find highly captivating.

Staring at her from across the ice and making it known to

at least one person—even if it's only Kane—that she and I are something more than what we portray has me reeling.

I'm being reckless, but at least I'm no longer in denial.

What started as something temporary is turning into something that I want to make permanent.

Fifty-Nine

SUNNY

I HELP LACE Ellie's skates and make sure her helmet is on straight before following the rest of the team's families onto the ice. Some I recognize, and some I don't. Scottie is already out there, flinging pucks at the net toward Emory, who continues to laugh with each one he catches.

"Okay, you're gonna have to help me," I say to Ellie. "I've never stepped foot on a rink before."

"What?!" she shrieks.

I laugh and follow her onto the ice.

Naturally, being the child of a pro hockey player, she does just fine. She spins around once, and I try to mimic her. Except, I'm in shoes, and I have zero traction. My foot slips, and I instantly think about how this was an awful idea, considering I was in an accident two days ago.

"Have you lost your mind? If you fall..." Rhodes swoops me up a millisecond before I land on the hard ice. It's unbelievable how often he catches me when I fall.

I try to hide my surprise and wrap my hands around his neck. "Are you a vampire?"

His eyebrows fold. He tries to hide his amusement, but I see the hint of humor on his lips. "What?"

"You're so fast," I explain. "You're somehow always ready to catch me mid-fall, even when you're not even paying attention. I'm going to start calling you Edward."

He looks disgusted at the thought. "Please don't."

I'm surprised he knows what I'm referencing, and now that I know he doesn't want me to call him that, I'm going to have to make a point to do it.

"That's an upgrade from Oscar."

He grunts.

When I realize he's making no effort to put me down, I decide to press his buttons. "Put me down...*Edward.*"

A burly growl rumbles from his chest, and he tightens his arms around me. People are starting to look at us like we're something that we're not.

"For the record, I'm always paying attention to you," he admits.

I roll my eyes. "You are not."

He looks at me with his vibrant green eyes that look more like a dare than anything. "I'm watching you even when you think I'm not, Sunshine."

He is?

"You better put me down," I whisper. "Or else people are going to start thinking there's something more to us than me being your daughter's nanny."

His jaw flexes. "Good."

I stiffen. "What?"

"Then maybe my teammates will stop picturing you naked."

I flatten my lips and glance toward Ellie, who is playing hockey with a couple other younger kids of guys on the team.

Malaki, a kid himself, is in the middle of them, acting as the ref.

"They don't do that," I argue.

"Trust me, they do. They tell me."

Rhodes slowly skates us over to the bench. He sits me down and then takes a seat beside me and grabs his water.

"Well, I guess kudos to you for being the only one who actually knows what I look like naked," I joke.

He turns toward me and slants his head. His eyes darken, and there's a sudden shift in the air.

"You shouldn't say things like that while we're in public."

My heart falls when I look out onto the ice. *He's right.*

"I don't think anyone heard me," Most of the kids are skating with the team, and the rest of the families are watching from the other end of the arena. "But you're right."

Talk about being a hypocrite. I just told him to put me down so no one thought anything and then I go and say that out loud?

Rhodes slips his gloves off one by one and places them on the other side of him. I sit back and watch Ellie playing with the other kids, laughing with Malaki as he blows a fake whistle for a made-up penalty.

"You took that the wrong way."

I slowly turn and stare at the side of Rhodes's sharp jaw. He keeps his focus pinned to the commotion on the ice, but I know he feels me looking. There's a little bit of scruff on his high cheekbones that I remember feeling against my skin the other night, and I can't stop staring at his flickering temple.

"How so?" I ask.

"I meant you shouldn't say things like that while we're in public, because now seeing you naked is the only thing I can think about."

My lips open with surprise.

Rhodes snaps his attention to me, and the air sizzles.

I start to sweat when he stares at my mouth.

Oh my god. Is this all it takes? One glance and I'm burning for him?

He turns away with an exhale, and I do the same.

I do my best to focus on the rink, but when he scoots an inch closer, my heart leaps out of my chest.

If he touches me, I'm a goner.

I watch Ellie skate circles around the other kids. It's a desperate attempt to distract myself so I stop wondering what's happening with me and Rhodes, but then his body heat surrounds me.

My hands fall beside my legs so I can grip the bench. A shaky breath tumbles from my tight chest, and by the faint groan I hear from Rhodes, he hears it.

Kane starts playing with the kids, joining the losing team. He glances at us and stares for a beat too long. One quick nod in our direction, and Rhodes's finger grazes mine.

Excitement rushes through me, as if I've never been touched before.

Each brush of his skin against mine leaves a fire behind.

I can't breathe.

"What are you thinking about?" His voice is velvety. Smooth and silky against my skin.

I continue to stare at the ice, but I can't see a single thing. "I'm thinking that what you do to me isn't normal." My breaths are ragged, and my heart beats so hard it hurts.

He laces our fingers together. The grip is heavy and grounding, yet I'm floating.

I turn with the sound of his heavy inhale, and our gazes clash. "You told me to be the rational one."

He nods. "I did."

"Which isn't hard for me to do. I've been making rational decisions all my life," I say.

His throat bobs with a slow swallow.

My teeth sink into my lip, and it draws his attention. "But what if I don't want to be rational when it comes to you?"

There's a wild look in his eye. My heart leaps when he pulls me to my feet.

The rink disappears at our backs as he pulls me down the long hallway leading to the locker rooms.

"Rhodes!" I exclaim. "What are you—"

He seals his mouth against mine.

It's an intense kiss and one that erases reality.

Rhodes is hungry, and I willingly open up to feed him. His hands dive beneath my sweater, and a shiver runs through me.

"I love it when you do that," he groans.

He goes right back to kissing me with force, and I match every last stroke of his tongue.

Someone could walk down the hall at any given second.

Ellie could come searching, wondering where we disappeared to.

"Rhodes," I murmur.

His finger fiddles with the button of my jeans, but he pauses and peers down at me with worried eyes. "You want me to stop?"

I glance behind me. "Well, no, but what if someone sees—"

He silences me by pulling me farther around the break in the hall. "Kane is keeping watch."

What? He is?

Rhodes, in his practice gear, seeming so much bigger than without it, pushes me against the wall while keeping a hold of my hips. "Can I keep going now?" His tongue slips from his mouth, and he wets his lips.

Unable to deny him, I grab onto his jersey and pull him in fast. He watches me with a held breath and so much hope in his eyes. "Yes." I embrace the thrill of him taking me like this, right here. "And don't stop."

Sixty

RHODES

SHE'S JUST as into this as I am.

My sweet Sunshine, always bright with a smile on her face, is nowhere in sight. Instead, there is a sexy-as-sin woman who makes my blood sing by just existing.

"I can't get enough of you," I admit, pulling her pants down. "I've never been so addicted to something before."

I graze her neck with my lips and slip my hand in between her legs. One brush against her clit and she's quietly whimpering. She's already wet, and I'm in a frenzy.

I'll never be able to replace the high she gives me.

It makes me irrational.

Her delicate hand falls to my chin, and she brings my face back to hers. Those pretty eyes show all her dirty thoughts that I can't wait to explore. When our mouths touch again, I finger her, relishing in the way she feels.

I hastily shove my pants down.

She helps me, which makes me even more eager.

When her warm hand grabs a hold of me, I clench my eyes.

Fuck.

Look at us.

I've never been so rash before.

She pumps me a few times, and I can't take it. With an eagerness, I grab her tiny wrist and slap it above her head. The seductive smile she wears does me in.

"I can't decide which version of you I like best." I push the rest of her jeans down and move them off to the side for better access. With my knee, I open her legs up farther and angle myself at her entrance. "The sweet, innocent version of you..." Moving her hair out of her face so I can see her better, I push myself in slowly.

Her mouth opens with a silent moan, and a fire burns between us.

"Or"—I tug on her lip with my teeth and let it plop away —"this sexy, wild version of you."

Her tongue slips out, and she wets the spot I bit. "You can have both."

I push into her harder.

It feels so fucking good that I don't even care if someone walks down the hall to find us.

Having her like this makes me want to tell every last person in this arena that she's mine and only mine.

I pull out and turn her around. She presses up against the wall and gives me better access. I push into her again, and my favorite noise escapes, echoing around the empty space.

"Shh, Sunshine." I brush away her braid and run my nose against her neck. She backs her ass up against me, and I'm so deep I can't think straight.

"Fuck."

Sunny moves against me, finding the angle she wants, and

the faster she goes, the more I succumb. My fingers clench her braid. The pleasure is out of this world.

"Don't stop, baby. You're almost there." It's hard to keep a hold of my thoughts with her like this.

She clenches around me, tightening her hold on my cock.

She's so close, and I'd give up everything to watch her.

"Let me see you come, Sunshine. It's my new favorite thing." I tug on her braid, and it brings her head back to my shoulder. I bury myself deep, chasing the pleasure. Those white teeth sink into her bottom lip, and then she's spilling her cum all over my dick.

"Jesus Christ," I grit. "I'm going to come from the sight."

I tap on her hips for her pussy to let me go.

No condom *again*. It's reckless and irrational.

But that's what she does to me. She makes me act so possessive that the thought of putting a baby inside of her doesn't scare me like it should.

"Sunny," I groan in desperation.

She lets me loose, and I pull myself out.

I stop dead in my tracks when she drops to her knees in front of me. She grabs a hold of me and guides my cock into her mouth.

"What the fu—"

I see nothing but Sunny on her knees, sucking me off. Her throat opens, and she takes me in deep. My hand blindly finds the wall, and I brace myself. I try to go easy on her, but her mouth is too much.

Look at her.

On her knees for me.

I clench my eyes shut with the intense tingling of my balls and come down her throat with force.

My knees weaken.

That's twice she's given me such a high that I can hardly stand afterward.

I'm a man with restraint, but it's long gone when she's near.

After I'm done, Sunny takes me out of her mouth and peers up at me from below. I quickly pull her to her feet and stare at her swollen lips and face full of mirth. Her eyes are watery, likely from me ramming my cock down her throat.

I hate that I love it.

It does something fucking terrifying to me.

I quickly adjust my hockey uniform and slip her panties and jeans back up her legs.

She buttons them as I brush the stray hairs out of her face. Her chin is so small in my hands, and her warm gaze is enough for me to burn the world down if she asked me to.

Her blinks are slow and lazy as I run the pad of my thumb beneath her healing cut. I stare at her with my heart fumbling in my chest.

I'd give it to her if she asked for it.

Shit.

Am I in love with my daughter's nanny?

The longer I gaze in her eyes, the more I feel myself making room for her in my heart. I didn't think I had room for anyone other than Ellie, but leave it to Sunny to prove me wrong.

"We should go before someone comes looking," she whispers.

I blink once.

Then twice.

A slow smile creeps on my face. "I think I'm going to keep you, Sunny Edwards."

Her quiet laugh is music to my ears. "Oh, yeah? For how long?"

I grab her hand and interlace our fingers. "For forever."

———

The locker room buzzes with energy. My teammates stretch their legs and pop their necks. Rival games hit differently, and with our record on the line, we're craving a win.

We're hungry for it, salivating at the thought.

Some of the guys are becoming vocal, glancing at me to see if I'm going to quiet their threats about the violence they promise the other team.

I remain quiet and poised, which is probably because I was able to release some of my energy earlier.

Right down Sunny's throat.

I lace my skates, tightening them with force.

She's on my mind, amongst other things.

Do I tell her?

Is it going to scare her off?

Or does she feel it too?

The last time I was this bent out of shape over something was when I became a father. It was a life-changing event. Loving Sunny feels that way too.

I glance up at the sound of someone walking into the locker room. A man dressed in a suit stands with his hands on his hips, staring at us like we owe him something.

Emory shifts his attention to me, and being team captain, I take the mental shove and stand.

"Wrong locker room?" I flick my chin at the door he walked in. "Down the hall and make a left. That's the visitor's locker room."

There's a small cut on the bridge of his nose, and I briefly wonder if he's been in a fight of some sort.

"I'm in the right place, Volkova." With a quick glimpse around the locker room, gaining everyone's attention, he says, "I'm Coach Tarvo."

Oh.

Weird introduction, but alright.

I hold my hand out and wait for him to shake it. When he does, annoyance runs through me. His grip is firm. A little too firm.

"Welcome to Chicago." My welcome is clipped, and though he is our new skills coach, I don't appreciate his introduction.

Coach Jacobs comes out of his office just in time.

A remark is on the tip of my tongue, but it probably won't sit well with Coach Tarvo, and it doesn't set the best example for the team either.

"We'll meet you guys on the ice." Coach Jacobs turns and directs Coach Tarvo to his office.

The door latches, and I stare at it long enough for Kane to slip beside me.

"I don't get a good vibe from him."

Emory, in his goalie gear, leads the guys out of the locker room, leaving me with Kane, Malaki, and Hayes.

Malaki snorts. "I can already tell this isn't going to work out."

"How?" Hayes asks, always attempting to be the mediator on the team.

"By the way Rhodes is staring at the door."

I smooth my face and shake it off. "It'll work out if he helps us win." Though, I agree with Kane too, which *never* happens. The vibe is off.

"Let's get on the ice," I say.

The feeling of unease stays with me until I catch sight of my girls.

Ellie and Sunny are smiling from the first row, opting to sit closer than usual for this game.

It was something that Sunny was originally against because she didn't want the cameras on her, but with Ellie never in the spotlight anyway, one game shouldn't hurt.

They both throw up their devil horns, and I quickly skate over, flinging ice up onto the glass.

I wink at them, and just like that, my worries fade, and I'm ready to play.

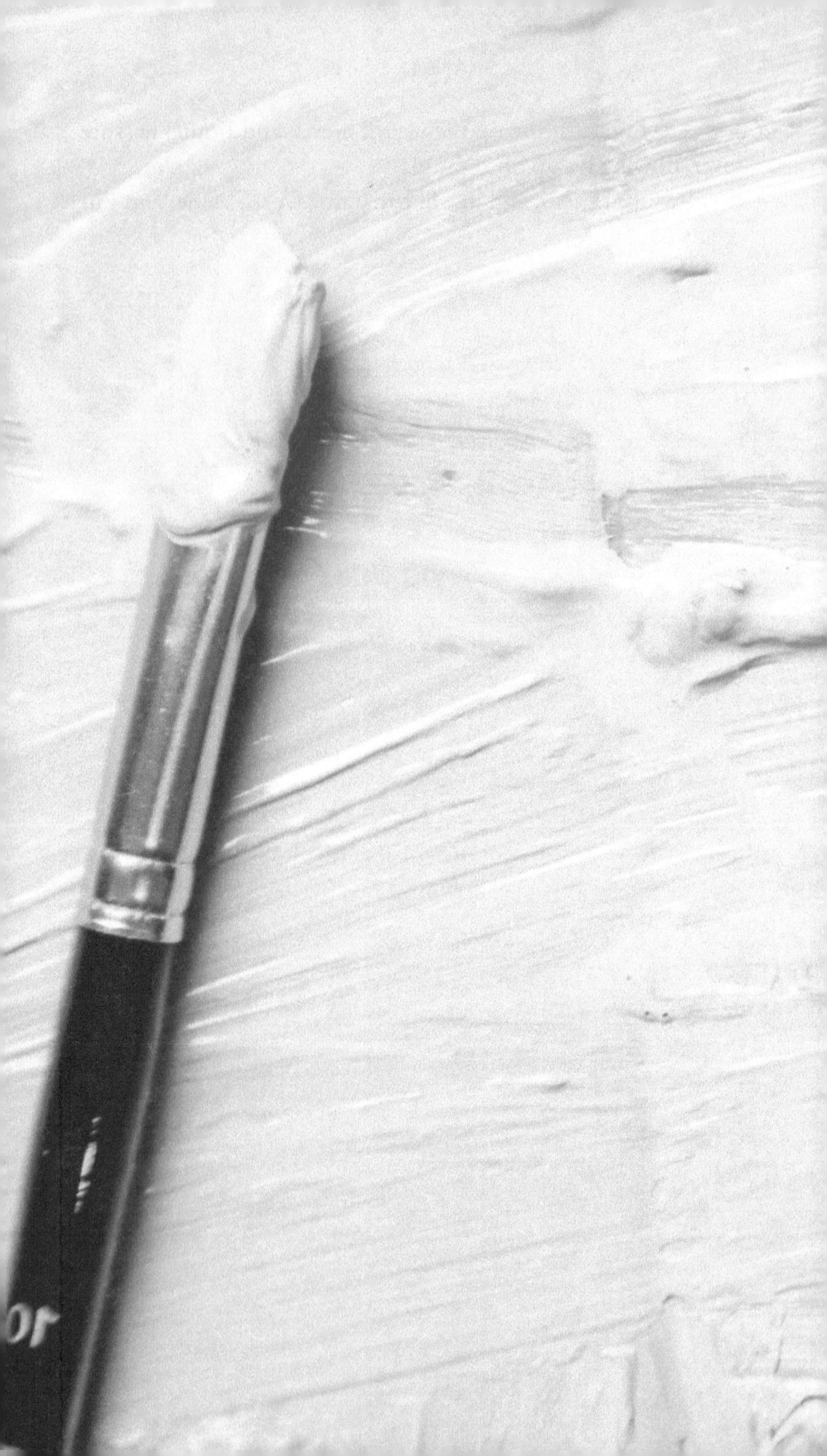

Sixty-One

SUNNY

"LET'S GO!" Ellie throws up the devil horns, and to appease her, I do the same.

She giggles, and I can't help but laugh alongside her.

Rhodes, being the very last to climb on the ice, skates over to us and small ice chunks spray the side of the glass.

He winks, and my stomach dips.

A few young boys and their dads bang on the glass from a couple seats down. Rhodes taps his stick against the glass, nodding at them.

They lose their minds. Ellie and I hide our smiles.

"Daddy is popular," she whispers.

She knows that Rhodes doesn't like her in the limelight, and she takes that very seriously–never indicating to anyone who her father is.

But she's right. He's popular.

To more than just young boys and their hockey-loving hearts.

The Volkova jersey that I'm wearing doesn't stand out at

all. There are so many other women wearing Volkova jerseys in the stands that I can't help but feel a little jealous.

But for all they know, I'm just another fan of the game.

The other team comes onto the ice, and the boys beside us start to boo.

Ellie grins and starts to do it too. "Booooooo!"

I snap a picture of her with her thumb pointing down and her lips forming an O. I send it to Rhodes, knowing he'll get it during intermission.

The game starts off without any issues.

Both teams are fast and aggressive.

I wince each time the puck flies in our direction. At one point, Rhodes slams against the glass in front of the boys, and my heart leaps in my chest.

Ellie, unworried, jumps to her feet and claps.

Rhodes ends up making a connection with the puck and sends it to Malaki.

The whistle blows, and the play stops.

Offsides.

The guys reposition, and they look tired already. It's been four minutes and only one line change—one that Rhodes wasn't a part of.

We win the puck drop, and it flies to the left, heading in the right direction.

"Yes!" I shout, grabbing onto Ellie's hand.

She squeezes mine, and then we both sit and wait for the play to unfold.

I keep my gaze pinned to Rhodes.

Watching him play hockey is captivating. He is focused, driven, and patient. With his chest rising, he glances to the bench and nods, taking off in that direction.

I follow him like a magnet. I selfishly want him to look at me, but I know he's too into the game for me to pop into his head like he continues to pop into mine.

My cheeks warm when I slip my gaze to the hallway that leads from the bench.

What we did earlier was so uncharacteristic of the both of us, but walking back out onto the ice during Family Day, I don't think either one of us regretted it.

I bite my lip and find him on the bench again.

To my surprise, he's staring right at me.

His eyebrow lifts, and I roll my lips.

He caught me.

There's a quick shake of his head paired with his smirk, and suddenly, he's standing again to get back on the ice.

I cover my smile with my hand and shift my gaze over the rest of the team, only to pause.

My smile falls along with my heart.

The entire arena blurs. Panic rushes to my fingertips.

I grip the sleeve of Ellie's sweatshirt.

I hear her voice, yet I can't pull away.

I'm pinned with shock, and reality comes crashing around me like I'm in the middle of a burning building with no way out.

The devil himself smiles at me.

What is *he* doing here?

What is *he* doing behind the Blue Devils bench in a suit, like he's coaching?

My heart stumbles back to life, and I turn toward Ellie.

"Sunny? Are you okay?" Her eyes grow wide, and worry lines curve around her little mouth.

I swallow past the lump of dread and confusion.

Is this a coincidence?

Too many questions hit me from every direction, and my thoughts spiral.

"I think I'm sick." It's not a lie. I'm so sick to my stomach that I have to grab a hold of it. "Let's go get you to the box so you can be with Scottie. Is that okay?"

Ellie nods quickly, more concerned with me than she is the game at this point.

What am I going to do?

He's not even supposed to be near me, yet he's here? Coaching?

There was no flicker of surprise on his face when he saw me, which is beyond concerning.

And then there's Rhodes. What do I tell him? That I used to nanny for his new coach, and he's the reason why I left Washington?

I feel the blood drain from my face.

Is he still stalking me? Did he find out that I was living in Chicago, and that's why he's here?

"Hey, girls!" Scottie and the other wives cheer when Ellie drags me into the box. Scottie rushes toward me when she sees the look on my face. "Whoa, are you okay? What's wrong?"

"She's sick," Ellie answers for me.

"You're sick? Here, come sit." Scottie grips my hand and guides me to sit. I'm so nervous that I'm shaking. I don't want her to let go.

"Here's some water." Someone hands me a bottle of water, but I make no move to drink it.

Scottie places her hand on my forehead. "You're cold and pale."

My eyes are watery, and the shaking gets worse.

"Hey." She bends down and gets on my level. "What's going on?" She keeps her voice low, somehow knowing that something is *really* wrong, and it isn't that I'm ill.

"I need to leave," I whisper, afraid Ellie will freak out.

She glances around before swinging her attention back to me. "Okay. I've got Ellie."

A tear slips down my cheek, and I angrily swipe it away.

"Did something happen?"

Not yet, and it's going to stay that way.

I suck up my emotions and shake my head, knowing I have to remain calm for Ellie.

She's shown such improvement lately, and the last thing I want to do is ruin it by panicking in front of her.

I pull her in close. "Are you okay to stay here and enjoy the game without me? I'm not feeling well, and I don't want to get anyone else sick."

I don't want to leave her, even though I know she's perfectly fine with Scottie. There's a nagging thought in the back of my head that keeps rearing its head, making this harder than it should be.

I can't leave her.

"Yes, I'll stay here and root for Daddy."

I force a smile.

Ellie's face turns serious. "If you need to borrow my puke bowl, it's in my bathroom, okay? Daddy cleaned it the last time I got sick."

Puke bowl? An abrupt laugh leaves me, and I welcome the quick break from my worries.

After saying goodbye, I turn and walk out of the box, knowing it'll probably be the last time I'm in there.

I send Rhodes a quick text.

> Me: I've come down with something, and I'm not feeling well. Ellie is with Scottie in the box. She'll get Ellie to you after the game.

I call an Uber since Marco is still recovering from the wreck.

My thoughts spin, and although I know Nicholas is standing behind the Blue Devils bench, coaching, I'm convinced he'll leave and follow me throughout the arena.

I still feel his gaze pressing against me.

It isn't until I'm tucked away safely in a stranger's car that I feel safe again.

I pull open my phone, and there are two texts waiting for me.

My finger shakes as I open the first.

> Unknown: What a coincidence. I had no idea you were in Chicago.

My heart breaks when I open the second.

> Rhodes: I wondered where you went. Stay in bed. I'll take care of you when I get home. If you need anything, text me and I'll pick it up on my way home.

If I need anything?
What I need is to tell him the truth.
But what I'm going to get is something so much worse.

Sixty-Two

RHODES

"APPARENTLY, that nanny of yours is our good luck charm." Kane sighs, throwing his glove to the ground from the loss.

He took a hard hit to the face, but unfortunately, it didn't knock any sort of restraint into his system, because shortly after, he found himself in the penalty box, and he's still bound with aggression.

"That's what you guys think you need? A good luck charm?"

I glance at Nicholas Tarvo, irritated by the sound of his voice.

He was awfully fucking quiet during the game, half the time searching in the stands more than looking for ways to tighten our offense.

I'm antsy and irritated.

Sometimes we lose. It's hard to accept, but it happens.

I stand up, ignoring our new coach because I'm not a fucking fan of him.

"It seems like you all have forgotten what it feels like to lose. It happens." I glance at Kane and his flexing jaw. "Get the anger out of your system, however that may be, and get back here in the morning to review tapes. The only way forward is to fix our mistakes and keep going."

Coach Jacobs takes over, talking about our next game and how we need to come together and figure out the best way to beat them instead of finding ourselves in another situation like this one.

I'm dressed and ready to go before he's even done talking, worried about Sunny and eager to grab Ellie.

It makes sense why the ones in relationships are always the first to leave the locker room. I now know what it's like to have someone waiting for you at home, despite a loss or win.

Emory and I walk out together, knowing Scottie is going to meet us in the parking lot with Ellie. Crew Hart, the new guy who only dressed for the game instead of playing, bumps fists with Emory, walking in stride with us.

"You guys played hard," he says. "I'm impressed. I can't wait to get on the ice for the next game."

Unable to keep quiet about our new coach, I scoff. "You know what I'm not impressed with? Tarvo."

Emory is the goalie, so he doesn't have to deal with anyone but his own line of coaches, but even he noticed. "Yeah, what was up with that? Is he a silent participant and will go heavier during practice tomorrow?"

Crew seems level-headed, and I know he's played against Tarvo's past line of offense. I lean forward and raise a brow. *Got anything to add?*

He shrugs and slings his bag up onto his shoulder. "I've heard some weird shit about him through the chatter."

"Like?" Emory pokes.

"Well, I heard that Washington was forced to fire him because of some legal obligation. He and his wife got divorced, and I'm pretty sure she put a restraining order on him."

Interesting.

Doesn't have anything to do with his coaching ability, though.

I'm curious to see how he acts during tomorrow's practice. It's unlikely that I'll like him, but here's to hoping he has some pointers to help us get to the playoffs.

The scent of Sunny's body wash fills the upstairs, and just like that, my stress is gone.

Ellie cuddles in my arms, fast asleep from the drive home, per usual after a game. Her little voice was raspy from shouting during the game, and I've never been prouder to have such a superfan.

After placing her into bed and kissing her head, I move onto Sunny.

She said she was sick, and Scottie seemed concerned when I met her and Ellie at the truck. Apparently, Sunny was pale and clammy.

It worries me because of her recent concussion.

I push on her door and hear the shower running.

My dick pulls to attention, and I stare down at it. *Stop.*

The glow from the bathroom shines into her room, and coconut fills my senses. I inhale and walk farther inside, prepared to ask if she's feeling better.

Slowly creeping past her bed, I catch a glimpse of her laptop.

I do a double take when I see two tabs open and on full display.

Why is she on the nanny website? The same one I used to find her.

Skipping my gaze over to the other tab, I catch the first line and lose my footing.

I'm writing to inform you of my immediate resignation. I

have found several replacement nannies that I know would be a great fit for Rhodes Volkova and his daughter...

My stomach falls to the floor.

I blink through my blurry vision and refocus on the screen.

I reread the email three times before I hear the shower turn off and watch her step out of the tub with a towel wrapped around her.

My pulse thrums angrily, and the scent of coconut instantly pisses me off.

What the hell is this?

I stand mere feet from her bed and wait.

The longer I watch her, the more I feel myself close off.

Like a trap door moving in front of my heart, I smooth the shock from my face and let the resentment replace the unbearable pain drowning me.

The cut digs in deep, and although I only feel it for a quick second, I'm not sure it'll ever fully heal.

"Rhodes." My name falls from her lips in a surprised whisper.

My nostrils flare.

Those dreamy brown eyes of hers widen.

My heart pounds in my chest with swift speed.

She shifts her gaze to the laptop resting on her bed, and I flex my jaw.

"What—" I clear my throat because she winces at my tone. "What is this?"

If I wasn't so angry, I'd be impressed with her ability to remain calm. Months ago, fear would have been obvious as it worked over her features. But she is impressively composed at the moment. It makes me wonder if I made up this entire thing between us.

Was I the only one who believed that we were more than what we were?

How could I let myself get this sucked in?

"I..." She exhales.

I take a step back. I can't even stand to look at her.

"You wanted to slip into our lives just to leave when things finally became normal?" My tone is anything but kind.

A flash of hurt moves over her face, but she quickly whisks it away. Her arms cross against her towel, and I'm so disoriented that I can't think straight.

"Normal?" she whispers. "This isn't normal."

She's referring to us.

It may make me less of a man to act desperate, but I make the move to do so anyway.

"You're right," I say. "You and I and...this thing between us...we can put a stop to it."

Anything to make you stay.

A soft, sarcastic breath fills my ears, and I hate that I love the sound of it.

"Do you really believe that, Rhodes?"

"If it makes you delete that email, yes."

Stay. Please.

I don't know if I want her to stay for Ellie's sake or mine.

I think it may be both.

"I can't." She won't meet my eye. "But I have a list of great nannies that will be able to replace me. I know each of them personally and—"

"I don't want another fucking nanny!" I shout.

I want you.

She jumps, and her gaze falls to the floor.

I spin and put my back to her.

In the worst way, I want to stalk over to her, grab her by the waist, and press her onto the wall, demanding she explain herself.

It doesn't make sense.

It's so sudden.

I don't understand, but with her proving to be like all the rest, I don't even want to try to.

I'm not going to stand here in denial and beg her to stay when she clearly doesn't want to.

She fooled me, and that's my fault.

Not hers.

"I want you gone first thing in the morning."

"Rhodes."

Focusing on the door, I walk over to it like it's my lifeline. *Get me the fuck out of here.*

"Can I at least say bye to Ellie? Explain it to her?" she asks.

I turn and glare at her over my shoulder. "Explain what? How you broke your promise?"

Her face falls. "My promise?"

"You promised me you wouldn't leave her." I shake my head with disappointment. "And look at you...*leaving.*"

That hurt her.

She winces.

It says something that her hurting hurts me, but I pretend it doesn't.

"I promised you I wouldn't fall in love with you." I dig the knife in a little further because it's the only way I'll let her go. "Looks like I'm the only one who knows how to keep a promise these days."

A line of hurt appears in between her eyebrows. I clench my teeth together to keep myself from telling her the truth, because let's face it. Not loving her is the biggest lie I've ever told.

———

I don't even want to speak.

Sunny was gone the next morning, her belongings all fitting into the two bags she showed up with. I deleted the footage from the cameras, not trusting myself to keep from watching them over and over again.

Ellie is pretending to be fine, but she's back to being quiet and reserved.

I hate it.

I hate it because I'm partly to blame.

We got too invested. I trusted myself to let Sunny into our lives. I even allowed her to move in, knowing *damn well* that she was hard to resist.

I skated the line, crossed the line, and then erased the entire thing altogether.

Now look at me.

Angry, resentful, hurt, and full of guilt.

"I meet the new nanny in a few days, Printsessa. But Marco is going to stay with you until I get back from my games, okay?"

Two away games, back-to-back. What shitty timing.

Marco is still a little sore from the crash, but he insisted he stay with Ellie to help me out.

Ellie glances at me from her bowl of cereal but says nothing. I see her fiddling with something in her lap. When she goes back to eating, I slowly walk around the island and glance to see what's in her hand.

My stomach falls.

Shit.

It's the little clay Pascal figurine that Sunny made her. The little clay trinkets were all over the house, and I quickly threw them into a box and hid them on a top shelf in the garage the day she left. I should have thrown them out, but I didn't have it in me to do so, and I clearly forgot to get the ones out of Ellie's room.

"What's that?" I nod to Ellie's lap, already knowing what it is.

Her fingers clamp onto it, like she's afraid I'll take it.

I hide my emotions and lean against the counter. "Sunny make that for you?"

Ellie lowers her head with a tiny nod.

She's hurting, and I hate myself for fucking everything up.

I place a tender kiss on top of her head and say nothing. I head upstairs to get our things ready for the next few days.

We're going through the motions at this point.

Cereal for breakfast, messy house, school drop-offs, rushing to the arena, and a stomach full of stress over the thought of being away from Ellie.

That's not the only issue either.

I can't stop thinking about the hurt I saw on Sunny's face when she decided to leave—like she didn't want to at all.

But if she didn't want to, then why did she?

Sixty-Three

RHODES

COACH JACOBS SLAPS me on the shoulder as he stands behind me on the bench. "I've never seen you in the penalty box this much. What the fuck is going on?"

I flex my jaw.

I'm *pissed*. Obviously.

"His good luck charm is gone," Coach Tarvo mutters.

Kane stiffens beside me, and Malaki mumbles something that I can't hear over my heartbeat in my ears.

Coach Tarvo has been on my shit list since he got here.

Day four with him, and I swear to god, he has it out for me, like he's just trying to get under my skin.

"How about you do your fucking job and help our offense instead of worrying about my personal life?" I look him dead in the eye and could strangle him.

He's probably the one who stuck the sun sticker on my locker too—for "*good luck.*" None of the guys fessed up to it, not that I thought they would after I snapped my stick in half and threatened the entire team.

When I came back for the second intermission, the sticker was gone.

I didn't find it funny.

Tarvo smirks from down the line and looks back out onto the ice.

Crew comes flying toward the bench, and I stand at full height to replace him.

I skate with vigilant speed, knocking opponents down left and right. The other team is offsides, and I pull my guys in and make a call that goes against Tarvo's, because the only thing he's done since getting here is make things worse.

Kane wins the puck drop. It shoots out to the left. Hayes swoops around and chucks it back and forth, teasing the defensemen. Once I sweep behind the net and get into position, I tap the ice, and the puck slides to me. I shoot it over to Malaki, who sends it flying toward the net. It hits the top bar and drops in perfectly.

After skating over to give him a tap on the helmet, I look directly at Tarvo.

He's glaring at me.

His frustration stays well after the game, following me to the locker room.

I'm setting a shit example by pulling my phone out mid-speech, but to be honest, there are zero fucks left to be given.

Kane snorts from beside me, though I don't think anyone else notices.

I glance at my notifications, checking on Marco and Ellie, but notice one from an unknown number.

Unknown: Hi. I know this may be really strange, considering you shooed me away from your house a week ago, but I really need to get ahold of Allison Edwards. I've tried messaging her, but I can't seem to get through. I swear I'm not crazy. This is just really important.

My heart skips.

I know exactly who is texting me.

A woman with long blonde hair showed up at the house a week ago and fed me some excuse about needing to talk to me. I immediately threatened to call the police, thinking it was another single woman trying to worm her way into my house like in the past, but now I'm intrigued.

I wait until I'm settled on the bus and in my own seat to message her back.

Me: How do you know Allison?

It feels weird to type Allison instead of Sunny.

Unknown: She used to be my son's nanny.

A moment later, a photo comes in.

There she is, radiant as ever, with a warm smile on her face. A little boy with dark hair, close to Ellie's age, is making a silly face beside her, and the same woman that came by the house the other day is in the photo too.

Me: Okay? And?

Did she leave you high and dry too?

Unknown: I just really need to get ahold of her. I can't seem to get through. It's about my ex.

Okay, now I'm on edge. Did something happen between Sunny and her ex?

A thought crosses my mind, but I refuse to fall for it. Sunny may have broken her promise to me, but deep down, I know her heart. She is too genuine to be a homewrecker.

Is that what this is about? Is this lady trying to figure out if something happened between her ex and Sunny?

I sigh while typing out my response.

Me: She's no longer my nanny.

It isn't until we're back to the hotel that her message comes through.

Unknown: Do you know where she is or how I can get ahold of her?

I may be pissed at Sunny, but I'm not really up for giving out any of her personal information, especially not when it comes to a crazy ex. I mean, how did she even get my number?

I swipe away her message and lie in bed, willing myself to sleep.

Ellie is safe with Marco, and I played one hell of a game. Yet, it's the same as every other night with Sunny gone.

I can't sleep.

I can't do anything but think about her and wonder what exactly made her go so quickly.

If there's one thing I've learned about Sunny, it's that she is sensible. She makes logical decisions. She isn't rash when it comes to any of them.

Besides, maybe...letting me touch her.

I pull up her name and stare at it for so long Emory turns out his light and rolls over to go to sleep.

I'm angry with her, but there's something in me that can't let it go.

I quickly type a message and hit send before I can rethink it.

> Me: This woman is trying to get ahold of you. Says you used to nanny for her. I haven't given her any information but thought you should know.

I attach the photo and hit send but the text bounces back.

Number no longer in service?

My world comes crashing down.

The covers fall to my lap when I sit up quickly in bed.

Panic seizes me. I shake my head with denial.

I refuse to let it be true that Sunny is out of my life for good.

Anger and resentment aside, there is a sliver of hope lingering beneath it all. I'll be here until the end of time, waiting for her to come back or feed me some explanation as to why she just up and *left*.

A voice in the back of my head tells me that I should have tried harder to get her to stay. Instead, I put her in the same group that I threw all the other women into, and that wasn't really fair because she isn't like them in the slightest.

Pulling up another number, I type something out that seems unhinged, but desperation makes a man do wild things.

> Me: I need a favor.

Mel and I are longtime friends, going all the way back to high school. He's the one I turn to for background checks on the nannies.

SGT Mel: Another background check?

Me: No. But are you able to pull police records? Even if they're buried?

After I learned that Sunny was attacked, I may have stayed up late one evening and searched public records for some type of police report. Nothing came up, though.

SGT Mel: Depends on what you mean by buried. Give me the name.

Me: Allison Edwards.

He texts back right away.

SGT Mel: I will send you what I find.

I click my phone off and roll over to my side, knowing very well I won't be getting any sleep until his text comes in.

———

I slept like shit, practiced like shit, and we're playing like shit.

All of us, not just me. Playing on the road is never easy, and it's even worse when we have a new coach who makes idiot calls and a captain with a bad attitude.

The captain being me.

I try to pull myself together and breathe in and out of my nose.

Ignoring the roaring crowd, Tarvo's stupid face glares in my direction, and Coach Jacobs's vein is bulging from stress. I climb back onto the ice.

"We need momentum," I say to Kane.

He grunts and gets in position for the puck drop.

The clock is ticking down, with only thirty seconds to go in the second period. We're on a power play, and that means we can really do some damage and hopefully get back on track.

Despite my stomach in knots while waiting for SGT Mel's text, I have to focus.

At the end of the day, hockey may not be the first thing on my priority list, but Ellie is, and if I didn't have hockey to ground me *and* pay the bills, I'm not sure where we'd be.

Malaki connects with the puck after Kane wins the puck drop. I skate with determination and plow down a player in white as we both head for the puck.

Malaki has the momentum we need.

I skate to a halt, knocking another player down. I'm about to be on their shit list, but when the puck slips right between their goalie's legs, it's hard to care.

The buzzer sounds, and the team flows into the locker room on a high note.

We've taken back the lead, and that's always a good thing going into the third and final period.

"Good work." I tap helmets with Malaki and plop down beside Hayes. Emory is the last to enter with his full goalie gear.

Then in comes Coach Jacobs.

Tarvo has stayed away, which I'm not angry about.

His face is the last thing I want to see after being on a high from the last play.

Coach Jacobs gives some words of inspiration and encouragement and then proceeds to go over some new plays he wants to run in the next period.

Kane and I give him some ideas on how to change things up. Being that we've been up close and personal with their best players, we see things from a different angle.

After making a few adjustments, we're due back on the ice.

Per usual, I grab my phone.
I have two messages.
One from Marco, telling me Ellie has fallen asleep.
And the other from SGT Mel.
I fumble with the device and swipe the message open.
It's a photo of some type of document.
I zoom in, enlarging the tiny font as much as I can.

To the Honorable Court of Washington:

The Petitioner, <u>Allison Edwards</u>, respectfully requests the Court to issue a Temporary Protection Order against the Respondent, <u>Nicholas Tarvo</u>, based on the following facts:

- Nature of Relationship: Petitioner was a nanny for the Respondent's child, hired under both parents.

- Acts of Abuse/Threats:
  - Respondent attempted to engage in a sexual manner with petitioner on a number of occasions after petitioner declined such behavior.
  - Respondent verbally abused petitioner after resignation letter was filed.
  - Respondent damaged property belonging to the petitioner upon attempting to leave the residence with the child for safety.
  - Respondent sexually assaulted petitioner after resignation.
  - Respondent portrayed physical violence, causing petitioner to fear for the child's safety and her own.
  - Respondent stalked petitioner from his residence to various outings - i.e., the mother

of child's house when petitioner continued nannying for her until a replacement was found.

- Fear of Imminent Harm:

I, Allison Edwards, fear for the safety of Atlas Tarvo and myself due to the threats from Nicholas Tarvo. I have been physically abused by Nicholas Tarvo when trying to leave the residence, and in addition, Nicholas threatened his son to stay quiet regarding the manner, putting him in imminent danger as well. I petition the court for a protection order of all parties involved.

My hand shakes.

I clench my jaw so tightly my head throbs.

There's no way.

Tarvo.

The locker room has cleared out. I hear the footsteps of someone coming to get me because the period is about to start.

I pray and hope it's him.

I read over the protection order two more times, hoping my eyes are playing a fucking trick.

But they're not.

Tarvo isn't here because of this "amazing opportunity" he was given by Coach Jacobs. He came here in search of Sunny, and the second he found her, she slipped right through *my* fingers.

The complaints make my blood run cold.

It all makes sense.

Her fear of hospitals, her fear of men, her request to stay out of the media's limelight. And to think he put her in the position to fear for her safety by stalking her on top of everything else?

My phone falls to the floor when I stand.

I brush past Kane, who must've been sent to grab me. He says something, but I can't hear a word he says.

The hallway opens up, and I turn for the bench. My teammates are on the ice, the ref coming toward them with a puck in hand.

"Where are your gloves? And stick? Get it together, Volkova!"

I move to the side, out of Coach Jacobs's line of sight. Tarvo is leaning against the glass behind the bench.

The smug fuck.

I've never been so angry.

I want to fucking strangle him.

"Hey, Tarvo!" I shout.

The entire team glances down the line at me.

"Atlas is on the phone for you."

He pops forward. "Atlas? My son?"

An animalistic growl rips through me. That's all the confirmation I need.

Kane is stalking up the hall behind me. I crack my neck and step onto the ice.

The whistle blows from the team having too many Devils on the ice, but it cancels out when I skate right in front of Tarvo.

His brow is furrowed, that cut on the bridge of his nose looking nearly healed. Too bad for him, I'm going to open it right up.

"Bro, what the fuck are you doing?" Malaki stands from the bench, but he quickly moves out of the way when my ungloved hands grip Tarvo's stupid fucking tie. I pull him onto the ice with force.

"I know why you're really here," I say into his ear, mid-tug. "And I'm going to teach you a fucking lesson on how to treat a woman."

He tries to hit me first, but I skate backward just in time to land a punch on his jaw before the rest of the team moves toward us.

"Not just any woman." I grab him around the neck. "But mine."

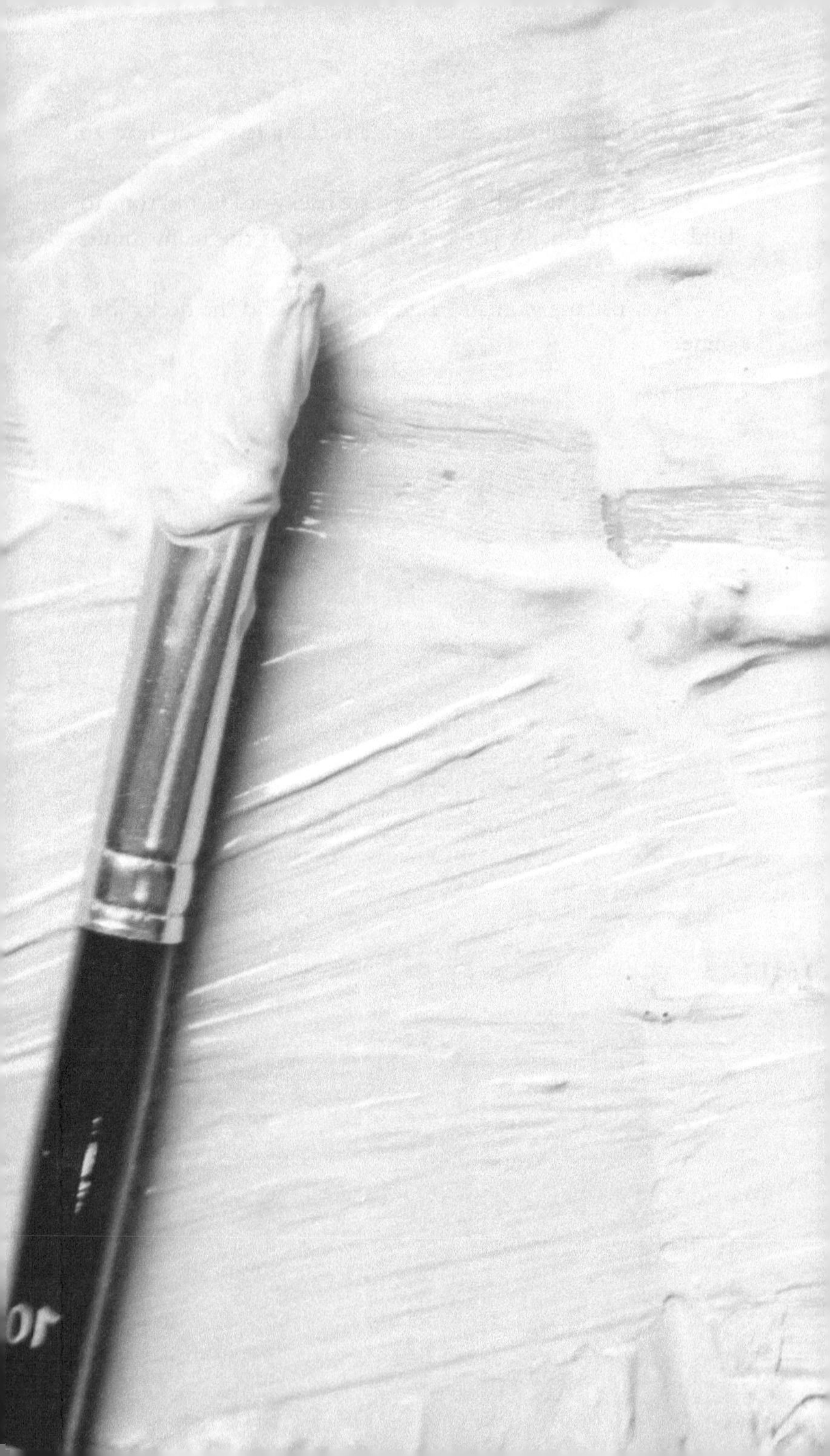

Sixty–Four

SUNNY

"GET UP RIGHT NOW."

I jump up from a dead sleep and stare at Ruby from across the room of her tiny apartment. "What? Why?"

My heart races.

"Is he here? Did he find me?"

The disheveled bun on top of her head bounces back and forth with her answer. "No, and I don't think he's going to."

She pulls me out of bed and drags me to the living room.

Some guy is on the couch, wearing nothing but a low pair of pants with his feet propped up on the coffee table.

"Never mind him," she whispers. "Turn it up, Preston!"

The guy—I'm assuming one of her "friends"—grabs the remote and turns up the volume. My eyes burn from the sudden brightness of the TV, but they adjust quickly when I spot a shade of blue that I'm all too familiar with.

"What the hell?" I rasp.

My eyes open wider.

It's a brawl.

I'm too confused to sit. I stand behind the couch and stare at the fight unfolding on the TV.

The commentators are at a loss. Stunned with silence. Clearly, they're confused as well.

"Tell her what you told me," Ruby urges in Preston's direction.

He tips his head back at me from the couch. "The fight isn't between the two teams. It's the Blue Devils against one of their coaches."

Oh no.

My hands dig into my hair. I pull on the strands and begin to panic.

Did Nicholas attack Rhodes, and the team responded and attacked him?

"It looked like one of the Blue Devils..." The announcer on TV pauses. A replay comes on the screen.

I'm going to be sick.

I wrap my arm around my waist from the sudden nausea.

"One of the Blue Devils grabbed a coach... Is that Nicholas Tarvo from Washington?"

"Looks like it, Pete."

"It looks to be Volkova as the instigator. He pulled Tarvo off the bench and threw him down. Then the entire team seemed to join in."

Eventually, they cut to commercial as the refs and other coaches sweep in and pull their players off the two stars of the fight: Rhodes and Nicholas.

This isn't good.

I slowly sink to the floor and wrap my arms around my knees. Preston sits up taller and mutters, "I think that is my cue to go."

Ruby whispers back to him, "I think that'd be a good idea."

"Call me if you need anything, yeah?"

She walks him to the door, handing him his shirt on his way out.

When the door shuts, our eyes crash.

"He seems nice," I say, desperate for anything but the attention to be on me.

She rolls her lips. "But would he fight for me on national television?"

I shoot her a look, and she snorts. "I'm sorry. It isn't funny, but I'm sort of afraid you're going to have a panic attack, so I thought I'd try to lighten the mood."

My bottom lip wobbles. I place my head on my knees and grab onto my legs tighter. "I thought leaving would fix things."

The plan was to leave things on a good note, which did *not* happen. My fight-or-flight kicked in. I felt safe, *finally*, after almost an entire year of bouncing around and hiding. Rhodes and Ellie became my home, and there was no way I was going to jeopardize that because of Nicholas.

I won't let him ruin anything else. Not another home. Not *my* home.

I knew if I told Rhodes who Nicholas really was that it would end badly.

But not telling him did the same.

How did he find out?

Was that what the fight was over?

Me?

What if he ruins his career over this? Fights in hockey aren't unusual, but an entire team attacking a hockey coach, in the middle of a game, on the ice? I think that's unheard of.

And Ellie. Was she there? I hope not.

I hope Atlas wasn't watching either.

Last I knew, they had no contact, but things can change.

"I think you should call him." Ruby slides down the back of the couch to sit beside me.

I peek at her, and she's holding an entire bottle of wine. I eye it, and she gingerly holds it out for me.

I grab the neck and bring it to my lips. "And say what?"

"Explain why you left without giving him a real explanation. If he's beating the shit out of Tarvo, he probably already knows."

I gulp the dry wine down and crinkle my face at the taste. "I highly doubt he wants to talk to me. You didn't see his face that night."

An ache digs deeper into my chest each time I picture it.

He was so hurt and confused.

Then he turned angry and bitter.

Regardless of my good intentions and attempt at making the right decision, I still broke my promise to him and Ellie. I *left*.

"Then maybe you tell him that you left because you love him and Ellie. Not because you don't."

I pause and stare at my best friend. She raises an eyebrow, like she's daring me to argue.

"Don't try to deny it." She takes the wine from my hand and swallows another gulp. "You put them first, even if they don't see it like that. That's something someone only does when they're in love."

I hate it when she makes sense.

"We weren't practical," I argue. "We were never meant to be anything serious. Rhodes has always been up front with me. He wanted a nanny that didn't have other intentions."

"And he got you." Ruby grabs my hand and gives it a squeeze. "Someone who *didn't* have other intentions. That's why it works."

I swallow two more gulps of wine.

"You're wrong," I argue.

All the reasons why Rhodes and I aren't meant to be are

scattered all around me. But the more I drink with my best friend on the floor of her apartment, the hazier they become.

My heart stings, even with the buzz of alcohol in my system.

I feel empty.

Like everything is just wrong.

I may be physically in Washington, but every other part of me is back in Chicago.

A tear crests over my cheek.

Ruby eventually pulls me over to her, and I rest my head against her lap and cry.

It's eerily similar to when I showed up at this exact apartment with a busted lip and fear wrecking my nervous system.

Only, this time, I'm not afraid.

I'm devastated.

Sixty-Five

RHODES

EMORY SEETHES FROM BESIDE ME. "You're lucky you're not in fucking handcuffs."

He paces back and forth in front of the trainer's room as I get my face stitched up. My knuckles are swollen, but most of my aggression is on hold from the staggering events that led to this moment.

We lost the game.

I was ejected for leaving the bench to fight.

It helped matters that Tarvo threw the first punch, but I did pull him onto the ice, so I think I'm still fucked. But what does everyone expect?

Even Kane, who has a heart the size of a piece of gravel, got a few hits in. He loves a good fight, but I know why he was the first to come to my aid.

He's the one who got Tarvo thrown out of the game, pleading with the refs and explaining why I went ballistic.

It's all very hush-hush, but the team is aware of my reason

for attacking Tarvo. According to Malaki, a few of the men from the other team backed Kane up too. We may be enemies on the ice, but when it comes to something like this, we're neutral.

You just don't fuck with another man's girl, and you most definitely don't do what Tarvo did.

According to the rest of Mel's text—that I just so happened to ignore before attacking Tarvo—there wasn't a formal investigation because charges were never pressed.

I'm not sure why she didn't press charges, but I know Sunny, and I've seen the fear on her face.

He's guilty.

"Let me see the report," Emory says.

I grind my jaw. It's sore.

I try not to wince with the last touches on my stitches. When I'm finished, I toss my phone to Emory with the report on the screen.

His forehead furrows, and then it furrows some more.

He flicks his gaze to me, and the room grows tight.

"Does Jacobs know about this?"

I hop down from the bench. "He probably does now."

"I like it here, and I like this team." He steps in line with me as we leave the training room and head down the hall toward the locker room. "I don't want to believe that he hired Tarvo knowing about his reputation."

The team should be gone and back at the hotel. The game ended at least an hour ago, the media even clearing out.

"Charges were never pressed," I say.

Why didn't she press charges?

Emory pushes on the door.

"Well, that's fucking ridiculous—"

Emory stops mid-sentence.

I'm afraid to look at the locker room. If the police are here to arrest me for assault, we're going to have problems. What would be worse is if Tarvo was waiting for round two.

"What are you guys still doing here?"

I open my eyes, and the shock grounds me.

The entire team, Coach Jacobs included, is waiting.

Kane stands up in the middle of the quiet locker room.

I continue to stare, fully fucking confused.

He claps.

It starts off slow, and eventually, the rest of the team is standing on their feet, and they're clapping too.

I glance at Coach Jacobs, and the slight nod in my direction is enough of an acceptance as any other.

"We're a team," Kane announces, once the clapping dies down. "We play together, we fight together, and we support each other."

Malaki pipes up. "Even if that means jumping into a fight for reasons unknown."

The team laughs, some of them throwing up devil horns.

A year ago, the locker room would have been cleared out without an ounce of support.

But this year is different.

Our mentality has changed, along with other things.

I clear my throat. "I appreciate you guys, and I apologize for not being present for the third period."

"Fuck Tarvo!" someone shouts from the back.

Kane points at them. "Fuck Tarvo."

I want to laugh, but I don't. Although I got some of my aggression out, the pain of losing Sunny remains.

"Tarvo is taken care of," Coach Jacobs interrupts the chatter. "I've made it clear that he is no longer welcome. He won't come near our arena."

That's great.

But what about going near Sunny?

———

"Daddy, where are we going?" Ellie quickly chases after me with her yellow backpack hanging off her one shoulder.

I stop right outside of our gate and wait for her to catch up.

She's out of breath, and I laugh. I scoop her up and put her on my shoulders.

"Mr. Volkova." One of the flight attendants nods at me as I walk through the doors. The rest of the team is flying out tomorrow, but I cleared it with Coach to fly out a day early to take care of some things.

Ellie and I rarely get to travel together. The only time we do is when we take our yearly Christmas trip to Russia.

"Are we going to see my babushka?" The glimmer of hope in her eye is the most emotion I've seen from her since Sunny left.

I shake my head, and the disappointment lands on her shoulders.

Once we're settled in our seats, she straps her seatbelt and reaches inside her bag. Instead of pulling out her tablet and headphones, she grabs onto a little container of clay. Her fingers work furiously as she tries to form something with the material.

I'm assuming that's her way of feeling close to Sunny without being with her.

Like mother, like daughter. Except, in this case, it's like nanny, like Ellie.

Right before we take off, I steal a piece of her clay and start to knead the material in my own hands.

Ellie growls with frustration.

I lean into her space and hope I'm not fucking myself with my spoiling where we're going.

"You want to know where we're going, Printsessa?"

Her angry brow smooths. "Yes."

"We're going somewhere...*Sunny*."

She thinks for a second, and like a lightbulb, her green eyes light up.

I grin, and she does the same.

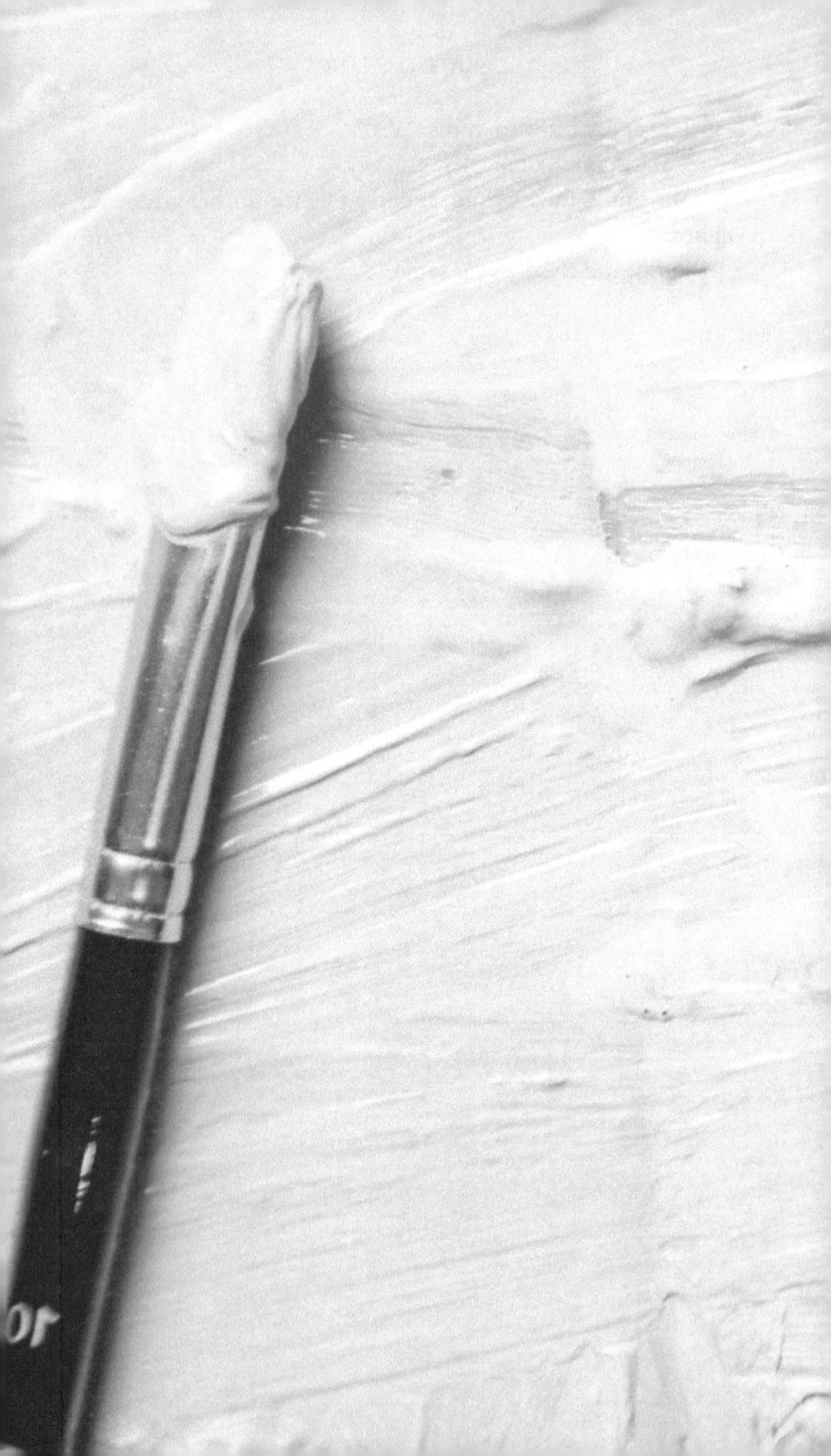

Sixty-Six

SUNNY

I KNOW I'll feel better after I see my nana. She may think it's December, but she's not too far gone that she won't recognize me when I walk into her room.

"Allison!" Nurse Jamie comes around the corner of the reception desk and gives me a big hug. It's warm and comforting. She has no clue that it's needed. "How are you?"

I've been better.

"I'm good. How are you? How is Cole doing in college?"

I made friends with just about everyone in the nursing home before moving. I'm happy to know they still welcome me with open arms.

After Jamie tells me all about Cole and his time at college while walking toward my nana's room, she grabs onto my arm. "Wait a second."

I pause. "Is everything okay?"

It's going to be about Nana. Her memory is getting worse, I know it.

"There's been a woman who has been looking for you over the last month or so," she says.

"Nana mentioned that, but I wasn't sure if she was confused or not."

Jamie pats her scrubs. She pulls out her phone and searches. "She gave me her number, said her name was Andrea."

Andrea Tarvo.

Shock ripples through me.

"Oh," I say. "Would you mind if I give her a call on your phone? I forgot mine."

Forgot it...disconnected it...doesn't matter the difference.

"Sure, sweetie. I'll be at my desk when you're done."

I smile and wait until she's out of sight.

I press the call button and nibble on my thumbnail while I wait.

"Hello?"

"Andrea," I say her name quietly, like Nicholas is somewhere nearby, ready to become irrationally angry with me that I'm talking to her like before.

"Oh my god. Finally," she sighs loudly. "I've been trying to get a hold of you for over a month."

I apologize to her, and she brushes it off, telling me she understands.

Of course she would.

She, too, had to disable her number at one point.

"I take it that you already know what I've been trying to tell you."

I press against the wall and continue to nibble on my nail. "Nicholas is in Chicago. Yeah, I sort of ran into him."

"That is not a coincidence." Her voice brims with a seriousness I've only heard a handful of times.

She and Atlas are a lot alike. Fun, goofy, and carefree. It

wasn't until the divorce that she grew grave when it came to her ex-husband.

"I know," I say quietly. "I left."

"He's still there," she says. "I have a private investigator."

I don't blame her.

"How is Atlas?" I slide down against the wall and sit on the floor. Standing seems too hard with the gravity of the phone call, and I'm exhausted from the fear.

"He's good." I hear the smile in her voice. "He's *so* good, Ally. He misses you."

"I miss him."

I picture his face. He's a good kid, just like Ellie.

"He is at the age now where he understands a little more about his father." There's a pause on the other end of the phone. "You know, he said he would testify if you ever changed your mind."

I'm quick to repeat the same thing I said a year ago. "I'm not putting him through that."

"Then you need to extend the protection order," she urges. "He's been watching you for months, Ally."

"I don't have proof of that, though."

"I do," she argues. "I have proof that he was involved in a hit-and-run too."

I quickly climb to my feet. "Wait, what did you say?"

"My private investigator called me about a week ago and said that he had followed him one evening and that he was involved in a wreck but left the scene. He took photos and everything, but he couldn't quite catch up to the person that Nicholas hit. By the time he got back in his car to make sure they were okay, they began driving off."

I press my hand to my mouth. Nicholas hasn't changed at all. In fact, I think he may have gotten worse.

"Ally?"

"I'm here," I force out. "Send me all the information you have on him."

"To this number?" she asks.

"No, send it to…" I rattle off my old email, knowing it's still active.

"And Ally?"

"Yeah?" My chest is wound with fear. I'm terrified that Nicholas is going to do something to Rhodes—or worse, Ellie. Did he hit us because he thought Marco was Rhodes?

"I'm so sorry I brought you into our lives." She sniffles. "He wasn't always like this."

My eyes sting, but I quickly brush the emotion away.

"Everything happens for a reason," I say.

We hang up after I promise her that I'll be in touch via email and stand on shaky legs. I gather myself on the way to Jamie's desk and slide the phone over to her.

"All good?" she asks.

I nod with a tight smile.

"Can I head to my nana's room now?"

She walks with me and talks about Cole some more, but the only thing I can think about is how I'm going to take care of Nicholas.

I need Nana.

The moment I lay eyes on her, my eyes gloss over.

"Oh, now, don't do that." She opens her arms up to me, and my heart swells.

There is nothing quite like a hug from the one person that has always been there for me, no matter what.

"Sorry, Nana," I choke out. "I just missed you."

I kneel beside her and continue to give her a hug. My head rests on her woven afghan, and she pats my head with her weathered hand.

"I know you better than that, Allison. Does this have something to do with that man?"

Which one?

I slowly pull back and eye her.

She doesn't know about Nicholas.

Does she?

Did he come here, or is she confused?

"Who?" I ask with skepticism.

"Me."

My breath catches.

I can hardly stand. The room spins when I lock onto his angular jaw with his usual scruff lining the edges.

"Rhodes."

What is he doing here?

Something squeezes my heart, and I don't know what to do.

It doesn't matter, though, because Ellie zips around his legs and jumps into my arms.

I almost don't catch her, but at the last second, I do, and we both collapse to the floor.

I can't help but smile when she pops up laughing with her wild, messy braid swinging over her shoulder. "What are you doing here?" I ask her.

She climbs off me. "All I know is that Daddy said we were going somewhere Sunny."

"Sunny?" Nana repeats. "It's colder than a polar bear's toenails outside."

I glance at Nana. She used to say that to me as a child, and every time, I'd do exactly what Ellie does: laugh.

"Come here, you!" She opens her arms to Ellie, and to my surprise, Ellie walks over and gives her a hug.

Rhodes watches the embrace with a soft expression. His hands are in his jeans pockets, and the longer I look at him, the more I realize how much I care about him. He was so angry when I left...and hurt.

He swings his expression over to me, and I stop breathing. "Can we talk?"

"Oh yes, you two go talk." Nana grabs Ellie's hand and pats it. "We will play a game."

"A game?" Ellie is excited.

Nana pulls out the brand-new tablet that Rhodes bought her and clicks an app. "Have you ever played bingo?"

I hide a laugh.

Bingo is her new favorite thing.

Rhodes turns and walks out of the room. I gingerly follow after him with my pulse racing and my legs heavy.

Everything I've found out in the last twenty minutes comes rushing to the tip of my tongue. I have to tell him about the wreck, how Nicholas has been following me for months, and how I plan to take the evidence to the police and make sure that he and Ellie are included in the protection order. Then I need to apologize for bringing a man like him into their lives, particularly Ellie's, because she could have been harmed in the wreck.

I exhale shakily and look at the floor.

"Rhodes—"

He grips my wrist and pulls me into him. The words surrender on my lips when he wraps his strong arms around me in a tight embrace.

Home.

He feels like home.

He backs away, putting very little space between us, and gazes into my eyes. "I lied."

"You lied?" I whisper.

He nods slowly with a tight jaw. I stare at the cut on his cheek, and guilt hits me.

"I said you were the only one who broke your promise."

I glance away.

I did break my promise. Even if my intentions were valid, it hurt me all the same.

His thumb and first finger land on my chin. He turns my face so I'm forced to look at him again.

My eyes are watery, but so are his.

I've never seen him so...vulnerable.

"I lied." He swallows thickly. "I promised I wouldn't fall in love with you, and I did."

My heart beats so hard I press my hand against my chest.

"I understand now why you made me promise not to fall in love with you. I understand why you left too." He cups both sides of my face with his hands.

"You do?" I choke out.

He nods. "You're scared, Sunshine. He made you think that love is dangerous. You're terrified to have someone love you because of what he's done."

My nose scrunches while I try to hold back my emotions.

"And I was terrified to love someone because I didn't think I had room for that in my life...my heart." Rhodes rubs the pad of his thumb over my cheekbone, and my face presses into his hand. "After you ran, I realized that the only thing I'm truly terrified of is losing you."

I open my mouth, but he shakes his head.

"I love you, Sunny."

Before I can even ask how Ellie feels about this, he stops me.

"Ellie loves you. *We* love you."

A choked noise leaves me, and a tear slips over the side of my face.

"Tell me you trust me enough to keep you safe," he pleads. "Tell me that I'm deserving of your heart." His hands tighten against my face, and I can't speak. "Tell me you love me too. *Please.*"

I do.

God, I do.

I nod quickly and gather myself enough to form a sentence.

"I didn't leave because I didn't trust you enough to keep me safe," I say. "I left because I wanted to keep you and Ellie safe. You two are my home, Rhodes. I had to protect it."

He shuts his eyes before bringing his lips to my forehead.

"You're the most deserving man I know," I whisper.

I close my eyes, relishing in his kiss against my skin. "And I do love you. Ellie too."

His chest heaves, and then his mouth is on mine. My back presses against the wall beside Nana's room, and we kiss for so long my lips are swollen when we finally break apart.

I stare into his green eyes, and though there are still things we have to discuss, I feel complete. He and Ellie make me whole.

"Moy Solnechnyy svet," he whispers, peering down at me.

"That means *my Sunshine*," Ellie says.

I jump, but Rhodes keeps ahold of me. We both turn to look, and sure enough, Ellie and Nana are spying on us through the crack in the door.

Ellie spots me and doesn't even try to hide. She smiles. "I'm teaching your babushka Russian."

Rhodes and I both burst out laughing.

Hand in hand, we go back into the room and listen to our girl teach a foreign language to Nana, who will likely forget it within the hour.

RHODES

I THANK my lucky stars daily for putting Sunny into our lives, but especially today.

Three sets of giggles hit my ears as I climb the stairs to the freshly remodeled loft. What was once an empty space full of cobwebs is now filled with the scent of acrylic paint, hardening clay, and canvas-covered walls.

Nana and I have become awfully close, and she let me in on a little secret, telling me where all of Sunny's old paintings were stored. Naturally, I had them sent here and hung them up so she could feel even more at home while dipping her toes into painting again.

Sunny already knows all my hopes and dreams: hockey, Ellie's happiness, and *her*. Not in that order. But when I asked about hers, ending up in an art museum one day was near the top of her list, so I'm going to do everything in my power to help her reach that goal. She might take some classes at the art school up the street to finish out her degree, and I've even encouraged her to start making those mesmerizing time-lapse videos again of painting.

Everything else in the house remains the same, besides Sunny moving into my room and extra security around the perimeter, because neither of us trust a flimsy piece of paper stating that Nicholas can't come near us.

If he knows what's good for him, he'll stay in Canada, which is where he ran off to shortly after paying his fines for the hit-and-run. If it were up to me, he'd be in prison, but when you have deep pockets and a good lawyer, that isn't always the case.

Standing along the opening to the loft, I watch Sunny concentrate while she puts two facemasks on Ellie and her new friend, Jacie.

Ellie has made so much improvement at school, and she actually has a friend. When she had asked if Jacie could spend the night for a slumber party, I panicked. *A slumber party?* I had no idea what that entailed, but leave it to Sunny to swoop in and save me. *As always.*

Star-shaped twinkle lights hang above the window, and two light-blue sleeping bags lay on the floor with an abundance of pillows and snacks.

"There." Sunny scrunches her nose and smiles at the girls. "You two are going to have fabulous skin."

They giggle and remain still, not wanting the masks to slip off their faces.

When Sunny peeks up and sees me leaning against the opening, her smile grows wider. It knocks the breath right out of my chest. Since bringing her back to Chicago with me, we've gotten even closer than before. I've always felt like I've known her all my life, but being able to share all my thoughts with her instead of hiding them has erased any line that was there before.

We know each other's hopes and dreams.

We know each other's worst fears.

We've shared our happiest and worst childhood memories, and I've planned our Christmas vacation. First Russia, so she can meet my mother, who is beyond excited that I've finally found someone to give my love to instead of being against it due to my father's broken promises, which is something I've never shared with anyone—except for Sunny.

Then we will go to Washington to spend time with Nana.

It won't be long before we move her closer to us.

Being apart from her makes Sunny sad, and that's unacceptable to me.

I watch Sunny tilt toward the girls with her sights set on me. The flirty glint sends me reeling as she whispers something in their ears. I have to behave, though, because tonight is all about Ellie and her slumber party. The girls giggle, and then all three stare at me with amusement.

"I'm not sure I like the look you three are giving me," I joke.

"Daddy," Ellie quips. "Your turn."

My eyebrows rise. "Huh?"

Sunny laughs, and I flick my eyes past Ellie and her friend. She is holding another facemask in her hands with a teasing smile.

"I am not putting a facemask on," I say in a panic.

Ellie and Jacie both laugh. My mouth twitches because they look ridiculous with an entire sheet covering their faces. All I see are two eyes, a nose, and a mouth split into giant smiles from both of them.

"*Pozhalusta,*" the Russian word for please slips with ease from Sunny's mouth, and my stomach dips.

She is playing dirty.

My eyes narrow.

Sunny knows exactly what she's doing by using that word. Quick snippets of her beneath me in bed from the night before fill my head, and all I hear is her quiet voice full of pleasure, saying *please* in Russian over and over again.

Damn her for asking Marco to teach her the language during the day while Ellie is at school so she's "prepared for our trip." She's been using it to her advantage since the first lesson.

I'm not going to lie, though. I *love* it.

Sunny opens her mouth, and my eyes flare. I reluctantly agree to the facemask, just to keep her from saying the word again. It wouldn't be appropriate for me to steal her from the girls and disappear to some hidden part of the house to have my way with her, so I quickly stop her before I can't stop myself.

After the facemask is on, and the three of them get over their fits of laughter, Sunny snaps a photo and lets me take the horrible thing off.

It smells like coconut, which reminds me of her, so I *guess* there's a benefit in the end.

"Here we go," I say after I get the projector set up so the girls can watch *Tangled* while snuggled in their sleeping bags.

The movie is playing on a sheet that Sunny hung from the exposed wood, and the girls are fully engrossed. She comes over and stands in between my legs while I sit on her favorite stool. Her back presses against my front, and I wrap my arms around her waist, bringing her in even closer.

God, I fucking love her.

Ellie and Jacie giggle at Pascal, and a thought slips into my head that would've scared me months prior, but now it no longer does, especially with her in my arms.

A bigger family would be nice.

Seeing Sunny pregnant with my baby would be nice too.

I press my head onto her shoulder and skim my nose along the slender part of her neck. She shivers, and I smile against her skin.

Her whisper is only loud enough for me to hear. "Better stop it. You know I'm sleeping up here with the girls, right?"

I want to pout, because she's mine. But then I remember that I'm in my thirties, and it's a bit much to throw a tantrum.

"Mm-hmm," I whisper back. "I'll miss you, though."

A faint laugh leaves her. "You will not."

"Will too," I argue.

Her warm hands fall to mine wrapped around her waist. "I'll miss you too," she admits.

A question rushes from the tip of my tongue. "Do you want kids?"

Her spine stiffens.

It's a question that packs a heavy punch, and I'd be perfectly fine with whatever she wants. Though, again, the thought of her carrying my baby is *so* enticing. "You can tell me," I stress quietly.

"I do," she answers. "But—"

"Should we try now or later?" I ask, interrupting her.

Her head jerks over her shoulder, and our eyes snag. I grin, and she presses her lips together to hide a smile.

"You already have one," she notes.

I snort. "I'm well aware. And thank god for that or else I never would've met you."

Fate has a way, though. Sunny belongs to me, and I would've found her one way or another.

"I'll give you a baby, Solnushka."

Sunny's white teeth sink into her bottom lip, and I want to kiss her so bad.

"But first you've gotta marry me," I add.

I wink at her, and a blush blossoms over her cheeks.

I expect a flirty eye roll or something to that extent, but as always, she surprises me.

"Okay, Oscar." She smiles, and my entire world lights up. "I'll marry you."

I'm crazy in love with her, and having her in my arms after hearing those words has me skating the line yet again with *Tangled* on in the background and two happy little girls in their sleeping bags, paying us no mind. I stare at her lips, and desire flows through my veins.

Sunny smacks my hand when I start to rub circles against the little bit of skin peeking out from below her shirt. "Knock it off," she warns.

I smirk. *Fine.*

"Zhena," I mutter the word *wife* in Russian when she turns back around to watch the movie.

Before she relaxes back against me, I hear her faint whisper. "Muzh."

Husband.

My chest swells.

Sunny Volkova, I think to myself.

What a perfect name.

The End

Ready for another Blue Devil? Head to **sjsylvis.com** for information on the next book in the series: ***Rush the Edge***

Standalones

Three Summers

Yours Truly, Cammie

Chasing Ivy

Falling for Fallon

Truth

Acknowledgments

This book hit differently. I expected to have it finished much sooner than it ended up being (it was a lot longer too LOL) but life always has a way of throwing curve balls.

In the middle of writing Skate the Line, my grandpa passed away. I know that having a grandparent pass is never a surprise when you're at the age that I am (32), but his parting hit me hard. My grandpa wasn't just a "grandpa". He was my father figure and a constant love that never wavered. I'm one of those "suffer in silence" types, always wanting to be the shoulder to lean on, so I've been very quiet when dealing with the loss except for when I think about *this* book.

I escaped between the pages of Skate the Line on the plane ride to my hometown and on the plane ride home (during the three hour delay, too). The way Sunny refers to her Nana and Gramps, is very much how I refer to my grandparents. Both are/were such strong pillars in my life and I feel like I owe a lot of my success (and this book) to them.

Grief is messy however this book is anything *but*. Writing Sunny and Rhodes helped me grieve and cope. When I reread the book during edits, I was blown away. I thought it was going to be awful and need a lot of edits, but I was wrong. It felt messy while writing, but *god*, I loved every single word.

So, thank you to both of my grandparents for your love, support, and wisdom. Thank you for always being a safe place for me to come back to when I need it the most. Thank you for loving me. <3

And of course, thank you to each and every person who

had a part in making sure this book was up to par. Emma, Bri, Kari, Jenn, Mary, Sarah, Ashlee, VPR, my agent, TU group chat, my besties, husband, and every reader who shares, makes content, reads, etc. I am so thankful for you all and wouldn't be where I am with you!!

xo

SJ